The baby.

She was still cryin was muffled, it was their location. Tess

And then he saw her.

Tessa saw him, too.

She didn't stop. With the baby gripped in her arms, she threw open the glass door and was within a heartbeat of getting outside to the parking lot. She might have made it, too, but Landon took hold of her arms and pulled her back inside.

As he'd done by the barn, he was as gentle with her as he could be, but he wasn't feeling very much of that gentleness inside.

"Please, just let me go." Her eyes filled with tears. "It's not safe for you to be with me."

"What the hell does that mean?" Landon snapped.

She closed her eyes, the tears spilling down her cheeks. "I'm not who you think I am. And if you stay here with me, they'll kill you."

LANDON

BY
DELORES FOSSEN

First Published in Great Britain 2016
By Mills & Boon, an imprint of HarperCollins*Publishers*
1 London Bridge Street, London, SE1 9GF

© 2016 Delores Fossen

ISBN: 978-0-263-91921-9

46-1116

Our policy is to use papers that are natural, renewable and recyclable products and made from wood grown in sustainable forests. The logging and manufacturing processes conform to the legal environmental regulations of the country of origin.

Printed and bound in Spain
by CPI, Barcelona

Delores Fossen, a *USA TODAY* bestselling author, has sold over fifty novels with millions of copies of her books in print worldwide. She's received a Booksellers' Best Award and an RT Reviewers' Choice Best Book Award. She was also a finalist for a prestigious RITA® Award. You can contact the author through her website at www.deloresfossen.com.

Chapter One

Deputy Landon Ryland was looking for a killer.

He stood back from the crowd who'd gathered for the graveside funeral, and Landon looked at each face of the fifty or so people. Most he'd known since he was a kid, when he had visited his Ryland cousins here in Silver Creek, Texas.

But today he had to consider that one of them might have murdered Emmett.

Just the thought of it felt as if someone had Landon's heart in a vise and was crushing it. Emmett and he were cousins. But more like brothers. And now Emmett was dead, and someone was going to pay for that.

Especially considering how, and why, Emmett had died.

Landon knew the how, but it was the why that was causing his sleepless nights. He intended to give the killer a whole lot worse than just lack of sleep, though.

He glanced out of the corner of his eye when he sensed someone approaching. Landon didn't exactly have a welcoming expression, and everybody had kept their distance. So far.

Since he was on edge, he slid his hand over his gun,

but it wasn't necessary. It was Sheriff Grayson Ryland, yet another of his cousins.

Grayson, however, was also Landon's new boss.

The ink was barely dry on his contract with the sheriff's office, but he was the newest lawman in Silver Creek. Newest resident, too, of the Silver Creek Ranch since he'd moved to the guesthouse there until he could find his own place. Landon just wished his homecoming had been under much better circumstances.

"You see anything?" Grayson said. He was tall, lanky and in charge merely by being there. Grayson didn't just wear a badge—he was the law in Silver Creek, and everybody knew it.

Grayson was no doubt asking if Landon had seen a killer. He hadn't. But one thing was for certain: *she* wasn't here.

"Any sign of her yet?" Landon asked.

Grayson shook his head, but like Landon, he continued to study the funeral attendees, looking at each one of them from beneath the brim of his cowboy hat. Also as Landon had done, Grayson lingered a moment on Emmett's three brothers. All grief stricken. And that didn't apply just to them but to the entire Ryland clan. Losing one of their own had cut them each to the bone.

"Tessa Sinclair might not be able to attend, because she could be dead," Grayson reminded him.

Yes. She could be. But unless Landon found proof of that, she was a person of interest in Emmett's death. Or at least, that was how Grayson had labeled her. To Landon, she was a suspect for accessory to murder since Emmett's body had been found in her house. That meant she likely knew the killer.

She could even be protecting him.

Well, she wouldn't protect that piece of dirt once Landon found him. And old times wouldn't play into this. It didn't matter that once she'd been Landon's lover. Didn't matter that once they'd had feelings for each other.

Something that didn't sit well with him, either.

But despite how Landon felt about her and no matter how hard he looked at the attendees, Tessa wasn't here at the funeral. With her blond hair and starlet looks, she would stick out, and Landon would have already spotted her.

Grayson reached in his pocket, pulled out a silver star badge and handed it to Landon. It caught the sunlight just right, and the glare cut across Landon's face, forcing him to shut his eyes for a second. He hoped that wasn't some kind of bad sign.

"You're certain you really want this?" Grayson pressed.

"Positive." He glanced at his cousin. Not quite like looking in a mirror but close enough. The Ryland genes were definitely the dominant ones in both of them. "You haven't changed your mind about hiring me, have you?"

"Nope. I can use the help now that I'm short a deputy. I just want to make sure you know what you're getting into."

Landon knew. He was putting himself in a position to catch a killer.

He clipped the badge onto his shoulder holster where once there'd been a different badge, for Houston PD. There he'd been a detective. But Landon had given that up when Emmett was murdered, so he could come home and find the killer.

Too bad it didn't look as if he would find him or her here.

"I'll see you back at the sheriff's office," Landon said,

heading toward his truck. It was only about a fifteen-minute ride back into town, not nearly enough time for him to burn off this restless energy churning inside him.

This is for you, Landon.

The words flashed through his head and twisted his gut into a knot so tight that Landon felt sick. Because that was what the handwritten note had said. The note that had been left on Emmett's body. Someone had killed Emmett because of Landon.

But why?

Landon had thought long and hard on it, and he still couldn't figure it out. Since he'd been a Houston cop for nearly a decade, it was possible this was a revenge killing. He'd certainly riled enough criminals over the years, and this could have been a payback murder meant to strike Landon right in the heart.

And it had.

Somewhere, the answers had to be in his old case files. Or maybe in the sketchy details they'd gotten from witnesses about the hours leading up to Emmett's death. Something was there. He just had to find it.

He took the final turn toward town, and Landon saw something he sure as hell didn't want to see.

Smoke.

It was thick, black and coiling from what was left of a barn at the old Waterson place. The house and outbuildings had been vacant for months now since Mr. Waterson had died, but that smoke meant someone was there.

Landon sped toward the blaze and skidded to a stop about twenty yards away. He made a quick 911 call to alert the fire department, and he drew his gun just in case the person responsible for that blaze was still around. However, it was hard to see much of anything, because of the smoke. It was stinging his eyes and making him cough.

But he did hear something.

A stray cat, maybe. Because there shouldn't be any livestock still inside that barn.

Landon went to the back of the barn, or rather what was left of it, and he saw something that had his heart slamming into overdrive.

Not a cat. A woman.

She had shoulder-length brown hair and was on her side, moaning in pain. But she was only a couple of feet from the fire, and the flames were snapping toward her.

Cursing, Landon rushed to her just as the gust of the autumn wind whipped some of those flames right at him. He had to put up his arm to protect his face, and in the same motion, he grabbed her by the ankle, the first part of her he could reach, and he dragged her away from the fire.

Not a second too soon.

A huge chunk of the barn came down with a loud swoosh and sent a spray of fiery timbers and ashes to the very spot where they'd just been. Some of the embers landed on his shirt, igniting it, and Landon had to slap them out before they became full-fledged flames.

The woman moaned again, but he didn't look back at her. He kept moving, kept dragging her until they were finally away from the fire. Well, the fire itself, anyway. The smoke continued to come right at them, and it sent both Landon and her into coughing fits.

And that was when he heard that catlike sound again.

Landon dropped down on his knees, putting himself between the woman and what was left of the fire. Part of the barn was still standing, but it wouldn't be for much longer. He didn't want them anywhere near it when it finally collapsed.

"Are you okay?" he asked her, rolling her to her back so he could see her face. Except he couldn't see much of her face until he wiped off some of the soot.

Ah, hell.

Tessa.

He felt a punch of relief because she was obviously alive after all. But it was a very brief punch because she could be hurt. Dying, even.

Landon checked her for injuries. He couldn't see any obvious ones, but she was holding something wrapped in a soot-covered blanket. He eased it back and was certain his mouth dropped open.

What the heck?

It was a baby.

A newborn, from the looks of it, and he or she was making that kitten sound.

"Whose child is that?" he asked. "And why are you here?"

Those were just two other questions Landon had to add to the list of things he would ask Tessa. And she would answer. Especially answer why Emmett's body was found in her house and where the heck she'd been for the past four days.

"You have to help me," Tessa whispered, her voice barely audible.

Yeah, he did have to help. Just because he didn't like or trust her, that didn't mean he wouldn't save her. Landon didn't want to move her any farther, though, in case she was injured, so he fired off a text to get an ambulance on the way.

Both the baby and she had no doubt inhaled a lot of

smoke, but at least the baby's face didn't have any soot on it, which meant maybe the blanket had protected him or her.

"Did you hear me?" he snapped. "Why were you near the burning barn? And whose baby is that?"

He wanted to ask about that dyed hair, too, but it could wait. Though it was likely a dye job to change her appearance.

Landon couldn't think of a good reason for her to do that. But he could think of a really bad one—she was on the run and didn't want anyone to recognize her. Well, she'd picked a stupid place to hide.

If that was what she'd been doing.

She stared up at him. Blinked several times. "Who are you?" she asked.

Landon gave her a flat look. "Very funny. I'm not in the mood for games. Answer those questions I asked and then tell me about Emmett."

"Emmett?" she repeated. She touched her hand to her head, her fingers sliding through her hair. She looked at the ends of the dark strands as if seeing them for the first time. "What did you do to me?"

Landon huffed. "I saved your life. And the baby's."

At the mention of the word *baby*, Landon got a bad feeling.

He quickly did the math, and it'd been seven months, more or less, since he'd landed in bed with Tessa. And he hadn't laid eyes on her since. Seven months might mean...

"Is that our baby?" he demanded.

As she'd done with her hair, she looked down at the newborn who was squirming in her arms. Tessa didn't gasp, but it was close. Her gaze flew to his, the accusation all over her face.

"I don't know," she said, her breath gusting now.

That wasn't the right answer. In fact, that wasn't an acceptable answer at all.

He didn't hold Tessa in high regard, but she would know who'd fathered her child. If it was indeed Landon, she might also be trying to keep the baby from him. After all, they hadn't parted on good terms, and those *terms* had gotten significantly worse with Emmett's murder.

Damn.

Were Tessa and he parents?

No. They couldn't be. The kid had to be Joel Mercer's and hers, and even though Landon had plenty of other reasons for his stomach to knot, just thinking of Joel's name did it. That night, seven months ago, Tessa had sworn she was through with Joel, but Landon would bet his next two paychecks that she had gone right back to him.

She always did.

In the distance, Landon heard the wail of the sirens from the fire engine. It'd be here soon. The ambulance, too. And then Tessa would be whisked away to the hospital, where she could pull another disappearing act.

"Start talking," Landon demanded, getting right in her face. "Tell me everything, and I mean *everything*."

The baby and the ends of her brown hair weren't the only thing she looked at as though she'd never seen them before. Tessa gave Landon that same look.

"Who are you?" she repeated, her eyes filling with tears. "Whose baby is this?" Tessa stopped, those teary blue eyes widening. "And who am *I*?"

Chapter Two

She couldn't catch her breath. Couldn't slow down her pulse. Nor could she fight back the tears that were stinging her eyes. Her heart seemed to be beating out of her chest, and everything inside her was spiraling out of control.

Where was she?

And who was this man staring at her?

Except it wasn't only a stare. He was glaring, and she could tell from the tone of his voice that he was furious with her.

But why?

With the panic building, she frantically studied his face. Dark brown hair. Gray eyes. He was dressed like a cowboy, in jeans, a white shirt and that hat. But he also had a gun.

God, he had a gun.

Gasping, she scrambled to get away from him. She was in danger. She didn't know why or from what, but she had to run.

She clutched the baby closer to her. The baby wasn't familiar to her, either, but there was one thought that kept repeating in her head.

Protect her.

She knew instinctively that it was a baby girl, and she was in danger. Maybe from this glaring man. Maybe from someone else, but she couldn't risk staying here to find out. Somehow she managed to get to her feet.

"What the hell do you think you're doing?" the man snarled.

She didn't answer. It felt as if all the muscles in her legs had disappeared, and the world started to spin around, but that didn't stop her. She took off running.

However, she didn't get far.

The man caught her almost immediately, and he dragged them to the ground. Not a slam. It was gentle, and he eased his hands around hers to cradle the baby. While she was thankful he was being so careful, that didn't mean she could trust him.

She heard the sirens getting louder with each passing second. Soon, very soon, there'd be others, and she might not be able to trust them, either.

"I have to go," she said, struggling again to get away from him.

But the man held on. "Tessa, stop it!"

She froze. *Tessa?* Was that really her name? She repeated it several times and knew that it was. Finally, something was clear. Her name was Tessa, and she was somewhere on a farm or ranch. Near a burning building. And this man had saved her.

Maybe.

Or maybe he just wanted her to think that so she wouldn't try to run away from him.

"How do you know me?" she asked.

He gave her that look again. The one that told her the answer was obvious. It wasn't, not to her, anyway. But he must have known plenty about her, because he'd asked if the baby was theirs.

She didn't know if it was.

Mercy, she didn't know.

"You know damn well who I am," he snapped. "I'm Landon Ryland."

That felt familiar, too, and it stirred some different feelings inside her. Both good and bad. But Tessa couldn't latch on to any of the specific memories that went with those feelings. Her head was spinning like an F5 tornado.

"Landon," she repeated. And she caught on to one of those memories. Or maybe it was pieces of that jumble that were coming together the wrong way. "I was in bed with you. You were naked."

That didn't help his glare, and she had no idea if she'd actually seen him without clothes or if her mind was playing tricks on her. If so, it was a pretty clear *trick*.

A fire engine squealed to a stop, the lights and sirens still going, but Tessa ignored them for the time being, and she gave the man a harder look. She saw the badge then. He was a lawman. But that didn't put her at ease, and she wasn't sure why.

"Can I trust you?" she came out and asked.

He grunted, and then he studied her. "Is this an act or what?"

Tessa shook her head. Not a good idea, because it brought on the dizziness again. And the panic. "I don't remember who I am," she admitted, her voice collapsing into a sob.

He mumbled some profanity and stood when one of the firemen hurried toward them. "An ambulance is on the way," the fireman said. "Is she hurt?"

"Maybe. But there's also a baby with her."

That put some concern on the fireman's face. Concern in her, too, and she pulled back the blanket to make sure the baby was okay. Something she should have done minutes ago. But it was just so hard to think, so hard to figure out what to do.

The baby was wearing a pink onesie, and she appeared to be all right. Her mouth was puckered as if she were sucking at a bottle, and she was still squirming a little but not actually fussing. Tessa couldn't see any injuries, thank God, and she seemed to be breathing normally.

"I'll tell the ambulance to hurry," the fireman said, moving away from them.

And he wasn't the only one rushing. The firemen were trying to put out the rest of the blaze, not that there was much to save. There were also other sirens, and she saw the blue lights of a cop car as it approached.

She caught on to Landon's hand when he got up and started toward that car. "Please don't let anyone hurt the baby."

That seemed to insult him. "No one will hurt her. Or you. But you will tell me what I need to know."

Tessa didn't think this had anything to do with that memory of them being in bed, but she had no idea what he expected from her. Whatever it was, he clearly expected a lot.

Landon pulled his hand out of her grip and started toward the man who stepped from the cop car. The second man was tall, built just like Landon.

A brother, perhaps?

The second man and Landon talked for several moments, and she saw the surprise register on the other man's face. He kept that same expression as he made his way to her.

"Tessa," he said. Not exactly a friendly greeting. "I'm Deputy Dade Ryland. Landon's cousin," he added, probably because she didn't say anything or show any signs of recognizing him. "We need to ask you some questions before the ambulance gets here."

Tessa nodded because she didn't know what else to do. The baby and she were at the mercy of these men. Her instincts told her, though, that she should get away, run, the first chance she got.

Maybe that chance would come soon. Before it was too late.

But it wasn't Dade who asked any questions. It was Landon. He put his hands on his hips and stared down at her. "We need to know what happened to Emmett."

"He's dead," she blurted out without even realizing she was going to say it. "And so is his wife, Annie. Annie was killed in a car accident."

Where had that come from?

"That's right," Dade said, exchanging an uneasy glance with Landon. "Emmett and Annie are both dead." As Landon had done earlier, Dade knelt down, checking the baby. Then Tessa. Specifically, he looked into her eyes. "She's been drugged," he added to Landon.

"Yeah," Landon readily agreed.

The relief rushed through her. That was why she couldn't remember. But just as quickly, Tessa took that one step further.

Who had drugged her?

The drug had obviously messed with her head. And maybe had done a whole lot more to the rest of her body.

She had a dozen bad possibilities hit her at once, but

first and foremost was that if someone had drugged her, they could have done the same to the baby.

The panic came again, hard and fast. "Did they give the baby something, too?"

"I don't think so," Dade said at the same moment that Landon demanded, "Tell me about the baby."

Tessa latched on to what Dade said about the baby, but she had to be sure that the newborn hadn't been drugged. It was something they'd be able to tell her at the hospital.

It's not safe there.

The words knifed through her head, and she repeated them aloud. And something else, too. "Don't trust anyone."

They weren't her words but something someone else had said to her. Important words. But Tessa didn't know who'd told her that.

Or why.

Obviously, that didn't make Landon happy. He said some more profanity. Added another glare. "She keeps dodging questions about the baby."

That caused Dade to give her another look. This time not to her eyes but rather her stomach. Not that he could see much of it, because she was holding the baby, but he was no doubt trying to see if she had recently given birth.

"Did you set this fire?" Dade asked her, easing the baby's legs away from Tessa's belly.

Tessa flinched, and Dade must have thought he'd hurt her, because he backed off. But that wasn't the reason she'd reacted that way. She'd winced not from pain but from his question.

"Someone set the fire?" she asked.

Landon didn't roll his eyes, but it was close. "Take a whiff of the air."

She did and got a quick reminder of the smoke. The breeze was blowing it away from them now, but Tessa could still smell it. And she could also smell something else.

Gasoline.

"Someone, maybe you," Landon continued, "used an accelerant. Based on how the fire spread, I'm guessing it was poured near the front of the barn and was ignited there."

And the person had done that while the baby and she were still inside.

Oh, mercy. That was a memory that came at her full force with not just the smells but the sensation on her skin. The hot flames licking at her. Her, running. Trying to get away from…someone.

She also remembered the fear.

"Someone tried to kill me," she said.

Dade didn't argue with that, but it was obvious she hadn't convinced Landon. Well, she didn't need to convince him. There weren't many things Tessa was certain of, but she was positive that she'd just come close to being murdered. Or maybe the person who'd set that fire had been trying to flush her out.

But why would she have been hiding in that barn?

Tessa didn't get to say more about that, and maybe she wouldn't have anyway, because the ambulance came driving toward them. The moment the vehicle stopped, two paramedics scrambled out, carrying a stretcher, and they headed straight for her and the baby.

She studied their faces as they approached, trying to see if she knew them. She didn't, but then, no one looked familiar. Well, except for Landon, and she didn't have enough information to know if she could trust him.

Don't trust anyone.

But if she hadn't trusted Landon, why had she landed in bed with him?

After cutting his way past Dade and Landon, one of the medics checked her. The other, the baby. And they asked questions. A flurry of them that she couldn't answer. How old was the baby? Any medical history of allergies? Were either of them taking medications?

"She claims she doesn't remember anything," Landon snarled. "Well, almost nothing. She knows Emmett's dead."

Yes. She did know that. But that was it. Heck, she wasn't even sure who Emmett was, but even through her hazy mind, it was obvious that these two lawmen believed she knew a whole lot more than she was saying.

Or maybe they believed she was the reason he was dead.

While Tessa kept a firm hold on the baby, the paramedics lifted them both onto the stretcher. "Will you be riding in the ambulance with them?" one of them asked Landon.

Landon stared at her, nodded. "Please tell me once these drugs wear off that she'll be able to remember everything."

"You know I can't guarantee that. She's been injured, too. Looks like someone hit her on the head."

Landon glanced back at the barn. "She could have gotten it there. When I got here, she was on the ground moaning. Maybe something fell on her."

The paramedic made a sound of disagreement. "It didn't happen today. More like a couple of days ago."

"Around the time when Emmett was killed," Landon said under his breath, and he looked ready to launch into another round of questions that Tessa knew she couldn't—and maybe *shouldn't*—answer.

However, one of the firemen hurried toward them, calling out for Landon before he reached him. "You need to see this," the fireman insisted.

Landon cursed and started to walk away, but then he stopped and stabbed his finger at her. "Don't you dare go anywhere. I'm riding in the ambulance with you to make sure you get there."

It sounded like some kind of threat. Felt like one, too.

The paramedics lifted the stretcher, moving the baby and her toward the ambulance, but they were also carrying her in the same direction Landon was headed. Tessa watched as the fireman led him to the front of what was left of the barn.

Whatever the fireman wanted Landon to see, it was on the ground, because both men stooped, their attention on a large gray boulder. Dade did the same when he joined them.

She saw Landon's shoulder's snap back, and it seemed as if he was cursing again. He pulled his phone from his pocket and took a picture, and after saying something to Dade, he came toward her. Not hurrying exactly, but with that fierce expression, he looked like an Old West cowboy who was about to draw in a gunfight.

"What do you know about this?" Landon demanded. "Did you write it?" He held up his phone screen for her to see.

With everything around her swimming in and out of focus, it took Tessa a few seconds to make out the words. When she did, she felt as if a Mack truck had just slammed into her.

Oh. God.

Chapter Three

While he waited on hold for Dade to come back on the line, Landon glanced around the thin blue curtain to check on Tessa again. Something he'd been doing since they arrived at the Silver Creek Hospital. She was still sitting on the examining table, feeding the baby a bottle of formula that the hospital staff had given her.

Tessa was also still eyeing Landon as if he were the enemy.

That probably had plenty to do with the message that'd been scrawled on the boulder back at the barn. *This is for you, Landon.*

The same words as in the message that'd been left on Emmett's body. Except this time, there was a little more. *Tessa's dead now because of you.*

Reading that obviously hadn't helped lessen the fear he'd seen in Tessa's eyes. Hadn't helped this knot in Landon's stomach, either. He had to find out what was going on, and that started with Tessa.

She'd insisted on the baby staying with her, so they had both been placed in the same room, where the doctor was checking them now. Maybe the doc would be able to give her something to counteract whatever drug Tessa had been given.

Or taken.

But Landon had to shake his head at that thought. Tessa wasn't a drug user, so someone had likely given it to her. He needed to know why.

This is for you, Landon.

Someone clearly had it out for him. And that someone had murdered Emmett and had maybe now tried to do the same thing to Tessa and that innocent baby.

The baby had to be cleared up for him, too. If she was his child… Well, Landon didn't want to go there just yet. He already had enough to juggle without having to deal with that. The only thing that mattered now was that the baby got whatever medical attention she needed, and Landon could go from there.

"There were no prints on the boulder," Dade said when he finally came back on the line.

Landon groaned, but he really hadn't expected they would get that lucky. The person who'd set all of this up wouldn't have been stupid enough to leave prints behind. But he or she had left a witness.

One whose memory was a mess.

"The crime scene folks will do a more thorough check, of course," Dade went on. "Something might turn up. Anything from Tessa yet?"

"Nothing. The nurse drew her and the baby's blood when they got here. Once we have the results of the tox screen, we'll know what drug she was given. And if that's what is affecting her memory."

Of course, there was still that lump on her head.

The doctor had examined it, too, right after checking the baby, but like the paramedic, the doc said it was an injury that Tessa had gotten several days ago. In the doctor's opinion, it was the result of blunt-force trauma.

Landon figured the timing wasn't a coincidence.

"I don't think she's faking this memory loss," Landon added to Dade.

Tessa must have heard that, because her gaze slashed to his. Of course, her attention hadn't stayed too far away from him since this whole ordeal started. And after seeing that message on the rock, he knew why.

"All of this is definitely connected to me," Landon said to Dade. "The second message proves it."

Or at least, that was what someone wanted him to believe—that both Emmett's murder and this attack were because of something Landon had done.

"Did you find anything else in the old arrest records you've been going through?" Dade asked.

Landon had found plenty. Too much, in fact. It was hard to narrow down a pool of suspects when Landon could name several dozen criminals that he'd had run-ins with over the years. But there was one that kept turning up like a bad penny.

"Quincy Nagel," Landon answered. The name wouldn't surprise his cousin, because Landon had discussed Quincy with Grayson, Dade and the other deputies in Silver Creek.

Landon had put Quincy behind bars four years ago for breaking and entering. Quincy had sworn to get even, and he was out on probation now. That made him a prime suspect. Except for one thing.

Quincy was in a wheelchair.

The man had been paralyzed from the waist down in a prison fight. It would have taken some strength to overpower Emmett and to club Tessa on the head. Strength or a hired thug. But while Quincy had plenty of money from his trust fund to hire a thug, there was no money trail to indicate Quincy had done that.

"I'll keep looking," Landon said to Dade. Though the looking would have to wait for now, because the doctor stepped away from Tessa, and that was Landon's cue to go in the room.

Landon knew the doctor. Doug Michelson. He'd been a fixture in Silver Creek for years, and while Landon had moved away when he was a kid, he still remembered the doc giving him checkups and tending to him on the various emergency room trips that he'd had to make.

"The baby's fine," Dr. Michelson said right off. "But I want to get a pediatrician in here to verify that. I'm guessing she's less than a week old since she still has her umbilical cord."

Since Landon didn't have a clue what to say about that, he just nodded.

"Is she yours?" Dr. Michelson asked.

Landon didn't know what to say about that, either, so he lifted his shoulder. "I'm hoping Tessa can tell me."

The doctor scratched his head. "Probably not at the moment but maybe soon she can do that. I can use the baby's blood test to run her DNA if you give me the go-ahead."

"You've definitely got the go-ahead for that. And put a rush on it just in case Tessa's memory doesn't come back."

"Will do. I did manage to get Tessa to let a nurse hold the baby so I could get an X-ray of her neck," the doctor continued, but he stopped, obviously noticing the renewed surprise on Landon's face.

"What's wrong with Tessa's neck?" Landon asked.

"She's got a small lesion." The doctor pointed to the

area where his neck and shoulders met. "It's too big for it to be an injection site for the drugs she was given. Besides, I found the needle mark for that. Or rather the needle *marks*. There are two of them on her arm. One is at least a couple of days old, and there was bruising involved."

"Bruising that probably happened around the same time she was hit on the head?" Landon asked.

"Yes. The other is more recent. I'd say an injection given to her within the last couple of hours."

So she'd been drugged twice. "Then what's with the lesion?"

The doctor shrugged. "I might know once I've had a chance to look at the X-ray. For now, though, I need to get an OB in here to examine Tessa."

Landon heard something in the doc's voice. Concern maybe? "You think something's wrong?"

"She doesn't trust me, so I'm thinking she might not trust an OB to do an exam, either. But an exam is a must since we have to rule out problems other than just the head injury." The doctor patted Landon's arm. "Talk to her. Convince her we're the good guys."

He'd have an easier time convincing Tessa that the sun was green. Still, he'd try. Plus, the doctor didn't give him much of a choice. He headed out, no doubt to round up the OB and pediatrician, leaving Landon alone with Tessa and the baby.

"Tell me what's going on," Tessa demanded.

Since that was what Landon wanted to ask her, they were at an impasse. One that he hoped they could work through fast. While he was hoping, he needed those drugs to wear off—now.

"Tell me," she snapped when he didn't jump to answer.

He didn't jump because Landon wasn't sure where to start. The beginning seemed like a lifetime ago.

"Stop me at any point if this is old news," he began. "A year ago, you moved to Silver Creek to open a private investigations office. We met shortly afterward, had a few dates, and I ran into you again at the Outlaw Bar when I was in town visiting my cousins."

He paused, waiting for her to process that. "Is that when you were naked in bed with me?" she asked, setting the baby bottle down beside her.

Of course she would remember *that*. But then, if the baby was his, she probably had it etched in her memory. Landon had it etched in his for a different reason. Because of the white-hot attraction that'd been between them.

But that wasn't something he needed to remember now. Or ever.

"Yes. The following morning, you told me you couldn't get involved with me," Landon continued. "And then your scummy boyfriend showed up. Joel Mercer. Remember him?"

She repeated the name, shook her head. "If I had a boyfriend, why did I sleep with you?"

Landon had asked himself that many, many times. "You said he was an ex, but he sure didn't act like it." He stopped, huffed. "Look, are you sure you don't remember simply because you'd rather not be talking about this with me?"

"I'm not faking or avoiding this conversation. Now, tell me about Joel. Why did you say he's scummy?"

"Because he is. He's a cattle broker—at least, that's what he calls himself, but it's really a front for assorted felonies, including gunrunning and money laundering.

That's why I was surprised when he showed up and said you two were together."

Judging from her expression, Tessa was surprised, too. But it wasn't the same kind of surprise that'd been on her face that morning seven months ago. Landon had seen the shock, and then she'd changed. Or something. She'd become all lovey-dovey with Joel and told Landon to leave.

But Landon hadn't forgotten the look that'd gone through her eyes.

After he'd walked, or rather stormed, out, he'd gone back to Houston and hadn't seen her since. And apparently neither had any of his cousins. Tessa had closed her PI office, and while she'd kept her house in Silver Creek, she rarely visited it.

That was maybe why no one had known she was pregnant.

Because if his cousins had known, they would have told Landon. Plenty of people, including a couple of his cousins, had seen him leave the Outlaw Bar with Tessa that night.

"What does Joel have to do with Emmett?" she asked.

Everything inside him went still. Until now he hadn't considered they could be connected.

But were they?

Landon decided to try something to jog her memory. "Four nights ago, someone murdered Emmett in your house." Man, it was still hard to say that aloud. Just as hard to think about his cousin dying that way. "Your cleaning lady found his body. He'd been shot three times, and there was a note left on his chest."

"'This is for you, Landon,'" she whispered.

"How the hell did you know that?" He hadn't intended

to raise his voice, and the baby reacted. She started to whimper.

"I'm not sure. But I saw your reaction when Dade showed you what was on the boulder. I guessed it must have been something to do with Emmett since the majority of your questions had been about him." She rocked the baby, kissed her forehead. "And her."

Yeah. And he would have more questions about *her* when he was finished with this.

Landon took out his phone, and even though he knew the picture was gruesome, he searched through his pictures and found the one he'd taken at the crime scene.

Emmett's body in a pool of blood.

There'd been blood on the note, too.

"Does this look familiar?" Landon asked, putting the phone practically in her face.

She gasped, turned her head and closed her eyes for a moment. "No." And she repeated it in a hoarse sob.

Landon didn't have a heart of ice. Not completely, anyway, and whether he wanted to or not, he was affected by that look on her face. Affected, but not to the point where he was stopping with the questions.

"Why was Emmett there at your house, and how did you know he was dead?" he pressed.

She shook her head. "I honestly don't know." Tessa paused, swallowed hard. "There's something about that photo that seems familiar, but I don't know what."

Good. Because if it was familiar, then it meant she was possibly there and might have seen who had done this.

Landon went to the next picture. A mug shot this time of Quincy Nagel. "Recognize him?"

Tessa moved closer for a long look and gave him another head shake. "Who is he?"

"A person of interest." Too bad Landon hadn't been able to find him yet. "A thug I arrested who might have wanted to pay me back by killing my cousin."

Tessa kept her attention on the baby, but because Landon was watching her so closely, he saw the small change in her. Her mouth tensed. A muscle flexed in her cheek. He hoped that was because she was concerned for the baby rather than because she was withholding something about Quincy. The little girl went beyond the whimpering stage and started to cry.

"So I slept with you, got pregnant." Tessa stood and rocked the baby. "Or maybe you believe she's Joel's daughter? You're not sure, but you'll demand a test so you can be certain."

He nodded. Though he would be surprised if she was Joel's. Yes, Tessa had been more than just friendly with Joel, but Landon didn't think she was the sort to go from one man straight to another. But he'd been wrong about stuff like that before. He didn't think so this time, though.

"Or maybe she's not my baby at all," she added. Tessa shuddered, dodged his gaze.

Landon lifted her chin, forcing eye contact. "Are you remembering something?"

"No."

Her answer came much too fast, and Landon would have jumped right on that if his phone hadn't buzzed. It was Grayson, which meant it could have something to do with the investigation. Since the baby was still crying, Landon stepped just into the hall so he could hear what the sheriff had to say.

"We found something," Grayson said the moment Landon answered. "A car on a ranch trail not far from the barn. The plates are fake, the VIN's been removed, but it has some baby things in it. A diaper bag and some clothes."

Tessa's car.

Or one that she'd "borrowed."

"We'll process it, of course," Grayson went on, "but something really stuck out. The GPS was programmed to go to your house in Houston."

Landon wanted to say that wasn't right, that there'd been no reason for her to see him, but if the baby was indeed his, maybe Tessa had been on the way to tell him. Of course, that didn't explain the other things: the dyed hair, the hit on her head, fake tags, no vehicle identification number on the car. Those were all signs of someone trying to hide.

Landon stepped out of the doorway when he saw Dr. Michelson approaching. There were two other doctors with him. The pediatrician and the OB, no doubt, and maybe one of them could talk Tessa into having the examination.

"What about the area leading from the car to the barn?" Landon asked Grayson. "Were there any signs of a struggle?"

"None, but something might turn up. In the meantime, ask Tessa why she was going to see you. Hearing about the GPS might trigger her memory."

He ended the call, intending to do just that, but Dr. Michelson pulled back the blue curtain and looked at him. "Where's Tessa and the baby?"

Landon practically pushed the doctor aside and looked

into the room. No Tessa. No baby. But the door leading off the back of the examining room was open.

Damn.

"Close off all the exits," Landon told the doctor, and he took off after her.

He cursed Tessa, and himself, for this. He should have known she would run, and when he caught up with her, she'd better be able to explain why she'd done this.

Landon barreled through the adjoining room. Another exam room, crammed with equipment that he had to maneuver around. He also checked the corners in case she had ducked behind something with plans to sneak out after he'd zipped right past her.

But she wasn't there, either.

There was a hall just off the examining room, and Landon headed there, his gaze slashing from one end of it to the other. He didn't see her.

But he heard something.

The baby.

She was still crying, and even though the sound was muffled, it was enough for Landon to pinpoint their location. Tessa was headed for the back exit. Landon doubted the doctor had managed to get the doors locked yet, so he hurried, running as fast as he could.

And then he saw her.

Tessa saw him, too.

She didn't stop. With the baby gripped in her arms, she threw open the glass door and was within a heartbeat of reaching the parking lot. She might have made it, too, but Landon took hold of her arms and pulled her back inside.

As he'd done by the barn, he was as gentle with her

as he could be, but he wasn't feeling very much of that gentleness inside.

Tessa was breathing through her mouth. Her eyes were wide. And she groaned. "I remember," she said.

He jerked back his head. That was the last thing Landon had expected her to say, but he'd take it. "Yeah, and you're going to tell me everything you remember, and you're going to do it right now."

But she didn't. Tessa just stood there, her attention volleying between him and the parking lot.

"Please, just let me go." Her eyes filled with tears. "It's not safe for you to be with me."

"What the hell does that mean?" Landon snapped.

She closed her eyes, the tears spilling down her cheeks. "I'm not who you think I am. And if you stay here with me, they'll kill you."

Chapter Four

Tessa tried to move away from Landon again, but he held on to her.

"Explain that," he demanded.

She didn't have to ask exactly what he wanted her to tell him. It was about the bombshell she'd just delivered.

If you stay here with me, they'll kill you.

There were plenty of things still unclear in Tessa's head, but that wasn't one of them.

She glanced behind her at the parking lot on the other side of the glass door. "It's not safe for us to be here. Please, let's go somewhere else."

Landon stared at her, obviously debating that, and he finally maneuvered her to the side. Not ideal, but it was better than being in front of the glass, where she could be seen, and at least this way she had a view of the hall in case someone came at her from that direction.

"Now that the drugs are wearing off, I'm remembering some things about Emmett's murder," Tessa admitted.

His eyes narrowed. "Keep talking."

"I didn't see the killer's face." Though Tessa tried to picture him, the bits and pieces of her memory didn't cooperate. "I came into my house, and this man wearing a ski mask attacked me. Emmett was there, and they fought."

Landon stayed quiet for a long time, clearly trying to process that. "Why was Emmett there?"

She had to shake her head. "I don't know. I don't know why the other man was there, either. Maybe he was a burglar?"

That didn't sound right at all, though. No. He wasn't a burglar, but clearly there were still some blanks in her memory. And because he was wearing a ski mask, she didn't have even fragmented memories of seeing his face.

Tessa looked down at the baby. Did that man have something to do with the newborn?

"A *burglar*," Landon repeated, "wouldn't have left a note like that on Emmett's body. His killer was connected to me and obviously to you since the murder happened in your house." He tipped his head to the baby. "And where was she the whole time this attack on you was going on?"

"In my arms." Tessa was certain of that. "She was also in my arms when I ran from the man. No, wait." More images came. Then the memory of the pain exploding in her head. "He hit me with his gun first." That explained the bump on her head. "Emmett tried to stop him, and that's when I think the man shot him."

Landon dropped back a step, no doubt taking a moment to absorb that. Those details were still fuzzy, and Tessa was actually thankful for it. She wasn't sure that right now she could handle remembering a man being murdered. Especially so soon after nearly dying in that barn fire.

"You were close to Emmett?" she asked but then

waved off the question. Of course he was. And apparently she had been, too.

After all, Emmett had been at her house.

"I think his killer might have been a cop," Tessa added.

Landon huffed. "First a burglar, now a cop?"

She didn't blame him for being skeptical, but her mind was all over the place, and it was so hard to think, especially with that warning that kept going through her head.

That it wasn't safe here. That she couldn't trust anyone.

That she was going to get Landon killed.

"The killer held his gun like a cop," she explained. "And he had one of those ear communicators like cops use."

"Criminals use them, too," Landon was just as quick to point out.

True enough. "But he said something about a perp to whoever he was talking to on the communicator. That's a word that cops use." Tessa paused. "And when I saw your badge, I got scared. Because I thought maybe... Well, it doesn't matter what I thought."

"You thought I had killed Emmett," he finished for her. Landon added a sharp glare to that. "I didn't, and I need you to remember a whole lot more than you just told me."

So did she, but before Tessa could even consider how to make that happen, she saw some movement in the hall. Landon saw it, too, because he moved in front of her. From over his shoulder, Tessa saw Dr. Michelson and a security guard. But there was another man with him. Tall and lanky with blond hair. Wearing a suit. It took her a moment to get a good look at his face.

Her heart jumped to her throat.

"Joel," she said. Even with the dizziness, she recognized him.

Landon looked back at her, a new round of displeasure in his expression. "So you remember him now?"

She did. And unlike the other memories, these were a lot clearer.

Oh, God.

This could be bad.

Joel kept his attention on her, obviously studying her dyed hair, but she soon saw the recognition in his eyes, and he picked up the pace as he made his way toward her.

"Tessa?" Joel called out. "Are you all right?"

Landon didn't budge. He stayed in front of her. "Someone tried to kill her. What do you know about that?"

Until Landon barked out that question, Joel hadn't seemed to notice him. But he noticed him now. "What are *you* doing here?" Joel snapped.

Landon tapped his badge. "What I'm doing is asking you a question that you *will* answer right now."

Despite the fact that Landon's tone was as lethal as his expression, Joel made a sound of amusement when he glanced at the badge. "What happened? Did you lose your job as a Houston cop and have to come begging your cousin for work?"

That jogged her memory, too. Yes, Landon had been a detective with the Houston PD, but Tessa doubted he'd lost his job. He had likely come back to Silver Creek to solve Emmett's murder. Good thing, too, or else there might not have been anyone to save her from that barn fire.

But he couldn't help her get out of this.

"How did you know I was at the hospital?" Tessa asked Joel.

Obviously, that wasn't what he wanted to hear from her. He probably expected a much warmer greeting, because he stepped around Landon and reached out as if to hug her.

Landon, however, blocked his path. "How did you know she was here?" he pressed.

Joel looked at her. Then at Landon. And it must have finally sunk in that this was not a good time for a social visit. If that was indeed what it was.

"What happened to you?" Joel asked her.

"I'm not sure." That was only a partial lie. "Someone drugged me and then tried to kill me."

Joel nodded. "In the barn fire. My assistant got a call from a friend who works at the fire department. He told her that you'd been brought here to the Silver Creek Hospital. I came right away."

"Why?" Landon demanded.

Joel huffed as if the answer were obvious, but he snapped back toward Tessa when the baby made a whimpering sound. He peered around Landon, and Tessa watched Joel's face carefully so she could try to gauge his reaction.

He was shocked.

She hadn't thought for a second that the baby was his, because Tessa was certain she'd never slept with Joel. She definitely didn't have any memories of him being naked in her bed. But she'd considered that he might have known if she'd had a child.

If she had, that is.

Joel stepped back, the shock fading, and in his eyes,

she saw something else. The raw anger, some directed at her. Most of it, though, was directed at Landon.

"You two had a baby," Joel snapped. "That's why I haven't heard from you in months."

Months? Had it been that long? Mercy, she needed to remember.

"I didn't think things were serious with you two," Joel added. "You said it was just a one-time fling with him."

She figured Joel had purposely used the word *fling* to make it seem as if what'd happened between Landon and her had been trivial. Of course, that was exactly what she'd led Joel, and even Landon, to believe.

Tessa needed to settle some things with Joel, but she couldn't do that now. Not with the baby here. And not until she was certain that this jumble of memories was right.

"I want the name of the person from the fire department who contacted your assistant and told her about Tessa," Landon continued.

It took Joel a few moments to pull his stare from her and look at Landon. "I'll have to get that for you. My assistant didn't mention a name, and I didn't think to ask."

Well, it was a name that Tessa needed so she'd know if Joel had someone in the Silver Creek Fire Department who was on the take.

"I'll want that information within the next half hour," Landon added. "And now you'll have to leave because Tessa and the baby have to be examined by the doctors."

Joel turned to her as if he expected her to ask him to stay. And she might have if Tessa had had the energy to keep up the facade so she could try to get what info she could from Joel. She didn't. It was time to regroup and tell Landon what she'd remembered, but she couldn't do that in front of Joel.

"Landon's right. The baby and I need to be examined," Tessa stated to Joel. "Please just go."

She could see the debate Joel was having with himself, but Tessa also saw the moment he gave in to her request. "Call me when you're done here," Joel said. "We have to talk." And he walked away as if there were no question that she would indeed do just that.

Tessa and Landon stood there watching him, until Joel disappeared around the hall corner.

"I'll need a minute with Tessa," Landon told the doctor and security guard.

The doctor hesitated, maybe because Landon's jaw was clenched and he looked ready to yell at Tessa. But Tessa gave the doctor a nod to let him know it was okay for him to leave. As Landon and she had done with Joel, they waited until both men were out of sight.

Since she knew that Landon was about to launch into an interrogation, Tessa went ahead and got started. "I don't think the baby is ours," she said. "And I'm certain she's not Joel's."

"How would you know that?"

She got another image of Landon naked. Good grief, why was that so clear? It was a distraction she didn't need. Especially since the man himself was right in front of her, reminding her of the reason they'd landed in bed in the first place.

"I just know," she answered. An answer that clearly didn't please him.

"Then whose baby is that?" Landon snapped.

Even though Landon wasn't going to like this, she had to shake her head. "Memories are still fuzzy there, but

I don't have any recollection of being pregnant. I think I would have remembered morning sickness, the delivery…something."

"And you don't?"

"Nothing." She wasn't certain if he looked relieved, disappointed or skeptical. But she wasn't lying.

"The doctor will be able to tell once he examines you," Landon reminded her.

She nodded. "I do have plenty of memories about Joel, though." Tessa had to lean against the wall when a new wave of dizziness hit her. "And some memories about me, too. I'm not a real PI."

Landon stared at her as if she were lying. "But you have a PI's license. A real one. I checked."

Of course he had. Landon probably wouldn't have asked her out unless he'd run a basic background check on her. And he definitely wouldn't have slept with her.

Then she rethought that.

The sex hadn't been planned, and it'd happened in the heat of the moment. Literally.

"Yes, I have a license." Best just to toss this out there and then deal with the aftermath. And there would be aftermath. "But I had it only because of Joel. He said he wanted me to get it so I could help him vet some of his business associates. It's easier for a PI to do that because I had access to certain databases."

She got the exact reaction she expected. Landon's eyes narrowed. Tessa wasn't sure of all of Joel's activities, but there were enough of them for her to know the kind of man she was dealing with. Landon had called him scummy, but he was much worse than that.

Because Joel was a dangerous man.

With that reminder, she looked around them again.

Tessa could still see the parking lot and the hall, and Landon made an uneasy glance around, too.

"You'll want to keep going with that explanation," Landon insisted. "But remember, you're talking to a cop."

The threat was real. He could arrest her, but it was a risk she had to take right now. She needed Landon on her side so he could help her protect this baby. Maybe from Joel.

Maybe from someone else.

Mercy, it was so hard to think.

Tessa had to clear her throat before she could continue. "I think Joel might have murdered someone."

His eyes were already dark, but that darkened them even more. "Who? Emmett?"

But she didn't get a chance to answer.

Landon stepped in front of her, drawing his weapon. That was when she saw the man in the hall.

He was coming straight toward them.

And he had a gun.

Chapter Five

Landon had a split-second debate with himself about just shooting at the armed man who was coming right at them.

But he couldn't.

It would be a huge risk to start shooting in the hospital around innocent bystanders.

A risk for Tessa and the baby, too.

The man obviously didn't have a problem doing just that. He lifted his gun and took aim. Landon hooked his arm around Tessa and yanked her out of the line of fire.

Barely in time.

The bullet smacked into the concrete block wall where they'd just been standing. The noise was deafening, and the baby immediately started to cry.

Landon pulled Tessa and the baby to the side so that he could use the wall for protection, but it wouldn't protect them for long, because the idiot fired another shot and sent more of those bits of concrete scattering.

"Tessa?" the man called out. "If you want the bullets to stop, then hand the kid to the cowboy cop and come with me."

Because Landon still had hold of her, he felt her muscles turn to iron, and she held the baby even closer to her body.

"Oh, God," she whispered.

Landon mumbled something significantly worse. This was not what he wanted to happen.

Of course, Landon had known there could be another attack since someone had tried to kill Tessa in that barn fire, but he hadn't thought a second attempt would happen in the hospital with so many witnesses around. Plus, the guy wasn't even wearing a mask. That meant he either knew no one would recognize him or didn't care if they did. But whoever he was, one thing was crystal clear.

This thug wanted Tessa.

Later, Landon would want to know why, but he figured this had something to do with one of the last things she'd said to him before the guy started shooting.

I think Joel might have murdered someone.

Landon didn't doubt it for a second. Nor did he doubt this armed thug was connected to Joel. But why exactly did Joel want her? Had she learned something incriminating while she was working for him vetting his "cattle broker" associates?

"Tessa?" the man called out. "You've got ten seconds."

"He knows you," Landon whispered to her. "You recognize his voice?

"No," she answered without hesitating.

"Think about it," the guy added. "Every bullet I fire puts that kid in danger even more. Danger that you can stop by coming with me."

"He's right," Tessa said on a rise of breath.

She moved as if preparing herself to surrender, but Landon wasn't going to let that happen.

"Stay back," he warned her.

Landon leaned out, trying to time it so that he wouldn't get shot, and glanced into the hall. The guy was no longer out in the open. He'd taken cover in a doorway.

Hell.

Hopefully, there wasn't anyone inside the room where this man was hiding or he would no doubt shoot them.

On the second glance, Landon took aim and fired at the moron. The guy ducked back into the room, and Landon's bullets slammed into the door.

He couldn't stand there and trade shots with this guy, because sooner or later, the gunman might get lucky. Certainly by now someone had called the sheriff, and that meant Grayson would be here soon. Although it might not be soon enough.

"Let's go," Landon told her.

He leaned around the corner and fired another shot at the man, and Landon hoped it would pin him in place long enough to put some distance between those bullets and Tessa.

Staying in front of her while trying to keep watch all around them, Landon maneuvered her down the back hall toward the other end, where there was another line of patients' rooms. He prayed that all the patients and staff had heard the shots and were hunkering down somewhere.

The baby was still crying, and even though Tessa was trying to comfort it, her attempts weren't working. Too bad. Because the sounds of the baby's cries were like a homing beacon for that shooter.

Landon had no choice but to pause when he reached the junction of the halls, and he glanced around to see if there was a second gunman waiting to ambush them.

Empty.

Thank God.

But his short pause allowed the shooter to catch up with them. The guy leaned around the corner where Landon had just been, and he fired at them.

Since it was possible for the gunman to double back and come at them from the other end of the hall, Landon needed better protection. Again, it was a risk because he didn't know what he was going to find, but he opened the first door he reached.

Not empty.

And the young twentysomething woman inside gave him a jolt until he noticed that she wore a hospital gown and was hanging on to an IV pole. She was a patient.

He hoped.

"Go in the bathroom," he ordered the woman. "Close the door and don't come out."

She gasped and gave a shaky nod but followed his instructions. Landon would have liked to have sent Tessa and the baby in there with her, but he couldn't risk it. Anyone bold enough to send this gunman could have also planted backups in the rooms.

"Keep an eye on the woman," Landon whispered to Tessa.

Tessa's eyes widened, probably because she realized this could be a trap. Of course, that was only one of their problems. The baby was still crying, the sound echoing through the empty hall.

Landon heard the footsteps to his right. The gunman, no doubt. And he readied himself to shoot when the man rounded the corner. But the footsteps stopped just short of the hall junction.

He glanced back at Tessa to make sure she was staying down. She was, and she was volleying glances between him and the bathroom door. In those glimpses that Landon got of her face, though, he could see the stark fear in her eyes. He would have liked to assure her that they'd get out of this alive, but Landon had no idea how this would play out.

"Tessa?" the guy called out. "Time's up."

Landon braced himself for more shots. And they came, all right. The guy pivoted around the corner, and he started shooting right at Tessa and him. Landon had no choice but to push her deeper into the room.

"Deputy Ryland?" someone called out. It was the security guard, and judging from the sound of his voice, he was on the opposite end of the hall from the shooter. "The other deputies are in the building. They're on the way now to help you."

Good. Well, maybe. It could be a bluff since it'd been less than ten minutes since the shooting had started, and that would be a very fast response time for backup. Still, even if it was a bluff, it worked.

Because the shots stopped, and Landon heard the guy take off running.

His first instincts were to go after the guy, to stop him from getting away, but Landon had no way of knowing if the security guard was on the take. Hell, this could be a ruse to lure them out of the room so that Tessa could be kidnapped or killed.

Landon waited, cursing while he listened to the thug get away, but it wasn't long before he heard another voice. One that he trusted completely.

Grayson.

"Landon?" his cousin called out. "Don't shoot. I'm coming toward you."

It seemed to take an eternity for Grayson to make it to them, and when he reached the door, Landon could see the concern on his face. Concern that was no doubt mirrored in Landon's own expression.

"Come on," Grayson said, motioning for them to follow him. "I need to get the three of you out of here right now."

TESSA'S HEART WAS beating so hard that she thought her ribs might crack. Her entire body was shaking, especially her legs, and if Landon hadn't hooked his arm around her for support, she would have almost certainly fallen.

She hated feeling like his. Helpless and weak. But at the moment she had no choice but to rely on Landon and Grayson to get the baby and her away from that shooter.

The sheriff led them up the hall, in the opposite direction of where the gunman had fired those last shots. Since that back hall also led to the parking lot, Tessa suspected he was getting away.

That didn't help slow down her heartbeat.

Because if he escaped, he could return for a second attempt. But an attempt at what? He obviously had wanted her to go with him. Or maybe that was what he had wanted her to believe. If she'd surrendered, he could have just gunned her down, done the same to Landon. Heaven knew then what would have happened to the baby.

"This way," Grayson said, and he didn't head toward the front but rather to a side exit.

The moment they reached it, Tessa spotted the cruiser parked there, only inches from the exit and apparently waiting for him. When Grayson opened the door, she saw Dade behind the wheel.

Even though she now believed she could trust the

Ryland lawmen, seeing him and Grayson still gave her a jolt. If she'd been right about Emmett's killer being a cop, then it was possible the killer worked at the Silver Creek sheriff's office.

Landon hurried her onto the backseat, following right behind her, and the moment he shut the door, Dade took off.

"Are you all okay?" Dade asked, making brief eye contact in the rearview mirror.

Landon nodded but then checked her face. Tessa did the same to the baby. The newborn was still making fussing sounds, but she wasn't hurt. Thank God. That was a miracle, what with all those bullets flying.

When she finished examining the baby, Tessa realized Landon was still looking at her. Or rather he was staring at her. No doubt waiting for answers.

Answers that she didn't have.

Someone had attacked her twice in the same day. Heck, maybe even more than that since her memories were still hazy.

"Maybe he's one of Joel's hired thugs?" Landon asked.

She had to shake her head again. Then Tessa had to stop because a new wave of dizziness came over her. It was so hard to think with her head spinning. "I only got a glimpse of him before you pulled me back, but he didn't look familiar. I don't know why he came after me like that. Do you?"

"No," Landon snapped. "But I want you to guess why he attacked us. And the guessing should start with you telling me everything you know about Joel. The baby, too."

His tone wasn't as sharp as it'd been before, and his

glare had softened some. Maybe he was starting to believe that this wasn't her fault.

Well, not totally her fault, anyway.

Tessa tried to concentrate and latch on to whatever information she could remember. It was strange, but the memories from years ago were a lot clearer than the recent ones. In fact, some of the recent ones were just a tangle of images and sounds.

"Tell me about Joel," Landon pressed, probably because she was still trying to figure out what to say.

"Joel," she repeated. And Tessa went with what she did remember. "I started working for him two years ago as a bookkeeper. I didn't know what he was," she added. "I was an out-of-work accountant, and he offered me a job. Later, he wanted me to be a PI so I could run background checks for him."

"But you soon found out what he was," Landon finished for her.

Another nod. "But I didn't know how deep his operation went, and he was hiding assets and activities under layers of corporate paperwork." Tessa had to pause again, brush away the mental cobwebs. These next memories were spotty compared to the ones of her starting to work for Joel.

"Back at the hospital, you said you thought Joel had killed someone," Landon reminded her. "Who? Emmett?"

Tessa closed her eyes a moment, trying to make the thoughts come. Finally, she remembered a piece of a memory. Or maybe it was just a dream. It was so hard to work all of this out.

"No. Not Emmett. I think the murder might have had something to do with the baby's mother," she said.

"But…no, that's not right." She touched her fingers to her head. "It's getting all mixed up again."

"Her mother?" Landon questioned. "So you're positive she's not yours…ours?"

"Yes, I'm certain."

She couldn't tell if Landon was relieved about that or not. He didn't seem relieved about anything. Neither was she. The child might not be theirs, but Tessa still needed to protect the newborn.

But who was after the baby? And why?

Her gaze dropped to the baby. "I think I know the reason I have her, though. Because a killer was after her mother, and she left the baby with me for safekeeping."

"A killer," Landon said. "You mean Joel?"

"I just don't know." Tessa groaned softly. "If I could just rest for a while, maybe that would help me remember?"

"You'll get some rest later. For now, tell me what happened to the baby's mother," Landon demanded.

Tessa had no idea. But this wasn't looking good. If all of this had happened four days ago, then the mother should have come back by now. If she was able to come back, that is.

Landon cursed. "Is the mother dead or hurt?"

But before she could even attempt an answer, Dade was on the phone, and she heard him ask if there was any information on the baby's mother that would match the sketchy details she'd just given them.

"Is it possible the woman who had this baby didn't have anything to do with Emmett?" Landon pressed.

"I just don't know." She paused. "But maybe Emmett was helping me find some evidence against Joel?"

As expected, that didn't go over well with Landon.

He didn't come out and say that she should have contacted him instead of Emmett, but she knew that was what he was thinking.

"But why would Emmett have been helping me?" Tessa asked.

Neither of the men jumped to answer that, maybe because they didn't have a clue, but it was Landon who finally responded. "Emmett was a DEA agent in Grand Valley, and Joel had a business there."

The memories were coming but too darn slow. She huffed and rubbed the back of her neck. Or rather she tried to do that but yanked back her hand when her fingers brushed over the sensitive skin there.

"Does it hurt?" Landon asked. He leaned closer, lifted her hair and looked for himself.

"Some." Not nearly as much as her head, though. "Why? How bad does it look?"

"It looks like a wasp sting or something. But the doctor took an X-ray. If it's something serious, he'll let us know."

Now that the drugs were partially wearing off, she tried to remember what'd happened to cause this particular injury. But nothing came. Everything was still so jumbled in her head, and that couldn't last.

There were secrets in her memories, secrets that had caused someone to try to kill her, and until she unlocked those secrets, she wouldn't be able to figure out who had sent that gunman after the baby and her.

And figure out who'd killed Emmett and why.

"Good news, *maybe*," Dade said when he finished his call. "There have been no reports of a seriously injured or dead woman who gave birth in the past week, but Josh will keep calling around and see if something turns up."

"Josh?" she asked, hoping it was someone she could trust. Of course, at the moment Tessa wasn't sure she could trust anyone.

"Our cousin," Landon explained. "He's a deputy in Silver Creek."

Like Landon. Tessa prayed this Josh was being mindful of those calls and that he didn't give away any information that could put the baby's mother in further danger. Of course, it was possible the woman was dead. Just because the cops hadn't found a body didn't mean there wasn't one.

Oh, God.

Another wave of dizziness hit her, and Tessa had to lean her head against the seat. She closed her eyes, hoping it would stop. Hoping, too, that the car would soon stop, as well.

"Where are we going?" she asked. And better yet—how soon would they be there? But the moment she asked the question, Tessa got yet another bad feeling. That feeling only increased when neither Landon nor Dade jumped to answer.

"Where?" she repeated.

"Someplace you're not going to like," Landon grumbled.

Chapter Six

Landon had told Tessa that he was taking her someplace she wouldn't like. Well, it wasn't a place where
he especially wanted her to be, either, but his options
were limited.

And that was why Tessa was now sleeping under his
own roof.

Or at least, the roof of the guesthouse at the Silver
Creek Ranch where Landon had made his temporary
home. Until he could come up with other arrangements,
it would be Tessa and the baby's temporary home, too.
With more than a half-dozen lawmen living on the
grounds, it was safer than any other place Landon could
think to take them.

Landon poured himself a fourth cup of coffee, figuring he'd need a fifth or sixth one to rid him of the headache he had from lack of sleep, and checked on the baby
again. She was still sacked out in the bassinet his cousins
had provided. Maybe Tessa was asleep, as well, because
he didn't hear her stirring in the bedroom.

Since Tessa had been the one to do the baby's 2:00 a.m.
feeding, Landon had brought the infant into the living-
kitchen combo area with him so that Tessa could sleep
in. Of course, he'd done that with the hopes that he might

get in a catnap or two on the sofa—where he'd spent the night—but no such luck. His mind was spinning with all the details of the attack. With Tessa's situation. With Emmett's murder. And despite all that mind spinning, Landon still didn't have the answers he wanted.

But maybe Tessa would.

By now, those drugs she'd been given should have worn off, and that meant maybe she would be able to tell him not only who was behind the attack at the hospital but also who'd murdered Emmett.

Landon had more coffee and checked outside. Something he'd done a lot during the night and yet another of the reasons he hadn't gotten much sleep. No signs of gunmen. Thank God. But then, the ranch hands had been told not to let anyone other than family and ranch employees onto the grounds. Maybe that would be enough to stop another attack.

However, the only way to be certain of no future attacks was to catch the person responsible. Joel, maybe. He was the obvious person of interest here, but Landon wasn't ruling out Quincy. Too bad neither Landon nor any of his lawman cousins had been able to find any evidence to make an arrest for either man.

Landon heard the two sounds at once. The baby whimpered, and Tessa moved around in the bedroom. He didn't wait for Tessa to come out. Since it was time for the baby's feeding, Landon went ahead and got the bottle from the fridge and warmed it up, just as the nanny had shown him when they'd arrived yesterday. Thankfully, there were three full-time nannies at the ranch now, so he hadn't had to resort to looking up bottle-warming instructions on the internet.

He eased the baby from the bassinet, silently cursing

that his hands suddenly felt way too big and clumsy. The baby didn't seem to mind, though, and she latched on to the bottle the moment it touched her mouth.

Without the baby's fussing, it was easier for Landon to hear something else. Tessa's voice. She wasn't talking loud enough for him to pick out the words, but it seemed as if she was having a conversation with someone on the phone. The guesthouse didn't have a landline, but there was a cell phone on the nightstand for guests—something that apparently Tessa had decided to make use of. But before Landon could find out who she was calling, Tessa quit talking, and a moment later the bedroom door opened.

And there she was.

Landon hated that slam of attraction. Yeah, he felt it even now, and it was proof that attraction was more than just skin-deep. Because despite the bruises on her face, the fatigued eyes, and the baggy loaner jeans and shirt, she still managed to light fires inside him that he didn't want lit.

She opened her mouth, ready to say something, but then her attention landed on the baby. "You're feeding her," Tessa said in the same tone someone might use when announcing a miracle. Maybe because he didn't look like the bottle-feeding type.

"The nanny talked me through how to do it," he explained. "And since you'd done the other feedings, I figured it was my turn."

Tessa glanced around as if expecting to see Rose, the nanny, standing there, but the woman hadn't returned after she'd gotten them settled in the night before. That was Landon's doing.

"I didn't want to disrupt the nannies' routines any

more than we already have, so I told her to go home," he explained. "My cousins have a lot of kids."

Thirteen at last count. Or maybe fourteen. Sometimes the ranch felt a little like a day care.

"I remember," Tessa said.

Two words, that was all she said, but those two words caused Landon to release the breath he didn't even know he'd been holding. Because she wasn't just talking about remembering that his cousins had plenty of children. She was talking about the memories the drugs had suppressed.

"You know who killed Emmett?" Landon asked.

His relief didn't last long, because she shook her head. "No. I don't know the person's name, but I remember what happened." Tessa lifted her shoulder. "Well, some things are still fuzzy, probably because of the drugs, but I remembered about the baby. Her name is Samantha."

"Whose child is this?" he pressed when Tessa didn't continue.

"She belongs to a friend, Courtney Hager. She wanted me to keep the baby while she made arrangements to move. The baby's father was abusive, she said, and Courtney didn't want him anywhere near Samantha or her. She told me not to trust anyone, because the father had connections."

Landon would want to know more about those connections and the father, but for now he stood and handed Tessa the baby so he could fire off a text to his cousin Holden. Holden was a marshal and would be able to do a quick background check on this Courtney Hager. Of course, Grayson and the other deputies could do it, as well, but they were already swamped with the investigation.

In a way, Landon hated to ask Holden to do this, too. Because Emmett and Holden were brothers, and Landon knew that he and Emmett's other brothers were sick with grief over their loss. But Landon also knew that Holden and the others would do whatever it took to find Emmett's killer and that Tessa and this baby could be a connection.

"How long were you supposed to keep the baby?" Landon pressed.

"Courtney said it would only be a day or two. She's probably looking for us right now. Probably frantic, too."

Probably. Well, unless something had happened to her. "Was it Courtney you just called?"

She got that deer-caught-in-headlights look. A look that didn't please Landon one bit. "No. I called a friend," she said. "I didn't have Courtney's number memorized. It was on my cell, but I lost that somewhere in the last day or so. I wanted to try to figure out if this friend knew anything about what was going on, but he didn't answer the call."

She didn't remember Courtney's number, yet she remembered the number of this other "friend." Landon wanted to know a lot more about that, too, but it wasn't at the top of his list of questions.

"Did Courtney have anything to do with Emmett's murder?" he asked.

"No," Tessa jumped to answer. Then she paused. "But maybe her abusive boyfriend did. I don't know his name," she quickly added. "I've only known Courtney a couple of months, and I never met Samantha's father. She didn't talk about him much, but I know she's afraid of him or else she wouldn't have told me not to trust anyone."

That was something Holden might be able to uncover in the background check. Maybe this abusive guy had killed Emmett when Emmett was trying to protect the baby, though that didn't explain the note left on Emmett's body.

Tessa glanced down at the baby, brushed a kiss on her cheek. "Anything new on the attack? Did they find the gunman?" she added before he could press her for more information.

Landon would indeed press her for more, especially more about that "friend" she'd called, but for now he went with the update on the investigation. Unfortunately, he wasn't going to be the bearer of good news.

"Grayson and the deputies didn't catch the man," he said and paused the bottle-feeding just long enough so he could hit the button on his laptop. "It's surveillance footage from the hospital, and I want you to take a closer look. Tell me if you recognize the man who attacked us."

Maybe she would be truthful about that. Maybe.

Landon didn't look at the screen. He didn't need to, since he'd studied the footage frame by frame. Instead, he watched Tessa, looking for any signs that she knew the man who'd been trying to gun them down.

She shook her head, moved closer to the laptop. In doing so, she moved closer to Landon, her arm brushing against his. She noticed. Also noticed the scowl he gave her as a result, and Tessa inched away from him.

"I'm not positive," she said, her attention back on the screen, where she froze one of the frames, "but I think that might be the same masked man who attacked me at my house. The man who killed Emmett." Tessa pointed to the guy's hand. "See the way he's holding his gun, the way he's standing. He looks like a cop."

Could be, but Landon wasn't convinced. He could just as easily be a trained killer or a former cop.

"Who is he?" she asked.

"We still don't know. But I don't believe it's a coincidence that Joel was there just minutes before this clown showed up."

Tessa made a sound of agreement. "Has anyone questioned Joel yet?"

"Grayson did last night. Of course, Joel claims he had nothing to do with the attack. He also came up with that name of the fire department employee who told his assistant. It was the dispatcher, Valerie Culpepper, and she confirmed she did tell the assistant."

"You believe her?"

"Not sure. Of course, it's possible Joel paid the dispatcher to say that. He could have known you were at the hospital because he or his hired gun was at the scene of the fire and saw you'd been taken away in an ambulance."

Since there was only one hospital in Silver Creek and it wasn't that big of a building, Tessa wouldn't have been hard to find.

Landon's phone buzzed, and when he saw Holden's name on the screen, he stepped away to take the call. Not that he could step far. The guesthouse wasn't that big, but he went into the living room area.

"Dade told me what happened at the hospital," Holden said the moment Landon answered. "Any reason I didn't hear it from you?"

"I've been busy. I'm with Tessa."

"Yeah. I heard that, too." Even though Holden didn't come out and say it, Landon heard the disapproval in his cousin's voice. Probably because Holden knew how

Tessa had treated him. "I'm guessing Tessa's the reason you wanted me to find out about Courtney Hager?"

"She is. The baby that Tessa had with her belongs to Courtney." Landon nearly added some *maybes* in that explanation since he wasn't sure if Tessa was telling him the truth. Not the whole truth, anyway. But Holden would have automatically known that Landon had doubts about his former lover.

"I'll do a more thorough check," Holden continued a moment later, "but here's what I got. Courtney Hager is twenty-nine, unmarried and is a bookkeeper. Her address is listed in Austin."

"Have someone sent out there to do a welfare check on her," Landon suggested. That was only an hour away, but the local cops there could do that ASAP.

"She's in danger?" Holden didn't hesitate with that question.

"Possibly." And that was, sadly, the best-case scenario here. If she truly did have an abusive ex, then it was possible she was already dead. "If she's home, the locals need to take her into custody and bring her here to Silver Creek."

"Got it," Holden assured him. "What about Tessa? You want me to arrange a safe house for her?"

"Thanks, but I'm already working on it." Landon paused. "Are you...okay?"

It wasn't something he'd normally ask his cousin. Holden wasn't exactly the type to want anyone to ask that, either, but Landon wanted to make sure he wasn't pushing Holden too hard this soon after his brother's death.

"I just want to find the bastard who killed Emmett," Holden answered. "I won't be okay until then."

Landon knew exactly how Holden felt. He finished the call and turned to face Tessa.

"I'm going to a safe house?" she asked. Clearly, she'd heard the conversation.

Landon nodded. "The baby will, too. As long as the gunman's out there, you'll need protection."

She didn't disagree with that, but she made a weary sigh and sank down onto the chair. "Joel," was all she said. "It has to be him. He must have been the one who hired that guy who killed Emmett and attacked me. I've been hiding from him all these months, but he must have found me and sent a thug after me."

If Landon followed this line of reasoning, then it was also a thug who'd killed Emmett. "Do you remember why Joel would want you dead?"

She nodded, and since Samantha was finished with the bottle, Tessa put the baby against her shoulder to burp her. "I found out…something." She swallowed hard, and when her gaze met his, Landon saw the tears shimmering in her eyes. "I told you I believed Joel had murdered someone. It was a man named Harry Schuler."

The name didn't mean anything to Landon, but like Courtney, he'd soon find out everything he could about him. "How long have you known about this murder?" he asked.

"Several months."

Landon cursed. Then he bit back more profanity since it seemed wrong to curse in front of a baby. "Months? Why didn't you come to me with this? Or to anybody in law enforcement?"

"No proof. Not just about that but any of the other illegal things that I'm certain Joel was doing."

Landon was certain of those illegal things, too, and he motioned for her to continue.

"By the time Harry Schuler was killed, I'd stopped working for Joel," she went on after taking in a long breath. "But I pretended to stay friendly with Joel so I could keep digging into his business dealings."

"Define *friendly*," Landon snapped.

She flinched a little. "Nothing like that. But I didn't want Joel to know I was on to him."

"Good thing. Or he would have killed you, too. What kind of dirt did you have on Joel?"

Tessa shook her head. "Everything I found was circumstantial at best. Vaguely worded emails and part of a phone conversation I overheard. That's really why I jumped at the chance when Joel wanted me to become a PI, so I'd have the resources and contacts to look for something concrete that could be used for an arrest. I wanted to get some proof because I knew if I accused him and he didn't go to jail, that he would kill me."

Landon tried to process that while he fired off yet another text to his cousin. This time he asked Holden to get him more info on Harry Schuler.

"You said Joel wanted you to be a PI," he reminded her. "You think that's because he could use you in some way? Maybe so he could get access to those data bases you mentioned?"

"Could be, but he never asked me for any specific info from them. He only wanted me to vet potential clients to make sure they had the finances to cover whatever deal he was making with them."

But Joel was smart, and he might have been giving Tessa just enough rope to hang herself. "When specifically did this possible murder happen?"

Silence.

Oh, man. He didn't like this at all.

"That same week we slept together," she finally said. "*Before* we slept together," Tessa clarified.

That made the cut even deeper. She'd had sex with him while withholding something as huge as an alleged murder.

"If you believed Joel was capable of murder, then why leave with him that morning after you were with me?" Landon asked.

Oh.

He saw it in her eyes then. "You thought Joel would try to kill me," Landon concluded.

She nodded. "Maybe even kill both of us."

Landon had to bite back more profanity, and it took him a moment to get his jaw unclenched so he could speak. "Protecting me wasn't necessary, and it was stupid for you to go off with him like that."

"I thought if I went with him, then I'd be able to find the proof that he'd murdered Harry Schuler."

Landon jabbed his finger in her direction. "There's no argument, *none*, that you can make that'll have me agreeing with what you did." He tapped his new badge. "I'm a cop, and I could have handled this the right way."

And there was no chance she could refute that this had been anything but the right way. Now Emmett was dead, Courtney was heaven knew where, and Tessa had a killer after her.

"I was planning to come to you," she said after several quiet moments. "I got your address in Houston and had put it in my GPS, but then the baby kept fussing, so I decided to make a detour to my house here in Silver Creek."

Landon didn't have to tell her that the second part of that wasn't such a good idea. Even though her house was in town and near the sheriff's office, someone could have been watching it.

"Is that how the gunman found you?" he asked. "Were you going to your house?"

She nodded. "I didn't see him following me until it was too late. I tried to outrun him, and that's how I ended up near the barn. The memories are sketchy after that, though. I don't have any idea how I got from my car to the barn."

Because she'd been drugged a second time, that was why. While Landon hoped she would recover all her memories, including those, recalling an attack that'd nearly left her dead wouldn't help her sleep at night. Still, the devil was in the details of those memories.

Emmett's killer was.

And anything she could tell him might help him figure out who'd sent that ski-masked thug after Emmett and her. Or if it was indeed the same thug who'd committed this crime spree.

She stayed quiet a moment, her own jaw muscles stirring. "Tell me about that picture of the man you showed me. Quincy Nagel."

Since Landon was still trying to rein in his temper, it took him a moment to switch gears. "He's someone I arrested. And yes, it's possible he's the one who had Emmett murdered, but right now Joel is looking like my top suspect."

What he needed now was proof. And more answers. Landon thought he might get at least one of those answers on the bedroom phone that Tessa had used to call her friend.

He excused himself without telling Tessa what he was going to do, and he went into the bedroom. Landon went through the cache of recent calls, but Tessa had obviously cleared the one she'd made. There wasn't a good reason for her to do that, and he went back into the living room, ready to demand a full explanation as to what was going on. However, before he could do that, Landon's phone buzzed, and it wasn't his cousin this time.

It was Dr. Michelson.

Since it was barely 6:00 a.m. and nowhere near normal office hours, Landon figured it had to be important, so he answered it right away.

"I just got back the results of Tessa's tests," the doc said, skipping any greeting. "You need to bring her back to the hospital immediately."

Chapter Seven

Tessa couldn't stop herself from thinking the worst. Easy to think the worst after everything she'd been through. But it wasn't the memories of the attacks that troubled her most right now.

It was what she couldn't remember.

Those hours right after she'd been given the drugs were still a blur, and she needed to recall every second of what'd happened to her. Maybe then she would know who had done this to her.

"Any idea what it is?" Dr. Michelson asked Landon. They were looking at what the doctor had just extracted from her neck. It was only about a quarter of an inch long and looked like a tiny bullet.

"I think it's a tracking device," Landon answered.

Tessa's stomach dropped. To think she'd been walking around with that in for heaven knew how long, and she couldn't even remember how she'd gotten it. Of course, it wasn't very big, but she still should have known that something wasn't right, and it sickened her to think of what else this unknown monster could have done to her.

"I'll need it bagged as evidence," Landon instructed the doctor, and he glanced back at her. "You okay?"

Tessa lied with a nod, and even though Landon likely

knew it was a lie, he also understood something else. It could have been much worse.

Now that she'd had a thorough exam, Tessa knew she hadn't been sexually assaulted and that her captor had given her a powerful barbiturate cocktail. She also knew that she hadn't given birth, but then, she hadn't needed an exam to confirm that. Her memories of Courtney calling her and asking her to come and get the baby were clear.

She also had clear memories of how afraid Courtney had been.

Tessa had hurried next door to Courtney's rental house when she'd heard that fear in the woman's voice, and when Courtney had begged her to take the baby for safekeeping, Tessa had done it. After she'd tried to talk Courtney into going to the authorities, that is. Courtney had flat-out refused that, though.

"Why would someone have injected Tessa with a tracking device?" the doctor asked Landon.

"Probably in case she escaped. That way her captor could find her."

Oh, God. "The baby." Tessa tried to get off the table, despite the fact the nurse was still bandaging her neck. "Someone could have used the tracking device to follow us to the ranch."

Landon motioned for her to stay down, and he made a call to the ranch, where they'd left Samantha with a nanny and several of his lawman cousins. The ranch had security, but it wasn't a fortress, and a gunman might be able to get onto the grounds and hurt the baby.

"Everything's fine," Landon relayed after he finished his short call. "The ranch hands are all on alert, and they'll let one of my cousins know if they see anyone suspicious." Landon walked closer to her. "Besides, this tracking device was on you, not the baby."

Yes, he was right. Maybe that meant the gunman wasn't after Samantha at all but just her. That didn't help with the tangle of nerves she was feeling. The newborn could be in danger all because of her.

"Will you be able to tell who was getting information from the tracking device?" she asked once the nurse was out of the room. It wasn't that Tessa didn't trust the woman, but she wasn't sure she fully trusted anyone right now.

Landon lifted his shoulder. "We'll try, but it's probably a microchip that can be tracked with a computer. It does make me wonder, though, why someone would go to the trouble of injecting you with it."

Tessa gave that some thought but had to shake her head. She didn't know why, either, but it was obvious whoever had attacked her had wanted to be able to find her if she escaped.

Unless...

"Maybe this person wanted me to come to you," she said on a rise of breath.

"I'm not a hard man to find," Landon pointed out. "But this could mean the person didn't want you dead. Not when he or she put that tracker device on you, anyway."

True. If someone had gotten close enough to do that to her, they could have easily just killed her. Not exactly a comforting thought.

Dr. Michelson put the tracking device in a plastic bag and looked at Landon. "You want me to have Grayson or one of the other deputies pick this up?"

"No. I'll take it. When will she be free to go?"

The doctor looked at her. "She can leave now but keep an eye on her. The barbiturates have worn off, but she still could experience some dizziness."

Yes, the dizziness was there, and her head still felt a little foggy. Still, it was better than not knowing who she was. At least now she could start to look for the person behind this.

Either Landon had noticed she was wobbly or else he was just being cautious, because he took hold of her arm and helped her from the examining table. "Come on. I can drop off this tracking device at the sheriff's office, and we can give our statements about the attack."

That wasn't exactly a surprise for Tessa. She knew they needed to do the paperwork, but that meant facing yet more Ryland lawmen who wanted answers she didn't have. Even after regaining most of her memories, she didn't know who'd murdered one of their own.

With Landon's grip still firm on her arm, they made their way to the exit. Since Dade had driven with him, she expected to see him waiting in the cruiser just outside. But Tessa stopped in her tracks when she saw the scowling man. Not Dade.

But Deputy Mason Ryland.

None of the Rylands had been especially friendly to her, but Mason had a dark and dangerous edge to him, and right now he was aiming some of that intensity at her.

"Dade had to leave for a parent-teacher thing at the school," Mason growled. "I drew the short straw."

Clearly, he wasn't happy about that, but then, she'd never actually seen Mason happy. "Thank you," Tessa told him, but that only intensified the scowl.

"As soon as you drop us off at the sheriff's office, you

can head back to the ranch," Landon told him Landon's eyes met hers as they got into the backseat of the cruiser. "Mason's retiring as a Silver Creek deputy. That's why Grayson offered me the job."

Tessa knew Mason pretty much ran the sprawling ranch and had done so for years, so that was probably why he was giving up his deputy duties. But she also suspected that Landon had pressed for the job. So he could catch his cousin's killer.

"Who did you call this morning?" Landon asked out of the blue. Except it probably wasn't out of the blue for him. He was like a dog with a bone when he latched on to anything to do with the investigation. And sadly, this might have something to do with it. Of course, it wouldn't be a simple explanation.

Or one that Landon would like.

"His name is Ward Strickland," she said and tried to figure out the best way to spill all of this.

"A boyfriend?" Landon didn't hesitate. He also continued to glance around, no doubt to make sure that they weren't being followed or that the gunman wasn't nearby, ready to launch another attack.

"Hardly. I haven't had a boyfriend since you." She hadn't meant to blurt that out, and it made her sound even more pathetic than she already was. Telling him about Ward wouldn't help that, either. "He's a Justice Department agent." Tessa paused. "But I'm not sure I can trust him."

She hadn't thought anyone's scowl could be worse than Mason's, but she'd been wrong. Landon beat him. "Explain that now," he demanded.

Tessa took a deep breath first. "You already know I was looking for dirt on Joel. Well, Ward said he was, too, and he contacted me to see if I had anything he could use to make an arrest. I didn't, but Ward kept hounding me to dig deeper. He wanted me to tell him anything I found out about Joel."

Landon fired off a text, no doubt to have one of his cousins run a background check on the agent. "Why aren't you sure you can trust him?" Landon asked.

"Gut feeling." She braced herself for Landon to groan. He didn't. "Once I found an email that Joel had sent. It possibly connected him to some illegal arms. *Possibly*," she emphasized. "Anyway, the day before Emmett was killed, I gave Ward a copy of the email, but a few hours later, I noticed the email had been deleted off Joel's server. I'd been checking for things like that, hoping to find something to use to have Joel arrested."

Landon stayed quiet a moment. "You think this agent could be working for Joel and just wanted to figure out if you were on to anything? Or maybe he wanted to make sure you didn't find something?"

There it was in a nutshell. "If Ward is on Joel's payroll, maybe he's the one behind the attacks."

No quiet moment this time. Landon cursed. "So why did you call him this morning? And I'm guessing it wasn't because you thought he could help you find Courtney."

"No. He doesn't know Courtney. I told you that because I didn't want to explain who he was. Not until I'd found out more about what was going on."

Landon made a circling motion with his finger to indicate he wanted this explanation to continue. He also hoped she understood that he wasn't happy with the lie she'd told him.

"I called Ward to feel him out, to try and see if he had

anything to do with this. But he didn't answer. The call went straight to voice mail, so I left a message just to tell him I'd been attacked. And before you tell me that it was risky, that I could have led Ward straight to the ranch, I remember Dade saying it was a prepaid cell, so I knew Ward wouldn't be able to trace it."

More profanity from Landon, and Mason even grumbled some, as well. "If you're that worried about this guy, you should have said something before now. I'm trying to find out who came after us, and I need the names of anyone who could have been involved. *Anyone*," Landon emphasized.

Tessa couldn't argue with that. "I just didn't think you'd want to rely on my gut feelings."

"A disappearing email is more than a gut feeling," Landon verified as Mason pulled to a stop in front of the sheriff's office. "Anyone connected to Joel is a suspect."

No argument there, either. "But Joel doesn't need to hire a federal agent to come after me. I'm sure he already has plenty of hired thugs."

Landon didn't answer. In fact, he was no longer looking at her. Instead, his attention was on the two men who were entering the sheriff's office. One of the men was in a wheelchair, and the other, much larger man was helping him through the door.

"Did Grayson call him in for questioning?" Landon asked.

"No," Mason snarled. "He was going to wait until after he questioned Joel again later this morning. Maybe I should take Tessa back to the ranch while you deal with this?"

Tessa wasn't sure why Mason had said that until she

got a better look at the man in the wheelchair. Landon had shown her his mug shot. Quincy Nagel.

And he was yet another suspect.

Quincy had barely made it into the office when Landon stepped from the car. Quincy turned his wheelchair in their direction, and much to Tessa's surprise, the man smiled.

"Thank God you're here," Quincy said. But he wasn't looking at Landon when he spoke. He was looking at Tessa. "Where's the baby? I'm here to take my daughter home."

LANDON HADN'T BEEN sure what exactly Quincy would say to him, but he hadn't expected *that*.

Clearly, neither had Tessa, because she got out of the cruiser to face the man. In case this was some kind of ploy to get her out in the open so someone could gun her down, Landon hooked his arm around her and maneuvered her into the sheriff's office. Mason followed.

The place wasn't exactly quiet. Two deputies were at their desks in the open squad room, and Landon spotted Grayson in the hall outside his office. Like the deputies, he was in the middle of a phone call, but when he spotted them, he disconnected and headed for them.

"Trouble?" Grayson immediately asked.

Probably. Trouble and Quincy often went together.

"No trouble, Sheriff," Quincy insisted. He didn't sound like the thug that Landon knew he was. Didn't look like one today, either. He was wearing a dark blue suit and so was the linebacker-sized guy behind his wheelchair.

"You said something about a baby?" Tessa asked.

Quincy smiled. "Samantha. I understand you've been keeping her for Courtney."

Landon looked at her to see if this was yet something else she'd kept from him, but she looked as shell-shocked as Landon felt. That precious little girl was Quincy's?

"So where is she?" Quincy asked.

"I don't know what you're talking about," Landon said before Tessa could speak. No way was he handing over a newborn to this man.

Quincy's thin smile didn't stay in place for long. "But you do know." His jaw tightened. Eyes narrowed. "Quit playing games with me and give me my daughter. I know that Courtney gave Tessa the baby, but that's only because she couldn't find me. Well, I'm here now, so give Samantha to me."

Landon needed to stall him until he could either get in touch with Courtney or find out what the heck was going on.

"Tessa and I don't have your daughter," Landon said. "The baby we have is ours."

The squad room suddenly got very quiet. Grayson knew Landon had just lied through his teeth. Mason, too.

Quincy looked Tessa over from head to toe. "You expect me to believe that you just had a baby?"

Even though Tessa was wearing loose loaner jeans, they skimmed her body enough to show her flat stomach. But Tessa didn't panic, and she stepped right into the lie by taking hold of Landon's arm and leaning against him.

"Tessa kept the pregnancy from me," Landon added. "But she had no choice but to come to me when someone tried to kill her. What exactly do you know about that?"

Quincy shook his head as if trying to figure out what was going on, but then Landon saw the moment the man pushed his surprise aside to deal with the accusation. "Nothing. You believe I tried to hurt Tessa?"

"Did you?" Landon didn't even try to sound as if Quincy might be innocent. Plain and simple, Quincy hated him, and he hated Emmett, too, for testifying against him. That hatred could have bubbled over to Tessa.

Except Quincy might not have gone after Tessa because of any ill will he was feeling for Landon. This could indeed be connected to the baby.

"Where's Courtney?" Landon asked.

Quincy shook his head again, and Landon got a flash of the thug behind the newly polished facade. "You tell me. Are you hiding her from me?"

"Is there a reason I'd do that?" Landon countered.

Oh, Quincy did *not* like that. The anger slashed through his eyes. "You have no right. Courtney is my lover, the mother of my child. Tessa knows that."

"No, I don't," Tessa argued. "Courtney's never even mentioned you, but she did tell me that Samantha's father was abusive."

"That's a lie!" Quincy shouted. "I never laid a hand on Courtney."

The goon behind his wheelchair leaned down and whispered something to him. Landon didn't know what the guy said, but it caused Quincy to rein in his temper.

"I want my daughter, and I want her now," Quincy insisted. "And don't say you don't have her, because I know you do."

Landon lifted his shoulder. "You're mistaken." And Landon left it at that. "Now, let's talk about Emmett. About his murder."

The rein on Quincy's temper didn't last long, and

Landon could practically see the veins bulging on the man's neck. "I had nothing to do with that."

"I don't believe you. I think you killed him to get back at me."

The goon whispered something else, or rather that was what he tried to do, but this time Quincy batted him away. "You have no proof linking me to Emmett's death."

"Wrong." Landon decided to test out his latest theory. "You went to Tessa's, looking for Courtney and the baby, and Emmett was there. You got violent, Emmett tried to stop you, and you killed him."

Despite his tense muscles, Quincy managed a smile. "I didn't know you believed in fairy tales. I've never stepped foot in Tessa's place, and that means there's not a shred of physical evidence to link me to it or Emmett's murder." He made a show of gripping on to his wheelchair. "Besides, how could I overpower Emmett when I can't even walk?"

"You don't need to walk to shoot someone," Landon argued. "Or to hire a thug to shoot someone. With the trust fund your parents left you, I'm betting you've got plenty of funds to hire plenty of thugs."

"Prove it," Quincy snapped. He motioned for his goon to get him moving. "In the meantime, I'll work on getting a court order to force you to turn over my daughter to me. Neither Courtney nor you will keep her from me."

Landon considered holding Quincy for questioning, but the man would just lawyer up. It was best if Landon backed off, regrouped and figured out exactly how Quincy was involved in this.

Quincy's goon wheeled him out of the sheriff's office, but Landon didn't stand there and watch them leave. He moved Tessa away from the windows in case Quincy or his hired gun started shooting. Since Landon didn't have a private office, he took her down the hall to one of the interview rooms.

"I didn't know Quincy was involved with Courtney," Tessa said the moment they were inside. "I told the truth when I said she'd never mentioned him."

Landon believed her. "Quincy could have been lying about Courtney."

Tessa blinked. Shook her head. "But why would he do that?"

"I'm not sure." But Landon intended to find out. He took out his phone, and this time he didn't text his cousin Holden. He called him, and he put it on Speaker. Mainly because he knew Tessa would want to hear this, and he didn't want her standing too close to listen. "Please tell me you found out something, anything, about Courtney Hager."

"Bad morning?" Holden asked, probably because Landon hadn't even bothered with a greeting.

"I've had better. I just had a visit from Quincy Nagel claiming he's the father of the baby Tessa was protecting. Courtney Hager's baby."

"Quincy, huh? Haven't found a connection between Courtney and him. Uh, can Nagel even father a child?"

"His paralysis is in his legs, so yes, I'm guessing he could. But that doesn't mean he did. What did you find out about Courtney?"

"Not much at all. She has no criminal record, and she did have a baby just last week. She also moves around a lot. I mean like every couple of months. The local cops did a welfare check for me, but she wasn't home, and her neighbors said they hadn't seen her in days."

That was possibly because she was on the run, hiding

out from Quincy, but it was just as possible that she was hurt. Or dead. Quincy could have gotten to her before he came looking for his baby. If he had a baby, that is.

"Did you have DNA tests run on the baby?" Holden asked.

"Yes," Landon answered. "But I did that in case the child turned out to be mine. Now we could look for a match with Quincy, and it'll speed things up because Quincy's DNA is already in the system."

"I'll get to work on seeing if it's a match. And I'll keep looking for a connection between Quincy and her," Holden went on. "By the way, did Tessa remember anything else that could help us find Emmett's killer?"

"Nothing so far, but Grayson is questioning Joel later this morning. I'll be here for that—after I take Tessa back to the ranch."

Tessa's gaze flew to his. "I want to be here for Joel's interview, too," she insisted.

His first reaction was to say no, that she didn't need to go another round with Joel, but if Landon had been in her place, he would have wanted to hear what the creep had to say about the attack.

"I'll let you two work that out," Holden grumbled. "If I find out anything else, I'll call you."

Landon put his phone away and stared at her. "Tell me everything you know about Courtney. How did you meet? How long have you known her?"

"Like I already told you, I've only known her a few months. She moved into the rental house next to me, and while she was waiting on her internet to be connected, she came over and asked to use mine." She paused. "I did a computer check on Courtney, to make sure she wasn't someone Joel hadn't sent over to spy on me. I didn't find anything."

Good. Because a connection to Quincy was bad enough. Still, that didn't mean this wasn't all stirred together somehow. But at the moment Landon couldn't see how. If Quincy had arranged for Courtney and Tessa to meet, what could he have gained by that? It was the same for Courtney. If the woman had known about his affair with Tessa or Landon and Quincy's bad blood, why wouldn't she have said anything about it?

Landon was still trying to piece together some answers when his phone buzzed, and he saw the name on the screen of someone who just might be able to help him with those answers.

Ward Strickland.

Tessa must have seen it, too, because she pulled in her breath. "I want to talk to him," she insisted.

"For now, just listen," Landon instructed. Whether she would or not was anyone's guess. Like his, her nerves were sky-high right now.

"Deputy Ryland," Ward said the moment Landon answered. "Your cousin Holden told me you needed to speak to me. Is this about Tessa? Do you know where she is?"

Landon took a moment to consider how to answer that. "She's in protective custody. Someone's been trying to kill her," he settled for saying.

"Yes, I heard. She left me a message but didn't give me any details. Is she all right?" The man's tone sounded sincere enough, but Landon wasn't going to trust him merely on that.

"For now. But I need proof as to who's behind these attacks. I'm hoping you can help with that."

Even from the other end of the line, Landon heard the agent's weary sigh. "I'm sure Tessa would say it's Joel."

"Is it?" Landon pressed.

"Maybe, but I've been investigating Joel for a year now, and I haven't found any evidence to arrest him for a misdemeanor, much less the felonies that Tessa claims he's been committing."

Tessa shook her head and looked ready to launch into an argument about that, but Landon motioned for her to keep quiet.

"You believe Joel's innocent?" Landon came out and asked Ward.

"No, not totally, but I'm not sure I believe what Tessa said he did. In fact, I'm not sure I can trust Tessa."

Thankfully, Tessa didn't gasp or make a sound of outrage, though there was some anger going through her eyes.

"I need to talk to Tessa," Ward went on. "I tried to trace the call she made to me, but it came from a pre-paid cell, and she didn't leave a number where she could be reached."

"You want to talk to her even if you don't trust her?" Landon snapped.

"Of course." The agent paused. "Because I'm not just investigating Joel. I'm also investigating her. I believe they're working together, or else Tessa could be using Joel as a front man for several illegal operations. Specifically, gunrunning and money laundering."

Tessa no longer looked angry. But rather defeated. Landon couldn't blame her. She'd been attacked at least three times and had been drugged, and someone had injected her with a tracking device. Now here was a federal agent accusing her of assorted felonies.

"I want to take Tessa into custody," Ward continued. "If she's truly in danger, I can protect her. And if she's helping Joel, maybe I can learn that, too. When can I pick her up?"

Landon's first instinct was to tell his guy to take a hike, but there was no sense showing Ward his hand. "I'll get back to you on that. Gotta go." And Landon ended the call.

Tessa was shaking her head before Landon even slipped his phone back into his pocket. "I'm not going with Ward. He could be trying to set me up to cover for Joel."

She turned as if to bolt out of there, but Landon took hold of her shoulders to stop her. "You're not going anywhere with Ward."

Her breath rushed out. Maybe from relief, but her eyes watered. "I'm not helping Joel," she said, her voice more breath than sound. "And I'm not a criminal."

Landon wasn't made of ice, especially around Tessa, and seeing those fresh tears in her eyes melted the ice he wished were there. Cursing himself, cursing Tessa, too, he slid his arm around her waist and eased her closer.

She melted against him. As if she belonged there.

His body seemed to think she belonged, not just in his arms. But other places. Like his bed. Still, Landon pushed that aside and tried to do what any de-iced human would do—comfort Tessa. It seemed to work, until she looked up at him.

Hell.

He didn't want another dose of this, but he wasn't exactly moving away from her, either. In fact, Landon thought he might be inching closer.

Yeah, he was.

And he didn't just inch with his body. He lowered his head, touched his mouth to hers. Now would have been a really good time for her to come to her senses and push him away. Thankfully, she did. Tessa stepped back.

"I'll bet you're already regretting that," she said, pressing her lips together a moment.

"I regretted it before I even did it." Regretted even more that it would happen again.

Landon wanted to think he could add a *probably* to that—that other kisses would probably happen—but he wasn't a man who approved of lying to himself. The *probably* was a lie. If he was around Tessa, he would kiss her again. And that was a really good reason to come up with other arrangements for her protective custody.

Definitely not Ward. But maybe he could arrange for her to stay with Holden for a while.

There was a knock at the door, and even though Tessa was no longer in his arms, she moved back even farther. The door opened, and Grayson stuck his head inside. His attention went to Tessa, not Landon.

"There's a woman lurking across the street," Grayson said. "I haven't been out there, because I didn't want to spook her, but it's possible it's Courtney."

That got Tessa moving, and Landon had to hurry to get in front of her. "I don't want you outside," Landon reminded her.

He wasn't even sure she heard him, because Tessa was already looking out the window. Landon did the same, and it didn't take him long to spot the woman. Lurking was a good description since she was in the narrow alley between two buildings, and she was glancing over at the sheriff's office.

Landon had seen Courtney's driver's license photo,

but it was hard to tell if it matched this woman. The hair color was right, but she was wearing a baseball hat that she'd pulled low over her face. Also, with the baggy dark blue dress she was wearing, he couldn't tell if she had recently given birth.

"It could be her," Tessa said, shaking her head. "But I'm not sure."

"I'll go out and talk to her," Landon volunteered. "Wait here," he warned Tessa. "And I mean it."

Grayson stepped beside her and gave Landon a glance to assure him that Tessa was staying put. Good. One less thing to worry about.

Landon went outside, but he didn't make a beeline toward the woman. If this was Courtney, then she probably wouldn't trust him just because he was a cop. He first wanted to make sure it was her, and then he could try to coax her into going inside.

But the woman surprised Landon by calling out to him. "Are you Landon Ryland, the cop Tessa told me about?" she asked.

"I am." Landon went a little closer, wishing he could get a better look at her face.

And he did.

The woman moved out from the alley, not onto the sidewalk but just enough for him to see her.

Hell.

It wasn't Courtney. Landon didn't have a clue who she was, but when she lifted her hand, he saw the gun.

The gun she pointed right at him.

Chapter Eight

Tessa got just a glimpse of the woman taking aim at Landon before Grayson shoved her behind him.

"Get down!" Tessa managed to shout to Landon. But it was already too late.

The woman fired at him.

Landon dropped down, and the bullet slammed into the window. The glass was reinforced, so the shot didn't go through into the squad room, but Landon wasn't behind the glass. He was out there in the open.

Oh, God.

It was happening again. Someone was trying to kill them, and Landon was in danger because of her.

It was hard for Tessa to see around Grayson, and it got even harder when the other two deputies stepped up, as well. All three of them took aim, but it was Grayson who stepped out. He delivered a shot that had the woman ducking back into the alley, and the sheriff continued to shoot at her until Landon could scramble back inside.

"It's not Courtney," Landon relayed to her.

Tessa heard him, but she couldn't respond, because she had to make sure he wasn't hurt. There'd been a lot of shots fired, but Landon appeared to be unharmed.

And riled to the core.

"I don't want her to get away," Landon growled. "I'll go out back and see if I can get her in my line of sight."

"I'll do it," Grayson insisted. "In the meantime, take Tessa to my office. This could be some kind of trap."

Tessa hadn't even thought of that, but he was right. There were four lawmen in the building, and their instincts were no doubt to go in pursuit of the shooter. That might be exactly what their attacker wanted, and he could use this to come after Tessa again. Still, she didn't want Grayson hurt, either.

"Be careful," Tessa called out as the sheriff and one of the other deputies hurried toward the back exit.

Landon didn't waste any time taking her to Grayson's office, but he didn't go inside with her. He stayed in the hall with his gun ready while he volleyed glances at both the front and back of the building.

Another shot.

But Tessa didn't know if the woman had fired it or if it was Grayson.

"She wanted us to think she was Courtney," Tessa said, thinking out loud.

"Yeah. I believe she was sent here to draw you out."

And it'd nearly worked. If Landon hadn't held her back, Tessa would have indeed gone out there. But which of their suspects would be most likely to use a Courtney look-alike to do that?

Quincy Nagel.

Plus, the man had just left the building, so he could be out there somewhere watching his "handiwork." It sickened her to think of Courtney being involved with a man like that. Sickened her even more that Quincy might have already found Courtney and killed her.

"Hell," Landon growled. "I don't need this now."

Tessa could see why he'd said that, but it sent her heart pounding, and a moment later she heard a voice she didn't want to hear. Joel.

"What the hell's going on?" Joel spat out.

She heard some kind of struggle, maybe between Joel and the deputy, but Landon didn't budge. However, he did take aim in that direction, and every muscle in his body was primed for a fight.

"Keep your hands where I can see them," Landon ordered, and a moment later Joel scrambled into the hallway. He dropped down onto the floor, his back against the wall.

"If you demand a man come in for an interrogation," Joel snapped, "then you should make sure the place is safe first. Who the hell is shooting?"

"I thought you might know something about that," Landon countered. Now he was including Joel in those volleyed glances, and the man who crawled to Joel's side. His lawyer, no doubt.

Tessa knew that Joel was indeed coming in for an interview, and judging from the timing of the attack, this could make him appear innocent. Appear. But it was just as likely that Joel had orchestrated it just for that reason. If so, it was still risky since Joel could have been hit by a stray bullet.

More shots came.

These didn't seem as close as the others, but they still sliced through Tessa as if they'd been fired at her. Then everything stopped, and she held her breath, waiting and praying.

"Grayson's coming back," Landon relayed to her, but he still didn't budge. He stayed in front of her like a sentry.

Tessa managed to get a glimpse of Joel to see how he was dealing with this, but he was checking his phone. Obviously, being caught in the middle of an attack hadn't caused him to go into the panic mode, which only supported her notion that he could have set all of this in motion.

"I had to shoot her," she heard Grayson say. "She's dead." He didn't sound any happier about that than Landon was, and Tessa knew why. A dead shooter couldn't give them any answers.

"Get into the interview room and close the door," Landon told Joel and the lawyer, and he didn't say anything else until they had done that. "Did she say anything?" he added.

Grayson joined them in the hall, and he shook his head. "She had no ID on her, but she did have a phone. Josh is looking at it now."

Good. Maybe they'd find something to tell them who she was and who had hired her. Maybe.

Grayson tipped his head to the interview room. "Let Joel know it's going to be a while before I can talk to him. Then, you can go ahead and get Tessa out of here if you want."

She could see the debate Landon was having with himself about that. He no doubt wanted to be part of this investigation, but that wouldn't happen if he was with her at the ranch.

"As long as the baby's safe, I'll be okay here for a while longer," she offered.

"My cousins will call if there's a problem at the ranch," he said. Landon looked at the interview room. "But now that Quincy and Joel both know you're here, this is probably the last place you should be."

Ironic because it was a sheriff's office, but Tessa could see his point. As long as she was in danger, so were Landon and his cousins.

He went across the hall and opened the door of the interview room. Joel and his lawyer were huddled together, talking, but they hushed the moment Landon stepped in.

"You're going to have to wait for the interview," Landon insisted. He certainly didn't offer Joel the opportunity to reschedule.

"Who fired those shots?" Joel asked. "And don't bother accusing me, because I didn't do it. Nor did I hire someone. Was it Quincy Nagel?"

Because she was standing so close to Landon, she felt his muscles go stiff. Tessa was certain some of her muscles did the same thing. She stepped in the doorway next to Landon so she could face Joel.

"How do you know Quincy?" Landon asked, taking the question right out of her mouth.

Joel looked as if he was fighting a smile. "Really? You don't think I've made it my business to learn everything I can about both Tessa and you? I know you crossed paths with Quincy, and I know he wants to get back at you. I saw him and some guy in a suit just seconds before the shots started. Why was he here?"

"As you said, he wants to get back at me," Landon answered. Not exactly the truth, but she didn't want to discuss Quincy's possible paternity with Joel. "What'd you learn about Quincy?"

Joel stared at him as if trying to figure out if this was some kind of trick. It wasn't, but it was a fishing expedition.

"I know you arrested him," Joel finally answered,

"that he's paralyzed because of a prison fight. But I have no idea if he's the one who murdered Emmett."

"Anything else?" Landon pressed.

Joel did more staring. "What are you looking for on Quincy?"

"You tell me."

Joel chuckled. "It must make your hand really tired, holding your cards so close to the vest like that. Well, no need. I really don't know anything about Quincy."

Landon made a sound to indicate he didn't buy that. Neither did Tessa. Joel knew something…but what? Tessa would have definitely pressed for more, but from the corner of her eye, she saw Grayson motioning for them. Landon shut the door of the interview room and headed toward his cousin.

"We might have found something," Grayson said the moment they joined him. "Josh looked through the shooter's recent calls, and there's a name you'll recognize."

Tessa figured Grayson was about to say Joel's or Quincy's name. But no.

Grayson lifted the phone and showed them the screen, and Tessa had no trouble seeing the name of the caller.

Agent Ward Strickland.

WAITING HAD NEVER been Landon's strong suit, and this time was no different. Where the hell was Ward Strickland and why wasn't the agent returning Landon's calls? One way or another, he would find out why, but for now he had to wait it out.

Along with keeping Tessa and the baby safe.

That was the reason he'd brought Tessa back to the ranch, but at the time he'd done that, Landon had thought it would be only a couple of hours, but here it was nearly nightfall, and they still had nothing.

Tessa stared at him from over the dinner that the cook had brought from the main house. Fried chicken, some vegetables and homemade bread. Landon had eaten some of it. Tessa, too. But judging from the way she was picking at her food, her appetite was as off as his. Nearly being killed could do that.

"You think Ward could be dead?" she asked.

Landon had gone over all the possibilities, and yeah, that was one of them. The person behind this could have set up Ward with that phone call to the dead shooter and then murdered Ward. Without a body, it would certainly look as if Ward was guilty. And maybe he was. But Landon wanted to make sure. Tessa's and the baby's safety depended on it.

As if on cue, Samantha stirred in the bassinet. Since she'd probably want another bottle soon, Landon figured she'd wake up and start fussing, but she went back to sleep.

"So how long do we stay here?" Tessa asked.

Good question. Landon had gone over all the possibilities and for now had put the safe house on hold.

"I figured we'd need at least one of my cousins to go with us to a safe house, and that would mean tying up a deputy, one Grayson will need," he explained. "At least by being at the ranch, the hands can help with security."

She nodded but didn't look especially pleased about that. Maybe because she just felt as if she were in hostile territory here because of her connection to Emmett's death. Or maybe it was him.

Or rather that stupid kiss.

Their gazes met, and Landon knew which one it was.

Definitely the kiss. Clearly, Tessa wasn't any more comfortable with the attraction than he was, because she looked away and stood. Too bad Landon did the same thing at the exact same time, and in the small space they nearly bumped into each other.

The corner of Tessa's mouth lifted in a short-lived half smile. "It's a good thing we don't have time for this," she said in a whisper.

If he'd wanted to be a jerk, he could have asked her what she was talking about, but Landon knew. It was the attraction—the reason that kiss had happened. And she was right. They didn't have time for "this."

He had things he could be doing to try to move the investigation along. Calls to make. Of course, none of those calls had resulted in anything so far, but now that they'd finished eating, he needed to get back to it. So far, they'd yet to find a number for Courtney. There wasn't a phone in her name anyway, but she could have been using a prepaid cell.

But he didn't get back to the calls.

Like in the sheriff's office, his feet seemed anchored to the floor, and he couldn't take his eyes off Tessa. What else was new? He'd always had that trouble around her, but unlike at the sheriff's office, Landon didn't pull her to him. Didn't kiss her. Instead, he took out his phone to start those calls, but before he could make the first one to Grayson, there was a knock at the door.

Landon automatically put his hand over his gun, but when he looked out the window, he realized it wasn't a threat. It was his cousin Lieutenant Nate Ryland, a cop in the San Antonio PD, and he wasn't alone. He had four kids with him. The oldest, Kimmie, was Nate's eight-year-old daughter, but the other three were Nate's nieces and nephew.

"Supplies," Nate said after Landon opened the door. He had two plastic bags, one with disposable diapers and the other containing formula.

"And a dolly for the baby," Kimmie added. She held up a curly-haired doll for Landon to see.

The four kids came in ahead of Nate and made a bee-line for the bassinet. Tessa stepped back as if clearing the way, or maybe she was just alarmed by the sudden onset of chattering, running kids. Her nerves probably weren't all that steady yet, and Landon wasn't even sure she had much experience being around children.

Kimmie looked in at the baby, putting the doll next to the bassinet, but one of the other girls, Leah—at least, Landon thought it was Leah—hurried to him and hugged him. Since Leah and her twin sister, Mia, were only six years old, that meant the little girl ended up hugging his legs. Landon scooped her up and kissed her cheek.

"Are all these your children?" Tessa asked Nate.

Nate smiled. "Just that one." He pointed to Kimmie, who had her face right against Samantha's. "The boy is Grayson's son, Chet. He's five. And the twins belong to my brother Kade and his wife, Bree."

"And Uncle Landon," Leah corrected, snuggling against Landon. Landon was her cousin, not her uncle, but since Nate had five brothers, Landon figured the kids gave the uncle label to any adult Ryland male.

"Yep. I'm yours," Landon agreed, and that seemed to surprise Tessa, too. Or maybe the surprise was just because he was smiling. Landon certainly hadn't done much of that in the past couple of weeks.

"Can we keep her?" Chet asked, looking down at Samantha.

Nate didn't jump to answer, which meant he probably didn't know the situation. He knew that Samantha wasn't Landon's daughter, of course, but with the baby's mother missing, it was possible she might be at the ranch for a while.

"Don't you have enough cousins?" Nate teased the boy. He ruffled his dark brown hair.

Chet shook his head. "I don't have a sister. Once I get a brother or sister, it'll be enough."

"You'll need to talk to your mom and dad about that. Grayson and his wife, Eve, are thinking about adopting since they can't have any more children of their own," Nate added to Tessa.

Landon set Leah back down on the floor so she, too, could go see the baby, and once all four kids were gathered around the bassinet, Nate went closer to Landon and Tessa.

"I got a call from the crime lab a few minutes ago," Nate said, and he kept his voice low. Probably so the kids wouldn't hear. "Grayson asked me to try to cut through some red tape so he could get the baby's DNA test results and the tracking device the doctor took from Tessa. It's not good news on either front."

Tessa groaned softly. "Is Samantha Quincy's baby?"

"The results aren't back on that yet, but Quincy does have a fairly rare blood type, and it matches Samantha's."

Yeah, definitely not good. "Quincy said he was going to get a court order," Landon told Nate.

Nate nodded. "He's already started proceedings. Of course, his record won't work in his favor, but since he's served his time, a judge probably wouldn't block a demand for custody. That's why Grayson's pushing so hard to find the baby's mother. Still no sign of her, though."

Hell. It sickened Landon to think of Quincy getting anywhere near the newborn, much less taking her. If Courtney was still alive, Quincy could use the baby to force her to come back to him.

"What about the microchip taken from Tessa?" Landon asked.

"It's not traceable. There were thousands of them made, and the techs can't work out who, if anyone, was even monitoring it." Nate paused. "Though I'm guessing someone was monitoring it and that's how Tessa ended up in that burning barn."

Tessa made a sound of agreement. "And I don't remember who did that to me. In fact, I still don't remember much about the hours after the two times I was drugged."

That was too bad, but the doctor had already warned Landon that those memories might be lost for good.

"Are you two, uh, back together?" Nate came out and asked.

"No," Tessa said even faster than Landon.

Maybe it was the fast answers. Maybe their body language was giving off some signs of the attraction. Either way, Nate just flexed his eyebrows.

"All right, kids, let's go," Nate said.

That got varied reactions. The twins were already bored with the baby, probably because they had a baby sister of their own at home, but Chet lingered a couple of extra seconds.

"Can't we wait until she wakes up?" Kimmie begged.

"Afraid not. I gotta get ready for work, but maybe

you can come back in the morning with Uncle Mason when he stops by."

Despite Mason being the most unfriendly looking guy in the state, that pleased Kimmie. Probably because she had her uncle Mason wrapped around her little finger.

Landon got hugs from all four of them, but just as he was seeing them out, his phone buzzed, and he saw Grayson's name on the screen. Landon looked up while he answered it.

"We found Ward," Grayson greeted, but Landon could tell from the sheriff's tone that this wasn't good news. "Someone ran his car off the road, and he's banged up. He said he spent most of the afternoon at the hospital and that's why he didn't answer his phone."

"Could his injuries have been self-inflicted?" Tessa immediately asked. Landon hadn't put the call on Speaker, but she was close enough to hear.

"Possibly. I'll ask him about that when he comes in for questioning in the morning." Grayson paused. "But you should know that Ward is saying that Tessa's responsible, that she hired the person who tried to kill him." Another pause. "Ward is demanding that I arrest her."

Chapter Nine

Tessa's nerves were still raw and right at the surface, and walking into the sheriff's office didn't help. Neither would coming face-to-face with Ward, since he was accusing her of a serious crime that could lead to her arrest. Still, she wanted to confront him, wanted to try to get to the truth. But there was a problem with that.

Landon.

He didn't want her anywhere near Ward when the agent was being questioned. It had taken some doing for Tessa to talk him into allowing her to go with him and that had been only after she'd agreed she wouldn't take part in the interrogation. However, she would be able to listen and she was hoping Landon could convince Ward that she'd had no part in running him off the road.

"Move fast," Landon reminded her the moment they stepped from his truck.

He'd parked it directly in front of the sheriff's office, so it was only a few steps outside, but considering the hired gun had fired those shots just the day before, with each step, she felt as if she were in a combat zone. No way would Tessa mention that, though, since Landon was no doubt leaning toward the idea of having someone escort her back to the ranch so she could stay with the baby, his lawman cousins and the rest of his family. They'd left the baby with Mason and the nanny, and while she didn't want them to be inconvenienced for too long, this meeting was important.

"Is Ward here yet?" Landon asked Grayson the moment they were inside. Landon also moved her away from the window. Not that he had to do much to make that happen, since Tessa had no plans to stand anywhere near the glass.

Grayson nodded. "Ward's in the interview room. He still wants you arrested for hiring the person who ran him off the road," he added to Tessa.

Tessa had figured Ward wouldn't have a change of heart about that, but she had to shake her head. "Has he said why he believes I did that?"

"Not yet, but he's claiming he has proof."

Since Tessa knew she was innocent, there was no proof. But Ward might believe he had something incriminating.

"Well, we have proof of his connection to the dead woman who tried to kill us," Landon countered.

But there was something in Grayson's expression that indicated otherwise. "We checked the phone records. Ward didn't answer the call from her."

Tessa groaned because she knew that meant Ward could claim not only that he didn't know the woman but also that the call had been made to set him up.

And it was possible that was true.

Heck, it was possible that the same person was trying to set up both of them. Joel maybe? Or Quincy? Tessa knew why Joel or even Quincy might want to set her up, but what she needed to find out was if and how Ward was connected to this.

"Quincy's lawyer has been pestering us this morning," Grayson went on. "He's trying to find a judge who'll grant him temporary custody."

Landon cursed under his breath. "Then I need to find a judge who'll block his every move." He tipped his head to the interview room. "Speaking of our sometimes-warped legal system, did Ward manage to get a warrant for Tessa's arrest?"

Grayson shook his head. "But he claims he's working on it."

"I am," someone said.

Ward.

The lanky sandy-haired agent was standing in the doorway of the interview room and stepped into the hall. His attention stayed nailed to her.

It didn't surprise her that Ward had heard Landon and her talking with Grayson. In fact, he'd no doubt been listening for her to arrive so he could confront her with the stupid allegation that she'd tried to kill him.

"Tessa," Ward greeted, but it wasn't a friendly tone.

He walked closer. Or rather he limped closer. In addition to the limping, there was also a three-inch bandage on the left side of his forehead and a bruise on his cheek. It was obvious he'd been banged up, but Tessa figured she beat him in the banged-up-looking department.

Grayson tipped his head to the interview room. "You and I will go back in there and get started."

But Ward didn't budge. "Why do you want me dead?" he asked Tessa.

"I could ask you the same thing," she countered. It was obvious that neither Grayson nor Landon wanted her to confront Ward, but Tessa couldn't stop herself.

Ward scowled at her. "If I'd wanted you dead, I

wouldn't have hired some idiot gunwoman who just happened to be carrying a phone that she used to call me. Lots of people know my phone number. Even you."

That was true, but that didn't mean Ward was innocent. It could have been a simple mistake, or else done as a sort of reverse psychology.

"Why do you think I'm trying to kill you?" Tessa asked.

Ward glanced at Landon. Then Grayson. "That was something I'd planned on telling the Texas Rangers. I figure the Silver Creek lawmen are a little too cozy with you to make sure justice is served."

Landon stepped closer, and he had that dangerous look in his eyes. "I always make sure justice is served," he snarled. "And you'd better rein in your accusations when it comes to me, Tessa and anyone else in this sheriff's office."

The anger snapped through Ward's eyes, and she could tell he wanted to challenge that. But he wasn't in friendly territory here, and he was indeed throwing out serious accusations that Tessa knew he couldn't back up.

"Let's take this to the interview room," Grayson said, and it wasn't a suggestion. He sounded just as dangerous as Landon.

"You're not joining us?" Ward asked when she didn't go any farther than the doorway.

While she wanted to know answers, she didn't want to compromise the interrogation that could possibly help them learn about a killer. "I just want to hear whatever proof you claim to have against me."

Ward didn't say anything, but he took out his phone and pressed a button. It didn't take long for the recorded voice to start pouring through the room.

"Tessa Sinclair can't be trusted," the person said. "She paid my friend to try to kill you."

That was it, all of the message, and the voice was so muffled that Tessa couldn't even tell if it was a man or a woman. But it didn't matter. Someone was trying to frame her.

"Is there any proof to go along with that?" Grayson asked, taking the question right out of her mouth.

Ward's face tightened. "No. And the call came from a prepaid cell that couldn't be traced."

Even though Tessa already knew there wouldn't be real proof, the relief flooded through her. "Someone's trying to set us up."

"Why would you think Tessa had done something like this?" Landon asked as soon as she'd finished speaking.

Ward lifted his shoulder. "I figured it was all connected. Emmett's murder. Joel. And what with Tessa being involved with Joel—"

"I wasn't involved with him," Tessa interrupted. "At least, not involved in the way you're making it sound. I was trying to find proof to send him to jail. So was Emmett. That's why he was at my house the night someone killed him."

Ward shifted his attention to Landon. "And that someone left that note tying you to the murder?"

Landon just nodded, but Tessa could tell from the way his back straightened that the connection not only sickened him but was also the reason he'd moved back to Silver Creek.

"What do you know about Quincy Nagel?" Landon asked.

Ward just stared at him. "He's involved in this?"

Landon stared at Ward, too. "I asked first."

Ward clearly didn't care for Landon's tone, but Tessa didn't care for Ward's hesitation on what was a fairly simple question.

"Word on the street is that Quincy wants to get back at you for arresting him. He blames you for being paralyzed." Ward paused again. "But I don't know whether or not he's connected to any of this." He huffed and scrubbed his hand over his face. "In fact, I don't know what the hell is going on."

Tessa felt relief about that, too. At least he wasn't yapping about trying to have her arrested.

"I'm shaken up, I guess," Ward went on a moment later. But then there was more of that anger in his eyes when he looked at her. "Swear to me that you didn't have anything to do with trying to kill me."

This was an easy response for her. "I swear. Now I want you to do the same. That gunwoman fired shots into the building. I don't want Landon or anyone else hurt because you're gunning for me."

Ward huffed. "And why exactly do you think I'd be gunning for you?"

Tessa took a couple of moments to figure out the best way to say this, but there was no best way. "I thought you could be working with Joel."

A burst of air left Ward's mouth. Definitely not humor but surprise. "Not a chance."

"Ditto," Tessa countered. "I don't work for him, either."

The silence came, and so did the stares, and it didn't sit well between them. Tessa could almost feel the tension smothering her. It helped, though, when Landon's arm brushed against hers. She wasn't even sure it was intentional until she glanced up at him.

Yes, it was intentional.

Soon, very soon, they were going to have to deal with this unwanted attraction between them.

"Did your memory return?" Ward asked her.

The question was so abrupt that it threw her for a moment. "How did you know I'd lost it?"

"Word gets out about that sort of thing. Did you remember everything?" Ward pressed.

Everything but what mattered most to Landon—who'd murdered Emmett.

"My memory is fine," Tessa settled for saying, and she watched Ward's reaction.

At least, she would have watched for it if he hadn't dodged her gaze. "And the baby that was with you when Landon rescued you from that burning barn? How is she?"

Tessa decided it was a good time to stay quiet and wait to see where he was going with this. It was possible Ward thought she had indeed given birth, because they'd mainly dealt with each other over the phone and it'd been months since she'd seen him in person.

"The baby's okay, too," Landon answered.

Ward volleyed glances between them, clearly expecting more, but neither Landon nor she gave him anything else. If they admitted the baby wasn't theirs, the word might get back to Quincy. She didn't want him to have any more fodder for trying to get custody of the baby.

Ward's glances lasted a few more seconds before he turned his head toward Grayson. "Could we get on with this interview? I also want to read Tessa's statement on the attacks."

"We're still processing the statement," Grayson volunteered.

Since Tessa had made one the night before, she doubted there was any processing to do, but she was thankful that Grayson seemed to be on her side. About this, anyway.

Landon put her hand on her back to get her moving. Not that he had to encourage her much. Tessa figured she'd personally gotten everything she could get from Ward.

"You believe him?" Landon asked. "Do you trust him?" he amended. He didn't take her back into the squad room but rather to the break room at the back of the building.

"No to both. I believe he could have been set up with that phone call from the gunwoman. Just as someone set me up with that phone call to him. But I'm not taking him off our suspect list."

Our.

She hadn't meant to pause over that word, and it sounded, well, intimate or something. Still, Landon and she had been working together, so the *our* applied.

"I should call the ranch and check on the baby," she said. She'd already walked on enough eggshells today, and besides, she did want to check on Samantha.

Landon took out his phone, made the call and then put it on Speaker when Mason answered. "Anything wrong?" Mason immediately asked.

"Fine. We're just making sure Samantha is okay."

"Yeah, I figured that's why you were calling. Are you sure you aren't the parents? Because you're acting like the kid is yours."

Landon scowled. "I'm sure. And just drop the subject and don't make any other suggestions like you did last night."

She couldn't be sure, but she thought maybe Mason chuckled. She had to be wrong about that. Mason wasn't the chuckling type.

"Quincy's not backing off the custody suit," Landon explained. "He's the kind of snake who'd try to sneak someone onto the ranch to steal the baby."

"The hands have orders to shoot at any trespassers— even one who happens to be in a wheelchair."

"Good. Tessa and I won't be much longer, and we'll head back to the ranch as soon as Grayson finishes his chat with Ward."

Landon ended the call, but as he was putting his phone away, his gaze met hers. "What?" he asked.

Tessa hadn't realized she was looking puzzled, but she apparently was. "What suggestions did Mason make?" But the moment she asked it, Tessa wished she could take it back, because Landon looked even more annoyed than he had when Mason had brought it up.

"Mason thinks you and I are together again," Landon finally said.

Tessa wasn't sure how to feel about that. Embarrassed that Mason had picked up on the attraction or worried that what she felt for Landon—what she'd always felt for him—was more than just mere attraction.

"He suggested…" But Landon stopped, waved it off. "He suggested, since it already looks as if we're together, that we should raise the baby. If Quincy is the father, that is, but isn't granted custody."

She figured Mason had suggested a little more than that. Maybe like Landon and her becoming lovers again. Which was the last thing Landon wanted. She hadn't heard any part of his conversation with his cousin, because he'd stepped outside the guest cottage to take the call, but now Tessa wished she'd listened in.

But then she was the one to mentally wave that off.

She didn't need to be spinning any kind of fantasies about Landon, even ones that included the baby's future.

"That kiss shouldn't have happened," Landon said, and his tone indicated it wouldn't happen again. It did, though.

Almost.

He brushed a kiss on her forehead, and his mouth lingered there for a moment as if it might continue. But then they heard something that neither of them wanted to hear.

Joel.

"I have to see Landon and Tessa now," Joel practically shouted. "It's an emergency."

Mercy. What now?

Landon cursed again, and he stepped in front of her as they made their way back to the squad room. Considering the volume and emotion in Joel's voice, Tessa halfway expected to see the man hurt and bleeding. Maybe the victim of another attack. Or the victim of something staged to look like an attack. There didn't appear to be a scratch on Joel, though.

"What do you want?" Landon snarled, and he didn't sound as if he wanted to hear a word the man had to say.

Joel went toward them. His breath was gusting, and he held out his phone. At first Tessa couldn't tell what was on the screen, but as Joel got closer, she saw the photo of the woman.

Oh, God.

"That's Courtney," she said, snatching the phone from Joel.

Now, here was someone who looked hurt and bleeding, and Courtney's blond hair was in a tangled mess around her face.

A face etched with fear.

"Look at what she's holding," Joel insisted, stabbing his index finger at the screen.

But Joel hadn't needed to point out the white sign that Courtney had gripped in her hands. Or the two words that were scrawled on the sign.

Help me.

Chapter Ten

Landon groaned and motioned for Dade to have a look at the picture Joel had just shown them.

"You're sure that's the missing woman?" Dade asked Tessa.

"I'm sure it's Courtney," Tessa answered, though she had to repeat it for her response to have any sound. She was trembling now, and some of the color had drained from her face. "Where is she? How did you get that picture?"

The questions were aimed at Joel, and Landon was about to put the guy in cuffs when he shook his head. "I don't know who or where she is," Joel insisted. "Someone texted me that picture about twenty minutes ago."

Hell. Twenty minutes was a lifetime if Courtney truly did need someone to help her. Landon hoped that *if* wasn't an issue and that the woman wasn't faking this.

"That looks like the bridge on Sanderson's Road," Dade said after he studied the photo a moment.

It did, though it'd been years since Landon had been out there. There were two routes that led in and out of town, and Sanderson's Road wasn't the one that most people took.

"I'll call in Gage and Josh to head out there now," Dade added. He took out his phone and stepped away.

Joel moved as if to step away, as well, but Landon grabbed him by the arm. "Who's the *someone* who texted you that picture?"

"I don't know. Whoever it was blocked the number."

Landon would still have the lab check Joel's phone to see if there was some way to trace it. Or maybe there was even some way to figure out who'd taken the picture. It clearly wasn't a selfie, because he could see both of Courtney's hands, but whoever had snapped the shot was standing close to her.

"Why would someone text you about Courtney?" Tessa asked.

Joel lifted his hands in the air. "None of this makes sense, but what I don't want you doing is blaming the messenger. I did the right thing by bringing you this photo, and I don't want to be blamed for anything."

Landon would reserve blame for later, but Joel could be just as much of a snake as he was a messenger.

Dade finished his call and motioned for Landon to step into Grayson's office with him. Since Landon didn't want Tessa left alone with Joel, he took her with him.

"Gage said someone was spotted near the fence at the ranch," Dade explained.

That didn't help the color return to Tessa's face, and Landon had to step in front of her to keep her from bolting.

"The baby's okay," Dade assured her. "Everyone is. The person ran when one of the hands confronted him, but all of this is starting to feel like a trap."

Landon made a sound of agreement. "Have Josh and Gage stay put at the ranch. I'll get Joel and Ward out of here, and then while Grayson stays with Tessa, you and I can go look for Courtney."

Tessa was shaking her head before he even finished. "Courtney won't trust you. If I go with you, maybe we can get her out of there."

Now it was Landon's turn to shake his head. "You're not going out there."

"I agree," Dade said and then looked at Landon. "But I don't think you should go, either. The two of you are targets. I'll call in the night deputies, and Grayson and I can go after Courtney."

His cousin didn't wait for him to agree to that. Probably because Dade knew he was right. He went to the interview room to fill in Grayson, and Landon returned to the squad room to tell Joel to take a hike. But it wasn't necessary.

Because Joel was already gone.

Normally, Landon would have preferred not having Tessa around a creep like Joel, but it gave him an uneasy feeling that the man had just run out like that.

"I demand to know what's going on," Landon heard Ward say. "Someone's trying to kill me, and I need to know everything about this investigation."

"We'll fill you in when we know something," Grayson said. "Now leave. I'll have someone call you and reschedule the interview."

Ward came out of the interview room, but he didn't head for the exit. He stopped in front of Landon and Tessa. "Tell me what's going on." Then he huffed, and Landon could see the man trying to put a leash on his temper. "I can help," he added as if they would agree to that.

They didn't.

Landon didn't want help from one of their suspects. "Just go," Landon insisted.

Ward glanced at Tessa. Why, Landon didn't know. She certainly wasn't going to ask him to hang around, and while mumbling some profanity, Ward finally turned and stormed out.

Almost immediately Tessa's gaze started to fire around the room. No doubt looking for something she could do to help save her friend. Or at least, the woman she thought was her friend. As far as Landon was concerned, the jury was still out on that.

"Courtney's alive," Landon assured Tessa. "Hang on to that."

She shook her head. "Courtney was alive when that photo was taken. Just because someone sent it to Joel twenty minutes ago, doesn't mean that's when it was taken."

No, it didn't, and there was no way to assure Tessa otherwise.

"Dade and I will leave as soon as the night deputies arrive," Grayson said as Dade and he gathered their things. That included backup weapons.

Hell. Landon wanted to go with them. He wanted to help if his cousins were walking into a trap, but he caught a glimpse of something that reminded him of why he should stay put. Or rather a glimpse of someone.

And that someone was Quincy.

The timing sucked. It usually did when it came to Quincy, but this was especially bad. Landon didn't want Quincy to find out Courtney's last known location, since the woman was on the run, probably because of him.

"I need to see you, Deputy Ryland," Quincy said the

moment his goon helped him maneuver the wheelchair through the door.

"I don't have time for you right now," Landon fired back. "You need to get out of here."

But Quincy wasn't budging. He had some papers in his hand, and he waved them at Landon. "Here's the proof for me to take my daughter. Now, hand her over to me."

Landon really didn't want to deal with this now, but he was hoping that Quincy's proof was bogus.

"This is the result of the DNA test I had run yesterday," Quincy went on. "I paid top dollars to have the results expedited so I'd know the truth. You lied about the baby being yours, and you'll both pay for that lie. Did you honestly think you could keep my daughter from me?"

That was the plan, and Landon wanted to continue with that plan.

He went to Quincy and took the papers, and Tessa hurried toward them so she could have a look, as well. Grayson and Dade stayed back, watching, but both his cousins knew how this could play out if the test results were real.

And they appeared to be.

Appeared.

Landon handed off the paper to Dade so his cousin could call the lab and verify that a test had been done.

"Where did you get the baby's DNA?" Landon asked.

"From Courtney's place in Austin. There was a pacifier in the crib, and I had it tested."

Landon glanced at Tessa to see if that was possible, and she only lifted her shoulder. So, yeah, it was possible. But Landon had no intentions of giving Quincy an open-arms invitation to take a child he'd fathered. Any fool could father a baby.

"Did you just admit that you broke into your ex's house?" Landon pressed.

Clearly, Quincy didn't like that. He leaned forward and for a moment looked ready to come out of that chair and launch himself at Landon. "You can't keep my daughter from me," Quincy snarled.

Maybe not forever, but he darn sure could for now. "A DNA test is a far cry from a court order. I'm guessing even with that so-called proof, which can easily be faked, by the way, that you'll have trouble getting custody. Plus, you haven't proven that the DNA from the pacifier even belongs to the baby we have in custody. So leave now and come back when and if you have a court order."

Quincy would have almost certainly argued about that if the two trucks hadn't pulled to a stop in front of the building and the deputies hadn't hurried inside.

"What's going on?" Quincy asked.

Landon didn't answer, but he did motion for the goon to get Quincy moving. "Either you can leave or I'll arrest you both for obstruction of justice." A charge like that wouldn't stick, of course, but at least Quincy would be locked up.

Quincy glanced at all of them, and while it was obvious he thought this was somehow connected to him, he didn't argue. He said something under his breath to the hired goon, and the guy wheeled him out of the sheriff's office.

"This isn't over," Quincy said from over his shoulder. It sounded like the threat that it was.

"He'll try and follow you," Landon reminded Dade and Grayson.

Grayson nodded, and Dade and he headed out the back.

"I'm not giving Quincy the baby," Tessa insisted.

Just lately they hadn't been in complete agreement, but they were now. Landon put his hand on her back to get her moving to Grayson's office, but they'd hardly made it a step when Landon heard a sound of glass shattering behind them.

He turned to step in front of Tessa, but it was already too late.

The blast tore through the building.

ONE SECOND TESSA was standing, and the next she was on the floor. It took her a moment not only to catch her breath but to realize what had happened. Someone had set off some kind of explosive device.

Oh, God.

Just like that, her heart was back in her throat, and her breath was gusting. Someone was trying to kill them. Again.

Cursing, Landon drew his gun, and in the same motion, he crawled over her. Protecting her again. But not only was he putting himself in danger, Tessa wasn't even sure it was possible to protect her. The front door had been blasted open and one of the reinforced windows had broken.

"Car bomb," she heard Landon say, though it was hard to hear much of anything with the sound of the blast still ringing in her ears.

The words had hardly left his mouth when there was a

second explosion, and even though Tessa hadn't thought it possible, it was louder than the first.

Landon caught on to her, scrambling toward Grayson's office, and he pushed her inside. But he didn't come in. He stayed in the hall with the gun ready and aimed.

"The deputies?" Tessa managed to say. She wasn't sure where they were, though she could hear them talking.

"They're fine."

Good. That was something at least, but another blast could bring down the building. Plus, they had Grayson and Dade to worry about. They were outside, somewhere, and while they'd gone out through the back, that didn't mean someone hadn't been waiting there to ambush them.

If so, the photo of Courtney had been a trap.

That sickened Tessa, but if that was indeed what it'd been, that didn't mean Courtney had wanted this to happen. Courtney would have likely been forced to have that picture taken. Which meant she was innocent.

"Stay down," Landon warned her when Tessa lifted her head.

She did stay down, but Tessa crawled to the desk, opened the center drawer and found exactly what she'd hoped to find.

A gun.

She wasn't a good shot, but she needed some way to try to defend herself if things escalated. And they did escalate.

"There's a gunman!" Grayson shouted.

Tessa couldn't tell where the sheriff was, but the sound of the gunshot confirmed his warning. And from the sound of it, the gunshot came through into the squad room. It wasn't a single shot, either.

More came.

"Hell, there's more than one gunman," Landon grumbled.

Tessa was about to ask how he knew that, but it soon became crystal clear. Bullets started to smack into the window just above her head. The reinforced glass was stopping them. For now. But whoever was firing those shots was determined to tear through the glass.

But how had the shooter known Landon and she were inside the office?

Maybe their attackers had some kind of thermal scan or were on the roof of one of the nearby buildings. Not exactly a thought to steady her nerves, because it was daylight and any one of those shots could hit an innocent bystander.

"One of them is using an Uzi," Grayson called out. "Everybody stay down."

Tessa certainly did, but Landon didn't. He scurried toward her and maneuvered into the corner so that the desk was between the window and her. Not that it would do much good. The Uzi could fire off a lot of shots in just a few seconds, and it wouldn't be long before those bullets made it through the glass, and then Landon and she would be trapped. He must have realized that, too.

"We have to move," he said. "Stay low and go as fast as you can."

Tessa barely had time to take a breath before Landon had them moving. He stayed in front of her as they barreled out into the hall, and he didn't waste a second shoving her into the interview room where Ward had been just minutes earlier.

She caught a glimpse of the shooter then. One of them, anyway. The man had on a ski mask and was behind a car parked in front of the café across the street. The position gave him a direct line of sight into the sheriff's office, especially now that the door was open. And the shooter made full use of that.

He fired at Landon.

The bullet came too close, smacking into the wall right next to Landon's hand. Tessa latched on to his arm and pulled him into the room with her, and she prayed the deputies were doing something to stay out of the path of those shots. There was another hall leading to the holding cells on that side of the building, so maybe they'd used that.

More shots.

Maybe some of them were coming from Grayson or Dade, though it was hard to tell. Though it wasn't hard to tell when Landon fired. He leaned out the doorway, took aim and pulled the trigger.

"The shooter got through the window," Landon growled.

Mercy. That meant he was in the building, and if this was the gunman with the Uzi, he could mow them all down.

Landon fired another shot. Then another.

It was hard for Tessa to see much of anything, but she did catch a glimpse of a man peering out from Grayson's office. He, too, wore a ski mask and what appeared to be full body armor.

Landon had no choice but to duck back into the interview room when the guy started firing, but there was no way they could let this monster get any closer. Though she knew Landon wasn't going to like it, she lifted her head and body just enough to fire a shot.

She missed.

The bullet tore into the office doorjamb, but it must have distracted the guy just enough. Landon cursed—some of the profanity aimed at her—and he fired again. This time at the guy's head.

Landon didn't miss.

Tessa heard the shooter drop to the floor. Thank God. But she also heard someone else.

The shots stopped.

The relief washed over her. Until Grayson shouted out something she didn't want to hear.

"The second gunman's getting away!"

Chapter Eleven

Landon wanted to kick himself. Two attacks now at the Silver Creek sheriff's office. And either attack could have killed Tessa, his cousins or the other deputies. They'd gotten damn lucky that there hadn't been more damage and there had been no injuries.

Of course, one of the shooters hadn't had much luck today.

The guy was dead, but that wasn't exactly a dose of great news for Landon. Just like the gunwoman from the day before, dead shooters couldn't give them answers, but maybe Grayson and the others would be able to find the gunman who'd gotten away. While Landon was wishing, he added that the moron would cough up a name of who was behind the attacks.

And that they'd find Courtney.

The last might not even be doable. When the deputies had finally made it out to the bridge, there'd been no sign of the woman. If someone was holding her captive, then it was possible that person had taken her far away from Silver Creek.

Tessa got out of the truck and went into the guesthouse ahead of Landon. As instructed, she hurried, and that precaution was because of the stranger one of the hands had seen in the area just minutes before the attack at the sheriff's office. Landon doubted that was a coincidence, and because of the possible threat and the attacks, everyone was on high alert.

By the time Landon got inside, Tessa was already at the bassinet and was checking on the baby—who was sleeping. At least Samantha was too young to know what was going on. That was something.

Tessa sighed and touched her fingertips to the baby's hair. She didn't have to tell him that she was worried about both Courtney and the little girl. There were threats all around them, and not all of those threats came from armed thugs. The biggest threat could come from the child's own father.

Landon thanked the nanny and Gage for staying with the baby, but he didn't say anything to Tessa until the two had left. Since he was essentially planning a crime, it was best not to involve his cousin and the nanny.

"If Quincy gets the court order," Landon told her, "we'll take the baby from the ranch. I know a place we can go."

"A safe house?"

"Not an official one. I don't want to go through channels for that, but it'll be a safe place." He hoped. And not just safe. But a place they could stay until they managed to stop Quincy from taking the newborn.

She nodded, and Landon nearly told her to go ahead and pack. Then he remembered Tessa didn't have much to take with her. It wouldn't take them long at all to get out of there if Quincy showed up with the law on his side.

"Why don't you try to get some rest?" Landon suggested. "You've been through a lot today."

"You've been through worse," Tessa quickly pointed out. "You had to kill a man."

Yeah, a man he would kill a dozen times over if it meant neutralizing the threat. Except there was more to it than that, and even though Landon tried to push it aside, the thought came anyway.

He'd kill to protect Tessa.

Hell.

This was about that blasted attraction again.

"I'm sorry about all of this," she added, and when she turned away from him, Landon knew there were tears in her eyes.

She was coming down from the adrenaline rush, and soon the bone-weary fatigue would take over, but for now there was no fatigue. Just her nerves firing. Landon's nerves were doing some firing, too, but unfortunately, his body was coming up with some bad suggestions as to how to tame those nerves.

"This isn't your fault," Landon said.

They weren't just talking about the danger now. Somewhere in the past couple of seconds, they'd moved on from nerves, danger and gunmen to something so basic and primal that he could feel it more than the nerves.

"I'm sorry about this, too," Tessa whispered, and she went to him, sliding right into his arms.

And Landon didn't stop her. Heck, if she hadn't come to him, he would have gone to her. That meant this stupid mistake was a little easier to make.

Landon hated that she landed in his arms again. Hated it mainly because it was the only place he wanted her to be. Along with giving her some comfort, it was doing the same thing to him. But it was also playing with fire. Having her in his arms made him remember how much he wanted her, and sadly, what he wanted was a whole lot more than a hug.

"Don't," he said when she opened her mouth, no doubt to remind him, and herself, that this was a bad idea.

Since he'd stopped her from putting an end to this, Landon decided to go for broke. He lowered his head, brushed his mouth over hers.

Oh, man.

There it was. That kick of heat. And it wasn't necessarily a good kick, either. It made him go for more than just a mere touch of the lips. If he was going to screw up, he might as well make it a screwup worth making.

He kissed her, hard and long, until he felt her melt against him. Of course, the melting had started before the kiss, so it didn't take much for him to hear that little hitch in her throat. Part pleasure, part surprise. Maybe surprise that they were doing this, but Landon figured it was more than that. Every time he kissed Tessa, he got that same jolt, the one that told him that no one should taste as good as she did.

Especially when she had trouble written all over her.

But it wasn't trouble on her face when she pulled back a fraction and looked up at him. "This can't go anywhere," she said.

The voice of reason. It couldn't go anywhere. He couldn't lose focus, couldn't get involved with someone in his protective custody. Plus, there was that whole thing about not wanting his heart stomped on again.

All of that didn't stop him, though.

Worse, it didn't stop Tessa.

She slipped her hands around him and inched him closer. Of course, the closeness only deepened the kiss, too, and the body-to-body contact soon had them grappling for position. Landon knew what position he wanted—Tessa beneath him in bed. Or on the floor. At the moment, he didn't care.

But the baby had a different notion about that. Samantha squirmed, made a little fussing sound, and that was enough to send Tessa and him flying apart. She turned from him but not before Landon saw the guilt.

Guilt that he felt, too.

He would have mentally cursed himself about it if his phone hadn't buzzed. Maybe this would be good news to offset the idiotic thing he'd just done. No such luck, though. Landon didn't recognize the number on the screen.

While Tessa tended to the baby, Landon answered the call, but he didn't say anything. He just waited for the caller to speak first. He didn't have to wait long.

"It's me, Courtney Hager," the woman said. Her words and breath were rushed together. "Is the baby okay?"

"She's fine. Safe."

"You have to get a message to Tessa for me," she said before Landon could add anything else. "Please."

"Where are you? Are you all right?"

His quick questions got Tessa's attention, and she hurried back toward him. However, he also motioned for her to stay quiet. If someone was listening and had put Courtney up to this, he didn't want to confirm to that person that Tessa was with him.

"I'm just outside of town," Courtney answered after several snail-crawling moments, "but I won't be here much longer. I have to keep moving. If I don't, they'll find me."

"Tell me where you are, and I'll send a deputy to get you," Landon insisted.

"You can't. Not now. They know the general area where I am, and if they see a cop, they'll find me. Just tell Tessa that I need her to meet me on the playground of the Silver Creek Elementary School. And don't bring the baby. It's not safe."

You bet it wasn't. "It's not safe for Tessa and you, either," Landon pointed out.

"I know." A hoarse sob tore from her mouth. "But I don't have a choice. You can come with Tessa, only you, but don't bring more cops or else it'll just put us all in even more danger."

"Who'll put us in danger?" Landon pressed.

"I'm not sure, but I need to give Tessa something. Only Tessa. She's the only one I trust. If she doesn't come, I'll have to keep running. Tell her to meet me tonight after dark. And tell her to be careful to make sure she's not followed."

"Where are you right now?" Landon didn't bother to bite back the profanity he added at the end of that.

Another sob. "Please have Tessa come." No sob this time. Courtney gasped. "Oh, God. They found me again."

As much as Tessa wanted to get Courtney out of harm's way, she prayed she wasn't trading her friend's safety for Landon's. Nothing about this felt right, but then it'd been a while since Tessa had felt right about anything. Someone wanted her dead, and that someone might want Courtney dead, too.

And Tessa didn't know why.

But maybe Courtney could help with that.

Courtney had said she wanted to give Tessa something. Evidence maybe? Whatever it was, it could turn out to be critical. Or it could lead to Landon and her being in danger again.

"I really wish you'd reconsider this," Landon repeated to her, and Tessa knew even when he wasn't saying it aloud, he was repeating it in his head.

Landon didn't want her going into town, where they'd already been attacked twice, but like Tessa, he also wanted to find Courtney and get some answers. If they could protect the woman and if Courtney was innocent in all of this, then she could eventually take custody of the baby, and that meant Quincy wouldn't stand much of a chance of getting custody.

She hoped.

Of course, there were a lot of *ifs* in all of this.

Tessa wasn't sure where Courtney had been for the past few days, and it was possible the woman was involved in something criminal. After all, why hadn't she just gone to the cops instead of asking to meet Tessa?

Then there was the matter of the phone Courtney had used to call Landon. When Landon had tried to call her back, she hadn't answered, and it hadn't taken him long to learn that it was a prepaid cell. Of course, it was possible Courtney had lost her own phone. Tessa had. But then whose phone had she used to make that critical call to Landon?

They found me again.

Tessa had heard the terror in Courtney's voice and that wasn't the voice of someone faking her fear. At least, Tessa didn't think it was.

"You trust Courtney?" Landon asked as they drove toward town. He was an uneasy as Tessa was, and both of them looked around to make sure no one was following them.

"I want to trust her," Tessa settled for saying.

It wasn't enough, and that was why Landon had arranged for some security. There was a truck with two ranch hands following them. Two of his cousins, Gage and Josh, had been positioned on the roof of the school building for hours. Added to that, there were two deputies waiting just up the street. If anything went wrong, there'd be five lawmen and two armed ranch hands to help.

But that wouldn't stop another sniper with an Uzi.

Yes, this was a risk, and if Tessa could have thought of another way, she would have done this differently.

Landon had instructed the deputies and the hands to stay back and out of sight. Of course, anyone looking for Courtney would also be looking for any signs of the cops. If the person or Courtney spotted them, it might put a quick end to this meeting, but Tessa had no intention of doing this without backup.

"Remember, when we get there, I don't want you out of the truck," Landon instructed as they approached Main Street. "I'll meet with Courtney, get whatever it is she wants to give you and then talk her into coming back with us so I can put her in protective custody." He paused. "Any other ideas as to what it is Courtney wants to give you?"

They'd already speculated about the obvious—some kind of evidence. Evidence perhaps linked to the attacks. Or maybe even Emmett's murder. After all, Courtney had been at Tessa's place the night Emmett was killed, so maybe Courtney had seen something. Maybe she had even picked up a shell casing or something the killer had left behind.

Tessa had to shake her head, though. If she'd found

something like that, then why hadn't she just gotten it to the cops somehow? Unless…

"Maybe Courtney saw the person who killed Emmett," Tessa speculated. "Or maybe she found out Ward had hired the killer. If she saw Ward's badge, she might believe she can't trust anyone in law enforcement."

Landon made a sound of agreement, but his attention was already on the school just ahead. "If anything goes wrong, I want you to stay down."

Tessa wanted to tell him to do the same thing, but she knew he wouldn't. Landon believed that badge meant he had to do whatever it took to make sure justice was served. Even if this was just another trap.

"Someone could be holding Courtney," Tessa said, talking more to herself than Landon. She remembered the photo of Courtney's bruised face.

"That's my guess, too, but if someone's with her, Gage will let us know. He'll let us know when he spots her, as well."

Since there'd been no calls or texts from any of his cousins or the deputies, Courtney probably hadn't arrived yet. Or else she was hiding and waiting for Tessa to show.

At least there was one silver lining in this. The baby was at the main ranch house with Mason and Grayson. Both would protect the baby with their lives. Tessa just hoped it didn't come down to that.

Landon pulled to a stop next to some playground equipment, and he fired glances all around them. Tessa did the same, but the only thing she saw was the truck with ranch hands parking just up the road from Landon's own vehicle. When they didn't spot Courtney, Landon took out his phone, and Tessa saw him press Gage's number.

"See anything?" he asked Gage.

"Nothing. You're sure she'll show?" Even though the call wasn't on Speaker, Tessa had no trouble hearing him in the small cab of the truck.

"I'm not sure of anything. If she's not here soon, though, I'm taking Tessa back to the ranch."

"Agreed," Gage said, and he ended the call.

Landon hadn't even had time to put his phone away when it buzzed, and he showed her the screen. It was the same number Courtney had used for her earlier call. Landon pushed the button to take the call and put it on Speaker, but he didn't say anything.

"Is the baby safe?" Courtney asked the moment she came on the line.

"Yes. Now, help us to keep it that way."

"I tried. I'm *trying*," she corrected. "I told you to come alone with Tessa," Courtney continued. "There are two cops on the roof. Send them away, and we'll talk."

"We'll talk right now," Landon snapped. "Someone's trying to kill Tessa, and you put her at risk by having her come out here. The cops on the roof are my cousins. They're men I trust, and that's a lot more than I can say for you right now. Tell me why you dragged us out here."

Tessa pulled in her breath, waited. Courtney could just hang up and disappear. And that was why she had to do something.

"Quincy's trying to take the baby," Tessa blurted out. "He's getting a court order."

"Oh, God," Courtney said, and there was no way that emotion was faked. Tessa could feel the pain. "You can't let him have her."

"Then come out of hiding," Landon insisted. "Let us protect both Samantha and you."

"I can't," Courtney said, and this time Tessa heard more than just the fear. She heard the woman sobbing. "I'd hoped they wouldn't still be on my trail, that I could meet you face-to-face, but I can't. They're following me, and I'd just lead them straight to the baby."

"Who's following you?" Tessa and Landon asked at the same time.

"Gunmen. There are two of them. They caught me by the bridge and forced me to take a picture with a sign that said Help Me. I'm guessing they did that to lure you out to help me, but when they tried to shove me in a car, I managed to get away."

Tessa and Landon exchanged glances. "Why would those men send the picture of you to Joel Mercer?" Landon asked.

The moments crawled by before Courtney said anything else. "Are you sure the men didn't send the photo to Quincy? I figured they'd send it to him, that maybe they were trying to get money from him because Quincy would pay lots of money to find me."

That knot in Tessa's stomach got even tighter. She didn't like that Courtney had dodged the question about Joel. To the best of Tessa's knowledge, Courtney didn't know Joel. Or at least, Courtney hadn't said anything about knowing Joel, but if she didn't know him, then why hadn't she just come out and said that?

"So you don't think these men work for Quincy?" Tessa pressed. Later she'd work her way back to the subject of Joel, but for now she wanted to get as much information as possible, and she didn't want Courtney clamming up.

"I don't know. But it's possible they used to work for him. They could have gotten greedy and figured they could use me to get him to pay up. But it's not me Quincy wants. It's the baby."

"So he's Samantha's father," Tessa said.

Courtney didn't jump to answer that, either, and she gave another long pause. "How is he getting a court order to get custody? He's a convicted felon."

"He claims he's got DNA proof," Landon explained.

"No. He couldn't have," Courtney insisted. "Where does he claim he got it?"

"He says it's from a pacifier that he took from your house."

"Samantha never used a pacifier, so whatever he's saying about it is a lie. Have the cops already run a DNA test on Samantha?"

"Yeah. We're waiting on the results now. Anything you want to tell us about that?" Landon challenged. Probably because Courtney hadn't confirmed that Quincy was indeed the baby's father. In fact, her friend hadn't confirmed much at all at this point.

That made Tessa glance around again, and she tightened her grip on the gun Landon had given her. She reminded herself that if this was a trap, Gage and Josh would see an approaching gunman. Ditto for seeing Courtney, too, but it was possible the woman wasn't anywhere near the elementary school.

"When you called, you said you wanted to give Tessa something," Landon reminded Courtney.

"I left it underneath the slide on the playground."

Of course it was in the middle of a wide-open space. A space where a shooter could gun them down.

"What is it?" Tessa asked.

"I can't say over the phone in case someone is listening. Just take it and use it to protect my baby."

Tessa hoped there was indeed something to do that, but the only thing that would make it happen was for Courtney to have the evidence needed for them to make an arrest. But if it was that simple, why hadn't she just said what it was?

"We want to protect you, too," Landon said to Courtney. "Tell me where you are, and I can arrange for Samantha and you to be together at a safe house."

Tessa couldn't be sure, but she thought Courtney was crying again. "I can't risk him finding me in a safe house. For now, just protect my little girl. I'll call you again as soon as I can. I have to go."

"Wait," Landon snapped, but he was talking to himself because Courtney had already ended the call.

As Landon had done with her earlier call, he tried to phone her right back, but she didn't answer. Tessa listened to see if she could hear a ringing phone nearby but there was nothing. Not a sound. Of course, it was possible that Courtney had put that so-called evidence beneath the slide before she even made the original call to them.

Landon called Josh and filled him in on what Courtney had told them. Judging from Landon's tone, he was just as frustrated with what Courtney had said, and hadn't said.

"Josh is wearing body armor," Landon explained once he was off the phone. "He's going out there to retrieve what Courtney left, and Gage is going to keep watch from the roof to make sure no one comes in here with guns blazing."

That jangled her nerves again. She hated that Josh had to put himself out there like that, but whoever was behind this wasn't after Josh. They were after Landon and her. And Courtney. Well, they were if Courtney was telling the truth.

"Stay in the truck," Landon told her, and he opened the door.

Tessa caught on to his arm. "It's not a good idea for you to be out in the open."

"I won't be." He got behind his truck door, using it for cover. "But I want to be in a position to give Josh some backup if he needs it. Just stay down."

She did because Tessa didn't want to distract Landon, but she also kept her gun ready. It seemed to take an eternity for Josh to make his way from the roof to the playground, though she figured it was only a few minutes. With each step he took, her heart pounded even harder and her breath raced. Maybe, just maybe, there'd soon be an end to the danger.

Josh was being diligent, too, his gaze firing all around him, and he hurried to the huge slide that was in the center of the playground. She watched him stoop down and pick up what appeared to be a manila envelope. He didn't look inside. Instead he hurried back to the cover of the building.

Time seemed to stop again, and even though she was expecting the call, Tessa gasped when Landon's phone buzzed. Unlike with the other call, she wasn't close enough to hear what Josh said to him.

"Does it have a name on it?" Landon asked. Again, she couldn't hear, but whatever Josh had told him caused Landon's forehead to bunch up. "Go ahead and get in touch with the lab," Landon added. "Then text me the lab's number in case I need to talk to them, too."

Landon got back in the truck in the same motion as he put away his phone. "It's DNA results," he said.

Tessa's mind began to whirl with all sorts of possibilities. "Whose DNA?"

Landon shook his head. "There are file numbers, but the lab should be able to give us a name. It might take a court order, though."

Which meant more hours, or possibly even days, when they didn't have answers. Was the DNA connected to the baby or did this have something to do with Emmett's murder?

Landon started the engine just as his phone buzzed again, and Tessa was hoping that Josh had found something else in that envelope. But it wasn't Josh. Tessa saw Mason's name on the screen. This time Landon put the call on Speaker.

"We got a problem," Mason said. "Two men just tried to trespass onto the ranch. And Tessa heard something she didn't want to hear from the other end of the line.

Someone fired shots.

Chapter Twelve

Landon cursed, threw the truck into gear and started driving—fast. His first instinct was to head to the ranch, but that would be taking Tessa directly into enemy fire. Instead, he could drop her off at the sheriff's office so he could go and help Mason. Maybe he wouldn't get there too late.

"Are they shooting at the guesthouse?" Landon asked. Beside him, Tessa was trembling, and she had a death grip on the gun.

Mason didn't answer for such a long time that Landon had his own death grip on the steering wheel. "No," Mason finally said. "That was Grayson and Nate who fired, and they weren't anywhere near any of the houses. They shot the intruders. Both men are dead."

Landon figured that was the best possible news he could hear right now. "Are there signs of any other gunmen?"

"Doesn't appear to be, but the ranch hands will patrol the grounds all night to make sure. I'll also give Gage and Josh a call, but it might be a good idea for all of you to stay away from here until we give you the all clear."

Yeah, Landon agreed. The ranch was essentially on lockdown and needed to stay that way. "We'll be at the sheriff's office until we hear from you. Is the baby okay?"

"She's fine, but she peed on me. Went right through the diaper. I'm not sure why that keeps happening to me whenever I'm around kids."

If this had been another cousin, Landon might have thought Mason was saying that to give them some comic relief, but Mason wasn't the comic-relief type.

"Is Courtney alive?" Mason asked.

"For now. But she didn't show up for the meeting. She did leave us something, though. The results of a DNA test. I'll let you know as soon as we know exactly what it is."

Landon ended the call and raced back to the sheriff's office—though the place no longer felt exactly safe. The boarded-up front of the building had something to do with that. The explosion hadn't done any structural damage, but it would be a while before things returned to normal. That included any peace of mind. They weren't going to get that until this snake was captured and put away.

As soon as they were in the building, Landon moved Tessa back to the interview room. No windows in there, unlike Grayson's office, which also had some parts of it boarded up. He waited in the hall, and it didn't take long for Josh to come through the door. However, Landon could tell from his cousin's expression that it wasn't good news.

"The lab wouldn't give you the DNA results," he said to Josh. Tessa stepped into the hall with Landon.

"Bingo," Josh confirmed. "It's a private facility and can't release them. Hell, they can't even tell me who submitted the test or whose DNA it is."

Tessa nodded, let out a long breath and pushed her hair from her face. He hated to see the fear and frustration on her face. Hated even more that those feelings, especially the fear, were warranted.

"Maybe if you tell the lab it's connected to a murder investigation?" Tessa suggested.

"I already tried that," Josh assured her. "They still want the court order. But I'll get started on it right away."

Since this might take a while, Landon had Tessa sit at the interview table, and he brought her back a bottle of water from the break room fridge. It wasn't much, especially considering she'd hardly touched the sandwiches they'd had before leaving for the meeting with Courtney, but he figured Tessa's stomach had to be churning. His certainly was.

"Stating the obvious here, but Courtney's covering up something," Tessa volunteered.

It was obvious. Too bad the answers weren't equally obvious. "Any idea what?"

She took a deep breath first, then a long sip of water. "Keep in mind that I don't know Courtney that well, but she certainly didn't confirm that Quincy was her baby's father."

Landon nodded. "And she was adamant that Quincy couldn't have gotten Samantha's DNA from a pacifier."

Tessa made a sound of agreement. "Granted, I wasn't around the baby much before Courtney left her with me, but I never saw her with a pacifier. So why would Quincy claim something like that?"

Landon could think of a reason. "A shortcut. Maybe Samantha really is his child, but since he can't get a real DNA sample, he created a fake one."

Of course, that would have taken the help of someone who worked in a lab, but considering Quincy was a criminal, he wouldn't have had any trouble paying someone off to help him out.

"Did Courtney ever mention being with Quincy or any other man, for that matter?" Landon asked.

"No." Tessa didn't pause, either. "She just said things weren't good between her and Samantha's father and that she didn't want him to see the baby."

Hearing that gave Landon a bad feeling. If Courtney knew about Landon's connection to Tessa, the woman could have purposely concealed her involvement with Quincy. Or maybe Quincy had been the one to put Courtney up to meeting Tessa.

But why?

What could Quincy have hoped to gain by having his lover get close to Tessa? As sick as Quincy was, maybe he'd planned on trying to seduce Tessa or something so he could sway her into getting revenge against Landon. That was such a long stretch, though, that he didn't even bring it up to Tessa. Besides, Tessa obviously already had too much to worry about.

"Don't say you're sorry again," Landon warned Tessa when she opened her mouth.

Since she immediately closed her mouth, Landon figured he'd pegged that right.

"I've made a mess of your life," she said. Not an apology but it was still too close to being one, so Landon dropped a kiss on her mouth.

She didn't look surprised by the kiss. Which was probably a bad thing. They shouldn't be at the point where he could just give her random kisses and have Tessa look content about it. But that was exactly how she looked—content.

Then she huffed.

No explanation was necessary. The attraction was there, always there. And they didn't even need a little kiss to remind them of it. This time, though, the attraction didn't get to turn into anything more than a heated look and the half kiss. That was because Landon heard someone talking in the squad room. Someone he didn't want to hear talking.

Because it was Ward.

"What did you find?" Landon heard the man ask. Except it wasn't a simple question. It was a demand.

That got Landon moving back into the hall again, and he didn't bother to tell Tessa to stay put. Whatever reason Ward was there, it would no doubt involve her anyway.

"What are you talking about?" Josh asked.

Ward huffed as if the answer were obvious. "What did you find on the playground? And don't bother to lie and say you weren't there, because I had someone watching the sheriff's office, and he followed you."

Josh looked about as uneasy with that as Gage and Landon. Landon went closer, and he made sure it was too close. Since he was a good three inches taller than the man, Landon figured it was time to use his size to do a little intimidating. But even if he hadn't been taller, he would still have been mad enough to spit bullets, and he was about to aim some of that anger at Ward.

"What the hell do you mean, you had someone watching us?" Landon demanded.

Ward's chin came up, but the confidence didn't quite make it to his eyes. "I told him to stay back, not to interfere with your investigation, and he didn't."

No, but what was disconcerting was that no one had noticed this shadow. Of course, since it was probably a federal agent doing the spying, he could have used some long-range surveillance equipment.

Ward pointed to Josh. "He saw him pick up something, and I want to know what it was."

"Trash," Landon said with a straight face. "We don't like litterbugs around here."

If looks could kill, Ward would have blasted Landon straight to the hereafter. "It was something about Tessa, wasn't it? Or the woman you're looking for—Courtney."

Landon just stared at him. "If you're waiting for me to make some kind of buzzer sound to let you know you've got a right or wrong answer, that's not going to happen. The Silver Creek sheriff's office has jurisdiction over the investigation into the recent attacks, and if we found anything, we don't have to share it with the feds."

"This is my investigation!" Ward didn't shout exactly, but his voice was a couple of notches above normal conversation. This time he pointed at Tessa. "She's working for Joel. Can't you see that?"

Tessa came forward and faced Ward head-on. "I've had a very bad day," she said. No longer shaky, just pissed off. "And I'm tired of you accusing me of working for Joel. I loathe the man and nearly got myself and others killed because I was trying to find evidence to have him arrested."

"I don't believe that," Ward argued.

"Tough." Tessa's index finger landed against his chest. "Because until you have some kind of proof, I want you to stay far away from me and anyone connected to me." She turned to go back toward the interview room.

"I can't do that," Ward said. "Because I need to find Courtney Hager."

That stopped Tessa in her tracks, and she turned

around slowly to face him. "Why? How do you even know Courtney?"

The muscles got to working in Ward's jaw. He put his hands on his hips and lowered his head a moment. "I can't tell you. But she's part of a federal investigation."

Mentioning federal was probably a dig at Landon since he'd just played the local-jurisdiction card on Ward.

"A word of advice when it comes to Courtney," Ward continued a moment later. "Don't trust her and don't believe a word she says."

"Why?" Tessa repeated.

But Ward only shook his head. "If you find her, turn her over to me. I'm the only one who can stop her from being killed."

And with that, Ward turned and walked out. Landon didn't bother to follow him and press him for more. They might both have badges, but that was where the similarities ended. They clearly were on opposite sides here, but Landon had to repeat Tessa's *why*.

"If he knows Courtney," Tessa said, "then maybe all of them are connected somehow—Joel, Quincy, Ward and Courtney."

Yeah, but how?

"I'm calling Kade," Landon explained, taking out his phone. "He's still with the FBI, and he might be able to find a link if there is one."

When his cousin didn't answer, Landon left him a message to find out if Courtney was in some witness protection program or was a criminal informant. Those two were the most obvious connections, but when people like Joel and Quincy were involved, it was possible this was a plain and simple criminal operation.

And that Courtney was part of it.

"We can't keep letting this go on," Tessa said. "And I've got an idea how to stop it."

That got not only Landon's attention but his cousins' attention, as well.

"I'm sure it's all over town that I was drugged," she continued. "Everyone probably knows I can't remember all the details of what happened the night Emmett was killed."

"Because someone drugged you," Josh provided.

Tessa nodded. "But what if we spread the word that I am remembering, and the memories are becoming clearer. We could even say I'm planning to go through hypnosis or take some kind of truth serum so I can identify Emmett's killer."

Landon was the first to curse, but Josh and Gage soon joined in, all of them telling her variations of no way in hell was that going to happen.

Landon huffed after he finished cursing. "You would make yourself an even bigger target than you already are."

She lifted her hands, palms up. "Someone wants me dead. I can't imagine that target can get any bigger."

"Well, imagine it," Landon snapped. "This killer will stop at nothing to come after you."

"Apparently, he, or she, will come after me anyway. The killer, the person who hired him or both think I saw something that night. I don't think I did, but hypnosis couldn't hurt. Heck, I might remember exactly what we need to catch this person, and if I don't, the mere threat of me remembering could lure him or her out."

"And you could be killed." Hell. Landon didn't need to say that aloud. Especially since she could be killed with or without the hypnosis, but he wanted to find another way. One that wouldn't put a bull's-eye on Tessa's back.

"You don't want to hear this," Josh said to him, "but Tessa is right. This could work."

"You're right. I don't want to hear it." Landon cursed some more. It didn't help. Because damn it, Josh was right. It could work. Still, Landon couldn't make a call like that.

And that made him stupid.

Because he had done exactly what he'd said he wouldn't do—he'd gotten personally involved with Tessa. He'd lost focus. That could be doubly dangerous for Tessa, the baby and anyone else around them.

Gage went closer, tapped Landon's badge. "You need to be thinking with this right now. We could use the next twelve hours to get everything ready, and this time we could maybe get ahead of an attack."

Hell, Gage was right, too, but that still didn't make this any easier to swallow. Landon was about to do what he didn't want to do. Give in. But before he could do that, his phone buzzed, and he saw Grayson's name on the screen. He got an instant punch of fear because this call could be to tell them that there was another intruder at the ranch.

"What's wrong?" Landon said the moment he answered, and he hoped he was just jumping to conclusions.

He wasn't.

Landon could tell from Grayson's pause. And Tessa must have been able to tell from Landon's expression, because she hurried to him.

"Is it the baby?" she asked.

In case it was, Landon didn't put the call on Speaker. He just waited for Grayson to continue.

"The sheriff over in Sweetwater Springs called," Grayson continued. "They found a body."

"Courtney?" Landon managed to say.

"No. It's a man, and there's no ID yet, but there was a note."

Everything inside Landon went still. Everything except that gut feeling that he was about to hear something he didn't want to hear.

"The sheriff sent me a picture of a note," Grayson explained, "and I'm sending it to you now."

It took but a couple of seconds for Landon's phone to ding, indicating that he had a text, and it took a few more seconds for the photo to load.

Yeah, this was bad. And not bad just because the note was on a dead man's chest. But because the note was addressed to Landon. *This is for you, Landon. Keep protecting Tessa, and there'll be another dead body tomorrow.*

Chapter Thirteen

Tessa didn't regret putting this plan into motion. Especially after seeing the photo of the note that'd been left on a dead man. But it was hard to tamp down all the emotions that went with making herself bait for a killer.

At least the baby was safe. That was something. Before Landon and the other deputies had leaked the news about her impending hypnosis, they'd made arrangements for a safe house and moved Samantha from the ranch. Along with two lawmen and a nanny. Considering there'd been two attempts by intruders, that was a wise thing to do anyway. It got not only Samantha out of immediate danger but also everyone else on the ranch.

Judging from Landon's expression, though, that was the only thing he thought was *wise* about this plan.

But they'd taken other precautions that Tessa felt fell into the wise category. After Grayson and Landon had hashed out the details, they'd agreed that it would be too risky to actually bring in a hypnotist. The killer might try to stop that before the person could even get inside the building. Instead, Grayson had put out the word that the hypnosis session would be done via the computer with an undisclosed therapist.

While Tessa was at the sheriff's office.

That would keep the hospital staff safe, but what it wouldn't do was get Tessa the session that might truly end up helping her recover any lost memories. At least, she wouldn't get the session today. There hadn't been enough time to set that up, but if this trap didn't get them the killer, then that was the backup plan.

"All the reserve deputies are in place," Grayson said when he finished his latest phone call. All of the Ryland lawmen at the sheriff's office—Grayson, Dade, Josh and Landon—had been making lots of phone calls to set all of this up. All doing everything possible to make sure she was safe.

Maybe it would be enough.

"Where are the reserves?" Landon asked.

"Both ends of Main Street, and I've got the other two positioned on the roofs of the diner and the hardware store."

Good. That would stop someone from launching an attack like the previous two. Tessa also knew that security had been beefed up at the ranch just in case the snake after them hadn't gotten the word that the baby had been moved.

"The reserves have orders to stay out of sight," Grayson added. "I've also put out the word that most of the deputies are tied up with the two intruders who were killed at the ranch."

Tessa approved of that, as well. Their attacker might not come after them if he or she sensed this was a trap. Of course, the person had been pretty darn bold with the other attacks, so maybe that wouldn't even matter. Whoever was behind this had no trouble hiring thugs to do their dirty work. That was the reason Landon had insisted on having her wear a bulletproof vest, but she'd put it beneath her shirt in case someone had been watching her go into the sheriff's office.

"We struck out on the dead guy in Sweetwater Springs," Dade said, joining the others and Tessa in the center of the squad room. "He was a homeless guy and doesn't seem to have a connection to any of our suspects."

Which meant he'd been killed just to torture and taunt Landon. And it was working. Every muscle in his body was tight to the point of looking painful, and Tessa figured that wouldn't get better until this was over.

"What time is the hypnosis session supposed to take place?" she asked.

Grayson checked the time. "Right about now. Why don't you go into the interview room and pretend to get started?"

That room had been chosen because there were no windows to guard, and the only way to get in was through the door. A door that Landon was personally guarding.

Tessa sank down at the table to wait. She wasn't certain how long a real hypnosis session would take, but it was possible the killer would try to put a quick end to it. Which meant bullets could start flying at any moment. Or this trap might fail. After all, the killer could just go after her when she finally left the office, but then he or she wouldn't be able to put an end to those possible memories before she could tell anyone else about them.

"You can still back out of this," Landon assured her.

Yes, but everyone in the building knew that wasn't going to happen. Tessa only shook her head. "This could all be over this morning. And then your life can get back to normal."

Of course, it would never be normal for Landon or the rest of his family, because even if they caught Emmett's killer, Emmett would still be dead. It wouldn't even matter why he died, because it would always be such a senseless killing.

She heard the footsteps coming toward the interview room, and Tessa automatically went on alert. But it was just Josh, and he had a very puzzled look on his face.

"Something's going on with the baby's DNA test," Josh said. "I just got off the phone with the lab, and they told me the test results have been suppressed."

"Suppressed?" Tessa and Landon repeated together.

Josh shook his head. "Apparently the feds have removed both the DNA sample and the test results from the lab, and they aren't making them available to anyone else in local law enforcement."

Tessa had no idea what that meant. "Why would they do something like that? And what about the other DNA results Courtney gave us?"

"Those are being released," Josh explained. "Well, partially, and only to us. According to those tests, Quincy isn't the father." He paused. "Emmett is."

That brought Grayson and Dade into the hall with them, and the cousins were as stunned as Tessa was. But it was more than just being stunned. This didn't seem right.

"Emmett and Annie were in love," Tessa said. "Before Annie died, they were trying to start a family. They were happy. I can't believe Emmett would have cheated on his wife, much less gotten Courtney pregnant."

All of the lawmen made sounds of agreement, but she could also feel the doubts. They looked at her as if she might have solid information about this. She didn't.

But it did jog something in her head. Something Tessa hadn't remembered until now.

"Courtney and Emmett were talking when she came to my house that night he was killed. I didn't hear what they said, but the conversation was tense. Maybe even an argument."

Landon cursed. "Why didn't you tell us this sooner?" However, he immediately waved that off because he already knew the answer. He'd asked that question only out of frustration. Frustration that Tessa was certainly feeling, too. "Think hard. Did Courtney ever mention Emmett?"

"No. But Courtney wasn't exactly volunteering anything about her personal life." Which was too bad, because details, any details, would have helped now.

Landon looked at his cousins. "Any idea if Emmett was romantically involved with Courtney?"

Grayson and Dade shook their heads, but Josh shrugged. "You know how Emmett was—not one to spill much about his job or his personal life."

Tessa knew that. It was because as a DEA agent, Emmett often worked undercover assignments that he couldn't discuss, and it was possible that Emmett had wanted some information from Courtney about Quincy.

But she kept going back to Annie.

The one thing Tessa was certain of was that Emmett and Annie had had a good marriage and that he had been torn to pieces when she'd been killed eight months ago in that car crash.

Except…

"What else are you remembering?" Landon pressed.

Landon didn't appear to be fishing with that question, either. He was studying her expression, and that was when Tessa realized her forehead was bunched up.

"It's probably nothing," she said. And hoped that was true. "Annie and Emmett were going through fertility treatments, and Annie was desperate to have a child. Maybe Emmett wasn't as desperate as she was."

No one disagreed with that, and it put a knot in her stomach.

Grayson scrubbed his hand over his face. "Emmett was worried about what the treatments were doing to Annie. But that doesn't mean he would cheat on her. Their marriage was solid."

No one disagreed with that, either. So that meant there had to be some other explanation.

"Maybe the results Courtney gave us are fake," Dade suggested. "Maybe Courtney thinks we'll do more to protect the baby if it's a Ryland."

That could be true, though they were already doing everything humanly possible in that department. "Or maybe Courtney just wanted to make sure Quincy didn't get the baby, and this was her way of making sure of that." Tessa paused. "But that doesn't explain why the feds would suppress the DNA test."

Everyone stayed quiet a moment. "Perhaps the feds aren't suppressing the baby's DNA but rather Courtney's," Landon said.

"Why would they do that?" Though she'd no sooner thrown out that question than she realized why. "You think Courtney is a federal agent or some kind of informant?"

Landon lifted his shoulder. "She could be. If she was a deep-cover operative—a Jane, they call them—then her DNA wouldn't be entered into the system."

True. Because it could get her killed if someone she was investigating got access to the database and ID'd her as an agent. But Courtney hadn't given her any indications that she was in law enforcement.

And there was something else that didn't make sense.

"If Samantha is Emmett's baby, then why would Quincy believe the child is his?" Of course, Tessa knew the most obvious answer—that Courtney could have been sleeping with both Emmett and Quincy at the same time. No way would she want to tell Quincy that.

The conversation came to a quick halt when Grayson's phone buzzed, and a message popped up on the screen.

"One of the reserve deputies spotted Joel making his way here," Grayson relayed. "He's alone and doesn't appear to be armed."

That didn't mean he wasn't carrying a concealed weapon.

Landon snapped in the direction of the front door. "Hell," he said under his breath.

She certainly hadn't forgotten about Joel, and he was still a prime suspect, but Tessa hadn't expected him to show up. He was more the sort to send hit men to do his dirty work.

"We're busy," Landon snarled. "You'll have to come back."

"Yes, I heard about the busyness going on. Tessa's hypnosis. It's all over town, and I'm guessing you did that to draw out the person trying to kill her."

"Is that why you're here—to try to kill her?" Landon fired back.

"No." Joel stretched that out a few syllables. "I don't want Tessa dead."

She couldn't see his face, but Tessa could almost see

the smirk that was surely there. She stood to confront the man herself, but Landon motioned for her to stay put, and he pulled the door nearly shut so there was a crack of only an inch or so. That meant she would still be able to hear the conversation, but Joel wouldn't be able to see that she wasn't going through a hypnosis session.

"Did you miss that part about me saying you'll have to come back?" Landon snapped to Joel.

"No, I didn't, but you'll want me to stay when you see what I've brought you. You wanted proof that Quincy was up to his old tricks. Well, here it is."

Tessa hurried to the door and looked out as Joel handed Landon a piece of paper. She was too far away to see what it was, but it certainly got not only Landon's attention but also his cousins'.

"Where did you get this?" Landon asked.

Joel wagged his finger in a no-no gesture. "I can't reveal my source."

"And that means we can't use this to arrest him." Landon cursed. "Who gave this to you?"

"I meant it when I said I can't reveal my source," Joel insisted. "Because I don't know where it came from. Someone sent it to my office in an unmarked envelope."

Landon glanced back at her to see if she was watching, and Tessa didn't duck out of the way in time before Joel spotted her.

"Did you remember who killed Emmett?" Joel immediately asked her.

But Tessa didn't answer. She went back into the interview room and kept listening, though she knew Landon would fill her in on what was on that sheet of paper as soon as Joel left. Which would no doubt be soon. No way would Landon want one of their suspects hanging around.

"According to this, Quincy is into gunrunning and drugs," Grayson said, reading through the paper.

"Complete with dates of the transactions and those involved with Quincy," Joel bragged. "I'm not sure exactly who Quincy pissed off, but clearly, the person who sent this is out to get him."

Yes, and it made her wonder why that person hadn't just sent it to the police. Of course, all of this could be some kind of ploy on Joel's part to get the suspicion off him. In fact, Joel could very well be the one behind the gunrunning and drugs, and the names on that paper could be people he wanted to set up to take the fall.

"Say, do you smell smoke?" Joel asked.

Tessa immediately lifted her head and sniffed. She couldn't smell anything, but judging from the way Landon and the others started to scramble around, they did.

Oh, God.

Was this the start of another attack?

Her heart went into overdrive, and even though she'd tried to prepare herself for this, maybe there was no way to prepare for something like that.

"Get the hell out of here," Landon ordered, and it took her a moment to realize he was talking to Joel.

Joel obeyed, and as soon as he was out the front door, Landon hurried to her.

"Is there really a fire?" she asked, but Tessa soon got the answer, because she smelled the smoke.

"The reserve deputies didn't spot anyone other than Joel near the building," Grayson called out to them. "But there's definitely a fire in the parking lot."

Maybe someone had put some kind of incendiary device on a timer. And maybe it wouldn't stay just a fire once the flames reached a car engine. They could have another explosion.

"Hell," Grayson added a moment later. "There are two fires. Landon and Josh, go ahead and get Tessa out of here. We can't wait around here for the killer to show up."

She reminded herself they'd planned for this just in case they had to evacuate. Landon had parked a bullet-resistant cruiser directly in front of the sheriff's office, and he'd already told her if anything went wrong, he'd be taking her to a safe house. Not the one where they were keeping Samantha but another one so they wouldn't lead the killer straight to the baby.

"Are the reserve deputies sure there are no gunmen in the area?" Landon asked Grayson.

"They don't see anyone."

But that didn't mean someone wasn't out there. Someone hiding in a place the deputies couldn't see.

"You know the drill," Landon told her. "Stay low and move fast."

She did, and Tessa figured she was out in the open only a couple of seconds since she literally stepped right out the sheriff's office and through the back door of the cruiser that Landon had opened for her.

Josh and Landon, though, were outside longer—and therefore in danger—since Landon got behind the wheel and Josh got into the front seat with him. Landon took off right away, but that didn't mean they were safe. In fact, this could be playing right into the killer's hands.

"The reserve deputies will follow us," Josh relayed, and he handed her a gun that he took from the glove compartment. "But they're using an unmarked car."

Good. That meant they'd be close enough to provide backup but without completely scaring off the person responsible for the attacks.

"Where's the killer most likely to come after us?" she asked.

But Landon didn't answer. That was because his head snapped to the left, and Tessa saw the black SUV a split second later.

Before it smashed right into them.

The jolt slammed her against the side of the door so hard that it knocked the breath out of her. Tessa gasped for air all the way, praying that Landon hadn't been hurt or worse. After all, the SUV had slammed into the driver's side. But she couldn't see his arm or shoulder. Couldn't tell if he was bleeding.

"Hold on," Landon shouted, and he gunned the engine.

At least they were able to move and the collision hadn't left them sitting ducks. As soon as Landon sped away, Tessa heard the sound of other tires on the asphalt.

The SUV was in pursuit.

"There's not even a dent in the SUV's bumper," Josh growled, and he turned in the seat to keep watch. He also kept his gun ready, though it wouldn't do any good for him to fire, since the windows on the cruiser would stop his bullet.

That also meant it would stop the bullets of their attackers, but since they must have known that, Tessa figured they had something else in mind.

And they did. The SUV crashed into them again.

This time Tessa went flying into the seats in front of her, and she barely managed to hang on to the gun. Though it was too late, she grappled around and managed to get on her seat belt. Just as the third impact came. She looked behind her and saw that Josh was right—the SUV bumper was still in place, which meant it'd been reinforced.

Landon drove as fast as he could, no doubt trying to get away from Main Street so that no one would be hurt. Plus, they were headed in the direction of one of the reserve deputies though she wasn't sure what he would be able to do. If the bumper on the SUV had been reinforced, then the windows probably had been, as well.

"Hell," Landon growled.

Tessa looked behind her and saw why he'd cursed. The passenger's-side window of the SUV had lowered, and she saw someone stick out the barrel of a big gun. Except it wasn't just a gun. It was some kind of launcher.

Oh, God.

Were they shooting a grenade at them?

She heard the loud swooshing sound and tried to brace herself for an explosion. But it didn't happen. Instead, something smacked onto the back of the cruiser. Definitely not a grenade. It looked like a lump of clay.

"Get down on the seat!" Landon shouted to her.

Not a second too soon, because they hadn't avoided an explosion after all. The clay must have been some kind of bomb, because the blast tore through the car, shattering the windows and lifting the rear of the cruiser into the air. It smacked back down onto the pavement, stopping them cold.

Tessa hadn't thought her heart could beat any harder, but she was wrong. It felt ready to come out of her chest, but she forced her fear aside because they were about to have to fight for their lives.

The first shot came at them before she could even lift

her gun and get it ready to fire. Thank God that Landon didn't have that problem, though. He pushed her down on the seat and fired out the gaping hole in what was left of the back window.

Whoever was attacking them didn't waste any time, either. More shots came, and even though Josh and Landon were using their seats for cover, she knew that bullets could easily go through those.

She didn't dare lift her head, since the SUV was just a few yards from her, but Tessa could see the vehicle in the cruiser's side mirror. And what she saw sent her heart dropping to her knees.

The person in the passenger's seat stuck out that launcher again, and he aimed it right at the cruiser. Sweet heaven. The cruiser wouldn't be able to withstand another direct hit, and that was probably why both Landon and Josh started firing at the guy. He pulled the launcher back inside the SUV. For only a couple of seconds.

Then he took aim at them again.

Tessa prayed this wasn't it, that the three of them wouldn't all die right here, right now. But then she heard a welcome sound.

Shots.

Not ones coming from Josh or Landon. These shots were coming from up the street. Either the reserve deputies had arrived or this was Grayson and Gage coming to help. She hated they were now all in harm's way, but without their help, Landon, Josh and she wouldn't get out of this alive.

She cursed the men trying to kill them. Cursed the fact that she was so close to dying and didn't even know why.

Landon scrambled over the seat, covering her body

with his. What he didn't do was fire. Probably because he didn't want to risk hitting his cousins or the other deputies. Josh did fire but that was only when the thug tried to put the launcher out the window again.

The shots outside the cruiser continued, one thick blast after another until they blended together into one deafening roar. But even over the roar, Tessa could still hear another sound.

The squeal of the tires, followed by the stench of the rubber burning against the pavement.

The gunmen were getting away.

Chapter Fourteen

Landon knew they'd gotten darn lucky, but it sure didn't feel like it at the moment.

He'd banged his shoulder when the SUV had first plowed into them, and it was throbbing like a toothache. Josh was limping from a bruised knee. And while Tessa didn't have any physical injuries, she had that look in her eyes that let him know she was on the verge of losing it.

Landon couldn't fault her for that. They'd come so close to dying. Hell, lots of people had since the attack could have turned into a bloodbath on Main Street. However, other than Josh's and his minor injuries, everyone was okay. Again, he qualified that. Everyone was physically okay.

Tessa finished her phone call with the nanny and turned to Landon. "The baby's fine. No sign of any gunmen at the safe house."

That was a relief even though he would have been shocked if attackers had found the location. They'd been careful when they'd moved the baby. Of course, Landon thought he'd been careful with the arrangements he'd made for Tessa, and look how they'd turned out.

Now all he could do was regroup and keep her safe. Not that he'd done a stellar job of that so far, and that meant he had to make some changes. Landon had brought her back to the Silver Creek Ranch guesthouse, but this would be their last night here. In the morning he would put her in Holden's protective custody, and Holden could take her to a real safe house. Then Landon could focus on catching this SOB who kept coming after them.

"Do I need to remind you that the fake-hypnosis plan was my idea?" Tessa said.

She sounded as weary and spent as Landon felt. Maybe even more. He was accustomed to dealing with nightmares like this, but Tessa wasn't. Though lately she'd had way too much experience in that department.

"I'm the one with the badge," Landon reminded her. "I should have done a better job."

"Right, because of those superhero powers you have."

At first he wasn't sure if her smart remark was an insult to point out his shortcomings, but then she lifted her eyebrow. "It was my plan," she repeated. "You got stuck with the mop-up."

"It was more than mop-up," he grumbled. But what he meant to say was that *she* was more than mop-up.

He didn't.

There was already enough dangerous energy zinging between them without his admitting that he'd been scared spitless at the thought of losing her.

"Besides, I have superhero powers," he added because he thought they could use some levity. "If we ever have to jump a ditch, you'll see what I mean. And I can open medicine bottles on the first try."

She smiled. Which was exactly the response he wanted. But it didn't last. He saw her bottom lip tremble, and just like that the tears watered her eyes. She blinked them back, of course. Landon stayed put, though. That whole dangerous-energy thing was still there.

"I guess you'll be leaving soon," she said, her voice not much louder than a whisper. "Who'll be babysitting me after you leave?"

Landon hadn't said a word to her about the arrangements he'd made shortly after the attack, and he was pretty sure she hadn't heard, because he'd made them when the doctor was checking her. Clearly, Tessa's superhero power was ESP.

"Holden," he admitted. "He'll be here first thing in the morning."

She didn't curse, but some of the weariness vanished, and he was pretty sure she wasn't happy about being traded off to another Ryland. Of course, there couldn't be much about this situation that pleased her, and it was clear he sucked at keeping her out of harm's way.

"You know with me tucked away, it'll be harder for you to catch Emmett's killer," she added.

Hell's bells. He didn't like the sound of that at all. "You're not thinking about making yourself bait again." And it wasn't a question.

"No. I doubt I could get you or any of your cousins to go along with that. Just reminding you that the killer might just disappear until the dust settles. Or until I come out of hiding." She paused. "Unless you're planning to put me in WITSEC."

Yeah, he was. And since Tessa also hadn't said it as a question, either she truly did have ESP or else she knew him a lot better than Landon wanted her to know him. It was best if he kept some of his feelings from her. Especially the feeling that he was afraid for her, and there weren't many times in his life he'd felt like this.

Tessa scrubbed her hands on the sides of her borrowed dress. "Well, I should probably…do something." She moved as if to go into the kitchen.

And Landon should have let her go. He didn't.

Landon was certain the only thing he didn't want about this were the consequences. And there would be a price to pay, all right. A huge one. Because not only would this make him lose focus, it would take him back to a place he swore he'd never go. A place where he had Tessa in his arms. In his bed.

Knowing all of that didn't stop him from reaching for her.

She was already heading toward him anyway, and it would have been easy to slide right into this without thinking. Landon wanted to think, wanted to remember how he'd felt when she'd walked out on him.

He didn't think, though. Didn't remember.

One touch of his mouth to hers, and there was no turning back. No remembering.

"You don't want to do this," she said, her voice not even a whisper.

"You're wrong." And he proved it.

He slipped his hand around the back of her neck, pulled her against him. Until they were body to body. He'd already crossed a huge line, and there weren't enough superhero powers in the world to make him stop. Tessa seemed to feel the same way, because the moment he deepened the kiss, he felt her surrender. Heck, maybe the surrender had happened even before this. All Landon knew was that this seemed inevitable.

And necessary.

If he'd been given a choice between her and the air he was breathing, he would have chosen Tessa.

Of course, that was the logic of that brainless part of him behind his zipper, but Landon went right along with it. If he was going to screw this up, he might as well make it worth it, even though just being with her seemed to fill the "worth it" bill.

Tessa was still trembling, probably from the adrenaline crash, but Landon upped the trembling by taking the kisses to her neck. Then lower to the tops of her breasts. Even though they had been together but that once, he remembered just how to fire her up.

But Tessa obviously remembered how to do the same to him.

He had her neck at an angle so she couldn't use that clever mouth on him, but she made good use of her hands. First on his chest. She slid her palm all the way to his stomach. And lower.

Definitely playing dirty.

He already had an erection, but that only made him harder. And hotter. To hell with foreplay. If she wanted that, he could give it to her after he burned off some of this fire that she'd started.

Landon enjoyed the sound of surprise, then pleasure, she made when he shoved up her dress and pulled it off her. Now the body-to-body contact was even better because her nearly bare breasts were there for the kissing. Landon fixed the "nearly" part by ridding her of her bra so he could kiss her the way he wanted.

Man, he was in trouble here.

Tessa was the source of that trouble. "I'm not the only one who's getting naked here." And she robbed him of his breath when she shimmied off her panties. "Please tell me you have a condom."

"In my wallet," he managed to say.

Tessa obviously took that as a challenge to get it out, and since Landon was distracted by her naked body, he lost focus long enough for her to go after his wallet. Either she was very bad at that task or else she was doing her own version of foreplay, because by the time she was done, Landon was already lowering her to the sofa.

The moment she had his wallet, she went after his clothes. Landon let her because it gave him a chance to kiss some places he'd missed the first time they'd had sex. It slowed her down a little, and she made a sound of pure pleasure that Landon wished he could bottle. But it still seemed to take only the blink of an eye for her to get off his shirt and boots and get him unzipped.

Landon helped with the jeans and his boxers. Even though this was mindless wild sex, he didn't want anything in between him and her.

And so that was what he got.

He took hold of her, pulling her onto his lap, and in the same motion, he went inside her. Of course, she was familiar, but he still felt that jolt of surprise. Still felt both the relief and the building need. The relief wouldn't last.

The need would.

"We are so in trouble here," she whispered.

Even if he'd had the breath to answer, he wouldn't have argued with her. Because they were. This might be the last time they ever saw each other, and here they were complicating it with sex.

Great sex, at that.

It didn't take long for them to find the right rhythm. Landon caught on to her hips, and Tessa used the rhythm and motion to slide against him.

Yeah, definitely great sex.

He went deeper, faster. Until he could feel Tessa close.

That was when he kissed her. It slowed them down a little, but it was worth it. Worth it, too, to watch her as she climaxed. Definitely not a trace of fear or weariness. Only the pleasure.

Tessa gave it right back to him. She kissed him and gave him exactly what he needed to finish this. Landon gathered her in his arms and let go.

"HELL," LANDON SAID under his breath.

Even though it was barely a whisper, Tessa heard it. She'd figured it would at least be a couple of minutes before Landon started regretting this, but apparently not. *Hell* wasn't exactly the postsex mutterings she wanted to hear.

"Phone," he added.

And that was when Tessa heard the buzzing. A buzzing she'd thought was in her head, but apparently not. Landon moved her off him, frantically dug through the pile of clothes that they'd practically ripped off each other and took his phone from his jeans pocket.

She saw Grayson's name on the screen along with the words Missed Call.

Now it was Tessa who was cursing. This could be something important, a matter of life and death, even.

While he was calling back Grayson, Landon went into the bathroom. She didn't follow him, and he didn't stay in there long. By the time he made it back into the living room, Grayson had already answered.

Tessa hurried to get dressed, and she braced herself to hear that there was another intruder on the grounds. Thankfully, Landon put the call on Speaker, but he probably did that to free up his hands so he could get dressed.

"Everything okay?" Grayson asked.

"Yeah," Landon lied. "What's wrong?"

"Nothing. Well, nothing other than all the other wrong things that have been going on, but we might have gotten a break."

Tessa was so relieved that her legs went a little weak. Of course, that reaction might have had something to do with having a half-naked hot cowboy just a few inches from her. It was wrong to still notice that with the danger all around them, but her body just couldn't forget about Landon.

"That info Joel gave us panned out," Grayson went on. "Though we can't use it as evidence to get Quincy, Dade was able to find a criminal informant who verified that the illegal arms transactions did happen on the dates that were on that paper. Even better, the CI gave us the name of a witness. The transaction happened in San Antonio PD's jurisdiction, so Nate's on his way now to question the witness."

"How credible is this witness?" Landon asked.

"Credible enough. He's a businessman, no record. It appears he didn't know what was going on with the deal and that he got out of it as soon as he realized it was illegal."

It took Tessa a moment to process that, and while it wasn't a guarantee that it would get Quincy out of their lives, it was a start.

"As a minimum," Grayson went on, "this witness can put Quincy in the company of known felons, and that means he can be arrested for a parole violation. If we get lucky, we could have Quincy behind bars tonight, where he'll have to finish out the rest of a twenty-year sentence."

That would mean one of their suspects was off the

streets. But Tessa immediately felt the sinking feeling in the pit of her stomach that even that wouldn't help. So far their attacker had only sent thugs after them, and Quincy could still certainly do that from behind bars.

"Is that troubled expression for me or for something else?" Landon asked her the moment he ended the call.

"You and everything else," Tessa admitted. She sank down on the sofa to have "the talk" with him. "What just happened between us doesn't have to mean anything."

He didn't say anything. Landon just waited, as if expecting her to add a *but*. She didn't, because Tessa didn't want him to feel hemmed in, especially since her life was in the air right now.

Landon dropped down on the sofa next to her, took his time putting on his boots and then turned to her. She tried to prepare herself for anything from a thanks to some profanity for what Landon might see as a huge lapse in judgment.

That didn't happen, though.

He kissed her. Not a quick peck of reassurance, either. This was a real kiss. Long and scalding hot. A reminder that what'd just happened did mean something. Well, to her, anyway. It was possible that the kiss was just a leftover response to the attraction.

"Questions?" he asked after he finished that mind-numbing kiss.

Plenty. But she kept them to herself. Good thing, too, because his phone buzzed again. Not Grayson this time. It was Courtney. Landon answered it right away.

"What the hell is going on?" he demanded before Courtney even got a word in.

"I'm sorry," Courtney said after a long pause. "Is Samantha okay?"

"Yes. She's at a safe house. Now, talk."

Courtney didn't do that. Not right away, anyway. "Everything I've done has been to protect my daughter, and I hate that I put you in danger. But I'd do it again if it kept her safe."

"What did you do?" Tessa asked. "And is Emmett really Samantha's father?"

She heard Courtney take a long breath. "I don't want to get into this over the phone. Meet me and we'll talk."

"Talk first and then we'll consider meeting you," Landon countered, and he sounded very much like the lawman that he was. "But I'm not taking Tessa anywhere until I know what's going on, and maybe not even then. You know someone tried to kill her again?"

"Yes, I know. And I'm sorry. So sorry."

"I'm not looking for apologies," Landon snapped. "Answers. *Now.*"

Courtney took another deep breath. "I'm a Justice Department operative." And that was all she said for several long moments. "But you might have already guessed that."

"It was one of the theories. I figured that might be why you had Samantha's DNA results suppressed."

"It was. Partly," Courtney added. "And I also had them suppressed because the DNA sample you took from Samantha will prove that Quincy is her father."

Landon didn't say anything, but Tessa could see the relief Landon was feeling because this meant Emmett hadn't cheated on his wife. But she could also see the confusion.

"Right before Emmett was killed," Courtney went on, "he agreed that he would say Samantha was his so that Quincy couldn't get her."

That sounded like something Emmett would do, and that might have been what Emmett and Courtney had been discussing when she'd seen them together.

"You knew Emmett well?" Landon asked.

"Yes. We'd worked together on some investigations. I'm so sorry he's dead."

They all were. But Tessa hoped Courtney could give them some answers. "Do you know who killed him?"

"No," Courtney quickly answered, "and if I did, I would be figuring out a way to make sure his killer gets some payback."

Hard to do that with killers on their trails. "How the heck did you ever get involved with Quincy?"

"I was on a deep-cover assignment, and he helped me make some contacts. Ward introduced us."

That was not a connection that Tessa wanted to hear. "Ward knows you're an agent?" Tessa asked.

"No." Courtney groaned. "Maybe. But he's not supposed to know. I was posing as a criminal informant when I met him. I'm a Jane operative, and there aren't any records about me in any of the regular Justice Department databases, but it's possible Ward hacked into the classified files and found out my real identity. Maybe that's why all of this happened."

"What *did* happen?" Landon pressed.

Again, Courtney paused. "A little over nine months ago, Quincy arranged a meeting with me, and he drugged me. Rohypnol, I think. I blacked out, and when I woke up, I was naked and in bed with him."

Landon cursed, and Tessa couldn't quite choke back the gasp that leaped from her throat. Courtney had been sexually assaulted.

"I would have killed Quincy on the spot, but his thugs

came in. At that time he was paying some motorcycle gang to play bodyguard and do his muscle work for him. So I left to regroup, to figure out a way to bring him down. And then I found out I was pregnant."

"You're sure the baby is Quincy's?" Tessa said, though it was a question she hated to ask.

"I'm sure. I had a real DNA test done, but those test results have been destroyed. Emmett was helping with that, and that's why I saw him the night he was killed. He's the one who had those fake results created."

Landon jumped right on that. "You think that's why Emmett was killed, because he was helping you?"

"I hope not." The sound Courtney made was part moan, part groan. "But I don't know for sure. Quincy could have found out Emmett was helping me and sent this hired muscle after him. I can't rule out Joel, either, because Emmett was investigating him. Both Joel and Quincy certainly have the resources to hire guns not only to kill Emmett but to go after you."

"And Ward?" Landon asked. "Can you rule him out?"

"No," Courtney said without hesitation. "I don't have anything on him, though. I don't have anything to bring anyone to justice. That has to change. I have to make sure Samantha is safe. That's why I gave you those fake DNA results—to protect my baby. I knew Emmett would have done the same thing if he'd been alive."

"He would have," Landon assured her. "But why leave the fake DNA results on the playground like you did?"

"I was hoping Quincy would get word of it. After the fact," she quickly added. "I certainly didn't want him showing up on that playground. I also thought if you believed Samantha was a Ryland, that you'd do everything within and even beyond the law to protect her."

"That was a given," Landon assured her. "She doesn't need Ryland blood for us to do that."

Tessa made a sound of agreement. They were a family married to the badge, and they wouldn't have let a snake like Quincy take the baby. She'd learned that firsthand, but then, Courtney probably felt she needed some insurance with those altered DNA results.

"What do you know about the body that turned up in Sweetwater Springs?" Landon asked. "It had a note similar to the one left on Emmett's body."

"I have no idea." And it sounded as if Courtney was telling the truth. "But that goes back to Quincy, doesn't it? I mean, he's the one with a personal vendetta against you."

Yes, but either Ward or Joel could have used that to set up Quincy. Of course, after what Courtney had just told them about Quincy sexually assaulting her, Tessa wanted the man to pay and pay hard. But she also wanted the same for the person behind the attacks. That way they could get double justice if that person turned out to be Quincy.

"We don't have anything to help with pinning this on Ward or Joel," Landon explained, "but we might have something on Quincy. There's a witness who could possibly help us nab Quincy on a parole violation."

"That won't help. He'll still send someone after Samantha."

Neither Landon nor Tessa could argue with that.

"I'm still weak from the delivery," Courtney added. "That's why I've had such a hard time keeping out of the path of these thugs."

"If you're weak, that's even more reason to let me help you," Landon insisted.

"I do need your help," Courtney agreed. "I have a plan to draw out Quincy. A plan that will put him behind bars for the rest of his life. I'll text you the details. And, Landon, please come. I'm begging you to help me."

Kidnapping in Texas

plan to bring her baby to the park, but Quincy will see
no baby. She'll claim she left it. I'll see the danger
there, and once Courtney's at the playground, looking in-

Chapter Fifteen

As plans went, there was nothing about this one that
Landon liked. Because it stood a good chance of getting
Courtney killed. It was also a plan he couldn't stop, since
Courtney had already set things in motion.

And that *motion* involved Landon.

"Let me get this straight," Grayson said, sounding as
skeptical as Landon and Tessa were, and Landon had no
trouble hearing every drop of that skepticism from the
other end of the phone line. "Courtney wants you to pretend to bring her baby to the playground at the elementary school so that Quincy's hired guns will believe that
she now has the child?"

That was it in a nutshell, and it would put a huge target
on Courtney. "She said that Quincy knows Tessa and I
have the child, so it'll make it more believable if I show
up. Of course, it won't be the real baby. Courtney suggested a doll wrapped in a blanket."

Grayson cursed a blue streak—which had been Landon's first reaction, as well. "And then what? Quincy's
men gun her down and take the 'child'?"

This wasn't going to sound any better than the first
part of the plan. "Courtney believes they won't shoot her,
because they won't risk hurting the baby." Maybe that

would happen. After all, Quincy seemed determined to get his hands on his daughter.

"Then what?" Grayson snarled.

"Then she can use the child to draw out Quincy. When he tries to kill her and take the baby, then she can arrest him for conspiracy to commit murder, rape and other assorted felonies."

Grayson stayed quiet a moment, obviously processing that. "How much time do you have?"

"Not much. Courtney said she'll be at the playground in about thirty minutes from now. If I'm not there with the fake baby, then she said she'll just try to deal with the hired guns to draw Quincy out, that one way or another she's putting an end to this tonight."

More profanity. "And how does she know the hired guns will even be there?"

"Because they've been following her, and she's barely managed to escape them several times." Obviously, once they'd managed to capture her, because that was when the photo of her had been taken. "She said if she steps out into the open, the gunmen will be on to her right away."

"Call her back. Stop this plan," Grayson insisted.

"Already tried. Multiple times. She's not answering her phone."

Courtney probably didn't want Landon trying to talk her out of this, and part of him couldn't blame her. She was a desperate mother trying to protect her baby, but Courtney was taking a huge risk that might not pay off.

"Where are Tessa and you now?" Grayson asked.

"On the way to the sheriff's office. I wanted to leave Tessa behind, but—"

"If this is a trap, I don't want to have gunmen come to the ranch," Tessa interrupted. It was an argument Landon had had with her from the moment they'd read the text with Courtney's plan.

Grayson clearly wasn't pleased about that, either. Welcome to the club. If there was a pecking order for displeasure here, Landon was at the top of it. Taking Tessa out in the open like this was dangerous.

"You're coming here to the sheriff's office?" Grayson asked.

"Yeah." Though that was a huge risk, too, considering everything that'd happened there in the past couple of days. "I have two armed ranch hands and Kade following me into town. I thought it best if the others stayed at the ranch. Just in case."

Though the ranch would probably be the safest place in the county since Tessa, he and the baby wouldn't be there.

"The two night deputies are here," Grayson explained. "Tessa can stay here with Kade and them. I'll go with you and the ranch hands to drop off the doll. I just wish I had more time to bring in backup."

So did Landon, but since Courtney wouldn't even answer her phone, there was no chance of putting a stop to this meeting. "I'll see you in ten minutes." Well, he would unless they encountered gunmen along the way.

"Stay low in the seat," Landon instructed Tessa. This was a farm road, no streetlights and only the spare lights from the ranches that dotted the area. It would be the perfect place for an attack.

"You think this will fool Quincy's men?" she asked.

She was looking down at Kimmie's doll, which they'd wrapped in a pink blanket. Landon was thankful it had been at the guesthouse or they would have had to go looking for one. When the little girl had brought over the gift for Samantha, Landon hadn't known it would come in so handy.

"It's dark," Landon answered. "And I'll make sure the blanket covers the doll's face."

It was a little precaution, but he'd taken a few bigger ones, too. Like Tessa and him both wearing Kevlar vests. And asking Kade and the ranch hands for backup. Landon had asked them simply because they'd been outside the guesthouse at the time. Patrolling. Right now every minute mattered.

"If shots are fired," Tessa said the moment he made the final turn for Silver Creek, "swear to me that you'll get down."

"They won't fire shots. Not as long as they think I have the baby."

"Swear it," she repeated.

Landon figured the little white lie he was about to tell might steady her nerves. "I'll get down."

And that was partly true. He would indeed get down if he could, but it was a playground. Not exactly a lot of places to take cover. And then there was Courtney to consider. He couldn't just leave her out in the open to be gunned down.

He saw the lights from Main Street just ahead and knew they had only a couple of minutes before he had to drop her off. "If this doesn't work," he added, "you're going into WITSEC first thing in the morning."

Tonight if he could arrange it.

But even that was a lie. Because either way, she'd have to leave. Catching Quincy wouldn't put an end to the danger if it was Joel or Ward who was after them. However, it could get Courtney and the baby out of harm's way.

"So this is goodbye," she said, though judging from

the slight huff she made, Tessa hadn't intended to say that aloud.

Landon considered another white lie, but after everything that had happened between them, he couldn't do that to Tessa. "Yes. More or less, anyway. If we get Quincy, I'll be tied up with that, and Grayson can finish up the WITSEC arrangements."

She nodded and glanced at him as if she wanted to say more. She didn't. Not for several long moments, anyway.

"I'm in love with you," Tessa blurted out, and that time she looked as if that was exactly what she wanted to say.

Hell.

Landon sure as heck hadn't seen that coming.

"I don't expect you to feel the same way," Tessa added, "and I don't expect you to do anything about it."

But she probably did expect him to give her some kind of response, and he would have done just that—even though he didn't have a clue what to say.

But something caught his eye.

They were still several blocks from the sheriff's office, on a stretch of Main Street with buildings and businesses on each side, but he saw the woman.

Courtney.

Landon got just a glimpse of her before she darted into an alley. But he got more than a glimpse of the two men who were running after her. One of those men lifted his gun, aimed it at Courtney.

And he fired.

"GET DOWN!" LANDON SHOUTED to Tessa.

He pushed her lower to the seat, but she was headed in that direction anyway. She also threw open the glove compartment and took out a gun. But before Tessa could even get the gun ready to fire, another shot rang out.

The bullet slammed into the windshield of Landon's truck.

So much for their theory that these goons wouldn't fire because they wouldn't want to risk hitting the baby. If Samantha had been in the truck with them, she could have already been hurt. Or worse.

That gave Tessa a jolt of anger. Not that she needed the thought of that to do it, but it helped. She was fed up with someone putting Landon and the others in danger. Fed up with all these attempts to kill her. She wanted to shout out, demanding answers, but the gunmen obviously didn't have answers on their minds.

They fired more shots into the truck.

"Hold on," Landon said. "I'm getting us out of here."

He threw the truck into Reverse, hit the accelerator and just as quickly had to slam on the brakes. He cursed, and it took her a moment to realize why. The truck with Kade and the two ranch hands was behind them.

But so were two more gunmen.

There was one on each side of the street, and they were shooting into Kade's truck. While in Reverse, as well, Kade screeched out of there, getting out of the path of those bullets, but Tessa figured he would double back to help them.

"Text Grayson." Landon tossed her his phone. "He needs to stay the hell back for now. I don't want him hit with friendly fire."

Neither did she, and while she did the text, she got a dose of what could be friendly fire. Landon leaned out from his truck window and fired at the guys behind them.

That was like turning on a switch. Suddenly, shots started slamming into the truck, and they were trapped with gunmen both in front of and behind them. Landon put the truck back in gear, jerked the steering wheel to the right and drove into one of the alleys.

But it was a dead end.

"Come on," Landon told her. He took his phone and shoved it in his pocket. "Move fast."

She did. Tessa hurried out of the truck, but she had no idea where they were going. She knew all the shops on Main Street, but she certainly didn't know the back alleys. Thankfully, Landon did. With his left hand gripping her wrist, they ran toward a Dumpster, and he yanked her behind it.

Just as the next shot came.

This one smacked into the Dumpster, the bullet pinging off the metal, which acted like a shield for them. But it wouldn't be a shield for long if all four of those thugs came in there with guns blazing. For now the four stayed back, using the fronts of the buildings for cover.

"Shoot them if they try to come closer," Landon told her, and he began to kick at a wooden fence on the left side of the Dumpster.

Tessa kept watch and tried to tamp down her breathing. Hard to do, though, because she felt ready to hyperventilate. It didn't help when one of the men darted out. She fired.

Missed.

And she fired again.

She wasn't sure if she winged him or not, but at least it got him scurrying back behind the building.

Landon gave the fence a few more kicks, and it gave way. Tessa had no idea what was on the other side, but it was behind the secondhand store run by a local charity group. The area wasn't very wide but was littered with all sorts of discarded furniture and another Dumpster. That was where Landon took her.

There wasn't much light at the back of the building. The only illumination came from Main Street and a pale moon, and there were enough shadows that it would be easy for a gunman to be right on them before she saw him.

"Keep watch there." He tipped his head to the alley between the store and a hair salon. The alley where she'd seen Courtney running. But there was no sign of her now.

What had gone wrong?

Had Quincy realized this was a trick and sent his thugs after her? Probably. This plan had been so risky right from the start, and now Courtney was running for her life again. But then, so were Landon and she.

While he kept watch of the area they'd just left, he also texted Grayson. No doubt to let him know their location. The moment he did that, though, he eased his phone into his pocket and put his finger to his mouth in a "stay quiet" gesture.

And Tessa soon knew why.

She heard the footsteps, and they were coming from both sides of the thrift store. Either the four gunmen had separated and were now in pairs or else this was someone else.

Tessa pulled in her breath. Held it. Waiting.

Other than the footsteps, everything was so quiet. At least for a couple of heart-stopping seconds.

"Ryland?" someone called out. She didn't recognize the person's voice, but it was likely one of Quincy's hired guns. Or whoever's hired guns they were. "Do the smart thing and give us the kid. That's all we want."

So definitely Quincy's men.

Well, maybe.

Unless this was yet another attempt to set him up.

"The kid's not in your truck," the guy continued. "We checked. So tell us where you have her stashed and you and your kin won't die."

Maybe it was out of frustration or maybe just to let the jerk know he wasn't cooperating, but Landon fired a shot in the direction of the voice.

The man cursed, calling Landon some vile names.

"It's me you want," someone else shouted.

Courtney.

Tessa couldn't tell where exactly she was, but she was close. Maybe just one building over.

Now Landon cursed. "Stay down!" he yelled to Courtney.

"No. I'm not going to let Tessa and you die for me. Just promise me you'll take care of my baby."

And then it was as if the world exploded.

The blast came like a fireball to their right. In the same area where Courtney had just been. It was deafening, and the flurry of shots that followed it didn't help. Tessa couldn't tell where the gunmen were, but she had no trouble figuring out where they were aiming all those shots.

At Courtney.

"Don't get up," Landon told her.

But that was exactly what he did. He leaned out from the Dumpster and fired two shots. Even over the din of the other bullets, Tessa could hear that the last one he fired sounded different.

"I got one of them," Landon snarled.

Tessa hated that he'd been forced to kill a man, but she wished he could do that to all four of them.

The fact that one of their comrades had fallen didn't stop the other three from firing. And running. They were heading away from Landon and her and were almost certainly in pursuit of Courtney.

"Stay behind me," Landon instructed. "I need to get you to Grayson so I can help Courtney."

Tessa wanted that. Well, she wanted part of it, anyway. She wanted Landon to save Courtney, but Tessa wasn't certain she'd be any safer with Grayson than she was with Landon.

Landon got them moving again. This time toward the back of the hair salon. It was also the direction of the sheriff's office. Of course, that was still buildings away. To Tessa, it suddenly felt like miles and miles, and it didn't help that the shots were still ringing out.

And getting closer.

God, were those men coming back?

Part of her hoped that meant they'd given up on chasing Courtney, but her mind went to a much worse scenario. They could have already killed Courtney and were now doubling back to take care of the other lawmen, Landon and her. Since Kade, Grayson and heaven knew who else were out here, the thugs could be firing those shots at them.

There was no Dumpster at the back of the salon, so Landon pulled her into the recessed exit at the rear of the building. It wasn't very deep, just enough for them to fit side by side, and like before, Landon instructed her to keep watch. She did, and Tessa listened.

The shots had stopped, and she could no longer hear

footsteps. In fact, she couldn't hear anything, and that caused her heartbeat to race even more. Something was wrong.

And she soon realized what.

The door behind them flew open, and someone put a gun to Landon's head.

"Move and you die," the man growled.

IF IT WOULD have helped, Landon would have cursed, but it wouldn't have done any good. One of the thugs had a gun pointed at him, and that meant Landon had to do something fast before the thug killed him and then turned that gun on Tessa.

"Drop your guns," the man ordered. "Do it!" he added, and this time he put the gun against Tessa's head.

Landon couldn't risk it, so he did drop his gun, but he didn't drop it far. Just by his feet. Tessa did the same, and hopefully, that meant he could grab them if it came down to it. Of course, in the small space, Landon might be able to overpower the guy.

"Who hired you?" Landon asked.

Though he figured getting an answer, much less a truthful one, would be next to impossible. Still, he had to try while he also came up with a plan to get Tessa out of there.

The guy didn't say a word, but Landon could hear some chattering. Probably from a communications ear-piece he was wearing. Landon wished he could hear the voice well enough to figure out who was giving these orders.

Landon's phone buzzed in his pocket. Likely Grayson. But he didn't dare reach for it. Grayson would take his silence as a sign he needed help.

"There's no reason for you to keep Tessa," Landon tried again.

"Shut up," the man barked. Judging from the earpiece chatter, he was still getting his orders.

Landon looked at Tessa. He expected for her to be terrified, and she probably was, but that wasn't a look of terror in her eyes. It was determination.

And something else.

She didn't move an inch, but Tessa angled her eyes to the left. It was Landon's blind side because of where he was in the recessed doorway, but Tessa must have seen something. Grayson maybe? Then, she lowered her eyes to the ground for a second.

Landon hoped like the devil that he was making the right interpretation of what she was trying to tell him—to get down—and he readied himself to respond.

But nothing happened.

The moments just crawled by with the thug behind him getting an earful from his equally thuggy boss. And with Tessa and him waiting. Landon didn't want to wait much longer, though, because there were two other hired guns out there somewhere, and he didn't want them joining their buddy who had a gun on Tessa.

"Now!" Tessa finally said. She didn't shout it, but she caught hold of Landon's arms and dragged him to the ground with her.

Just as the shot blasted through the air.

Even though he'd been expecting something to happen, his heart jumped to his throat, and for one sickening split second, he thought maybe Tessa had been hit. But she wasn't the one who took the bullet.

It was thug number two behind them.

Both the thug and his gun clattered to the ground, and

Landon didn't waste any time gathering up their weapons and getting Tessa the heck out of there. Since he figured it was an ally who'd killed the guy, he followed the direction of the shot, and he got just a glimpse of Courtney as she ran away. She was the one who'd fired the shot.

But now someone was firing at her.

The bullets blasted into the walls of the building as she disappeared around the corner. Landon needed to disappear, too, or at least move Tessa out of what was to become a line of fire. It didn't take long for that to happen. The shots came, and Landon pulled her between the hair salon and the barbershop.

It was darker here than in the back and other side alleys. That was because the perky yellow window awnings on the side of the salon were blocking out the moonlight. Landon could barely see his hand in front of his face, and that definitely wasn't a good thing. He didn't want to run into one of the two remaining gunmen.

Of course, there could be more.

Since that wasn't exactly a comforting thought, he pushed it aside and pulled Tessa into a recessed side exit of the barbershop. They couldn't stay there long, but it would give him a chance to check in with Grayson.

"See who texted me," Landon said, handing Tessa his phone and her gun. Since he didn't want anyone crashing through the door as the other thug had done, he volleyed glances all around him. And listened for footsteps.

"Grayson," she verified. "He wants us to try to get to the bakery shop just up the street. He says we should go inside because the other deputies and he are creating a net around the area. They're closing in to find the gunmen, and they don't want us caught in cross fire."

Landon didn't want that, either, but the bakery had

been closed for months now and was probably locked up tight. It was also three buildings away from the barbershop. Not very far distance-wise, but each step could be their last.

"What should I text Grayson?" she asked.

Her voice was shaking. So was she. But then, she'd just had a man gunned down inches behind her. Thank God Courtney was a good shot or things could have gone a lot worse. Though Landon hated that Courtney was having to fight a battle when she'd given birth only a week earlier. It didn't matter that Courtney was a federal agent; her body couldn't be ready for this.

"Give Grayson our location and tell him we're on our way to the bakery." Landon hoped they were, anyway.

It was too risky to head to the street. The lighting would be better there, but it would also make it too easy for the thugs to spot them. Instead, he led Tessa to the back of the building again, and he stopped at the corner to look around.

Nothing.

Well, nothing that he could see, anyway.

He doubted Courtney was still around to take someone out for him, and that meant he had to be vigilant even though he couldn't see squat. However, he could hear. Mainly Tessa's breathing. It was way too fast, and Landon touched her arm, hoping it would give her a little reassurance. It was the best he could do under the circumstances because he had to keep her moving.

Landon dragged in a deep breath, hooked his arm around Tessa's waist and hurried out from the cover of the building. No shots, but Landon knew that could change at any second. As soon as he reached the other side of the barbershop, he stopped again and made sure there wasn't anyone in the alley ready to ambush them.

He cursed the darkness and the shadows, and he moved himself in front of Tessa, racing across the open space to the next building. Two more and they'd be at the bakery. Landon only hoped by the time they made it there, Grayson would have it secured.

"Let's move," Landon whispered to her, and they started across the back of the next building. But they didn't get far before Tessa stumbled.

Landon tightened his grip on her to try to keep her from falling, but she tumbled to the ground anyway. Then he darn near tripped, as well. That was because there was something on the ground. And Landon immediately got a sickening feeling in the pit of his stomach.

Because that something was a dead body.

Chapter Sixteen

Tessa barely managed to choke back the scream in time. A scream would have given away their position, but it was hard not to react when she fell onto the body.

The person was still warm. And there was blood. But Tessa had no doubt that the person was dead, because there was no movement whatsoever.

"Courtney," she whispered on a gasp.

"No, it's not," Landon assured her. But he did more than give her a reassurance. He got her back to her feet and moved her into the alley on the side of a building. Probably because the person who'd done this was still close by.

The light was so dim in this part of the alley that it took Tessa several heart-racing moments to realize Landon was right. It wasn't Courtney. It was a man.

Quincy.

His wheelchair was only a few feet from his body and had been toppled over. There was also a gun near his hand.

What had happened here?

Tessa could think of a couple of possibilities. Maybe he'd been shot in cross fire by the thugs he'd hired? Or maybe the thugs worked for someone else? It was also possible Courtney had done this. After all, Quincy was a threat to the baby, her and maybe anyone else who crossed his path.

It was hard to mourn the death of a snake like Quincy, but Tessa realized the goons were still around because she heard several more shots. If they did indeed work for Quincy, maybe they didn't know their boss was dead.

"We need to keep moving," Landon told her under his breath.

They did, and Tessa forced herself to start running. Landon helped with that again. He took hold of her, and they ran through the back of the alley to the next building. They were close now to the old bakery where Grayson wanted them to go, but it still seemed miles away.

More shots came.

And these were close. Too close. One of them smacked into the wood fence that divided the alley from the town's park, and the shot had come from the area near Quincy's body.

Tessa hoped that once the thugs saw that Quincy was dead, they'd back off, that no more bullets would be fired. But almost immediately, another shot rang out. Then another.

Landon slipped his arm around her, but it wasn't preparation to get them running again. He pulled her deeper in the alley, and his gaze fired all around them. He stepped in front of her when they heard some movement near Quincy's body, and Tessa got just a glimpse of not one of the gunmen but Courtney.

The woman was leaning over Quincy and touched her fingers to his neck. It seemed as if she was making sure he was dead.

"Courtney," Landon whispered.

Tessa glanced out again and saw Courtney's head whip in their direction. She got to a standing position and turned, heading their way.

Just as there was another shot.

This one smacked right into Courtney's chest, and Tessa heard her friend gasp in pain as she dropped to the ground.

Oh, God.

Courtney had been hit.

The new wave of adrenaline slammed into Tessa, and she would have bolted out to help her if Landon hadn't stopped her. Landon cursed and stepped out from the building, but he almost certainly couldn't see the shooter, since the bullet had been fired from the alley of the building over from them.

Courtney groaned, the sound of sheer pain, and while she was gasping for breath, she was also trying to lift her gun. No doubt trying to stop the gunman before he put another bullet in her.

"She's wearing Kevlar," Landon said.

Because her instincts were screaming for her to help Courtney, it took Tessa a moment to process that. The bullet had hit the Kevlar, not her, and that meant she might not die. Not from that shot, at least, but the next one went into the ground right next to her. The only reason it didn't hit her was that Courtney managed to roll to the side. But Courtney was still writhing in pain, still gasping for air and clearly couldn't get to her feet to run.

Landon's phone buzzed, and Tessa saw Grayson's name on the screen. He passed it back to her so she could answer it.

"What's your position?" Grayson asked.

"We're still two buildings away from the bakery. We need help. Can you get to us?"

"Not right now. We're pinned down. There's a sniper on one of the roofs, and every time we move, he fires a shot. He hit one of the reserve deputies."

That didn't help steady her heart. "Courtney's been hit, too."

Grayson belted out some profanity. "We'll get there as soon as we can." And he ended the call.

Tessa knew that he would, but soon might not be soon enough. Plus, there was no way an ambulance could get anywhere near the scene. Not with all the gunfire.

"I've got to help Courtney," Landon whispered, but Tessa heard the hesitation in his voice. He made a split-second glance at her as she slipped his phone back into his pocket. "Stay put and keep watch around you."

That was the only warning Tessa got before Landon stepped out. He pivoted in the direction of the shooter, and he fired. Tessa prayed that would put an end to the immediate threat.

It didn't.

She saw the gunman's hand snake out, but this time he didn't fire at Courtney. He fired at Landon. Her heart nearly went out of her chest as Landon scrambled to the ground, using a pair of trash cans for cover.

As Landon had told her, she kept watch around her, but Tessa also tried to do something to stop that thug from gunning down both Courtney and Landon. Courtney was in the open, an easy target, and bullets could go through the trash cans where Landon had ducked down. She had to help. She couldn't just stand there and watch them die.

She waited, watching, and when she saw the gun-

man's hand come out again, she took aim and fired. Almost immediately, the guy howled in pain, and while she certainly hadn't killed him, at least she'd managed to injure his shooting hand. However, that didn't stop him from firing.

Again and again.

The man was cursing, and he was making grunting sounds of someone in pain, but that didn't stop him from pulling the trigger, and he was shooting at Landon. Maybe because he thought Landon had been the one to fire that shot at him.

Courtney moved again, managing to get on her side. And she even tried to take aim, but she was clearly in too much pain to defend herself. The gunman's next bullet slammed into her again, and Tessa heard Courtney's gasping sound of pain.

Mercy, she'd been shot, and this time Tessa didn't think the bullet had gone into the Kevlar. Landon must not have thought so, either, because he came from behind the trash cans and he raced out. Not toward Courtney.

But toward the alley where the gunman was getting ready to send another shot right into Courtney. To finish her off, no doubt.

Landon put a stop to that.

He pulled up, pivoted and double-tapped the trigger.

Even though there had been so many shots fired all around them, those two sent Tessa's heart into overdrive. Because now both Landon and Courtney were in the open, and if Landon's two shots didn't work, then the gunman would try to kill them both again.

Tessa was ready to do something to make sure that didn't happen when she heard the movement behind her. She started to whirl around, bringing up her weapon in the same motion, but it was already too late. Before she could even see who was behind her, someone hooked an arm around her neck. Stripped her gun from her hand.

And whoever it was put a gun to her head.

HELL. THE GUNMAN wasn't down.

Landon didn't know how the guy had managed to stay on his feet, not after Landon had put two bullets in him. He'd aimed for the guy's chest, figuring he, too, was wearing a vest, but two shots at this close range should have sent the guy to the ground. They didn't.

The man was gasping just as Courtney was doing, but he not only stayed upright but also pulled the trigger. Thank God the shot was off or Landon would have been a dead man.

Another shot came in Landon's direction, and he scrambled to the side. This time when he aimed, he went for the kill. As much as he would have liked to have this guy alive to answer questions, that wasn't going to happen. Landon put two bullets in his head. This time it worked, and the guy didn't manage to get off another shot before he collapsed onto the ground.

Just in case there was some shred of life left in the clown, Landon kicked away the man's weapon. There was no time to check and see if he was truly dead, because he didn't want to stay out of Tessa's line of sight for another second. Plus, he could still hear gunshots just up the street, which meant Grayson and the others were fighting for their lives.

He hurried to Courtney to see how bad her injuries were. There was blood, but from what Landon could tell, the injury was to her shoulder, a part of her that the Kevlar hadn't protected. She would live. Well, she would if she didn't bleed out, and that meant he had to clear the area so they could get her an ambulance.

"Clamp your hand over the wound," he instructed Courtney.

He dragged the wheelchair in front of her so she'd have some cover, and then he turned to check on Tessa.

Landon's heart slammed against his chest.

Tessa was barely visible at the back corner of the building where he'd left her. But she wasn't alone. Landon couldn't see who was with her, but whoever it was had a gun.

"I'm sorry," Tessa said. "I didn't see him in time."

Landon hated that she even felt the need to apologize. With all the bullets flying and the chaos, it would have been hard to hear someone coming up behind her. Besides, they hadn't even known the locations or even the number of the other gunmen. With this guy and the sniper on the roof, there were at least two, but Landon figured there could be others waiting to strike.

For now, though, he had to figure out how to get Tessa away from this goon before one of his comrades showed up to help. To do that, he had to stay alive, so he, too, ducked behind the wheelchair. It was lousy cover, but it was metal and might do the trick. Besides, he didn't plan to be behind cover for long. Not with Tessa in immediate danger.

Even though the timing sucked, Landon thought of what she'd said to him in the car.

I'm in love with you.

Landon hadn't had a chance to react to that, hadn't even had much time to think about it, but now those words troubled him. Because if Tessa was indeed truly in love with him, she might do anything to try to keep him safe. That might include sacrificing herself.

"I don't know what you want," Landon said to the guy, "but tell me what it'll take for you to release Tessa."

Nothing. For some long heart-pounding moments. Then Landon saw the person lean forward and whisper something in Tessa's ear. He couldn't hear what the guy said, but he got a better look at him. He was wearing a ski mask like the other thugs who'd been trying to kill them.

Not good.

Because it was hard to negotiate with someone who would murder for money.

"He wants Courtney," Tessa relayed. Her voice sounded a lot steadier than Landon figured she actually was. Trying to put on a good front.

Or maybe it was more than that.

She sounded angry. Perhaps because the guy had managed to sneak up on her, or maybe he'd added something else to that whisper.

"Courtney?" Landon questioned. "Why her?"

Landon figured he wasn't going to get a straight answer to that question, and he didn't. In fact, he didn't get an answer at all.

But it did make him think.

All along they'd believed the attacks were about Tessa, about what she possibly saw the night Emmett was murdered. The other theory they'd had was the attacks were connected to him, that Quincy was behind them. But maybe Quincy was after only Courtney and the baby, and Tessa and he just got in the way.

"Quincy's dead," he told the thug in case he hadn't noticed the body. "I hope he paid you in advance or you're out of luck."

The guy whispered something else to Tessa. "He still wants Courtney. He wants you to step aside."

Well, hell. Quincy must have left orders to kill Courtney even if something happened to him.

"If you kill Courtney, you'll make the baby an orphan," Landon tried again. "Whatever Quincy paid you or planned to pay you, I'll give you double. All you have to do is let Tessa go."

Of course, that might just prompt the guy to take her hostage, but every second he had a gun to her head was a second that could take this situation from bad to worse.

And it got worse, all right.

Landon heard the sound of an engine. Not a car. But rather a motorcycle. And it was coming at them fast. It didn't take long for it to come barreling up the alley, and Landon saw yet one more thing he didn't want to see.

Another ski-mask-wearing thug.

He brought the motorcycle to a stop right beside Tessa and his partner in crime. Landon wanted to send a shot right into the guy's head, but the thug holding Tessa might retaliate and do the same to her.

"I can pay you off, too," Landon told the second thug. He practically had to shout to be heard over the motorcycle engine. "With Quincy dead, wouldn't you rather have all that money than end up dead?"

"I got no plans to die," the one on the motorcycle shouted back. He was bulky, the size of a linebacker and armed to the hilt.

He killed the engine and climbed off, and Landon could have sworn his heart skipped some beats when he saw what was happening. The thugs switched places, and the whispering one who was holding Tessa dragged her onto the motorcycle with him.

Hell. Time was up. Landon couldn't let the guy just drive off with Tessa, because he was certain he'd never see her alive again.

"When you're ready to give us Courtney," the bulky guy said, "then you'll get Tessa back."

Landon doubted that. No way would they leave Tessa alive. "Take me instead," Landon bargained.

Tessa frantically shook her head and moved as if ready to cooperate with this stupid plan that would get her killed. Yeah, she'd been right about that *I'm in love with you*. She was putting her life ahead of his, and that wasn't going to happen.

"Lawmen don't make good hostages." The bulky guy again, though the other thug, the whisperer, said something else to Tessa. Something that Landon couldn't catch.

But whatever it was caused Tessa's shoulders to snap back.

"Landon, watch out!" she shouted.

The bulky guy took aim at Landon, and Landon had no choice but to fire.

Chapter Seventeen

The man who still had hold of Tessa yanked her to the side of the motorcycle. Just as the sound of two shots cracked through the air. One of those shots had come from Landon. The other, the thug who'd ridden up on the motorcycle.

Tessa hit the ground, hard, so hard that it knocked the breath out of her, but she fought to get up because she had to stop the big guy from shooting at Landon again. She managed to catch on to his leg, and it off-balanced him just enough to cause his next shot to go up in the air.

Landon's didn't.

His bullet went into the guy's shoulder. It didn't kill him, but it sent him scrambling for cover.

The uninjured gunman didn't do anything to help his partner. He latched on to Tessa's hair, dragging her back in front of him. Once again, she was his human shield, and Landon wouldn't have a clean shot to put an end to this.

"Get down!" she shouted to Landon.

He didn't, but at least he hurried back behind the wheelchair next to Courtney. Courtney was still moaning in pain. Still bleeding, too, from the looks of it, but at least she was alive. For now. And so was Landon. Tessa needed to do something to make sure it stayed that way.

"I'll go with them," she called out.

"No, you won't!" Landon answered. "They'll kill you."

Almost certainly. Tessa didn't want to die, but at least this way, Landon would be safe, and he would be able to get Courtney to the hospital. Samantha wouldn't be an orphan. Of course, if these men killed her, it wouldn't end the danger to Courtney, Landon or the baby, but maybe Landon could get them all to a safe house before the gunmen could regroup and attack again.

Tessa tried to hold on to that hope, and since she was hoping, she added that she could find a way to escape. Maybe she could do that once they had her wherever they were going to take her. All she would need was some kind of distraction.

The injured thug crawled to his partner and whispered something to him that Tessa didn't catch, but whatever it was, it got her captor moving. He had his left hand fisted in her hair, and with the gun jammed against her temple, he hauled her to her feet, keeping behind her. He then began to back his way to the motorcycle.

"We'll trade Tessa for Courtney," the wounded man shouted out to Landon. "You've got thirty seconds to decide."

Tessa knew that wasn't going to happen. No way would she make a trade like that, even though Courtney immediately tried to sit up. Tessa got so caught up in trying to figure out how to stop this that she nearly missed something.

Something critical.

Why was the wounded man doing all the talking? He

was having trouble breathing and couldn't stand, and yet the whispering guy had let him bark out the order for the trade.

Why?

Was it because she might recognize his voice?

Even though her mind was whirling, she tried to recall those whispers, but he'd purposely muffled his voice, and that meant this was likely either Joel or Ward. Too bad the men were about the same height and build, or she would have been able to tell from that.

So Tessa went with a bluff. Except in this case, she figured her bluff had a fifty-fifty chance of succeeding.

"The man holding me is Ward," she shouted.

Bingo.

Even though it'd been a bluff, she knew she was right when she heard him mumble some profanity under his breath. Then he cursed some more, much louder.

Yes, definitely Ward.

This time it was Landon who cursed. "How the hell could you do this? You're supposed to uphold the law, not break it."

"Breaking it pays a lot more than upholding it," Ward answered. "Now, bring Courtney to me, or I start shooting."

"You're going to start shooting no matter what I say or do," Landon countered, but Tessa saw him readjusting his position. Probably so he could take the shot if he got it, but Ward was staying right behind her.

But Ward wasn't staying put, either. He was inching her backward, but Tessa couldn't tell if he was trying to get her on the motorcycle or simply closer to his hired gun. Yes, the guy was injured, but that didn't mean he couldn't kill her.

"Who killed Quincy? You?"

"Possibly. He got in the way. He was here to get Courtney, but I never had any intentions of letting him have her."

"Because you want to kill her yourself," Landon concluded.

"She knows too much."

"About what?" Courtney asked, her breath gusting through the groans of pain.

"You don't really want me to go into that here, do you? Because then I'd have to kill Landon."

"I already know," Landon assured him.

It was a lie, but Tessa could feel the muscles in Ward's arm turn to steel.

"This is about your dirty dealings with Joel," Landon went on. "Both Tessa and Courtney were investigating him, and you believed they were on to you. They weren't, but I was."

Tessa hadn't thought it possible, but Ward's arm stiffened even more. "Joel will turn on you," she said.

"Joel's dead," Ward whispered. "Or soon will be. Before he dies, he'll confess to all of this. Including Courtney's murder. And yours."

She was pretty sure that wasn't a bluff. In fact, Ward had no doubt already arranged for Joel's death, and with Ward's connections in law enforcement, he could indeed set up Joel. Then Ward could walk away a free man with all the money he'd made from his business deals with Joel.

Well, he could walk if Landon, Courtney and she were dead.

That meant no matter what Landon and she did, the bottom line was that Ward would kill them. And he would do that before Landon got a chance to tell anyone else. That meant Tessa had to do something fast.

But what?

She went with the first thing that popped into her head. "Landon, did you record Ward's confession with your phone?" she called out.

"Sure did," Landon answered. She doubted he had, but judging from the way Ward started cursing, he didn't know it was a lie. She could see Landon put his left hand in his pocket. "And I just sent it to Grayson. Now every lawman in Silver Creek knows you're a dirty agent."

A feral sound came from Ward's throat, and Tessa knew he was about to shoot her in the head. She didn't waste a second. She dropped to the ground. Or rather that was what she tried to do, but Ward held on to her hair, yanking it so hard that she couldn't choke back a scream of pain.

Not good.

Because her scream brought Landon to his feet. He bolted toward them, firing a shot at the wounded gunman. Tessa wasn't at the right angle to see where his bullet had gone, but since the gunman didn't return fire, she figured Landon had hit his intended target.

Ward moved his gun, too. Aiming it at Landon. But Tessa rammed her elbow into his stomach. It didn't off-balance him, definitely didn't get him to drop his gun, but he had to re-aim, and that was just enough time for Landon to make it to them.

Landon plowed into them, sending all three of them to the ground.

Tessa felt the jolt go through her entire body, and while she didn't lose her breath this time, Ward's gun whacked against the side of her head. At first she thought it was just from the impact, but he did it again.

The pain exploded in her head.

But even with the pain, she heard Landon curse the man, and he dropped his own gun so he could latch on to Ward's wrist with both hands. It stopped Ward from hitting her again. Stopped him from aiming his gun at either of them, but Ward let go of her hair so he could punch Landon with his left hand. And he just kept on punching and kicking him.

Tessa tried to get out of the fray just so she could find some way to stop Ward, but it was hard to move with the struggle going on. She fought, too, clawing at Ward's face, but the man was in such a rage that she wasn't even sure he felt anything.

However, she did.

Ward backhanded her so hard Tessa could have sworn she saw stars. She fell and landed against the hulking hired gun—and yes, he was dead—but before she could spring back to her feet, Landon and Ward were already in a fierce battle. Landon was punching him, but Ward was bashing his gun against Landon's face.

Mercy, there was already so much blood.

Tessa frantically looked around and spotted the dead guy's gun. She wasn't familiar with the weapon and prayed it didn't go off and hit Landon. Still, it was the only thing she had right now. She scooped it up and tried to aim it at Ward.

But she couldn't.

Ward and Landon were tangled together so that she couldn't risk firing. Someone else had no trouble doing that, though. In the distance she heard a fresh round of gunfire. Grayson, the deputies and that sniper. Maybe she could try to put an end to this so she could help them. Until the area was safe, the ambulance wasn't going to be able to get to Courtney to save her life.

Maybe Landon's, too.

In that moment she hated Ward so much that she wanted to jump into that fight and punch him. But that wouldn't do Landon any good. He was battling for his life. For Courtney's and her lives, too, and Tessa was powerless to help him.

She waited, praying and watching for any opening where she would have a shot. But then she saw something that caused her breath to vanish.

Ward quit hitting Landon with the gun.

And Ward managed to point it at him.

He fired.

Tessa thought maybe she screamed. She screamed inside her head, anyway, and the scream got louder when Landon dropped back.

Oh, God. Had he been shot?

She'd heard that when some people died, their lives flashed before their eyes, and even though she wasn't dying, it happened to her. Tessa saw everything. Her time with Landon. All the mistakes she'd made. All the chances she'd lost to have a life with him.

Ward could have just taken all of that away. He was trying to make sure he killed Landon. He took aim at him again.

Everything inside her went still. And then the rage came. Even though Landon was still too close to fire, she shot the gun into the ground next to the dead man.

Ward whipped his head in her direction, turning his gun toward her. But Landon reacted faster than Ward did. Landon lunged at the man, twisting his wrist so that the gun was pointed at Ward's chest.

Ward fired.

Like his hired thugs, Ward was wearing a bulletproof vest, so Tessa expected him to make the same groan of pain that she'd heard from Courtney. But what she heard was a gurgling sound. Because Ward's bullet hadn't gone into his vest but rather his neck.

He was bleeding to death right in front of them.

Tessa didn't care. If fact, she wished him dead after all the hurt and misery he'd caused. Instead, she looked at Landon and was terrified of what she might see.

His face was bloody. So was his left arm.

"The bullet just grazed me," he said.

It looked like more than a graze to her, but at least he wasn't dead or dying.

The relief came so hard and fast that she probably would have dropped to her knees if she hadn't heard Courtney groan again.

"Check on her," Landon instructed. "I'll watch this snake."

Tessa nodded, and she somehow managed to get her feet moving. Though she'd made it only a few steps when she heard Ward speak.

Or rather he laughed.

"You think you got Emmett's killer," he said, his voice not much louder than a whisper. Still, Tessa had no trouble hearing it. "You didn't. He's still on the roof, and he's probably killing more Rylands right now."

And with that, Ward drew the last breath he'd ever take.

Chapter Eighteen

Landon didn't want to be stitched up. Hell, he didn't want to be in the hospital ER. He wanted to be out there with Grayson and the rest of his cousins so they could catch Emmett's killer. At least, he was dead certain he wanted that until he took one look at Tessa.

She was staring at him as if she expected him to keel over at any moment.

He was probably looking at her the same way, though.

She'd already gotten a couple of stitches on her forehead where Ward had hit her with his gun. Half of her face was covered in bruises, and there was way too much worry in her eyes. Of course, none of that worry was for her own injuries. It was for Courtney's and his.

"I'm fine," Landon told her, something he'd already said a couple of times. Judging from the way she was nibbling on her lip, he might have to keep repeating it.

"You were shot. Courtney was shot. And Emmett's killer is still out there."

"The only thing that you left out is that Courtney and I are going to be fine."

The doctor had already told them that. Courtney had lost plenty of blood, but the bullet was a through-and-through, so she wouldn't even need surgery. She'd been admitted to the hospital, though, for a transfusion, and Landon had made sure the security guard was posted outside her door. If that sniper, aka Emmett's killer, managed to get away from Grayson's team, Landon didn't want the snake slithering into the hospital to try to finish off a job for his dead boss.

"Are you going to be fine?" Landon asked Tessa the moment the nurse stepped away from him.

She nodded, but he wondered if that was the biggest lie of the night. This nightmare was going to stay with her for the rest of her life, and it wasn't even over yet.

Landon got up from the examining table, trying not to wince. He pretty much failed at that. It felt as if he'd just gotten his butt kicked, but if he could have pretended he wasn't aching from head to toe, he would have. Each wince caused Tessa to look even more worried.

He shut the door and went to her. Not that he thought they needed the privacy, but his mind was still on that sniper showing up. Or at least it was on the sniper until Tessa leaned in and kissed him.

Gently.

Both of them had busted lips, so anything long and deep would have caused some pain. Even that light touch seemed to cause her to flinch, just a little.

"Sorry," he said.

"Don't be. You saved my life." There were tears in her eyes now.

"You saved mine, too."

And since he wanted to do something to rid her of those tears, he risked the pain and kissed her for real. There probably was some pain involved, but his body must have shut it out. Tessa's, as well. Because the sound she made wasn't one of pain. It was that silky little purr of pleasure.

Landon might have just kept on kissing her if the door hadn't opened and Grayson hadn't walked in. Tessa tried to move away from Landon as if they'd been caught doing something wrong, but Landon kept his arm around her.

"Are all the deputies okay?" Landon immediately asked.

"Everyone's fine. We caught the sniper," Grayson said.

Those six words made Landon feel as if a ten-ton weight had been lifted off his shoulders. And his heart. Even though one of the reserve deputies had been injured, none of his cousins had been hurt in this fiasco, and they had Emmett's killer.

Landon cleared his throat before he spoke. "The sniper's alive?"

Grayson nodded. "And he's talking. His name is Albert Hawkins, a former cop. Once he heard Ward was dead and had fingered him for Emmett's murder, I guess he figured if he talked, it might get him a plea deal with the DA or at least get the death penalty off the table."

Landon wasn't sure he wanted deals to be made with his cousin's killer, but as long as he spent the rest of his life behind bars *and* gave them some answers, then he could accept it. Well, he could accept it as much as he could anything about Emmett's murder. And while he didn't like that a killer would be giving them those answers, the man who'd orchestrated all of this—Ward—was past the point of being able to explain the hellish plan he'd set in motion.

"Did Ward have Emmett murdered because of me?" Landon asked, and he hoped it was an answer he could live with.

Grayson took a moment, probably because this was

as hard for him as it was for Landon. "No. It wasn't because of you. Ward sent Hawkins to kidnap Tessa so they could use her to find Courtney. Emmett showed up to talk to Tessa about Joel, and when he tried to stop the kidnapping, Hawkins killed him."

Tessa shuddered, shook her head. "So I'm the reason Emmett was killed."

Landon wanted to nip this in the bud. "No, he died because he was doing what was right." Landon would have done the same thing in Emmett's place. But it might take him a while to convince Tessa that this wasn't her fault.

"I wish I could remember," she whispered.

Landon hoped she didn't get that wish. Judging from Grayson's expression, he felt the same way.

"Hawkins gave you a huge dose of drugs that night," Grayson explained. "He said you were fighting like a wildcat, so he hit you on the head and drugged you and he's the one who put that tracking device in your neck."

Landon gave that some thought. "So the plan was to let her go so that she'd lead him to Courtney?"

Grayson gave another nod.

Landon had to hand it to Ward—it was a plan that could have worked. Even if Tessa had remembered who'd murdered Emmett, she wouldn't have necessarily connected the killer to Ward. Plus, Tessa had the baby with her, so Ward must have believed that Courtney would come for the child.

But something didn't fit.

"Then who put Tessa in the burning barn?" Landon asked.

"Hawkins. On Ward's orders, though. After Tessa didn't lead him to Courtney, Ward figured it was time to cut his losses and get rid of her. He didn't want Tessa coming to any of us for help in case we figured out what was going on. So he used the tracking device to find her, drugged her again and put her in the barn."

"Any idea why he didn't just kill me?" Tessa's voice wasn't exactly steady with that question.

"Again, Ward's orders. He wanted your death to look as if it was connected to Landon. That's why he wrote what he did on the boulder."

It turned Landon's stomach to think about how close Ward had come to making this sick plan work. If Landon hadn't seen the burning barn, he might not have gotten to them in time.

"Hawkins also admitted to putting the note on Emmett's body," Grayson went on. "That was Ward's idea, too, he says. He also says Ward staged those injuries he got and murdered the other guy just so he could leave another of those taunting notes."

It was a good thing Ward was dead, because Landon wanted to pulverize the man for that alone. It'd been torture for Landon to believe he was the reason Emmett had died.

"Please tell me you've arrested Joel for this deadly partnership with Ward," Tessa said. "Or was Ward telling the truth when he said he was going to kill him?"

"No, he's dead, all right. It was set up as a suicide, but I think Ward was tying up loose ends."

And those loose ends included committing more murders tonight. Or rather trying to commit more. It was stupid that so many people had died to cover up a dirty federal agent's crimes.

"The cops did find something interesting near Joel's body," Grayson continued. "Proof of payment for the hit on a man named Harry Schuler."

Landon knew the name, and clearly, so did Tessa. She touched her fingers to her mouth for a moment. "One of the reasons I was investigating Joel," she said, "was because I believed he murdered Schuler."

"And he apparently did," Grayson verified. "I figure Ward had the proof all along and decided to leave it next to Joel's body."

They might never know why Ward had done that. Perhaps to "prove" that Joel had been overcome by guilt from all the illegal things he'd done. But Joel wasn't a man with that kind of a conscience. He might have had no conscience at all.

"So with Joel and Ward dead, the danger is really over," Tessa said. But she didn't sound overjoyed by that as much as just relieved.

"It is," Grayson verified, and he checked the time. "By the way, as soon as we caught Hawkins, I called the safe house and asked them to bring the baby. They should be here soon. I figured Courtney would want to see her daughter."

"She will," Landon agreed.

But Courtney wouldn't just want to see the baby. She would take custody of her. As she should. After all, Courtney was the baby's mother, and she'd been through hell and back to make sure Samantha was safe. Still, Landon felt a pang of a different kind. Not just because they'd all been through this nightmare but because the baby would no longer be part of his life.

Oh, man.

When had that happened?

When had he gone from being married to the badge to missing holding a newborn? For that matter, when had his feelings for Tessa deepened?

And there was no mistaking it—they had deepened. But just how deep were they? Deep, he decided when he glanced at her.

"Are you okay?" Grayson asked him.

Landon didn't want to know what had prompted Grayson to ask that, but he hoped he didn't look as if he'd just been punched in the gut. Though it felt a little like that. A gut punch that made him also feel pretty darn happy.

Grayson tipped his head to Landon's arm, which the nurse had just stitched. "You're sure? You both look beat up."

They were, but Tessa and he nodded. Being beaten up wasn't something Landon wanted to experience again anytime soon, but it could have been a lot worse.

Grayson volleyed glances at both Tessa and Landon and hitched his thumb to the door. "I need to get back to the office. Will you let Courtney know the baby's on the way?"

They assured Grayson that they would, and Tessa and Landon went out into the hall as soon as Grayson walked away. Courtney wasn't far, just a couple of doors away, but Landon had something on his mind, and he didn't want to wait any longer.

"Before all hell broke loose, you told me you were in love with me," Landon said to Tessa.

A quick sigh left her mouth. "I'm sorry about that."

His stomach dropped, and he stopped, caught on to her shoulder. "You're sorry?" And yeah, his tone wasn't a happy one.

"I know how your mind works," she explained. "Hearing that will make you feel obligated in some way, and that's not what I want you to feel."

She would have started walking away if he hadn't held

on. He did remember to hold on gently, though, because her shoulders were probably bruised, too.

"What do you want me to feel?" he came out and asked. Except it sounded like an order. So Landon softened his tone and repeated.

And he kissed her, too, just in case she needed any help with that answer.

When he pulled back from the kiss, she was looking at him as if he'd lost his mind. Which was possible. But if so, this was a good kind of mind losing.

She kept staring at him as if trying to gauge his mood or something. So Landon helped her with that, too.

"Tessa, do you want me to be in love with you?"

Still more staring, but her mouth did open a little. "Do you want to be in love with me?" she countered.

Hell. This shouldn't be this hard. He was fumbling the words. Fumbling *this*. So he went with his fallback plan and kissed her again. This time he made it a lot longer, and when he felt her melt against him, Landon thought this might be the time to bare his heart to her.

He was in love with her.

Desperately in love with her.

However, he didn't get out the words before he heard the commotion in the hall. He didn't draw his gun, though, because this commotion was from laughter. He soon saw the source of the laughter when Gage and Kade came into sight. Kade had the baby bundled in his arms.

"Told you," Gage said before they even made it to Landon and Tessa.

Kade chuckled. "Yep." Then Kade glanced at Landon and smiled. "Gage and I were just saying that it wouldn't be long before you two were back together."

"And that caused you to laugh?" Landon asked.

Gage shrugged. "We were just wondering if you'd have that thunderstruck look on your face when you realized you couldn't live without Tessa. You got that look. And Tessa's got that same look about you."

Landon glanced at Tessa, and he frowned. And not because he didn't feel that way about Tessa. He did. But he wasn't especially pleased that his cousins and Tessa had figured this all out before he did. Because Tessa did have that look on her face, and that meant he did, too.

Well, hell.

What now?

Landon got that question answered for him because the baby started to fuss, and besides, Courtney had already waited too long to be with her daughter.

"We can talk about this later," Tessa said, taking Samantha from Kade. Gage dropped kisses on both Tessa's and the baby's cheeks, and his cousins strolled away, still smiling like loons.

Landon gave the baby a cheek kiss, too. His way of saying goodbye. Tessa did the same before they opened the door to the hospital room. Courtney was clearly waiting for them, because the moment she spotted the baby, she got out of the bed. Since she still had an IV in her arm, Landon motioned for her to stay put, and they brought the baby to her.

He could see the love, and relief, all over Courtney's face.

"Thank you," Courtney said, her voice clogged with the emotions. "Grayson had the nurse tell me that the danger was over, but I didn't know I'd get to see Samantha so soon." Tears spilled down her cheeks, but Landon was certain they were happy tears. She tried to blink back some of those tears when she looked at them. "I can't ever thank you enough."

"No," Landon teased, "but you can let us babysit every now and then."

The moment he heard the words leave his mouth, he froze. It was that "us" part. It sounded a lot more than just joint babysitting duties.

And it was.

A lot more.

"I'm in love with you," Landon blurted out, causing both Tessa and Courtney to stare at him.

"I'm guessing you're not talking to me," Courtney joked. She snuggled her baby closer, pressing kisses on her face.

Since Courtney needed some time alone with the baby and since Landon didn't need an audience for the more word fumbling and blurting he was about to do, he gave the baby another kiss. After Tessa had done the same thing and hugged Courtney, Landon led Tessa back into the hall.

"You don't have to tell me that you love me," Tessa tossed out there before he could speak.

"I have to say it because it's true," he argued.

She stared at him as if she might challenge that, so he hauled her to him and kissed her. It was probably a little too rough considering their injuries, but Tessa still made that sound of pleasure.

Landon suddenly wanted to take her somewhere private so he could hear a lot more of those sounds from her.

"Here's how this could work," Landon continued after the kiss had left them both breathless. "We could be sensible about this, and I could just ask you out on a date. One date could lead to a second, third and so on—"

"Or I could just remind you that I'm crazy in love with you, and we could skip the dates and move in together."

He liked the way she was thinking, but Landon wanted more. Heck, he wanted it all.

"We could have lots of sex if I move in with you." She winked, nudged his body with hers.

He liked that way of thinking, too. Really liked it after she gave him another little nudge, but Landon wanted to finish this before his mind got so clouded that he couldn't think.

Landon looked her straight in the eyes. "How long will I have to wait to ask you to marry me?"

Tessa didn't jump to answer, but she did smile. Then she kissed him. "Two seconds," she said with her mouth against his.

"Too long. Marry me, Tessa."

Landon let her get out the yes before he pulled her back to him for a kiss to seal the deal. This was exactly the *all* that he wanted.

* * * * *

Look for more books in USA TODAY
bestselling author Delores Fossen's series
THE LAWMEN OF SILVER CREEK RANCH,
coming in 2017.

*And don't miss her
brand-new trilogy,*
A WRANGLER'S CREEK NOVEL,
beginning in January in ebook with
THOSE TEXAS NIGHTS.

*You'll find all of these titles wherever
Mills & Boon books and ebooks are sold!*

"With this ring, I thee fake wed. I promise to save your butt, should the need arise. . .again. And should you try anything without my permission, I promise to hurt you." Kate raised her brows. "Got it?"

He held up his hand. "Got it. I won't try anything without your permission." As Kate took his upraised hand and slipped the ring onto his finger, Montana muttered, "I don't try. . .I do."

Kate glared at him. "This marriage is fake. Don't forget that."

"Trust me. I won't." Montana leaned forward and pressed his lips to hers in a brief brush of a kiss.

A blast of electricity ripped through Kate, followed by heat, searing a path through her chest and down low in her belly. She pressed her fingers to her lips. "Why did you do that?"

"Only seemed fitting, after tying the knot." He winked, sending another rush of heat rushing through her veins. "Want me to take it back?"

NAVY SEAL SIX
PACK

BY
ELLE JAMES

MILLS
BOON

First Published in Great Britain 2016
By Mills & Boon, an imprint of HarperCollins*Publishers*
1 London Bridge Street, London, SE1 9GF

© 2016 Mary Jernigan

ISBN: 978-0-263-91921-9

46-1116

Our policy is to use papers that are natural, renewable and recyclable products and made from wood grown in sustainable forests. The logging and manufacturing processes conform to the legal environmental regulations of the country of origin.

Printed and bound in Spain
by CPI, Barcelona

Elle James, a *New York Times* bestselling author, started writing when her sister challenged her to write a romance novel. She has managed a full-time job and raised three wonderful children, and she and her husband even tried ranching exotic birds (ostriches, emus and rheas). Ask her, and she'll tell you what it's like to go toe-to-toe with an angry three-hundred-and fifty-pound bird! Elle loves to hear from fans at ellejames@earthlink.net or www.ellejames.com.

This book is dedicated to my editor, whom I adore, Patience Bloom, for all the love, care and feeding she gives me as an author. She's a pleasure to work with and a wonderful person. I wish her all the happiness in the world, because she brings me joy and happiness just by being who she is.

Chapter One

Navy SEAL Benjamin "Montana" Raines leaned against the side of the nondescript building in downtown Washington, DC. Anyone looking at it would guess it was nothing more than another office building filled with businessmen or lobbyists there to buy a congressman or senator into their way of thinking.

Montana liked being outside, even if it was on a busy street in DC. He preferred the open air and big skies of his home state, Montana, but this city was a nice change from the heat, humidity and mosquitoes prevalent at his duty station in Stennis, Mississippi. Not that he minded Mississippi all that much. That little backwater town was home to the Pearl River and some of the best riverine training in the country.

For the past four years, Montana had been with SEAL Boat Team 22, or as he and his team called it, SBT-22. The men on the team were more family than his own family back home. He'd been to hell and back with his fellow SEAL teammates and he'd give his life for each and every one of them.

Trained to conduct covert operations in river and jungle environments, Montana was feeling a bit out of his element and naked in DC. Instead of trees, brush and bugs, his surroundings consisted of concrete, cars and pavement. What bothered him most was that he couldn't openly carry a weapon, and he wasn't wearing any kind of protection—no Kevlar helmet or body armor. Civilian attire was the uniform of the day, with orders to try to look like he belonged in Washington, DC. Most of all, be on the lookout for his new partner.

His team had picked him for this operation because he was good at camouflage and he had experience with bombs. Whether it was in a desert, forest, golf course or city, he could blend in. From what he'd been told, his partner had similar skills. Which could be why he hadn't spotted her yet.

The need to blend in would be useful in a city where blending in normally wasn't the goal. Everyone in DC was, or wanted to be, someone. From the politicians always aware of the next election, to the lobbyists or leaders of the political action committees. All mingling with the rich and famous who hoped to manipulate the lawmakers with promises of campaign funding and vacations on fully staffed, luxury yachts.

None of that appealed to Montana. He'd rather be riding a horse on the prairie or staring up at the big sky on a starry night. He couldn't even see the stars in DC. The light pollution was off the scale and visible from the International Space Station like a gaudy jewel in a long chain of similarly gaudy jewels lining the East Coast.

A bicycle courier stopped on the sidewalk at the corner of the building Montana leaned against. The basket on the front of his bright yellow bicycle was overloaded with small packages and thick envelopes, precariously stacked. He toed the kickstand and dismounted. One by one, he removed the larger packages, lining them up against the building. Then he carefully rearranged them in the basket. A moment later he mounted his bicycle and rode off.

The courier passed Montana and crossed the street.

Montana glanced back the direction from which the cyclist had come and frowned. A small package lay against the brick of the building.

Montana spun toward the cyclist and yelled, "Hey!"

The young courier either didn't hear him or ignored him, hurrying toward his next delivery. Which could have been to deliver the package he'd left behind. Already he was too far away to hear someone shouting at him over the sounds of the traffic on the street, or for Montana to catch him on foot.

Montana turned back to the package and walked toward it. Perhaps it had an address on it, or the phone number of the delivery service. He could call and have them send the courier back to retrieve it.

He had just about reached the package when a flash of motion made him look up in time to see a jean-clad female, with shoulder-length, straight blond hair, flying at him.

The crazy woman bent over and plowed into him, her shoulder hitting him square in his gut, sending him staggering backward. She didn't stop plowing until he'd been pushed several yards along the sidewalk, tripped over his feet and landed hard on his back. He lay still for a moment, the breath knocked out of his lungs, not only from the fall, but from the woman landing on top of him.

When he could drag a breath of air in to fill his

lungs, he grabbed the woman's shoulders and pushed her to arm's length. "What the hell?"

"Stay down!" she shouted, and covered the back of her head with her arms, burying her face in his chest.

Not sure why he should keep down, he recognized the command in her voice and remained on the ground. He even threw his arm over his face.

Several seconds went by. People passed them on the sidewalk. A woman giggled, a man snorted and a child asked, "Mama, what's that woman doing to that man?"

"Shh," the woman said. "I'll tell you when you're older."

At that point, Montana opened his eyes and looked around. "Is something supposed to happen?"

His assailant leaned up on her arms and looked behind her. "The cyclist left a package. It could be full of explosives."

Montana chuckled. "Or it could be full of cookies, or paper clips, or someone's special-ordered dentures." He stared up into steely-gray eyes and studied the woman who'd tackled him. "Not that I mind letting the woman be on top, but I prefer it to be in the privacy of my bedroom, not a sidewalk crowded with people."

The female pushed to her feet and stared at the small box leaning against the side of the building, her eyes narrowed. "It could be a bomb," she said, as the bright yellow bicycle sailed past her.

Montana rose behind her, recognizing the cyclist from a few minutes earlier.

The rider barely came to a stop before he dropped to the ground and scooped up the box. Back on the bicycle, he jerked the handlebars around and sped away, hitting the street to weave in and out of the slow-moving traffic.

"Tragedy averted," Montana couldn't help saying. "Thank you for saving me from a fate worse than Grandma's cookies."

The woman stiffened, color rising in her cheeks. "Excuse me." With her chin lifted high enough that she couldn't possible see her feet, she marched away.

Montana resumed his post next to the entrance of the Stealth Operation Specialists headquarters, his gaze following the woman with the steely-gray eyes and sandy-blond hair.

She'd crossed the street and stopped to stare at the numbers on the building in front of her. Performing an about-face, she retraced her steps and stopped in front of him to stare at the number on the outside of the building.

With a chuckle, Montana asked, "You wouldn't happen to be Kate McKenzie, would you?"

She closed her eyes briefly, then opened them and nodded. "I am."

"Since we already know each other on an intimate level, let me introduce myself. Benjamin Raines, but my friends call me Montana. I hear we're going to be partners."

KATE WANTED TO sink into the concrete sidewalk and die of mortification. Instead, she sucked it up and held out her hand as if she tackled perfect strangers on a regular occurrence. "Nice to meet you. I don't suppose you'd keep our little…incident to yourself, would you?"

"It'll be our secret." He took her hand, his strong, callused fingers wrapping around hers. She had no doubt he could crush her bones with one tight squeeze, if he wanted. A ripple of awareness feathered across her senses.

When she'd been lying on top of him, she'd felt the rock-hard muscles of his chest and thighs. He was built as solid as an armored tank. When her old college roommate, Becca, had briefed her on this mission, she'd told her she'd be paired with a Navy SEAL. The image in her mind had been one of a scruffy man with a beard and intense eyes. Not this ruggedly handsome, clean-shaven man wearing blue jeans, cowboy boots and a blue chambray shirt. He could have been a model for a jeans commercial, the kind of jeans best suited for horseback riding, not hanging out on street corners in the city.

"We've been waiting for you," he said, his voice deep and smooth like warm chocolate being poured over her skin, seeping into every crevice. "Come with me."

To the end of the earth. The thought leaped into her mind and she quickly banished it. Kate had more than proved herself a lousy judge of men and matters of the heart. But she couldn't stop the shiver that slipped down the back of her neck as she passed him and entered the building.

Montana led the way to the elevator and waited for her to enter before he punched a button on the panel.

As the car rose, Kate held her tongue. What could she say after making a complete fool of herself? "Do you know what this so-called mission is all about?"

Montana nodded but didn't enlighten her. While the elevator car rose, he leaned against the wall, studying her.

"I take it you're not going to clue me in." Kate hit him with a brief but unswerving glare, and then jerked her gaze away, avoiding direct eye contact, afraid of repeating her own history. Hadn't she fallen for a handsome colleague once before? Drawn into his world, his life, she'd been hard-pressed and embarrassed to admit she'd fallen for the oldest double cross in the book.

Maybe she deserved to be a desk jockey for the remainder of her career as a CIA special agent. Determined not to fall under any man's spell ever again, Kate watched the numbers blink on the display over the door. Two. Three.

A loud boom echoed in the air. The elevator jerked to a halt so suddenly Kate was thrown to her knees. Lights blinked out and absolute darkness descended on the enclosed box.

"Are you all right?" Montana's deep voice filled the abyss.

"Yeah." She pushed to her feet, bracing her hand on the wall. "What happened?"

"I think your bomb exploded."

No sooner had the words left his mouth than another explosion rocked the elevator and dust sifted through the air vent. Thrown sideways, Kate crashed into the hard body of the Navy SEAL.

His arm circled her waist, pulling her tightly against him.

Kate waited in silence, her chest crushed to his, listening for the next explosion, sounds of sirens or voices.

After a couple minutes and nothing else exploding, Kate broke her silence. "You can let go of me. I think that was the last one."

"We can't be sure," he said, his arm tightening, his fingers digging into the small of her back. "Give it another minute or two."

The longer she waited in the circle of his arm, her body absorbing his heat, the more time she had to take in just how tall and firm this man's body was. From what she'd felt, he didn't have an ounce of fat anywhere. And he smelled of outdoors and fresh air. She inhaled, deeply.

"You were right. It was the last one," he said, his breath stirring the loose strands of hair on her cheek. His arm loosened.

For a long moment, Kate remained pressed against him, her thoughts in a whirl, her blood hammering through her veins. Then she remembered to let go of the breath she'd been holding, and backed away. "I don't suppose you have a flash—"

A light blinked on in the darkness.

When her eyes adjusted to the sudden illumination, Kate shook her head. "You don't look like the kind of guy who carries a penlight."

Montana grinned. "I'm not. But Becca's boss gave me this one. It also contains a hidden camera. I might be a cowboy at heart, but the James Bond in me goes all techno-geek with stuff like this." He shined the light at the control panel. "Suppose the emergency button will work without electricity?"

"Only one way to find out." She pressed the button and waited. No sirens nor flashing lights came to life. She shrugged. "Help me pry the doors open so we can see where we are."

Montana placed the penlight between his teeth, dug

his fingers between the sliding doors and pulled hard enough that Kate could get her fingers between, as well.

"On three," she said. "One…two…three."

They pulled hard in opposite directions. At first the door didn't budge much. Kate leaned back as hard as she could, digging her feet into the floor for leverage. Inch by hard-earned inch, the door opened, until there was enough room for one of them to squeeze through.

Montana shone the light, starting at their feet. The dark wall of the elevator shaft stared back at them. He swept the beam of light upward to the top, where they could see a four-inch gap to what Kate assumed was the fourth floor.

Montana gave her a sideways glance. "You don't suppose you could fit through?"

She shook her head. "I'm smaller than you, but I'd have to be a cat to squeeze through that narrow gap."

Montana trained the light at the ceiling of the car. "Then there's only one other way out of here. Here, hold the flashlight." He handed it to her, cupped his hands and bent down. "Check it out."

She stared at his cupped hands and didn't move.

He glanced up. "Unless you want to boost me. I warn you, I'm a little heavier than you are."

"I'll go." She stepped into his hands and raised her arms over her head.

Montana straightened, lifting her up as he did.

She found a loose panel in the ceiling, pushed it upward and then poked her head through. "I can see the fourth floor landing. We should be able to get out through here."

"I'm going to raise you high enough to get your arms through, and you can take it from there."

Montana lifted her until Kate got her arms through the hole, braced her elbows on the sides and pulled herself up to sit on the edge. Once she had her breath, she pushed to her feet and shone the light back into the elevator car. "Your turn. Need me to lend you a hand?"

"No, thanks." He jumped, his fingers catching on the sides of the panel opening.

Kate backed up as much as possible, directing the flashlight beam near Montana without blinding him. He pulled himself up, his biceps flexing, stretching the shirt tight around his chest and shoulders. Squeezing his shoulders through the tight space, he soon had the rest of his body through and stood beside Kate.

She handed him the light and stepped over to the fourth floor landing and down onto the hallway floor.

Emergency lighting glowed softly, giving just enough light to guide them.

"Follow me." Montana led the way, turning left at the end of the corridor. Midway down the next hall, he pushed through a doorway. "Everyone okay in here?" he called out.

A strong flashlight beam shone in his face.

Montana raised an arm to shade his eyes.

"Montana, is that you?" a voice called out.

Kate entered the room behind the Navy SEAL to find it crowded with guys as big and brawny as Montana, crowded around a couple of battery-operated lanterns. Interspersed with the big men were a few women and a white-haired man who appeared to be as physically fit as the younger men.

"Anyone sustain injuries?" Montana asked.

"We're all good here. Thankfully, we were in the war room when the explosion occurred," the white-haired man said. "I'm glad we put the extra money in the construction. It's built like a bunker." He stepped forward. "I'm betting this is our chameleon, Kate McKenzie. Hi, I'm Royce Fontaine, the head of Stealth Operations Specialists—or SOS, as we like to refer to it."

"SOS?" Kate raised her brows. "Just what does SOS do?"

Royce nodded, a smile tipping the corners of his mouth. "Stealth Operations Specialists is a team of agents called in when the FBI, CIA and Secret Service can't quite get the job done. Or the situation is highly sensitive and needs the utmost secrecy. Unfortunately, most of my agents are assigned at this time, thus the need to call in reinforcements." He swept his arm out, his gaze circling the room. "Glad to have you all on board for this operation. We can use all the help we can get."

Kate nodded, her gaze seeking and finding her old roommate from college, Becca Smith. "I didn't realize there'd be an entire team of people on this gig."

Becca pushed through the others and hugged Kate. "I couldn't say much over the phone. We needed you here, where others can't listen in on the conversation. As we've learned the hard way, we can't trust anyone but the people in this room."

"And based on the explosion outside the building," Royce said, "there are those who will stop at nothing to keep us from doing our jobs. Don't worry. I have people checking the structure. They will alert us if we need to evacuate immediately. When we had the structure built, we hardened it for just such an occasion. We could potentially continue to work out of this office, but coming and going from a targeted location will be dangerous."

Kate leaned toward Becca and whispered, "What are you getting me into?" Her body quivered with excitement. She'd trained for covert ops. This was what made her blood sing.

Becca took her hand. "Come into the conference room. Geek is working on getting the computers and lighting back online so we can brief you. Then I'm sure we'll move to our backup location. This building has been compromised."

As Becca led her through another door, Kate glanced over her shoulder, searching for and finding Montana. Though she'd met him only a few minutes before, he seemed to be the anchor in this sea of people, with their plans that threatened to sweep her away from a desk job she loathed.

Becca had promised her a way to redeem and reclaim her status in the CIA, if they could pull off this mission. By the looks of it, and the people squeezing into the war room, they could well be a small army gathering to overthrow the government, for all Kate knew.

What had she gotten herself into?

Whatever it was, it sure beat the hell out of pushing paper.

Chapter Two

Montana followed everyone into the conference room, amazed they weren't evacuating, despite Fontaine's assurance that the building could withstand a bomb blast.

Several flashlights and a couple of lanterns provided enough illumination that he could get around without tripping on the many people crowded into the large room.

"Take a seat," Fontaine commanded. "The lights should come on momentar—"

The fluorescent bulbs blinked overhead and then glowed brightly.

A collective sigh and smiles were shared all around. Montana pulled out a chair for Kate and waited while she sank into it. Then he sat beside her. Now that everyone was in and seated around the large table, he had a chance to study the people Fontaine had gathered.

"I want to start by introducing everyone," Fontaine said. "You're all to be part of the team in one fashion or another." He pointed to the man who entered carrying a laptop. "The heart of this group is Geek, our computer guru and all-around technical genius." The white-haired man waved his hand toward the man helping Geek with wires and switches. "Lance will be working with him in the office or in a communication van, wherever we need him to support the operation."

Fontaine waved next at a woman Montana knew from their failed attempt to vacation in Cancun, Becca Smith, who worked directly for Fontaine as one of his SOS agents. "Becca Smith has a stake in this operation. Whoever is behind all the assassinations and attempts killed her father and tried to kill her father's close friend, Oscar Melton. Both of them were top-notch CIA agents working with the congressional Subcommittee on Terrorism, Drug Trafficking and International Operations."

Turning to his left, Fontaine held his hand out to a nice-looking woman with blond hair and blue eyes. She, too, had been involved in the chaos of Cancun. "Natalie Layne is another SOS agent who has been a part of the ongoing issues we've encountered thus far. Her sister was one of the women abducted, with the intent to sell her in a human trafficking ring located out of Cancun, Mexico."

Fontaine continued around the table. "Besides the SOS operatives, please welcome Kate McKenzie, an agent with the CIA. We've also been augmented by six Navy SEALs, on loan to us from Stennis, Mississippi."

Starting around the room, Fontaine introduced them. "Dutton Callaway, who goes by Duff. Sawyer Houston, Quentin Lovett, Jace Hunter, Cord Schafer, who goes by Rip, and Benjamin Raines, nicknamed after his home state of Montana."

Montana nodded acknowledgment.

"A six pack of SEALs," Geek muttered, as he connected the laptop to an Ethernet cable and clicked a remote that lit a projection screen at one end of the long room.

"Are we planning to start a war with all of these people in the room?" Duff, one of Montana's SEAL teammates, asked.

Fontaine shook his head, his jaw tightening. "No, but by the looks of it, we might be stopping one that's been going on longer than we knew." He turned to Geek. "Ready?"

Geek nodded. "Someone get the door."

Navy SEAL Quentin Lovett, standing near the back of the room, shut the door.

At the same time, Geek clicked a handheld remote control device and the image on his laptop projected onto the screen. He touched the keyboard and the screen filled with a lot of what appeared to be random numbers.

"This is what we have so far," Fontaine said. "Thanks to Becca's father, God rest his soul, who knew he was in trouble and might not live to tell about it."

"All I see are numbers," Montana pointed out. "Do they represent something?"

"Geek has spent the past week crunching these numbers, trying to decode them, thinking they were a special message." Fontaine nodded toward him. "Tell them what you discovered."

"Well, I couldn't make secret messages out of them, and I was getting really frustrated, until I took a step back and just stared at the groupings. Then it hit me." He stood and pointed to the wall. "This half of each sixteen-digit number is a date." He pointed to the other half. "The other eight digits could have been bank accounts, safe-deposit box numbers or anything else in the world. Given that they were all eight digits in length, I made a calculated guess and ran a program, entering them as coordinates."

He walked back to the computer and clicked another key. A world map replaced the numbers. Bright red dots overlaid the map.

Montana leaned forward, his eyes narrowed, and studied the information depicted on the image.

Geek zoomed in on the map, focusing on Europe. He walked toward the screen again. "On the date for this location, in Paris, France, a terrorist attack took place, killing everyone in a certain restaurant, including Harmon Whitlow, his wife, son and daughter-in-law."

"I heard about that," Sawyer said. One of the six SEALs at the table, he knew the most about politics. As the son of a former US Senator, he kept up with the political scene, though he claimed he couldn't care less.

He always amazed Montana with his insight on what was going on in Washington, DC.

After the fiasco in Cancun, where someone had attempted to kill him and his father, Sawyer had been a little less adamant about his distaste for politics. With his father now in the equivalent of the witness protection program, starting a new life as someone else, Sawyer had volunteered for this mission, determined to find the person or persons responsible for trying to kill them. "Harmon Whitlow was the undersecretary for political affairs in the US State Department," he stated.

Geek nodded and pointed to another dot, this time on the map of the US. "On this date in New York City, a bomb went off near a set of bleachers during the NYC Marathon. Two people died in that attack, over two hundred people were injured and one went missing."

"Who?" Kate asked.

"Emily Brantley, daughter of Trevor Brantley, multi-millionaire." Geek pressed a key on the laptop, displaying a photo of a pretty young lady standing between a man in a suit and a well-dressed woman. "She was running the marathon. When the smoke cleared, she was gone. Her bodyguards had been killed not by the bomb, but by bullets that expertly pierced their skulls."

Montana knew about Brantley's missing daughter. It had been all over the news, with pleas and a reward posted from the Brantleys for their daughter's safe return.

Fontaine interjected, "The authorities assumed it was a terrorist bombing by members of ISIS, a copycat of the 2013 attack at the Boston Marathon. *We* think it was a diversion allowing the bombers to kill the bodyguards and nab the Brantley woman."

"How soon after the bombing was Trevor Brantley murdered?" Montana asked.

Geek pointed to a larger dot on the map in the vicinity of Washington, DC. "On this date, at this coordinate, less than two weeks later, Trevor Brantley was gunned down in his mansion here."

Sawyer pointed at the double dots on the Yucatan Peninsula. "Were those the dates and locations of the attempts on my life and my father's?"

Geek nodded. "Yes. Obviously those attempts weren't successful."

Becca Smith, her face pale, asked, "Was one of those dots on the nation's capital the day my father was killed near his apartment here? Is that why there are more dots in the DC area? Multiple killings?"

Geek's lips twisted. "The date your father died and

the date there was an attempt on his colleague Oscar Melton's life were both on that list, with the coordinates of the attacks."

Montana's teammate Quentin Lovett slipped an arm around Becca's waist. "We know the connection between Marcus Smith and Oscar Melton. What connection is there between them and all the others?"

"Besides investigating the drug and human trafficking issues worldwide, the two CIA agents were investigating these codes. I can only assume they thought they were connected. Marcus Smith was able to mail the disk containing the information to Becca before he was killed. Oscar Melton is still in critical condition in a coma."

"We suspect Sawyer's father, Rand Houston, was targeted because he was on the Subcommittee for Terrorism, Drug Trafficking and International Operations," Fontaine said. "What we can't connect is Trevor Brantley and his family to the others. Which leads me to one more introduction, for those who haven't had the pleasure of meeting her." He turned toward the door, smiled and held out his hand. "Perfect timing. Please, come in."

A woman with long dark hair, wearing a tailored gray skirt suit, stepped into the room. Montana remembered her from their operation to rescue women in Cancun. She'd come undercover as a potential buyer. Montana recognized the man following her as Rex, her bodyguard.

Fontaine took the woman's hand. "This is Mica Brantley, Trevor Brantley's widow. Since her husband's death, she's made it her mission to find and bring her stepdaughter, Emily Brantley, home."

Mica nodded at the roomful of people. "Thank you for volunteering for this mission. I won't rest until Emily is home safe and my husband's killer is brought to justice."

"Mrs. Brantley was not in the country on the date her husband was murdered in their home," Fontaine said. "She's had multiple attempts made on her life but managed to get here despite her pursuers."

Mica nodded. "Since Trevor's death, I've lived aboard my yacht and traveled, searching for Emily. I'll never give up hope of finding her. I love the girl as if she were my own."

Fontaine nodded. "She's taken a huge risk to come back to DC, offering herself as bait to catch the killer."

Mica gave a brief, sad smile. "I've spent a lot of money and time searching and thus far haven't found the source of all the tragedy. Royce has been in contact with me since the incident in Cancun. When he learned about the disk, he thought I should know." She lifted her chin. "I'm tired of running. If I can put myself up as the target, maybe we can flush out the killer, or catch one of his hit men and interrogate him."

"That's a dangerous proposition," Kate said. "You're willing to risk your life for this effort?"

"I am." Mica turned to Fontaine. "With the understanding that, should I die in this attempt, someone continue to look for Emily."

Fontaine nodded. "We'll do our best to keep you alive and find Emily." He glanced around, making eye contact with everyone in the room. "We're all in this together. We have to stop those behind all the murders and attempted murders in this case."

As one, everyone in the room nodded.

Montana's sense of justice refused to let him back down from this mission. He'd seen the women held captive for auction. No woman, or her family, should be subjected to the horror of human trafficking. He wanted to get to the bottom of the case as much as Mica Brantley did.

Montana tipped his head toward the screen, ready to get on with solving the case. "What about the rest of the dates and coordinates?"

"We connected the dots with a couple of 'accidents,'" Geek said. "Richard Giddings drove off a bridge into the Potomac. He worked with Senator Houston on the same subcommittee. Percy Beardon, an avid cyclist, fell from his bike at this coordinate on the date indicated."

"What's the deal on Beardon?" Duff asked.

Fontaine shook his head. "His claim to fame was that he was one of the survivors of the Syrian attack on the US Embassy in Turkey a couple of years ago."

"Most of the dates are past," Sawyer said.

"Like notches on a bedpost?" Quentin asked.

Montana's lips twitched. Trust Quentin to make it about sex. The man was an expert ladies' man and charmer. At least until he'd met his match. Becca had been good for him. She made him work to woo her. And now that they were in a committed relationship, they were seldom apart.

Montana was glad for his friend. Quentin had needed someone to come home to. He'd settled down and quit going out as much. Too bad they worked so far apart, with Becca based out of Virginia and Quentin out of Mississippi. But then Fontaine didn't care where his SOS operatives lived, as long as they could deploy at a moment's notice. Montana suspected Becca would soon base out of Mississippi, to be closer to Quentin when she wasn't working an assignment.

Familiar with those conditions, Montana didn't envy Quentin and Becca's relationship. As often as SBT-22 was deployed, and given the nature of Becca's work, the two would be hard-pressed to get together on a regular basis, even if she was based out of Mississippi.

Montana had always considered that as long as he was on active duty as a Navy SEAL, he'd be better off steering clear of entanglements. Being a bachelor was the safest bet.

He glanced at his new partner, Kate McKenzie. The woman seemed no-nonsense and decidedly kick-ass. He shouldn't have a problem sticking to his intent to stay single and emotionally unavailable to women. Especially one who'd tackled him before they'd been properly introduced.

Those steely eyes didn't inspire him to lose himself in her. Her athletic body and shoulder-length, straight, sandy-blond hair didn't make him want to run his hand through it to ascertain just how silky the strands were.

Well, maybe just a little. And her eyes were a startling steel-gray, rimmed with a darker pewter outline.

When she'd lain on top of him, protecting him from potential shrapnel, he hadn't been all that turned on by the rounded swells of her breasts against his chest.

Okay, so maybe he had noticed her breasts. They had been smashed against him for what had felt like an eternity. When he'd rested his hands on her hips, his body had naturally reacted to having a female on top of him. A lot of time had passed since he'd been with a woman.

He turned to study his new partner and frowned. It was so much easier to work with men. They didn't threaten his determination to remain footloose and single.

Dragging his attention from Kate, he focused on Fontaine. "Most of the dates are past. That means some of them are in the future. Like a schedule of events to come. You agree with that, don't you?"

Geek and Fontaine nodded simultaneously.

"That's exactly what we've learned," Fontaine said.

"So how do we fit in with this mission?" Kate asked. "Why did you need me when you had all of these people to run your operation?"

Fontaine faced Montana and Kate. "Becca tells me you are an expert chameleon, able to change your appearance to look like anyone you want."

Kate shrugged. "I did a lot of theater in high school and college. My skills with makeup came in handy as a field agent with CIA. I had a knack for transforming into whomever I needed to be." Her lips thinned and her jaw tightened.

Montana noted this little change in her expression. That she spoke in the past tense made him curious. Wasn't she still an agent in the CIA?

Fontaine nodded and his gaze shifted to Montana. "Raines, your team considers you the best at camouflage and bombs."

Montana frowned. "Sure. I can blend in with any tree, bush or desert location. But nothing like Kate."

"Your abilities to blend in were only part of the reason I chose you two for this assignment." Fontaine waved his hand. "If you could please stand, I'll show you the other reason."

Montana stood and held Kate's chair while she rose as well, her brows pulling together.

"Mrs. Brantley, I'd like you and your bodyguard to please stand by Raines and McKenzie."

The two complied.

Fontaine smiled. "Perfect. Kate, you're almost the exact height as Mrs. Brantley. And Raines, you're pretty close to Rex Masters's height and build."

"So?" Montana challenged.

Geek pointed to a dot on the map. "One of the dates indicates tomorrow at the yacht club."

Fontaine picked up from there. "Mrs. Brantley is listed as keynote speaker at the annual fund-raiser the club sponsors for the children's hospital."

"I've canceled every other engagement I've had since my husband's death," Mica said. "This was one I couldn't. The children's hospital is near and dear to my heart. After losing my baby to leukemia, I realized how much the hospital does for desperately ill children and their families. I'll be there."

"Based on the date and coordinates, someone knows you wouldn't miss the event," Fontaine said. "We can't be certain just who will be targeted, but we wanted to make sure you're safe. Raines and McKenzie will go as your guests. We created identities for them as newly rich recent members of the yacht club."

"Are we to supplement Mrs. Brantley's bodyguard support?" Kate asked.

"Yes, and more," Fontaine said. "I'll have several of the other SEALs and some of my agents augmenting the waitstaff at the club."

Geek added, "We can't be certain who they will target. Because whoever is orchestrating these attacks doesn't seem to be going after just the politicians and federal agents…" He paused. "They're taking out the family members, too."

Mrs. Brantley's face paled. "Perhaps I should call and cancel my speech at the fund-raiser. I'd hate for a bomb, targeting me, to take out innocent bystanders."

"That's why we'll have the SEALs and SOS team in place," Fontaine assured her. "I'll also have bomb-sniffing dogs make a thorough sweep of the entire building before the event commences, and we'll have security cordon off the area to keep vehicles from getting close."

Mrs. Brantley chewed on her bottom lip. "I don't want people hurt because of me."

"We don't know who they will be after," Geek said. "And as far as we can tell, nobody knows we have the list of dates and coordinates."

Fontaine turned to Montana. "Raines, you and McKenzie will be there not only to protect Mrs. Brantley, you are to watch and listen closely to the people she interacts with. If we determine she is a target, you two might have to take Mrs. Brantley's and Masters's places in the DC scene as their doubles for a while."

Montana exchanged glances with Rex Masters. It made sense that he would replace the man. They were similar in build and he could have his hair lightened to match Masters's dark blond cropped hair. Kate and Mica were the same height and close to the same build. Mrs. Brantley might have a tinier waist and bigger breasts, but Kate, if she was as good as she said she was, could make her face up to look just like Mica's. Colored contacts would help match Mica's dark brown irises.

"Why aren't you using your SOS agents instead of the SEALs?" asked Navy SEAL Jace Hunter, the youngest member of the SBT-22 team.

"I'm short staffed," Fontaine said. "They're on critical missions throughout the country and the world. Considering the successful kill rate of that list, we might need all the security and waitstaff we can get. The future dates and locations are in or around the DC area at major events. Geek and I conducted a thorough background check on the six of you SEALs. You all have exemplary records. I'd trust you with my life and that of Mrs. Brantley. Add to it the fact that most of you have already been involved in the attacks, and I think you have a stake in seeing it to a satisfactory conclusion."

"We usually work in combat environments," Duff said. "Mingling with the rich and famous might be a bit out of our league."

"Again," Fontaine said, "I don't know who else I could trust. When we took down the assassin after Oscar Melton, we found a mole in the CIA orchestrating some of the assassinations. We don't know how deep into our nation's security the problem exists."

Montana's fists clenched. They were all supposed to be on the same side. When the organization had bad seeds within it, people lost faith, and the infrastructure of that entity crumbled from within. After all they'd been through in Cancun, and the multiple attempts on his friend Sawyer's life, he would be happy to see this operation to the bitter end. "I'm in."

"WHY ME?" KATE faced Royce. "I'm with the CIA. As far as you know, I could be as rotten as the deputy director you brought down."

Her friend Becca stepped forward. "I vouched for you. My father and Oscar only had good things to say about your work and your integrity. They trusted you."

Kate's cheeks heated. "Even after my demotion?"

Becca nodded. "Especially after. You couldn't know your partner was a double agent. I'm betting you learned a valuable lesson from the whole affair."

Out of the corner of her eye, Kate saw Montana's face jerk toward her.

Well, to hell with him. People made mistakes. Unfortunately, she'd made a double-whammy mistake. Falling for her partner was bad enough. Not doing her homework to learn the man she was sleeping with was actually a Russian double agent was worse. Kate was lucky she hadn't been kicked out of the CIA. Being demoted from field agent to desk duty had been bad, but not the end of her career.

With a sigh, she pushed the past behind her and glanced at Mica. "I'll need to get inside your head and know your moves, expressions, likes and dislikes, as well as who your friends are, and known enemies."

Mica smiled. "I like the way you think." Her smile faded. "But if I *am* a target, and you take my place, you'll become the target." She shook her head and turned to Royce. "I can't put Kate in that position."

"If it helps uncover who's after you, I'm in," Kate said. "Hell, if it gets me out of desk duty, I'll do just about anything."

Royce glanced at Montana. "What about you, Raines? Are you up for playing dress-up and body-double?"

Montana shrugged. "As I said, I'm in."

Mica Brantley nodded. "Thank you both. I hope

nothing bad comes of the yacht club fund-raiser. It's supposed to be all about the children and raising money for them."

"Our aim is to make certain nothing happens," Royce assured her.

"Then I'll see you all at the event." Mica stared around the room. "In some form or fashion. Thank you for your assistance in this matter. I was running out of alternatives. I'm hoping with your help to recover my stepdaughter."

"We're looking into that. Geek and Lance have been searching the internet and backtracking through all the footage of the marathon."

Mica's eyes widened. "Anything new?"

Royce shook his head. "Nothing yet, but we're not done."

Her shoulders slumped. "Thank you for all you've done thus far."

With a dip of his head, Royce squeezed her hand. "Until tomorrow."

After Mica left the room with Rex, Royce returned his attention to the group. "Any questions?"

Her mind already ten steps ahead, Kate raked her gaze over Montana. "We'll need clothes and shoes."

"I have clothes and shoes," Montana said.

Royce grinned. "Trust Kate. You'll need new clothes and shoes. And they won't be cheap. Don't worry about budget or what to buy. I have one of my agents on standby at a local high-end clothier. She'll guide you two on selections and then arrange for your makeover."

Montana's brows dipped, and the SEALs around the table chuckled.

"Going preppy on us, Montana?" the man Royce had introduced as Jace Hunter asked.

"Don't go hookin' up with some rich hoochie mama," the one nicknamed Rip said. "Your country needs you as a SEAL, not a bonbon-eating gigolo."

Rip's comment had all the guys laughing.

Kate got a strange amount of enjoyment from Montana's discomfort. At the same time, she couldn't wait to see the big man decked out in a suit and tie. Then again...if she thought he was ruggedly handsome in jeans, with a T-shirt stretching tautly over his massive chest...she might have palpitations over this SEAL's magnetism in a suit or tuxedo.

Get a grip.

Kate squared her shoulders. "When do we start?"

"There's a company car pulling up to the back of the building now." Royce turned to the others in the room. "We could use some help clearing the building and moving to our disaster recovery site."

Everyone rose at once, talking and moving toward the door.

Kate went through first.

Becca caught up with her. "I'll show you the way out the back."

Once Montana joined them, they headed along the hallway, dimly lit by emergency lighting. Becca opened a door to a stairwell and they descended to the ground level.

When Becca reached for the exit door, Montana covered her hand with his. "Let me go first."

Becca snorted. "At this point, we're all tactical. Male or female, we're trained in urban warfare."

"You and Kate might be trained in urban warfare,

but I've *survived* urban warfare. And if that's not good enough, my mama taught me to open doors for ladies." He winked and stepped around her.

Kate's heart skipped several beats at the sexy wink.

Becca turned to her friend with a smile. "Oh, he's *smooth*, that one."

Montana exited the building, closing the door behind him. A moment later, he opened it and held it for the women.

Becca stood back. "I'm not actually going with you. I need to help move operations to the backup location."

Kate hugged her. "Thanks for thinking of me."

Her friend squeezed her tightly. "I figured you were perfect for this job. Stay safe."

"I will." Kate released Becca.

Montana stood beside a long, black, chauffeur-driven car, holding the door for her.

Kate gave him a crooked grin.

"I told you," he said. "My mama taught me to treat the ladies right."

"Your mother would be proud," she said, and slid into the backseat, scooting over far enough to allow room for Montana.

So this was it. The start of a potentially dangerous operation, with a hunk of a SEAL as her sidekick, and a chance to redeem herself if things turned out okay. She couldn't help but cross her fingers and pray this mission went off like clockwork, they nailed the persons responsible for the hits and brought the Brantley girl home alive.

Chapter Three

Montana hated shopping. After trying on the fourth set of trousers, the fifth button-down shirt and the third suit jacket, he'd had enough. "What's wrong with this one?" he asked. Other than he'd probably rip the damned thing when he went after the bad guys. One right uppercut and he'd bust out the stitches.

SOS Agent Nicole Steele, who preferred to go by her nickname of Tazer, shook her head. "We need to go another size larger. You can't move in that jacket. Good Lord, Ben, what do they feed men in Montana?" She waved to the attendant and asked him to bring another size larger. "We have a seamstress on standby to make the alterations quickly."

"Seriously, I don't need but one suit and a pair of casual pants."

"Not if you want to blend in with the rich and politically elevated," Tazer said. "Now quit bellyaching. How did you ever make it through BUD/S training?"

"I sure as hell didn't have to wear a suit and dress shirt. I only had to worry about drowning in the sea or falling flat on my face in the mud. For that matter, it was a cakewalk compared to this."

"Big baby. You'll be happy when it fits properly,"

Tazer said. "Hurry up. We still have to get Kate tricked out."

Kate sat beside Tazer, her lips twitching.

Montana pointed a finger. "Don't say a word."

She held up her hands. "Did I?"

"No, but I can feel you want to."

She drew a line across her lips. "My lips are sealed." Her gray eyes flashed. "But if I were to say something, it would be along the lines of 'think of these clothes as a uniform.'"

"Not helping," he said, and yanked the jacket off his shoulders.

The attendant handed him another jacket and quickly stepped back, as if afraid Montana would take a swing at him.

Montana shrugged into the garment. The sooner he got through this, the better. He knew what size jeans he wore and the brand that fit best. When he needed a new pair, he walked into the store, picked them out of the stacks and headed straight for the checkout counter. The end.

As the jacket settled around his shoulders, Montana hated to admit Tazer was right. This one wasn't nearly as constricting and actually felt good on his body.

"Much better. Now, button the jacket." Tazer and the attendant converged on him. While Tazer tugged, the clerk pinned. When they were done, Montana was afraid to move for fear of being stuck by one of the hundreds of pins sticking out of the material. He felt like a cross between a voodoo doll and a dressmaker's dummy.

Then they went to work on the trousers, tugging and tucking the hem and the waistband. When they were done, Montana was hot, cranky and ready to be out of the building.

"Let me have the jacket." Tazer held out her hands.

Montana started to take it off and was jabbed by a pin. "Ouch!"

"Here, let me." Kate stood, eased the jacket from his shoulders and handed it to Tazer.

Tazer handed the jacket to the attendant, who hustled out of the room, presumably to take the garment to the seamstress.

"Now, out of those trousers." Tazer held out her hands again.

Kate backed away. "Sorry. Can't help you there."

"Hurry up." Tazer snapped her fingers. "We don't have all day. Trust me, you don't have anything I haven't seen before."

Montana glared. "You haven't seen *my* anything before."

Kate's lips stretched into a wide grin and she turned her back, chuckling.

Montana stripped out of the trousers and slipped into his jeans.

"I'll be back shortly with the clothes you'll wear out of here." Tazer left the dressing area.

Montana buttoned his jeans. "You can turn around now."

Kate faced him. "I would have thought a SEAL would have no trouble stripping in front of a woman."

"My mama—"

Kate waved her hand. "Yeah, yeah. Your mama taught you better. But you're a SEAL. You fight hard and play rough."

He shrugged. "It's just who I am. I was taught to respect women, no matter how young or old."

Kate shook her head. "You can take the cowboy out of Montana, but you can't take the Montana out of the cowboy?"

"Something like that." He tipped his head toward her. "What about you? Where did you grow up?"

She shook her head. "I was a military brat. We moved fifteen times before I turned eighteen. I'm not *from* anywhere."

"What about your folks? Did your father retire somewhere you call home?" he asked.

Kate nodded. "He passed away. My mother has a condo in Wisconsin and she now works for a pediatrician."

"I take it you don't see her often." Montana sat in one of the chairs and shoved his foot into one of his cowboy boots.

She stared in the direction Tazer had gone. "Not often enough. What about you?"

"I haven't been back to Montana in two years. Just never seems to be enough time."

"Where in Montana?" Kate turned toward him, her gaze capturing his.

"On a ranch south of Bozeman."

"So you're the real deal, then."

"If you mean I'm a real cowboy, then yes. I've done just about everything that needs doing on a cattle ranch." He pulled the second boot on and stood. "Enough about me. What about you? Why did they demote you in the CIA?"

She turned away, her mouth thinning into a firm line. "I'd rather not talk about it."

"Suit yourself. But the more we know about each other, the better we will be able to work together. If I didn't know my buddies on my SEAL team as well as I do, I wouldn't be able to anticipate their reactions to different situations."

"Fine." She faced him, a frown pulling her brows together. "I screwed up. I fell for my partner, and he just happened to be a double agent for Russia." She sighed. "I was a green rookie. I thought everyone who signed on with the CIA had been fully vetted and loved our country as much as I do." Kate lifted her chin and stared straight into Montana's eyes. "I learned my lesson. Don't put your full faith and trust in anyone. And don't fall for your partner."

Montana nodded. "I'm sorry that happened to you. Must have hurt pretty bad." He stepped toward the door. "You don't have to worry about this partner. I'm a confirmed bachelor, and I've never even been to Russia." He winked at her. "Let's go find Tazer. It's your turn to play dress-up."

Montana had asked the hard question, but he'd rather know who he was working with and what made her tick. When the crap hit the fan, he wanted to know what she was made of and how she would react.

Kate McKenzie had taken a hit. More than likely, she wouldn't trust him easily. He'd have to ease into her confidence a little at a time. He sure as hell hoped they had time to make that happen. In a life-and-death situation, Kate needed to know he had her six. He already knew she had his, based on the flying tackle she'd initiated earlier.

While the seamstress worked on the suit jacket and trousers for Montana, Tazer led them to the exclusive shop next door. Where the men's shop was all dark wood and masculine, this one was light and airy. What amazed him was the lack of clothes racks. "Are they hiding the ladies' clothing?" he whispered into Kate's ear.

She glanced around. "No idea. Normally, I can't afford to walk into a shop like this. Royce must have one helluva budget."

The beautifully dressed and tastefully made-up attendant in high heels and perfect accessories shot a glance at Kate and Montana and then turned her attention to Tazer. "How might I help you?"

If the woman had thought to have an attitude about finding clothing for Kate, Tazer set her in her place quickly.

Tazer took Montana's arm, pointed to a cushioned seat and ordered, "Sit."

The attendant took Kate to a dressing room and then disappeared into the back of the shop with Tazer. They returned with a handful of dresses, blouses and trousers, and disappeared into the dressing room.

Already antsy and ready to be outside, Montana rose from the cushioned seat and paced.

Tazer emerged from the dressing room, looked around and spotted Montana. She pointed a finger. "You. Come with me."

She took him to the back of the salon, where a barber's chair stood in the middle of a small office. A woman with bright blue hair, armed with scissors and a comb, smiled at him. "Let's get started."

Unsure as to what they were to "get started" on, Montana shot a glance at Tazer.

She hooked his arm, led him to the chair and pointed. "Sit."

Montana's brows rose. "I'm beginning to feel like a dog in training."

"Then act like one, and do as instructed." Tazer clapped her hands sharply. "Come on, we don't have all day. You two have a meeting tonight."

"We do?"

"Yes. I'll fill you in once we're through the transformation."

Half bent toward the seat, Montana paused. "Transformation?"

Tazer rolled her eyes. "Trust me."

He figured hair grew back, but his buddies wouldn't let him live down blue hair. Still, he knew they didn't have time to argue, and Tazer seemed to know what she was doing.

Montana sat.

"By the way, I'm Karen," said the hairstylist. "This shouldn't take too long."

Her scissors flashed and hair flew around him. She shaved his face with a wicked-looking straight razor, trimmed his eyebrows and plucked some of the wild hairs.

So far, he didn't have a problem with what she'd done. He'd needed a haircut after being on vacation for two weeks, and his brows were a little on the bushy side. But when she brought out a bowl with powder and mixed in liquid from a bottle, he held up his hand. "What's that?"

"Bleach."

"For what?" he asked, leaning away from the bowl

and what appeared to be a wide, flat paintbrush she was using to stir the contents.

"I'm going to lighten your hair." She held up a photo of Rex Masters, Mica's bodyguard. "I'm told you need to have this hair color."

"Yeah, but will it be permanent?"

She shook her head. "It'll grow out in a couple months."

"Months!"

"Relax. It's just hair. With your tan, the blond will look fabulous on you."

Not liking the gleam in Karen's eyes, Montana sat back and allowed the stylist to do her job. Tazer chose that hour to be absent.

Figures.

By the time the stylist finished and dried his hair, Montana was ready to bust through whatever doors stood in his way to getting outside.

Karen slapped a handheld mirror in his palm. "See? You look great."

He glanced into the mirror, relieved he didn't have blue hair, and was amazed at the resemblance between him and Mica Brantley's bodyguard.

Karen had even lightened his eyebrows to a shade darker than his now sandy-blond hair.

"Good, you're done." Tazer appeared in the doorway with an armful of clothes. "Put these on."

"Ever consider the word *please*?" Montana asked. The SOS agent might dress like a fashion model, but she was as lacking in manners as some of his SEAL buddies.

"No time." Again, she clapped her hands. "Chop,

chop!" Tazer disappeared again, leaving Montana with the stylist, who was gathering the tools of her trade.

"Thank you, Karen." Montana pulled his wallet out of his pocket, prepared to tip the woman for a job well done.

She held up her hand. "No need to tip me. Miss Steele took care of everything. It was a pleasure." She held out a card. "Look me up if you're ever at a loose end." With a wink, she left the office, closing the door behind her.

Montana shucked his clothes and slipped into the trousers and matching suit jacket, freshly altered. Though he preferred jeans and T-shirts, he had to admit the outfit, now that it had been adjusted, fit like a second skin. He drew the line at putting on the silk tie. Dressed, buttoned and wearing the new patent leather shoes Tazer had delivered with the suit, he stepped out of the office and went in search of Tazer and Kate.

The female attendant he'd met earlier found him wandering through the warehouse of dresses and clothes, and took his arm. "Miss Steele asked that you wait in the viewing area until the ladies are ready." She ushered him into the lounge with the dressing room doors Kate had disappeared behind earlier.

Montana paced, his patience worn thin, his need to get outside an obsession.

Fifteen very long minutes later, Tazer walked out of the back warehouse area.

Kate followed, wearing a pale cream skirt suit that fit her long, athletic body like a kid glove. The matching high heels made her legs look even longer, the tight muscles of her calves bunching with each step.

Montana's groin tightened and he fought to keep his jaw from dropping to the floor.

Her shoulder-length hair had been swept back into one of those French twist things women liked to wear. She looked amazing.

Kate's gaze swept him from top to bottom. "I like you with dark hair better," she said. "But you'll do."

"Not to worry." Tazer nodded to the attendant. "Could you get the handbag I left in the back?"

She nodded and hurried through the door.

Once they were alone, Tazer handed Montana a bottle of dark liquid. "Before you go out tonight, put this in your hair and let it dry. You two are now Monty and Kayla Lindemann, good friends of the Brantleys. While you're Monty, you'll put the dye in your hair. When you have to switch to fill in for Rex, just wash it out."

"What about me?" Kate asked. "I can't just dye my hair black in a flash."

"No, but you can wear this." She handed Kate a bag.

Kate fished inside and pulled a wig halfway out. It was long, dark and straight, like Mica Brantley's hair. Kate nodded. "Got it."

"I've arranged for you and Mica to have matching outfits for the yacht club gala. You will arrive as the Lindemanns, but if anything happens that puts Mrs. Brantley in danger, we're pulling her and Rex out and putting you two in as their replacements."

"The event is tomorrow. What's happening tonight?" Montana asked.

"You're going to meet up with Mica at the Jefferson Hotel in downtown DC. She has the Martha Jefferson Penthouse Suite. The Lindemanns will be a floor below. You're having dinner together. We'll have the hotel covered with your SEAL team and SOS electronic surveillance." She handed Montana a leather briefcase. "Everything you'll need is in the case. Familiarize yourselves with the contents on the way over. Once inside the hotel, consider everything bugged. Act, live, breathe as if you really are the Lindemanns. We don't know how deep the traitors are entrenched and in what government entities. Trust no one but the members of the team."

Montana nodded, his free hand tightening into a fist. To think there were traitors within the organizations he would have thought he could trust made him all the more determined to take them down.

KATE AND MONTANA stepped through the front door of the dress shop and slid into the waiting limousine. Their new clothes had been packed into designer luggage and stored in the trunk of the car. They would take the long way around the city, be dropped off at the airport and later picked up by Mica Brantley's car.

Montana opened the case Tazer had given him and extracted their orders and a dossier detailing who they were supposed to be, how they'd met Mica and her husband and why they were visiting her at the Jefferson.

"Mica and Trevor introduced us to each other in Paris." Kate turned to Montana. "Have you been to Paris?"

His lips twisted. "I might prefer Montana to the big cities, but yes, I've been to Paris. How about you?"

She nodded. Her partner had taken her to Paris over a long weekend between assignments. Little had she known he had used their weekend away as an opportunity to pass information to his Russian contact. God, she'd been a fool, thinking he was in love with her and out getting little French pastries for their breakfasts. All along, he'd been working.

"Hey." Montana touched a finger to her chin. "We're supposed to be newlyweds. No long faces."

"Sorry." She read through the pages, committing the words to memory. "I've got this. Do you need to see it again?"

"No."

"It says to shred the documents." Kate glanced around the inside of the limousine. It didn't surprise her to find a shredder. One last glance at the pages and she pushed them through the device.

Montana extracted a ring box from the case and opened it. "Hold out your left hand."

Kate did as he asked.

"With this ring, I thee fake wed. I promise to have your six and pretend to love, honor and cherish you until this op is over." Montana slipped on the engagement ring with the huge emerald cut diamond and matching wedding band.

Kate snorted. "Cute." His big hands felt rough against hers, but warm and strong. She could imagine them sliding across her bare skin. With a start, she yanked her hand away. Now was not the time to be daydreaming about the man who would play her husband. "God, I hope this isn't real. It looks like at least three carats."

He removed the larger, plain wedding band from the box and started to slip it onto his ring finger.

"Wait." Kate took the band from him. "It's only fair."

Montana's lips quirked. "I've never been accused of being unfair."

"Well, don't start now," she said. "With this ring, I thee fake wed. I promise to save your butt, should the need arise…*again*. And should you try anything without my permission, I promise to hurt you." Kate raised her brows. "Got it?"

He held up his hand. "Got it. I won't *try* anything without your permission." As Kate took his upraised hand and slipped the ring onto his finger, Montana muttered, "I don't *try*…I *do*."

Kate glared at him. "This marriage is fake. Don't forget that."

"Trust me. I won't." Montana leaned forward and pressed his lips to hers in a brief brush of a kiss.

A blast of electricity ripped through Kate, followed by heat, searing a path through her chest and down low in her belly. She pressed her fingers to her lips. "Why did you do that?"

"Only seemed fitting, after tying the knot." He winked, sending another rush of heat rushing through her veins. "Want me to take it back?"

She rubbed the back of her hand over her mouth, her head spinning. "You can't take something like that back. Once given, it can't be returned."

"Oh well, I guess you'll have to keep it." He smiled and sat back against the plush leather seat.

"Well, don't do it again." Thankfully, the car pulled up to the curb at the Baltimore International Airport and dropped them off with their luggage.

Two minutes later, Mica Brantley's limousine arrived, picked them up and drove them back into the city.

Once they'd switched chauffeur-driven vehicles,

Kate remained silent, going over the script Tazer had given them. Not only did she have to know the details about the fictitious Lindemanns, she had to be prepared to step into Mica Brantley's shoes at a moment's notice. She had to know Mica's idiosyncrasies, which would be much harder to pull off if they ran into anyone who knew her and Trevor Brantley.

Over an hour since they'd left the shops, the limousine pulled up in front of the Jefferson Hotel, one of the oldest and most expensive hotels in downtown DC. Once Monty and Kayla Lindemann got settled, they were to meet Mrs. Brantley for dinner.

The chauffeur opened the door.

Montana slid out first and then bent to offer his hand to Kate.

Reluctantly, she placed her fingers against his. That same shock of electricity rippled up her arm and showered warmth throughout her body. He had her so stirred up inside, she tripped over the curb.

If Montana hadn't reached out and yanked her into his arms, smashing her against his chest, she'd have fallen face-first on the concrete sidewalk.

Instead, she was crushed to him, his arms like steel bands around her waist. When she got her feet under her, heat rose up her cheeks. "Sorry."

He leaned close and whispered in her ear, "I'm not." Then he hooked her with one of his big, capable hands and waved toward the door. "Ready?"

She nodded, though she couldn't remember ever being so ill-prepared as she was at that moment. What worried her most was that she had no doubt she could play the part required. Keeping her head on straight and not falling even a little bit for the handsome SEAL would be the real challenge.

While the bellman retrieved their luggage, Montana dealt with the reception desk. Royce and Geek had been busy securing reservations, backdating them to make it appear as though Mr. and Mrs. Lindemann had planned their trip to DC weeks ago.

Kate took a moment to casually glance around the lobby, searching for anything that stood out. Suspicious characters, security cameras, lurking staff members… anything that might set off alarm bells in her head.

Fortunately, or unfortunately, nothing did. She spotted the requisite security cameras placed throughout the lobby for the protection of the wealthy guests.

A warm, rough hand curled around her elbow. "Ready?" Montana's deep, rich voice filled her ear and spread over her body like melted butter—warm, smooth and penetrating every fiber of her being. She trembled.

How did he do that?

With a nod, she let him lead her through the lobby to the elevator.

Montana pushed the button for the seventh floor and then slipped his arm around her waist. "Feeling better?"

"I wasn't aware I was feeling poorly."

"You know…you don't have a stomach for flying." He pulled her against him.

"Oh, yes. I feel much better." Aware of the camera in the upper right corner, she leaned into Montana. The thin fabric of her suit did little to guard her against her body's reaction to his.

The elevator door slid open. Kate stepped out, afraid

if she stayed any longer, her knees would wobble and refuse to hold her up.

Their room was the last door near the end of the hallway. A stairwell was located at the very end, marked with a sign For Emergency Use Only.

Montana ran the key card over the lock and the green light blinked. When he pushed, the door swung open on oiled hinges.

Kate entered first. Expertly decorated, the suite contained a sitting room, sleeping chamber and a large bathroom with a shower big enough to fit two.

Montana set the briefcase on a desk in the corner and flipped the spring-loaded latches. He opened the case and extracted a small monitor Kate recognized as the kind she'd used to check for surveillance devices. Bugs.

"Do you need to freshen up before we meet with Mica?" Montana asked, as he crossed to her and slipped the monitor into her palm.

"Sure, but you can go first." She leaned up on her toes and pressed a kiss to his lips.

His irises flared and he caught her arm. "I'll only be a minute." Then he kissed her full on the lips.

Reeling from the rush of searing passion from the kiss, Kate stood in the middle of the room until Montana entered the bathroom and closed the door behind him.

Having been warned that they couldn't trust anyone, Kate had to assume even their room could be bugged. Until she swept the room to determine whether or not there were listening devices, she had to play the part.

While Montana took his time in the bathroom, she walked around the room, pretending to examine the decorations, all the while carrying the monitor in her palm. The alarm vibrated against her hand when she neared the nightstand on the right side of the bed. She leaned close and flicked the light on. A tiny metal object clung to the inside of the shade. First bug.

When she walked to the other side of the bed and leaned over the nightstand, the monitor again vibrated in her hand. As she switched on the light, she noted a second bug clinging to the inside of that shade. Walking through every part of the room and the adjoining suite, she located two more listening devices and a miniature camera affixed to the chandelier in the sitting room.

By the time she'd completed a thorough sweep, the bathroom door opened and Montana emerged.

Kate hurried toward him, plastering a smile on her face. She flung her arms around him and pulled his head down for a kiss.

"Mmm. To what do I owe the pleasure?" Montana wrapped his arms around her waist and held her close.

She leaned back. "Do I have to have a reason to kiss my husband?"

"No." He bent and kissed her, then nuzzled her neck. "What's up?"

"Bugs on both nightstands," she whispered in his ear, then nibbled his earlobe. "Mmm. Maybe we should skip dinner with Mica and stay here for dessert."

"You don't have to twist my arm," Montana responded.

"Camera in the chandelier and two more bugs in the sitting room," she breathed into his ear.

Montana gave her a very slight nod. "Mmm, you smell delicious," he said aloud. Then in a whisper Kate had to strain to hear, he added, "Leave them or destroy?"

Her pulse hammering and her blood burning through her system, Kate struggled to push away from Montana. "We'd better leave. Mica will be expecting us."

"Agreed." He kissed her once more and set her at arm's length. "We can pick up where we left off, later."

Kate's breath hitched in her chest and she hastily turned away before she fell back into the SEAL's strong arms. Just the thought of picking up where they'd left off made her heart skip several beats and then run on like she'd just finished a marathon.

"I need to powder my nose," she said, and dodged into the bathroom. A quick scan with the monitor located one more bug behind the mirror. After she'd located it, she took a moment to stare at her reflection, surprised at what she saw. Never had she looked so much like a model ready to hit the runway. This wasn't the Kate she knew. Nothing about the face staring back at her was familiar. Especially the way she felt inside.

Yes, she could understand her attraction to the SEAL. After all, he was built like a fighting machine, solid and muscular, with the bonus of being ruggedly handsome.

Hadn't she learned her lesson about falling for her partner? She wasn't a brand-new agent with stars in her eyes. Been there…done that…got the demotion to prove it.

Kate applied a fresh coat of lipstick, straightened her shoulders and marched out of the bathroom.

This assignment might prove to be the hardest one she'd ever undertaken. But she'd be damned if she went down without a fight. Even if she was fighting herself.

Chapter Four

Montana's lips still tingled from touching Kate's. He'd been more than tempted to follow through on his threat to ditch Mica and stay in the room with his partner.

When she'd ducked into the bathroom, he'd made his rounds of the suite, without appearing too obvious. All the bugs, and the camera in the chandelier of the sitting room, meant someone had been in there in preparation for their arrival. Since the hotel's computers and Mica's driver had known for less than a couple hours that they were coming, it had to have been an expert job to get all the bugs in so quickly.

These kinds of tactics were foreign to Montana. Give him a gun and a wedge of plastic explosives, and he could blast his way through the enemy. Not here. His adversary was elusive and hid among innocents in a highly populated urban area that didn't see the usual terrorist activities of a war-torn, third-world country.

The sound of the door opening made him turn around.

As when he'd first seen her step out of the high-end clothing salon's back room, Montana's breath caught in his throat. Kate was absolutely beautiful. The skirt suit hugged her body, accentuating every curve to perfection.

Again, he wanted to skip the meeting with Mica and explore the zipper and buttons he'd have to overcome to strip Kate out of the outfit. Then he'd get to her hair, pulling pins and whatever it was that tucked it behind her head in a smooth sweep.

She smiled. "Ready?"

"Yes." More than she'd ever know. He waved his hand, urging her to lead the way through the door, while he adjusted his trousers to accommodate his arousal.

In the hallway, he took her elbow and walked with her to the elevator, selecting the restaurant level, where they would meet Mica.

Kate slipped her hand into his, but remained silent all the way down.

As Montana stepped out of the elevator, the smells of food made his stomach rumble. It wasn't until then that he realized he and Kate hadn't had lunch.

They entered the restaurant and Montana glanced around for Mrs. Brantley.

"I don't see her. Do you?" Kate asked.

"No. Would you like a cocktail while we wait?"

Kate nodded. "Whiskey on the rocks."

He smiled.

Kate frowned. "What?"

"I was thinking something a little more…" He struggled for the right word.

"Fruity? You know me better." She shook her head. "I like my alcohol as strong as my men." Kate tossed her head and strode toward the bar, her hips swaying with each step.

Heat rushed through him and Montana tugged at the tie around his neck, feeling as if he might choke, break a sweat or both. Kate might prove to be more woman than he could handle. Given her training, she might even be able to kick his butt in hand-to-hand combat. The thought of wrestling with Kate made him even hotter.

She ordered her drink and turned to Montana.

"I'll have a Guinness," he said. Liquor dulled his wits. Not that he'd drink the entire beer. He still found it hard to believe they could be in danger. The bar was like any bar in the US. People came in, never expecting to be shot at or have a bomb go off next to them.

The bartender set the drinks on the counter in front of them.

Montana lifted the longneck bottle and touched it to her whiskey glass. "To old friends."

"And new adventures." She tipped the glass and drank a long swallow. "There she is." Kate nodded toward the door.

Mica Brantley entered, wearing a black dress, the neckline dipping low in front, and displaying a sparkling diamond necklace. Her hair was swept up into a smooth bun at the back of her head.

Rex Masters followed her, keeping close enough that he could throw himself in front of anyone who decided to rush the woman. His broad shoulders were a testament to a man who stayed in shape, ready for anything. The bulky lump beneath his jacket had to be a concealed weapon.

Mica glanced around the room. When she spotted them, she smiled and hurried forward. "Kayla, Monty! How wonderful of you to come for the gala."

Kate moved forward and air-kissed both of Mica's cheeks. "We wouldn't have missed it for the world."

Montana lifted Mica's hand to his lips and kissed her knuckles. He'd seen a secret agent in one of the thriller movies do that with a high-class woman. He hoped it wasn't just something they made up for the movies.

Mica frowned. "Really, Monty?" Holding on to his hand, she pulled him closer and kissed his cheek. "That's better. No need to be formal with me."

Beside him, Kate slid her hand through his bent elbow. "Shall we find a table? We're famished."

"Oh, good. The food here is above par. I've had no complaints anytime I've stayed here."

"How long have you been in town?" Kate asked, keeping up a running conversation.

"Got here today. Since Trevor's…passing, I haven't had the heart to go back to the house."

"I don't blame you. But where have you been staying?"

"Here and there." Mica waved her hand. "I can't seem to settle." Makeup couldn't hide the shadows beneath the woman's eyes. Her husband's death and her driving determination to find the one responsible were taking their toll on Mrs. Brantley.

Montana understood loss of a loved one. He'd lost more than one of his teammates in firefights. It wasn't something a person got over easily.

The maître d' showed them to their table. As they sat, a familiar voice spoke behind Montana. "Good evening, I'm Dutton. I'll be your server."

Montana fought to keep a grin from spreading across his face. Duff stood straight in a black waiter's uniform, a fringe of gray hair circling his seemingly bald head. Someone had done an expert job of blending makeup into the natural tanned tones of his skin, covering any of the lines from the skullcap wig, all the way around his head.

If Montana hadn't known the voice, he wouldn't have guessed the waiter was Duff. Based on the bland glances from the others at the table, they hadn't caught on to their waiter being one of the other SEALs on the team.

At one point after ordering their dinner, Montana rose under the pretext of going to the restroom. On the way, he caught Duff and asked for another napkin. On a much quieter note, he asked, "Anyone else?"

"The gang's all here," Duff whispered. Louder, he said, "If you'll wait right here, I'll have that napkin to you right away, sir." He spun on his heels, ducked behind a partition and returned with a cloth napkin. "Here you go, sir. Let me know if there's anything else I can do for you." Duff winked. "All you have to do is ask." He pressed the napkin into Montana's hand and squeezed.

Montana could feel something more than the napkin being pressed into his palm. He nodded. "Thank you." He folded the napkin, tucked it into his inside pocket and continued toward the bathroom.

Once inside the beautifully equipped oasis, he entered a stall, pulled out the napkin and carefully unfolded it. Inside was a small, flesh-toned earbud radio headset. He pressed it deep into his ear canal and listened.

Sawyer's voice came online. "Comm check."

"Rip here."

"Duff here."

"Loverboy here."

"Hunter here."

At that moment, the swish of a door opening and footsteps sounded. Knowing it was his turn to check in, Montana pressed the lever on the toilet at the same time as he said, "Monty here." He stepped out of the stall and crossed to the sink.

Whoever had entered the restroom had gone straight into one of the stalls and closed the door.

Sawyer continued, "All present and accounted for."

Montana washed his hands quickly and dried them, then stepped out of the restroom into the empty hallway.

"Geek has Lance and me positioned in a van outside the Jefferson," Sawyer said. "We're tapped into the hotel security system, but keep your eyes open."

"The monitoring device Montana had in his room recorded six bugs," Geek said. "We backed up the security footage on the hotel corridors and stairwells. There was a freeze-frame at two points today. Those two points were between the time Mrs. Brantley made arrangements for her car to pick up the Lindemanns at the airport, and the time they arrived two hours later." He paused. "Just to be clear…if things go south, our primary goal is to get Mrs. Brantley out alive."

Knowing his team had his six in the hotel, Montana felt better, less exposed, not like a sitting duck, waiting for something to happen. His buddies would be watching all angles, checking for anyone acting strange.

Back at the dinner table, Montana studied Mica's bodyguard. He'd been with her in Cancun when they'd blown open the human trafficking auction and rescued the women who were to be sold to the highest bidder.

Though Rex sat with them at the table, he didn't contribute to the conversation, except when Mica included him. Then he answered in cryptic responses. His gaze moved around the room constantly. Having chosen the seat with his back to the wall, he had a one-hundred-eighty-degree view of the dining room and its occupants.

Montana sat with his back to the door, not liking it one bit. But with Duff moving in and out, delivering food and drinks, he wasn't as worried.

Mrs. Brantley and Kate talked through dinner about their fake travels together in Paris and the upcoming gala at the yacht club.

Halfway through the meal, Mica passed a key card to Montana beneath the table. He assumed it was to her room, should they need it. He slid it into his trouser pocket.

When the meal was over, Montana was glad to stand and look around. The tables had filled with well-dressed businessmen and ladies wearing cocktail dresses, none of whom appeared to be spies or traitors ready to gun down Mica Brantley. But one never knew. Bad guys came in all shapes and sizes. Sometimes they were children with explosives strapped around them, sent into the middle of a group of soldiers.

The question roiling around in Montana's mind was, why was all the surveillance added to their room? Were the people stalking Mrs. Brantley trying to get to her through her friends?

Some things didn't make any sense in this case. Montana wished he could have an open discussion with Kate and Mrs. Brantley. Mrs. Brantley because she was the potential target. Kate because this was the kind of work she'd been trained for.

Frustrated and determined to get answers, Montana bided his time, acting as if he enjoyed the inane conversation about acquaintances Mrs. Brantley expected to see the next day at the club, and the usual big donors.

Montana made mental notes about the names Mrs. Brantley brought up, in case they ran across them at the gala. Tomorrow would be a more hectic day, trying to keep track of Mrs. Brantley and make sure she wasn't attacked, or that the politicians and wealthy donors weren't harmed. If Montana had his way, he'd have had the gala rescheduled. Or at the very least, he would encourage Mrs. Brantley to skip it.

All four of them entered the elevator together, along with two more of Mrs. Brantley's bodyguards. They rode to the seventh floor, where Montana and Kate got off, bidding Mrs. Brantley good-evening.

Once in their room, Montana still couldn't relax. Knowing they were being bugged and watched didn't help. He took off the suit jacket and tossed it over the back of a chair.

Kate unbuttoned her jacket. "It was good seeing Mica again, don't you think?"

"Mmm, yes." He stepped up behind her and helped her out of the jacket. "But it would be even better to see you naked in the shower." He felt her stiffen. Montana nibbled on her earlobe and whispered, "We can talk with the water on."

She nodded, leaned her head back and turned her mouth to kiss his neck. "The only way that's going to happen is to get out of these clothes." She cupped his cheek and pulled him down for a kiss on the lips. Then she stepped away from him, walking out of the jacket he held on to. "What are you waiting for?"

Montana grinned. "For my brain to engage." After hanging up her garment, he jerked the tie loose from around his neck and threw it toward the jacket on the back of the chair. It landed somewhere on the floor. Montana didn't care. He had to remind himself that Kate's come-on was an act, but it had the same effect as her come-hither looks would if they'd been real. He followed like a starving man to a smorgasbord.

Once inside the bathroom, they wouldn't have to keep up the pretense of stripping, but they had to be aware of the listening device located behind the mirror.

Montana turned on the faucet, giving it as much pressure as it would allow. The more water blasting into the shower stall, the better it would cover the sound of their voices.

When he turned, he was stunned to see Kate standing in nothing but her panties and bra.

"Need help getting undressed?" she asked.

"No, I just need to get protection. Unless, of course, you're ready to start a family."

She laughed. "Maybe in a year or two."

"Here, let me unclip your bra," Montana said for their listeners. He pulled the radio from his ear and held it up for her to see.

Her eyes widened and then she nodded. "Last one in is a rotten egg." She stepped into the shower, still wearing her bra and panties.

Montana stripped off everything and dug a condom out of his wallet. He didn't know where being naked with Kate might lead, but, by damned, he'd be prepared. Wrapping a towel around his waist, he stepped into the shower.

Kate had taken the pins out of her hair and applied shampoo. "I thought you had changed your mind," she said, loudly enough to be heard over the spray. Her eyes were closed to the soap bubbles running down her face and over her shoulders.

Montana set the foil package in the soap dish, trying but failing to keep his gaze from following the path of the bubbles as they dipped into the cups hugging the CIA agent's breasts. He stood with one hand holding the corners of the towel, regretting that he'd had to strip out of the expensive trousers. Seeing Kate almost naked had the natural effect of tenting the towel. He adjusted, holding the towel loosely, praying she didn't notice. *Fat chance.*

KATE COULD SENSE when Montana stepped into the shower. Not so much by the sounds, but by the way her body heated at his mere presence. Lowering her voice so that only Montana could hear, she said, "I had to get all the pins and hair spray out. It was making my scalp itch."

"Good. I like your hair down better," he said, his voice deliciously warm, like the water caressing her body. She wished she could have taken off her bra and panties and melted into Montana's rock-hard muscles. The man was tempting her more than her former partner ever had.

Kate wasn't the same naive newbie, green from school with stars in her eyes. She was a grown woman, with needs like any other red-blooded female. Sex didn't require giving her heart or trust to the man.

Surely she could keep those separate. What would it hurt to play this role all the way? The Lindemanns were a married couple. Making love in a hotel would be the natural thing to do, especially when they were in a shower, supposedly naked.

Her channel clenched and an ache built deep in her core.

She tried to tell herself that lusting after the SEAL wasn't getting the case solved. It would only get in the way of clear thinking and lightning reflexes.

She rinsed her hair, feeling the warm water rushing over her sensitized breasts and down her torso to soak her panties. Maybe she'd be better off giving in to her lust, seducing the SEAL and getting him out of her system.

Kate rinsed the suds out of her hair, braced herself to keep from giving away her carnal thoughts and blinked open her eyes.

Her glance swept over Montana, pausing on the tented towel. Heat rushed into her cheeks as she realized he was just as aroused. She jerked her gaze up to his and anchored there. "What's happening?" That was the question of the century. Hell, she knew what was happening between them, but she had to get her mind out of the towel and onto the case.

Montana's lips twitched at the corners. Speaking in a low, sexy tone, he said, "My team is here. They're tapped into the hotel security system and they're monitoring all movements in and out."

Even though Montana was only filling her in on his team's activities, Kate couldn't help the shiver of awareness trickling down her spine along with the warm soapy water. She drew in a steadying breath. "Good. Anything unusual?"

"They're concerned about us, since our room was bugged," he said, his hand shifting. Water drenched the towel, plastering it to his thighs and emphasizing his long, thick erection.

Holy hell. She wanted to reach out and touch him there, to take the towel from his hands and fling it to the shower floor.

"I don't care about us," Kate said, when it was far from the truth. She cared what would happen *between* them, not *to* them. "I'm worried about Mrs. B." Kate crossed her arms over her chest. "She's been here less than a day. It might be only a matter of time before someone goes after her."

"Based on the dates and coordinates, she might be the target for tomorrow's charity gala."

"That list was created before the events in Cancun. Everything could have changed. A new list could be out, or whoever is orchestrating the killings might have adjusted his schedule accordingly. Hell, he might be shooting from the hip now that he knows someone is looking for him and possibly getting closer."

"True. All the more reason to keep our eyes and ears open." Montana shifted, bumping into her.

That slight touch set off a spark of electricity that turned into a fire raging all the way through to her very core. Much more togetherness and she'd be helpless to resist.

Kate stepped back quickly. Her foot slipped on the tiles and she pitched forward.

Montana let go of the towel he'd been holding and

grabbed her around her waist, pulling her against him to steady her. His hardened staff pressed into her belly.

The air caught in Kate's lungs and refused to move in or out. "Um, thanks," she said.

"No problem," Montana replied through tight lips.

For a moment, they stared into each other's eyes.

"I guess it's not a secret that I find you incredibly attractive," he said, his erection shifting between them.

If possible, it was getting even longer and harder. Desperate to breathe, Kate sucked in some air, her body moving with the effort, her belly sliding ever so slightly over that velvety smooth, hard shaft between them.

Again, her lungs seized and her knees wobbled. Kate gripped his arms to stabilize herself. "Mmm. This could get awkward."

"Or not." His hands tightened around her waist. "We're supposed to be a married couple."

"But we're not," she reminded him and herself. "We're on a case, not vacation."

He nodded. "You're right."

When he started to back away, she tightened her grip, her hands responding to her body's desire, while her mind yelled, *What the hell are you doing?*

"I'm confused," he said. "When a woman says she's not interested, I don't push the issue."

"I didn't say I wasn't interested." She wet her suddenly dry lips. The shower spray was cooling, but did little to chill the passion raging inside Kate.

Montana's fingers flexed against her skin. "I'm just a cowboy from Montana. Be clear in what you want, or I let go and walk away."

The direct and searing look in his blue eyes bored through her resolve. Hell, who was she kidding? Kate couldn't walk away from what was happening between them. *Get it over with*, she told herself. *Get him out of your system, and get back to work.*

"We don't have much time," she said. "We don't know when or if someone will make a move."

"Darlin', time should never be the issue." He raised his hand to the back of her bra and flicked the hooks free. "Where there's a will, there's a way." He peeled the straps down her arms and flung the garment over the top of the shower stall. Then he hooked his fingers into her panties and dragged them down her legs.

When he reached her ankles, Kate couldn't wait a moment longer. She kicked the panties to the side. "Got protection?"

Montana nodded and straightened. As he did, he cupped her buttocks, lifted and pressed her back against the cool tiles. "Would you believe me if I told you I was a Boy Scout?"

"Mmm." She wiggled her bottom, inching downward toward his jutting staff. "I'm not in the habit of making love to a Boy Scout." She pressed her finger to his lips. "A little less talk, please."

"Got it." He grabbed the foil packet from the soap dish.

She snatched it from his hand, tore it open and applied it, all in a few swift, efficient moves. "Now, show me what you're made of." God, this was really going to happen. She was going to make love with a man she'd met only that morning. Either she was a fool or she was one gutsy, empowered female, taking her sexual needs and desires by the horn and riding them to the end.

She cupped his face between her palms and bent to capture his lips with hers. He obliged with no resistance, pushing his tongue past her teeth to caress hers in a long, slow glide she hoped would be his style when he entered her.

Whatever she was, she was hot, needy and impatient to consummate their fake marriage.

Chapter Five

Montana captured Kate's wrists in one of his hands and pressed them to the tile above her head. Then he crushed her mouth, kissing her hard, as if he could draw the breath from her into him.

With his shaft poised at her opening, he rocked his hips, dipping into her slick wetness.

Kate wrapped her legs around his waist and dug her heels into his buttocks, urging him to go deeper.

He complied, sliding in a little more, allowing her channel to adjust to his girth. He knew he was built a little bigger than most men, based on observation in the shower room. He didn't want to hurt her.

"More," Kate moaned. "Want more."

He inched deeper, glad for the water and the slickness of her juices lubricating his way. With every ounce of control he could muster, he held back, determined to take her slowly.

"Please," she begged. "Give me all you've got." Her thighs tightened and her heels dug into him, pulling him closer, harder, deeper.

"I don't want to hurt you," he whispered into her mouth.

She nibbled his bottom lip and sucked it between her

teeth. When she let go, she said, "I can handle it. Do it. Now." She sank down on him, her channel clenching around him.

His control slipped and he thrust deep, pushing all the way to the hilt. She felt good, wrapped around him, hot, tight and wet. Montana remained buried inside her, letting her adjust to his size for several long seconds, then he moved out and back in.

Her legs contracted and she fought to free her wrists. "Let go. I want to touch you." When he released his grip, she laid her hands on his shoulders, digging her nails into his skin as she rode him.

Montana pumped in and out, faster and faster until the sensations culminated in a rush of adrenaline and white-hot heat surging throughout his body. Starting in his shaft, surges rippled outward as he shot over the edge and rocketed into the heavens.

He thrust one last time and held her hips tight against him, as wave after wave consumed him.

When he came back to earth, he drew in a deep breath and leaned his forehead against hers. "Incredible."

"Yes," she said, her breathing ragged.

The cool water and wrinkled skin reminded Montana of just how long they'd been in the shower. He eased Kate to her feet, pulling out of her. Discarding the condom, he picked up the bar of soap, worked up a lather and glanced at her questioningly.

A smile spread across her lips and she raised her arms.

He started with her hands, running his soapy fingers over her arms and downward to the swells of her breasts. Pausing for a moment, he tweaked and teased the distended nipples until they hardened into little beads. Leaning her beneath the cooling water, he let the spray rinse away the bubbles, then he caught one nipple between his teeth and rolled it until she squirmed against him.

She grasped his head in her hands and moved him to the other nipple.

He tongued and flicked the tip until Kate's back arched and she moaned.

Sucking her breast into his mouth, he ran his hand down her torso, over her belly and lower, to the mound of hair at the apex of her thighs.

Her chest rose on a deep, indrawn breath and her hips pushed forward.

Encouraged, Montana slid his fingers between her folds and touched the little strip of flesh there.

Her hips rocked hard against him and she groaned.

Montana flicked and then skimmed a finger over the sensitive nubbin.

Kate dug her fingers into the hair at the nape of his neck. "Yes. There," she whispered.

He dipped his finger into her and stroked her with his thumb at the same time.

Her body quivered against his and she widened her legs.

Dragging his damp finger upward, he swirled and teased until she grew rigid in his arms, her breathing halted and she squeezed her eyes shut.

Then she cupped her hand over his, pressing hard as she rocked her hips. For a long moment he held her there, letting her ride her release all the way to the end. When she sagged against him, he rinsed them both, turned off the cold water and stepped out of the shower stall.

With a plush, terry-cloth towel, he rubbed the moisture from her body and hair, kissing her shoulder, neck and breasts as he worked.

Armed with a dry towel, Kate returned the favor until they were both dry and naked in the bathroom.

Montana wrapped her in a towel and wound one around himself. He mouthed the word, *"Ready?"*

She nodded.

Montana planted the radio in his ear and stepped out of the bathroom, carrying a hand towel. With a quick snap, he tossed the towel over the camera on the chandelier in the sitting room.

"Mmm," Kate said. "That's nice." She made it sound like he was kissing her, or making love to her again, but he knew she meant it was nice they could dress without someone watching.

In the bedroom, Kate skipped the beautiful negligee and sheer nightgown and opted for Montana's pajama top. Drawing it over her head, she let it fall over her body to hang down to midthigh. Then she pulled on a clean pair of panties from her suitcase.

Montana watched her dress, enjoying every movement. Kate made putting on clothes as sexy as taking them off. If he hadn't just spent himself in the shower, he'd consider making love to her all over again.

Instead, he dressed in pajama bottoms. Nothing else. He figured it was better than sleeping in the nude, wondering if they'd missed a camera somewhere. He had to admit he kind of liked it that Kate wore the other half of his nightclothes. It made her seem more real to him than the made-up Mrs. Lindemann.

Kate glanced at the bed. "Should we attempt to get some sleep?" she asked.

"The gala lasts a good portion of tomorrow evening, so we'll need all the rest we can get," Montana replied.

Kate nodded and slipped into the bed, pulling the sheet and duvet up to her waist.

Montana sat on the edge, his staff hardening at the thought of sleeping with the beautiful CIA agent. If something didn't happen soon, he'd be making love to her again, and maybe all night long.

As he swung his legs up into the bed, something popped in the suite. Montana leaped to his feet. "Did you hear that?"

Kate was out of the bed and on her feet in a flash. "I did. What do you suppose it could be?"

Montana shrugged. "Stay here. I'll check it out."

As he neared the doorway to the sitting area, his heart started racing at the same time as his skin grew cold.

"Sweetheart," he said. "You might want to get dressed. I smell smoke."

Kate joined Montana in the doorway, dragging one of the hotel bathrobes over her shoulders. She scanned the room with its antique sofa and Martha Washington secretary desk against one wall. "Where?"

Montana pointed. "There." He hurried toward an electrical socket. Smoke rose from the holes in the plate, spiraling upward.

Kate hurried around the room, looking in the coat closet near the door, checking behind armchairs. "If we had an extinguisher…"

Montana ran for the telephone and punched the zero. "We have a faulty electrical socket that just caught fire.

Please send someone up with a fire extinguisher, and notify the fire department. ASAP."

In the next second, the alarm system went off, the incessant whine filling the hallway outside their room.

"That's our cue to get out of here." Montana ran for the bedroom, shucked his pajamas and dragged on his jeans and shoes.

"Should we grab our things?" Kate asked.

"Leave them. We can replace things. You can't replace people."

Kate tied a robe around her pajama top, jammed her feet into a pair of slippers and ran for the door.

Montana was there first. He leaned close and whispered in her ear, "We're going up."

She glanced at him, her eyes wide. "Up?"

He nodded and murmured, "This could be a ploy to draw Mica out of her room." Louder, he said, "Ready?"

Kate nodded. "Ready."

He opened the door and looked before he stepped out. Two couples emerged from other rooms down the hall, heading for the elevator. As expected, the elevators weren't running. They turned toward the stairs as Montana shut the door behind him and waited for them to go ahead. Once they'd passed and entered the stairwell, he tapped the ear with the headset. "Talk to me."

"Where have you been?" Sawyer said. "Never mind, someone set off the fire alarm."

"That would be because of the fire I reported in an electrical socket in our suite," Montana said.

"That explains it. I suspect things are about to get crazy. I'm scrambling the cameras on seven and eight. You know where you need to go."

"Going." Montana grabbed Kate's hand and ran for

the stairwell. Instead of going down with the other couples, they turned and climbed to the next level. Using the spare key card Mrs. Brantley had passed to him beneath the dining table, Montana was able to gain access to the penthouse floor. He hurried toward the Martha Jefferson Suite. If Mica and Rex were still there, they'd need to get out soon. And they'd need all of them to keep Mrs. Brantley safe from whoever was after her.

KATE'S PULSE RACED as she ran toward the door to Mica's suite.

Montana swept the card over the reader. The green light blinked on and he pushed the door inward. A shot rang out, hitting the wall on the other side of the hall.

Kate's blood ran cold. Had Montana charged straight in, he'd have been hit in the head. Without weapons, they couldn't shoot back. But they couldn't stand out in the corridor, waiting for the shooter to kill Mica. Assuming he hadn't already.

"We have a shooter in the Brantley room," Montana said softly. "Could use some backup. I'm going in."

"I am, too," Kate added.

Montana glanced across the open doorway at her. He opened his mouth to say something, seemed to think better of it and shrugged. "Just don't give him a target. Okay?"

"Okay."

Montana dived into the sitting room of the suite and rolled behind a couch.

Kate drew in a deep breath and somersaulted into the room, rolling to a stop behind an antique sofa. Feeling naked without her gun, she waited and listened before calling out, "Mica? Rex?"

A loud crash sounded in another room, as if someone had broken a window.

Montana leaped to his feet and ran into the next room. "He's getting away," he called out.

Kate raced into a beautifully equipped bedroom. One of the windows had been broken. Montana leaned through the broken glass.

"The bastard went out the window," Rex Masters called out from a corner on the other side of the bed. He held his arm close to his chest, blood oozing from beneath his elbow.

Kate ran toward him. "Where's Mica?"

"Barricaded in the bathroom. Don't let him get away." He tossed his gun to Kate with his free hand. "I'm hit, or I'd go after him myself."

Montana grabbed a pillow from the bed, tore off the case and wrapped the ends around each hand. Then he was back at the window. "Cover me."

Before Kate could respond, Montana was over the ledge, walking backward down the side of the eight-story building, holding on to a thin cable with his hands wrapped in the pillowcase.

The shadowy figure farther down the cable leaped to the ground and pointed a gun up at Montana.

Kate leaned out as far as she could and fired down at the man on the ground. A bullet whizzed past her head, splintering the window frame above her.

Montana was halfway down the cable when someone burst into the room behind Kate.

She swung around and aimed at the waiter who'd worked their table earlier that evening. He carried a gun and had it pointing at her.

"It's me, Duff," he said.

Kate nodded. "Good." She tucked the gun into her robe pocket, grabbed a pillowcase and wrapped her hands in it. "Stay with them and cover us."

"Where are you going?" Duff asked.

"After Monty." Before Duff could stop her, Kate stepped out onto the ledge, lowered herself over the side and gripped the cable with her wrapped hands. Easing her way downward, she prayed she didn't lose her grip. As she slid toward the ground, her hands grew hotter and hotter, the pillowcase wearing through to her skin before she reached the bottom. She glanced behind her, watching the direction Montana took off as he hit the ground.

Anxious to be there, too, Kate dropped the last ten feet to avoid blistering her hands. She rolled to her feet, pulled the gun from her pocket and took off after the two men.

It wasn't long before she kicked off the slippers and ran barefoot across the street and through a back alley.

Gunfire sounded from around the side of a building.

Her heart hammering against her ribs and her breath coming in gasps, she slowed at the corner and peered around.

A man stood at the next corner. Between him and Kate sat a large industrial trash bin. A movement at the base of the bin caught her attention.

It was Montana, crouched low.

The man at the other end of the alley fired. A bullet pinged off the bin.

Apparently, the shooter hadn't noticed Kate yet.

He fired again. The shot ricocheted off the pavement next to Montana.

Kate aimed down the barrel of the unfamiliar pistol

Rex had thrown at her and fired. At that exact moment, the shooter turned and ran around the corner. Whether or not her bullet had hit him, she didn't know.

Montana turned. "Kate? What the hell?"

"He's getting away," she called out, running toward the other end of the building.

As she came abreast of Montana, he caught her around the waist and stopped her.

"Why are you stopping me?" she cried, fighting against his hold. "He'll get away."

"Give me the gun. You stay here, and I'll go after him."

"Fine." She shoved the pistol into his hands. "Go."

Montana took off after the gunman. When he reached the corner, he stopped.

Kate ran to catch up. "Why did you stop?"

"He's gone."

"Gone?" She started past him.

Montana's hand shot out. "A car took off with him in it. Trust me, he's gone. All I saw was the flash of taillights." He put the pistol on Safe and tucked it into his trouser pocket.

Now that she had stopped, Kate bent over, bracing her hands on her knees, fighting to catch her breath after the headlong race to catch up to the gunman.

"Damn it, Kate."

She glanced up, still struggling to catch her breath. "What?"

He pointed at her feet. "Where the hell are your shoes?" Before she could answer, Montana swept her up into his arms.

"They slowed me down." She wiggled her feet and tugged at the robe as it fell open, exposing most of her thigh. "Put me down. I can walk."

"Your feet are cut and bleeding."

She frowned, noticing for the first time he was right and her feet were cut, her big toe bleeding from the tip. "You'll be cut and bleeding if you don't put me down," she said, with a little less steam than she was aiming for. Now that she wasn't running after Montana, determined to save the unarmed idiot from being shot, she had time to think about her feet and how they were tender, scratched and bloody. Still…he didn't have to carry her back to the hotel.

He pressed his lips to hers in a brief kiss. "Just hush and let me be the man."

"You *are* the man," she said, her lips tingling. "But that doesn't mean you have to *man*handle me."

Montana shook his head, but held on to her and kept walking back to the hotel. "Do you ever stop talking?"

"Do you ever do as you're told?" she retorted.

"Only if it's the right thing." He stopped next to a van parked against the curb on a street a block from the Jefferson Hotel.

"Why did you stop?" she asked, and looked around.

He tapped his ear. "Open the van door."

The back door opened and Sawyer leaned out. "Damn it, Montana. Why the hell did you let him get away?" He reached for Kate and lifted her into the van. "How are you, Miss McKenzie?"

"Fine, except when your teammate decides I can't walk on my own two feet."

He set her on a cushioned office chair in front of an array of electronics and monitors. "And those two feet are pretty messed up." He reached into a cabinet over his head and extracted a first-aid kit.

Sirens sounded nearby, wailing toward them.

Kate craned her neck, searching for a window. "How do you see outside?"

"Through the camera." Sawyer pointed to a screen.

The monitor displayed the front of the Jefferson Hotel. Guests milled around in the street, some dressed in suits or cocktail dresses, others in bathrobes. A first responder fire truck raced by and stopped in front of the hotel. Men jumped out and ran into the building. A long-ladder truck sped by and halted in the middle of the street. Firefighters leaped to the ground and pulled hoses from the sides of the truck.

A figure dressed in a hotel bellboy uniform ran across the street headed for the van. A second later a knock sounded.

"Let Hunter in," Sawyer said, without turning away from the first-aid kit.

"Here." Montana took the alcohol pads from him. "Let me do this. You're supposed to be on the monitors."

"I got it covered," Lance, the SOS computer guy, said from a seat on the other end of the van.

Sawyer opened the door and Hunter leaped aboard. "We need to pick up a special delivery on the dock at the back of the Jefferson before the streets in and out are complete blocked."

Sawyer climbed into the front seat. "Hold on to your hats." He shifted into gear and drove through the gathering crowd of emergency personnel and hotel guests, turned on the side street leading to the back of the hotel and backed up to the loading dock.

Hunter flung open the rear door of the van.

A balding man with a gray fringe pushed a laundry cart full of sheets toward them. Flanking him were two more members of the SEAL team. Kate recognized them as Quentin and Rip.

Everyone crowded deeper into the communications van, making room for the laundry cart.

As soon as the door closed on all eight of the team and the cart, Duff, the balding man with the fringe, shouted, "Go!"

Sawyer hit the accelerator, sending the van shooting out into the street, heading away from the Jefferson Hotel and into the heart of DC.

At the first stoplight, the sheets shifted and a man's head emerged from beneath.

"Are we clear?" Rex Masters asked.

"Bring her up," Duff said. He pulled the sheets aside until a slim hand reached out. He grasped it and helped Mica Brantley out of the cart.

The light changed and the van surged forward.

Rex lurched and crashed into Rip and Quentin.

Duff caught Mica and held her steady.

"We need to get Rex to a doctor," she said.

"Royce has one on the way to our disaster recovery site," Lance informed them. "That's where we're headed now."

Kate glanced up at Montana, who calmly swayed with the motion of the van and applied a bandage to her cut toe.

Amid the commotion and insanity of the crowded van, he was Kate's rock, grounding her to a new reality. Once her toe was bandaged, he slipped his arm around her and held on until the van pulled up to an automatic overhead door. When it opened, the van pulled in and the door closed behind them, shutting out the traffic,

lights and noise that was a twenty-four-hour part of
Washington, DC.

Kate drew in a deep breath and leaned into
Montana's quiet strength, glad he was her partner for
this mission. Whatever the next day brought she could
handle, as long as he was by her side. The man had
her back.

Chapter Six

When the van came to a complete stop deep in the bowels of a subterranean parking garage, Montana held on tightly to Kate's hand. One by one, the occupants of the vehicle jumped down. Quentin and Rip each took a side and helped Rex out, half dragging, half carrying him through a doorway into a lit building.

The last ones out, Montana jumped down and held up his arms for Kate.

For once she didn't argue. Instead, she allowed him to lift her into his arms and carry her inside.

He liked holding her close. Sure, the ground inside the alternate SOS work site was swept clean of glass and debris found on city streets, but her feet had taken a beating when she'd chased after him. Whatever had possessed her to run through the streets barefoot, wearing nothing more than a bathrobe and not much else, had Montana shaking his head.

The woman was dedicated, that was certain. At least she had a robe to keep her warm.

Montana had taken time to slip into jeans and his shoes, but he hadn't stopped to throw on a shirt. No longer running, his body had cooled in the damp night air. The sooner they got new clothes, the better.

The team trickled past a guard and entered a corridor. Fontaine stood at the end, waving them into a room. "Hurry. We need to debrief and get some sleep before tomorrow. We have a lot to do." He pointed to Quentin and Rip, who had Rex leaning heavily on them for support, his face pale beneath his rugged tan.

"Take Mr. Masters into the infirmary two doors down. I have a doctor waiting to examine and treat him."

Rip and Quentin continued on to the room indicated and disappeared with the injured man.

"The rest of you can gather here in the conference room," Royce said.

Mica Brantley stopped in front of Fontaine. "I'm sorry we didn't get him this time. We didn't expect an attack from outside of the building."

"Blame that on me." Fontaine patted her hand. "We should have had surveillance on that side of the hotel. I'm just glad you and Rex are okay."

"I hope Rex will be okay. He took a hit to his side." She glanced toward the doorway down the hall.

"I'd like to have you in the debrief, since Rex is indisposed at this time."

"Anything I can do to help, I will." Mrs. Brantley entered the room.

Fontaine stopped Montana and Kate as they started through the door. "I can't let Mrs. Brantley continue to present herself as bait." He spoke in low tones none of the others could hear from the room beyond. "I need you two to step in."

Montana nodded. He understood what that meant. He and Kate would attend the yacht club gala the following day as Mica Brantley and her bodyguard, Rex Masters.

Tazer appeared. "Don't worry, I had the concierge collect yours and Mrs. Brantley's wardrobes from the hotel. Fortunately, the sprinkler system and smoke didn't damage the contents of your suitcases." She handed Montana a faded black T-shirt. "Sorry, this was all I had in my workout bag. You'll have to put up with Led Zeppelin. If you don't like him, sue me. I'm a huge fan." She waved toward the table. "We'll work on other alternatives after the meeting."

For the next hour, they went over the sequence of events that led to their failed attempt to capture the assassin who'd broken into Mica Brantley's room at the Jefferson. If Mica hadn't been in the bathroom at the time of the invasion, it might not have ended the way it had. Rex Masters had put up a valiant defense.

The attacker had scaled the eight-story building, shooting a cable up to the window ledge and using an automatic lifting device to get him to the top in a hurry.

"That technology isn't readily available to just anyone. Whoever it was had connections," Lance said.

After Mica Brantley imparted what she knew, she stood. "If you're done with me, I'd like to check on Rex."

She left the room and the others continued until there was nothing more to say.

Montana studied Kate during the exchange. She leaned forward, listening intently to the others as they discussed what they'd observed from the different points of view and angles, from the guys in the communications van to those inside the hotel, working as staff members. Since the attack had come from an angle none of them had considered possible, they compared notes and decided they couldn't count on the next day being any easier.

"We'd better get some sleep. Those of you signing on as waitstaff will want to be in place early in the morning," Fontaine said. "I have a team of bomb-sniffing dogs making a pass through the yacht club premises tomorrow morning," the SOS leader continued. "I want to be there when they go through. You all have your assignments. We'll convene in the morning."

The team split up. Lance showed the SEALs to a room farther down the corridor, where cots had been set up and a shower was available.

Fontaine pulled Montana and Kate aside. They entered the infirmary, where they found Rex lying on an examination table with Mrs. Brantley at his side, and a man in a white lab coat tying off a stitch in the patient's side.

The doctor cut the strand, bandaged the wound and gave Rex a bottle of pills. "These are antibiotics. Take them until you run out. You don't want that wound getting infected." The doctor washed his hands in a nearby sink and nodded toward Fontaine. "Let me know if you need further assistance."

"I hope I won't have to call you." Fontaine held out his hand and shook the doctor's. "Thanks, Cal. I owe you one."

"Don't mention it," the doctor said. "One day I might need your services."

"I hope you won't, but if you do—" Fontaine squeezed the man's hand "—you know you can count on me."

Once the doctor left the room, Fontaine turned to

the four of them. "Mica, you can't go to the gala tomorrow."

Rex sat on the edge of the examination table, his face pale, his hand pressed to the bandage on his side. "Agreed."

Mrs. Brantley's lips thinned into a straight line. "I refuse to be intimidated and forced to go into hiding."

"It's temporary, until we find the one responsible," Fontaine assured her.

Mica spun on her heel and paced across the narrow room, turned and paced to stand in front of Fontaine. "My husband has been gone for weeks. I've been in hiding and searching for his killer all that time. Do you call that temporary?"

Fontaine captured her arms in his hands. "I'm sorry this is happening to you, but going to the gala tomorrow is like painting a big bull's-eye on you. We had fewer people to sift through at the hotel today, and someone still got inside. We can't take the chance with hundreds of people at the club and multiple entry points."

Mrs. Brantley lifted her chin. "What if I want to take that chance?"

Montana admired the woman's spunk, but going to the gala was too dangerous. He shifted his gaze to Kate. Taking Mica's place would set her up as the target. Granted, she was a highly trained operative who could probably handle herself in hand-to-hand combat, but she couldn't stop a bullet. And he doubted she'd consider wearing a bulletproof vest beneath her Gucci dress or Prada blouse.

Rex slid off the examination table and swayed slightly. "If you're going, I'm going."

Mrs. Brantley's brows descended. "You can't. You're wounded. You should be in bed, recuperating."

"I go where you go, ma'am."

The widow's frown deepened. "I won't allow it."

Rex's jaw tightened. "You won't have a choice."

"I'll...I'll fire you," she said. Pushing back her shoulders, she stared into her bodyguard's eyes.

Montana knew what Rex's response would be before he put it into words.

"It won't change a thing. I'd still be there to protect you."

Montana had to admire the man's resolve, considering he looked like he was about to pass out on the floor. Blood loss had a way of doing that to you. Montana had seen some of his buddies running on adrenaline. When the action was over, and they realized they'd been wounded and lost a lot of blood, they dropped like a ton of bricks. Montana moved closer to Rex, just in case the man took a dive to the stone-cold concrete floor.

Mrs. Brantley opened her mouth to argue. Apparently, the hard stare she received from Rex made her think again. She snapped her mouth shut and turned to Fontaine. "If I don't go, will that stop the attack on the gala?"

The SOS leader shook his head. "We can't guarantee it. We are assuming the dates and coordinates had something to do with you. But the truth is, the guest list is a who's who of financial and political heavy hitters. They could be the ones targeted, not you."

"Shouldn't we call it off?"

"We have heavy security in place in and around the

club," Fontaine said. "What I want to propose is Kate and Montana taking your places as guests."

"As the Lindemanns?" Mrs. Brantley's brows twisted. "I thought you'd already arranged for them to attend."

Fontaine shook his head. "Not as the Lindemanns but as you and Rex."

Already the widow was shaking her head. "I can't let you do that. I won't let Kate and Montana take a bullet, or an explosive device detonating on them, when it should have been me."

"Ma'am, this kind of work is our job," Kate assured her. "We know what to be on the lookout for and what to do if things go south."

Mrs. Brantley shook her head. "I won't let you or anyone else be hurt on my account. No."

"They're going to be there, anyway," Fontaine insisted. "Going as you will give them the advantage of trust. The people who have come for the past decade are used to seeing your face at the event. They trust you and might talk to you."

"Me." Mrs. Brantley tapped her chest. "They would talk to me."

"We can make Kate look like you, wire her with a radio headset and body cam. You will see what she sees, hear what she hears, and can feed information to her to engage others."

Mica stared at Fontaine, her eyes narrowing. "I thought that was something that could only be done in the movies."

Royce laughed. "That technology is available and works quite well."

She turned to Kate. "And you're willing to do this?

To go as me to a gala you know nothing about? To possibly be a target for a bullet you don't deserve?"

Kate nodded and smiled. "Beats pulling desk duty."

Montana almost laughed, but the seriousness of the situation made him hold back.

Finally, Mrs. Brantley drew in a deep breath and let it out slowly. "Okay. I'll agree on one condition."

Royce grinned. "What condition?"

Mrs. Brantley touched Kate's arm with a sad smile. "You keep this lovely young woman alive at all costs. The killing has already taken too great a toll of lives."

Montana's heart clenched. He stepped forward. "That's my job." Raising a hand like he had when he'd sworn into the Navy, he said, "I promise."

"Hey." Kate took Mrs. Brantley's hand. "I'm pretty good at looking out for myself. I'm an expert in hand-to-hand combat. Even if I wasn't, I have all of Mr. Fontaine's resources looking out for me. I'll be okay, as long as I have you in my ear telling me what to say and do."

The widow squeezed Kate's hand. "I can do that." Her gaze shot to Fontaine. "At least I think I can."

"We'll get you set up in time to help Kate play the part."

Mrs. Brantley swept a hand over Kate's hair. "Although we're about the same height, I don't know how you'll get this blonde to look like me in time."

Royce chuckled. "I have access to a professional hairstylist and makeup artist. I think we can manage."

"Okay, then." Mrs. Brantley nodded. "I'm in."

Rex sighed. "Good, because I wasn't sure how I was going to remain standing much longer." He swayed, reached for the examination table, missed and would have fallen if Montana hadn't been there to catch him. "Thanks."

Montana looped Rex's arm over his shoulder. "Come on, I bet you could use a drink and a bed."

"Yes to both." Rex shot a narrow-eyed glance at his boss. "You aren't going anywhere, are you?"

Mrs. Brantley smiled. "No. Get some rest. I'll be here when you wake."

Montana helped Rex to the barracks-style room he would share with the SEALs and Royce's SOS agents.

Once he had the bodyguard settled, Montana glanced around at the men moving in and out, making use of the shower, one by one.

Sawyer settled in the bunk next to Montana's and linked his hands behind his head. He wore only a pair of boxers and his hair glistened with moisture. "Not the level of quality you had at the Jefferson, is it?"

"No." Montana dropped to the thin mattress and settled in, determined to catch some Zs so that he could be alert and ready to go for the next day's action.

"Kate seems to be a real ballbuster, doesn't she?" Sawyer said. "I can't believe she ran through the city streets barefooted and wearing nothing but a bathrobe. That's dedication, if you ask me."

"She's something, all right," Montana commented. Kate was as passionate about her job as she was in bed. And she was beautiful, toned and could kiss. Boy, could she kiss. But when she wrapped her legs around him and he sank inside her...

Montana swallowed hard to keep from groaning aloud.

"Yeah, you and Kate seem to make a good team."

Sawyer yawned. "It doesn't hurt that she's got a body that doesn't quit."

Montana's fists clenched and a stab of something he could swear was jealousy knifed through his heart. If he didn't know Sawyer better, he'd be mad at his comment. Thankfully, Sawyer was in a relationship with a wonderful woman back in Mississippi. They had even started looking at engagement rings.

Forcing his hands to unclench, Montana lay still, staring up at the ceiling in the dim light filtering in from the bottom of the door to the hallway. He wondered what Kate was doing. Would she be asleep by now? Were her feet sore from running barefoot through the streets? Was she thinking about the shower in the Jefferson, like he was at that moment?

Montana rolled to his side and closed his eyes. He needed to sleep, but how could he when all he could think about was Kate's wet, naked body pressed against the shower stall?

After lying awake for another hour, listening to the other members of his team snoring or the bedsprings creaking, he gave up, got out of the bed and wandered out into the hall, hoping to find a kitchen and a glass of water. If he happened to run into Kate…well, he'd check and see how she was.

KATE HAD BEEN assigned to an office with a couch containing a hide-a-bed. After washing up and brushing her teeth with the toiletries Royce had provided, she'd removed the cushions from the couch and attempted to pull the bed out. No matter how many times she tried, it refused to budge.

After thirty minutes, a broken fingernail and a

bruised ego, Kate gave up. One by one, she replaced the cushions, then lay on the couch, tucking the robe around her.

It wasn't the Jefferson with its ultrasoft mattress and goose-down comforter, but it would have to do for the night. Thoughts of the Jefferson set her on the path of remembering everything that had happened from the time she entered the room she'd shared with Montana to jumping out the window and racing after the bad guy.

No wonder her pulse still raced and she couldn't go to sleep. It had been an exciting evening. Even more exciting because of the shower she'd shared with Montana. Looking back, she should have felt a flash of guilt for making love with her partner, but it had felt so right she couldn't make herself feel wrong about it. She could still feel the cool tiles against her back and the way Montana had filled her so completely.

She rolled to her back and groaned. Making love to Montana was supposed to be a one-time thing, and then she was supposed to move on, get over him and banish him from her system.

"Yeah, how's that working out for you?" she whispered to the empty room. Sleep wasn't coming and she really needed rest to be on her toes the next day. Closing her eyes, she counted bullets in her head, then beer bottles and then sheep. Nothing helped.

Kate rolled off the couch and stood in her bathrobe, wondering if she could find a bottle of whiskey somewhere in the building. Maybe some of the fiery liquid would take the edge off her nerves and allow her to fall asleep.

With that goal in mind, she opened the office door,

stepped out into the corridor and ran into a solid wall of muscle.

An arm clamped around her and a warm, buttery voice said, "You really should look before you leap."

Kate glanced up into the eyes of the man who'd made her night sleepless. Her pulse jacked up and pounded through her veins. "What are you doing awake?"

He chuckled. "I suspect the same thing you are. I was thinking about a certain shower in a certain hotel." He shook his head. "Once I went down that memory lane, I couldn't begin to go to sleep."

Kate considered denying that she had been consumed by the same thoughts and images. When she opened her mouth, she said, "Me, too." Then she did something she never thought she'd do in a bunker beneath the city. She turned toward her open door. "I don't suppose you can help me pull the bed out of this couch?"

His lips twitched. "Sure. But what's in it for me?"

"What's in it for you?" After a quick glance down the hallway, Kate took his hand, led him into the room and closed the door behind her. "You get to sleep on it."

Chapter Seven

Montana woke the next morning with Kate's warm body spooned into the curve of his own. For a long moment, he lay still, listening to the sound of her breathing and smelling the herbal scent of her shampoo.

He'd never stayed until morning in any woman's bed. In the middle of the night, the walls always seemed to close in on him. Lying awake with a naked female next to him would make him anxious to get up and leave, as though he would suffocate if he didn't get outside.

With Kate lying next to him in the basement bunker of a downtown DC building, Montana waited for the feeling of being strangled to force him out of the lumpy hide-a-bed and back to the makeshift barracks farther down the hallway. But that feeling never came. He'd slept better than he'd slept in a long time, with Kate nestled against him, her naked body warming his.

Once he'd pulled the bed out and they straightened the sheets, he'd lifted her into his arms and kissed her like he'd wanted to since they'd left the communications van. She'd responded with equal passion. From there, it was only natural for them to fall into the bed and make love until they had slaked their thirst for each other.

Making love with Kate had helped him to release the tension that had been building and keeping him awake. By the time they lay exhausted beside each other, Montana was able to fall into a deep and dreamless sleep. Without a window to let in sunlight, he didn't wake until he heard footsteps in the corridor outside the room.

A light tap on the door was followed by Tazer's voice. "McKenzie, are you awake?"

Kate stirred in his arms and stretched. "Yeah." She stared into Montana's eyes. "I'm awake." She ran her hand over his chest and downward.

"We need to get started. Can I come in?" The door handle wiggled.

Montana's heart leaped and he jerked to a sitting position.

Kate sat up as well, pulling the sheet up over her naked breasts.

Though the handle wiggled again, the door remained closed. "You'll have to unlock the door."

"Uh. Give me a minute to get dressed." Kate swung her legs over the side of the bed, fighting to free them from the sheet. "I can meet you in the conference room in five." Failing to get her legs free, she rose, wrapped mummy-style, and fell forward.

Montana dived across the bed, catching her before she performed a face-plant on the concrete flooring. Dragging her back into the bed, he swallowed hard on the laughter threatening to rumble up his chest.

"Don't you dare laugh," she whispered.

"You okay in there, McKenzie?"

"Yes, I am," Kate responded.

Montana nibbled at her earlobe. "Mmm, yes. You're more than okay."

"Shh." Kate touched a finger to his lips and tilted her head, listening for Tazer's footsteps. When the woman had left her post out in the hall, Kate relaxed and shook her head. "Thank you for locking the door last night. I completely forgot."

"I'm good for more than unfolding hide-a-beds." He kissed her neck again and trailed his lips lower to capture a rosy-tipped nipple between his teeth.

"Ouch." She shoved him away. "Those aren't for consumption." Kate smiled, cupped his face and pulled him up to kiss her properly. "Much as I'd love to stay in bed all day, we have a job to do. Can we take a rain check for after the show?"

Montana sighed. "You're right. I'm sure my team will be wondering where I've been, as well." He sat up, untangled her legs and waited for her to rise from the bed before he stood.

Kate stretched, her naked body a silhouette in the wedge of light shining from beneath the door. God, she was beautiful, her body perfect in every way.

Montana stepped up to her and pulled her against him, liking the feel of her skin against his.

Kate laced her hands behind his neck and pressed her breasts against his chest. "You know you tempt me, don't you?"

"No, I think it's the other way around. What say you and I call in sick and stay in bed all day?"

Kate nuzzled his neck. "Think the boss would understand?"

"Probably not."

"That's too bad." She ran her hand along his jawline and down to his chest. "Yeah, frogman, you tempt me more than I care to admit."

"Tonight?"

"You're on." She leaned up on her toes and pressed her lips to his in a brief, chaste kiss.

Montana captured her around her waist and held her there, his mouth crashing down on hers in a kiss he hoped was more than a promise of what they would have after the big gala. He'd count the minutes until that night. In the meantime, they had a job to do.

Kate stepped away, her lips bruised, her eyes shining and a rosy color blooming in her cheeks. "I have to go." She pulled on the only clothing she had, his pajama top and the bathrobe. "Give me a minute lead before you come out. The less everyone knows about our business, the better."

Montana's gut tightened. The sudden urge to tell the world that Kate McKenzie was his lover nearly burst from his chest. But she was right. If Fontaine knew they were getting too close, he might assign one of his teammates to play the part of Rex Masters.

Montana couldn't let that happen. He wanted to be there when the operation went down. Kate might be fully capable of helping herself out of a situation, but no one could undo the damage of a bomb. Having set his share of explosive devices, Montana knew what to look for and what kind of damage an explosion could cause.

Kate left, pulling the door closed behind her.

Montana folded the bed back into the couch, restoring the room into the office it was meant to be. Having burned the appropriate lead time, he edged the door open and glanced out into the corridor.

It was empty, but he could hear voices farther down the hallway. He ducked into the shower, rinsed off and toweled dry. Wrapping a towel around his waist, he hurried to the room he should have slept in the night before.

The guys were up and dressed, gearing up for the day ahead.

"Nice of you to join us," Rip said, his lips pulled back in a smirk.

"We were about to send out a search party to find you." Duff dragged back the slide on a .45 caliber pistol, checked the chamber and released the slide. "We're almost finished getting ready to go to the club. Tazer's been looking for you and Kate. Says she has a stylist waiting to start the transformation."

Sawyer passed Montana and clapped a hand on his shoulder. "Better you than me. Couldn't stand to wear makeup."

"What do you think camouflage is?" Montana asked.

"It sure as hell isn't pink," Sawyer shot back.

The men all laughed out loud. After each had selected a gun and finished dressing in the uniforms of the yacht club employees, they filed past Montana.

The last one out was Duff. He clapped a hand on Montana's shoulder in turn. "Break a leg, bro."

"You, too. This will be one of those missions to tell your grandchildren about." Montana smiled. "When are you and Natalie going to tie the knot?"

Duff grinned. "I think I've found the right ring. When we get back to Mississippi, I'm going to take her out on the Pearl River and pop the question."

Montana stared at his friend. "The Pearl? Couldn't you take her on a beach vacation or at least to a nice restaurant to pop the question?"

"I want to take her fishing. If she still loves me after fighting the bugs and humidity, I'll know I've got a keeper."

"Seriously? The woman's already been through hell in Cancun. You don't think that was enough?"

Duff's lips twisted. "You're right. I thought about taking her to a spa in Biloxi and signing up for one of those couples' massages. I could pop the question there."

"Now you're thinking straight." Montana shook his head. "Asking a girl on the Pearl is a surefire way to get her to not only say no, but *hell* no. What were you thinking?"

"That I like fishing?" Duff said. "And that I couldn't think of anyone else I'd like to go fishing with for the rest of my life."

"Save the fishing for a different occasion, like maybe your twenty-fifth anniversary."

Duff left Montana shaking his head.

If he were asking a woman to marry him, he'd take her somewhere with a beautiful sunset—a beach, the mountains, a cabin on a lake. He'd found that spot once in the mountains of Montana. That would be the ideal spot, if he could find it again.

He'd wait for the perfect moment, when the sky was at its most beautiful, then he'd get down on one knee and tell her she was the one person in the entire world he wanted to share that sunset with. He'd tell her that she was the woman he wanted to have children with, and have sitting next to him in a rocking chair on his front porch when they grew old, wrinkled and gray. Then he'd ask her to marry him and make him the happiest man in the world.

An image of Kate popped into his mind. Would a mountain lake appeal to a woman like her? Was she open to horseback riding and hiking into the backcountry to find the perfect location for a proposal? Montana had dreamed of eventually returning to his home state to live close to the mountains south of Bozeman. Any woman he hoped to marry would have to be open to such a move. Not all women liked living in such wide-open spaces, where the nearest shopping mall could be hundreds of miles away.

Not that he was thinking of popping the question anytime soon. He had to have a girlfriend first. Kate was just his partner for this operation. So they'd had sex. He hadn't assumed it committed them to a relationship. Kate was a very independent woman, burned by her former partner.

How any man could use her so ruthlessly, Montana couldn't imagine. Kate was beautiful, passionate and beyond fantastic in bed. His groin tightened. Drawing in a deep breath, he fought for control.

"You ready to get this party started?" a voice called out from behind him.

He spun, remembering at the last minute he wore only a towel around his middle.

Tazer stood in the doorway, a smile curling her lips. "Is that a banana under your towel or are you just happy to see me?"

Montana cursed.

"When you're dressed and ready to think with your mind, you can join us in the conference room. I'll tell them you'll be a few minutes."

"Thanks," he grumbled, and turned away, his cheeks burning.

KATE SAT FOR an hour with a stylist Royce had brought in. Leslie Saunders had been a makeup and hair artist in Hollywood before moving to Washington.

Tazer told Kate that Leslie had been blindfolded before they brought her to the secret site beneath the city, thus keeping their location safe. "Though I completely trust her. Leslie's saved my butt on more than one occasion."

Leslie wore a long, silk, royal blue oriental robe over a white camisole and white leggings. Her beautiful platinum-blond curls were pushed back behind her ears and secured with ornamental peacock-shaped combs. Her makeup matched her robe, framing her eyes with royal blue eye shadow and coal-black liner.

Kate felt like the ugly duckling next to her ethereal beauty.

Leslie fluffed Kate's hair, running her hands through the fine strands. "What are we doing here?"

Mica entered the room. "She needs to be the spitting image of me." Mrs. Brantley had applied her makeup as usual and arranged her hair as if she were attending the gala, the long, smooth strands neatly pinned into a subtle but elegant twist at the back of her head.

Leslie made several laps around Mica, studying her face and hair closely. Finally, she nodded. "I can do this." She opened the suitcase she'd brought and extracted bottles of liquid foundation, pallettes of contouring powder, blushes and eye shadows. Then she laid several tubes of eyeliner and mascara on the table, along with fake eyelashes and eyebrow pencils.

For the next thirty minutes, she worked on Kate's face like a painter on a blank canvas. When she was through with the makeup, she dug into her suitcase again and removed several dark wigs with long straight hair. One by one, she held them up to Mica's hair until she found one that most closely matched the color.

She slipped it over Kate's head and anchored it with pins in the back and at the sides. Then she applied a liquid to blend the cap with Kate's forehead. Once it was in place, she applied makeup to completely hide the edge, and swept the long hair up into a loose twist, allowing strands to fall around her face and neck.

Finally, Leslie called Mica over to stand beside Kate.

When she stepped back, Tazer gasped. Then a grin spread across her face. "Honey, I knew you were good, but wow. Just wow."

Kate had yet to see her reflection in the mirror. Mica looked the same as she had when she'd walked through the door an hour before, but Kate had no idea how closely they matched.

Leslie dug again in her suitcase, extracted a large mirror and handed it to her.

Mica bent and looked into the mirror at the same time as Kate.

Kate's breath caught in her throat and her heart skipped several beats. If she didn't know better, she'd bet the two women in the mirror were identical twins.

"Amazing," Mica said, her smile spreading across her face. "You're going to pull this off." Then her grin faded and she placed a hand on Kate's shoulder. "You could still back out of this. I don't want you hurt."

Kate patted the woman's hand. "I'm going. It's my choice. You lost your husband to this madman. I lost my mentor in the CIA. Becca lost her father. This has to stop."

"But I could go instead," Mica insisted.

"No. You're not trained to fight. I am. You said it yourself—I can pull this off. With you in my ear, I'll be you. No one will know the difference." Kate modified her voice, raising it to the pitch Mica used when she was worried or adamant. "I've been listening to you and watching your gestures." Kate waved her hand in the graceful style Mica displayed when she was more animated in her speech.

Tazer shook her head. "I can't tell the difference when you do that. It's uncanny."

Mica turned to Tazer. "But she shouldn't have to place herself in danger."

Kate faced Tazer and assumed the same stance and facial expression, as well as the way Mica held her arms and hands. "But she shouldn't have to place herself in danger," she mimicked, matching Mica's tones and inflections exactly.

Tazer laughed and clapped her hands. "Perfect." She glanced at her watch. "We don't have much time. We need to fit you for clothes and shoes. The outfits we chose yesterday are similar in taste and style as what Mrs. Brantley would wear. Since it's a gala, she wouldn't be expected to wear something she'd worn somewhere else. So new is good." Tazer opened a closet and pulled out the three outfits they'd purchased the previous day.

Mrs. Brantley studied the first one, then held up the second and smiled at the third. "I'd wear this to the gala."

The dress was a long, shimmering silver gown with narrow straps and a deep neckline, both in the front and back.

Tazer nodded. "I thought you might like that one. And it looks amazing on Kate."

"And I have the perfect necklace to go with it. I was planning on wearing it to the gala. I'll be right back." Mica left the room and returned in a minute carrying a sparkling diamond necklace, each gem exquisitely encased in white gold.

Kate shook her head, drawing the bathrobe around her body. "I can't wear that. It probably cost a fortune."

"Darling, if you don't wear it, they'll know you're a fake for sure," Mrs. Brantley said. "Go on, get into the dress."

Kate dropped the robe and unbuttoned the pajama top, reluctant to let go of the one item of clothing she felt most comfortable in. That it was Montana's made it even harder to release.

Tazer held out the silver dress. She winked. "We're not prudes here, but if it helps, we can turn around." She started to do so.

"No, it's okay." Kate shrugged out of the pajama top and took the dress from Tazer. As she stepped into the garment, it slid across her legs and over her hips. She remembered liking the way it had felt in the dressing room at the shop.

Once Kate was zipped into the gown and the matching silver three-inch heels, Mrs. Brantley stepped behind her and placed the necklace around her neck.

Leslie handed her the mirror. "Honey, I couldn't have chosen better. You look fabulous."

Kate stared into the mirror. A different person stared back at her. If not for the gray-blue of her eyes, she wouldn't have recognized herself.

"Wait." Leslie dived into her bag again and came

out with a package of colored contacts. "You'll need the brown contacts or it'll be a dead giveaway. Attention to details pays off."

Leslie helped Kate insert the lenses.

She blinked several times before the contacts settled into place, at which point she could barely feel them.

"If you're ready, we need to get going." Tazer hooked her arm and led her toward the door.

"We have transportation that will take you to Mrs. Brantley's car. It's positioned at another hotel, where you're supposedly staying under another name," Tazer said. "Montana is waiting for you. The gala begins in less than an hour." She pressed a small radio earbud into Kate's hand. "Put this in your ear. It's your connection to Mrs. Brantley. And this rhinestone clip is just added bling to the dress. It contains a body cam. Mrs. B and the guys on the monitors will be able to see everything you see. Or at least everything you see at breast level." Tazer chuckled.

Kate's pulse picked up as she entered the corridor, her gaze searching for Montana. Her stomach clenched when she didn't find him.

Mrs. Brantley hurried alongside her. "You'll be deposited at the front of the yacht club onto a red carpet. The media will be there in full force. Remember to hold your head up and smile for the cameras. I'll be with you as soon as Lance gets me set up."

Kate smiled at Mica. "Thank you. I'll do my best to make you proud."

"Oh, and here." She pulled off her diamond wedding ring. "I wouldn't go anywhere without it." She held out her hand.

Kate reluctantly removed her fake wedding ring and

handed it to Mica. "I want that back," she said, taking Mica's giant diamond ring.

Mica grinned. "Ditto." She curled her hand around the fake ring. "And remember, I wouldn't be there at all if not for the children. It's all about the children." She slowed to a stop as they neared the building's solid steel doors leading into the garage.

Royce's long dark limousine was parked on the other side. A man in a tuxedo stood beside it. When he turned, Kate had to look closely. The man looked like Rex, but when he smiled, she knew it was Montana. Hell, she'd seen him naked more than she'd seen him in clothes. The tuxedo made him appear broader and taller. "Larger than life" was the phrase that came to mind.

His eyes narrowed and he glanced from her to Tazer and back. "Kate?"

Adopting Mica's tone and persona, she answered, "I decided this event was too important to miss. Kate will be working with the men in the computer room." She ran her gaze from the top of his head to his shoes. "You'll do as a double for Rex. Are we ready?" She didn't wait for him to respond, but sailed around him to the limousine.

As she passed Montana she felt a sharp slap on her behind.

"Hey." She swung around and glared at him.

Tazer laughed. "Go get 'em, Kate. You'll do great."

Montana's smile widened. "I knew it was you all along."

"Yeah, well, you didn't have to slap me to prove it." Kate lowered herself into the backseat of the limo and swung her legs inside.

Montana closed the door, walked around to the other side and slid onto the seat beside her. "I like the real Kate better." His lips twitched, curling into a smile, and he reached out to take her hand in his.

The ride to the staging hotel took only ten minutes. The driver dropped them at the rear of the hotel garden. Montana led Kate through a gap in the fence and onto the path leading through a fragrant array of rosebushes. They emerged near a swimming pool and entered the back door of the grand hotel.

Taking their time, they ambled across the lobby and out the front entrance to Mica's waiting limousine.

Kate stared hard at the chauffeur. If she wasn't mistaken, it was Duff behind the cap and sunglasses. Feeling better and better about the situation, she settled into the backseat and glanced out the window at the buildings as they drove through the streets of downtown DC toward the Potomac River and the yacht club where the event was to take place.

For all she knew nothing would happen. On the flip side, if someone had managed to get a bomb inside the building, this could be the last time she saw sunshine. It could be her last day on earth. She wished she'd had time for one more stolen kiss. Instead, Kate reached for Montana's hand and squeezed it as the limousine pulled up in front of the club.

Chapter Eight

No matter how different she appeared in the wig, makeup and dress, the woman beside Montana was still Kate, through and through. She held herself like royalty and, if things went south, he had no doubt she'd come out kicking butt.

He reached into his inside pocket and pulled out a small gun with a thin Velcro strap. "I was going to give this to you for protection, but I can't imagine where you'd hide it. That dress fits you like a second skin."

"I'll find a place." She took the small device from him.

"You know how to use it?"

"I do." Kate lifted the hem of her gown, exposing a good portion of her smooth, sexy leg.

Montana's pulse quickened. What he wouldn't give to be back on that damned hide-a-bed, locked in an office in the basement of the SOS building, making love to Kate.

She strapped the gun to the inside of her thigh, above the slit in the dress, and slipped the skirt back in place.

Montana swallowed hard and patted the gun he had tucked in a shoulder holster inside his jacket. "Ready?"

She touched her finger to the earbud. "Ready?"

Mica must have answered with an affirmative, because Kate looked up at Montana and nodded.

He got out of the limousine and turned to hold the door for Kate. She was beautiful and a dead ringer for Mica Brantley. If the assassin who'd come for the widow last night found his way inside the yacht club today, he'd have to go through "Rex" to get to the fake Mica.

Using his body as a shield, Montana placed himself between her and the waiting crowd, cordoned off the red carpet by a line of velvet ropes. Members of the media crowded in, cameras flashing and shoving microphones in her face.

"Mrs. Brantley, this is your first time out in public since your husband's death. How does it feel?"

Kate gave a stiff smile. "No comment."

Montana firmly pushed the reporter and his microphone out of the way, allowing Kate to proceed toward the door.

A female reporter came at her from the other side. "Mrs. Brantley, your dress is stunning. Who are you wearing?"

Kate paused and answered the woman, stating a name Montana had never heard. She turned and posed for the cameraman, placing her hand on her hip, turning slightly to the side.

Montana almost laughed. He could swear the Kate he knew was more comfortable in jeans and a T-shirt. But this Kate handled the press like a pro. Like a celebrity. The woman had actress potential. He made a note to himself to ask if that's what they taught CIA agents in training. He choked on a laugh when he thought that while he'd lugged logs in the waves off San Diego, she'd studied clothing designers and posing for cameras. She'd probably flip him over her hip and smash his face into the concrete if he said anything along those lines.

Another reporter jammed his microphone in Kate's face. "Mica, now that your husband is dead, are you having an affair with your bodyguard?"

Her eyes narrowed slightly, but she didn't respond to the question. Instead, she turned away from the man and climbed the steps toward the yacht club entrance.

Montana clenched his fists, holding on to his last nerve to keep from shoving his knuckles down the bastard's throat. Mica's husband was barely cold in the grave. How could the reporters be so heartless? Montana followed Kate's lead, refusing to rise to the rumormongers. He stayed close, keeping his body between her and the crowd.

Behind him, a reporter shouted above the melee, "Mrs. Brantley, did you murder your husband?"

Montana swung around, his gaze searching the throng for the man who'd had the audacity to accuse Mrs. Brantley of killing her husband.

Kate's hand on his arm stopped him from charging down the steps to crush the monster.

"He's not worth it," she said. "Let's do this."

Montana ground his teeth and shot a killing glare at the media, then turned on his heel, placed his hand at the small of Kate's back and followed her into the club.

Inside, the crowd wasn't nearly as pressing or overwhelming, but there were a lot of people milling about, dressed in their finest, strutting around like a flock of peacocks. Or was it a gaggle of peacocks, he wondered. No, it was something stranger... An ostentation!

Montana shook his head. Ostentatious was more like it. This group of men and women spent more on what they were wearing than most people earned in a month. All for a party. If they put all that money in with the amount they donated to the children's hospital, they'd amass a significantly greater amount for the cause.

"Mica, darling." A gray-haired woman in a dark blue dress rushed forward and would have engulfed her in a hug if Montana hadn't seen her coming and stepped between them at the last moment.

Kate placed a hand on his arm. "Rex, please. This is Mrs. Martin. One of our most generous patrons. I'm sure she's not here to harm me."

"Oh, certainly not," the woman said. "I love Mica like a daughter."

Montana eased out of the way, and the older woman hugged Kate so tightly, she grimaced.

"I was so sad to hear about Trevor. Such a good man. And he was so young."

"Thank you, Mrs. Martin."

"Are you doing well?" She stared into Kate's face. "You look a little peaked. You should go someplace where you can get some sun. Fresh air and sunshine helps when you lose a loved one."

Kate smiled. "I'll consider your advice when I plan my next trip."

Mrs. Martin patted her arm. "Please, if you need a place to stay while you're in the city, consider staying with me, not some cold, impersonal hotel. You're always welcome."

"Thank you, Mrs. Martin. You're too kind."

Mrs. Martin's attention darted to the left. "Oh, look. There's Janine Anderson. I must say hello. Will you be all right on your own?"

Kate nodded. "I have Rex to keep me company."

The older woman glanced at Montana as if noticing him for the first time. "Oh, yes. Of course you do. He is quite handsome. I think every woman should have a handsome bodyguard to keep her company in these dangerous times. Excuse me, I have to catch Mrs. Anderson." Mrs. Martin hurried away.

"One acquaintance down, only a hundred to go," Montana whispered.

"Thank goodness for technology," Kate whispered back. She smiled as another of Mica's friends approached her and engaged her in conversation.

Kate handled each person with care and dignity, much like Mrs. Brantley would have had she been there. With the woman feeding information into her ear, Kate was able to ask about one couple's daughter in college, another man's sickly mother and an elderly woman's son in the army.

Montana kept a close watch on Kate and looked around the crowded ballroom, searching for anyone who seemed out of place, angry or nervous. The security at the entrance was tight, but anyone who wanted to get into the yacht club badly enough would find a way.

On several occasions, he spotted his teammates, weaving in and out among the guests, carrying trays of hors d'oeuvres or glasses of champagne. Fontaine and Tazer appeared at the entrance as guests.

Tazer wore a long black gown, her blond hair piled high on her head, and long sparkling earrings hanging from her earlobes. Fontaine wore a black tuxedo that made his shock of white hair look even more prestigious. The man knew how to blend in to any crowd of people.

When the SOS leader glanced their direction, he gave the slightest dip of his head in acknowledgment. With six SEALs, two SOS agents and one CIA undercover operative at the gala, if something were to happen, they'd have an excellent chance of either stopping it or catching whoever initiated the fight.

Fontaine reported that the dogs hadn't come across anything that smelled even remotely like explosives. Not only had the team been through the building multiple times, they'd been at the loading dock for each delivery that day, up until the gala actually started.

Metal detectors had been set up at the entry points to scan for guns and weapons. All the right precautions had been taken. Still, Montana had a gut feeling something would happen that night. He'd been in enough firefights to trust his gut. He stuck to Kate throughout the evening. When it came time for her to address the gathering and laud the virtues of contributing to the children's hospital, he wasn't happy with how exposed she'd be on the stage.

As she started to climb the steps, he was right behind her.

Kate stopped halfway up and placed a hand on his chest. "I can handle this."

"No one can handle a bullet through the heart."

"I'll stay behind the podium," she said.

"It's made of wood. It'll only slow the bullet."

"Please." Kate smiled. "I'm here for the children."

"I'm here to make sure you live to *have* children," he insisted.

She stared into his eyes for a long moment. He held her brown-eyed gaze, refusing to back down, wishing he could see her gray eyes through the contact lenses.

"Okay." She straightened and continued upward. "But try not to look so big and intimidating. We want the people to donate, not run screaming."

Montana chuckled and fought the urge to slap her bottom. He followed her to the podium, standing back a few steps, putting on a poker face as he scanned the crowd, searching for anyone who looked like he might pull a gun and start firing.

Kate welcomed the guests with a smile and spoke eloquently the words Mrs. Brantley had prepared for her speech.

Montana half listened, balancing on the balls of his feet, ready to launch himself in front of Kate at any moment.

So FAR, THE event was going as planned, with no surprises and no attacks. Kate relaxed in her role, reading the speech Mrs. Brantley had given her before she'd left for the gala.

She'd been amazed at the statistics Mrs. B had compiled about all the children the hospital had helped at no cost to the families, and all the children who were still alive due to the care they'd received. At the conclusion of the speech, she called for people to open their hearts and wallets. She stepped back, thankful she hadn't been interrupted by gunfire and was able to do the speech justice for Mrs. Brantley.

A commotion at the side of the stage caught her attention. Montana stepped forward, using his body as a shield for hers.

Kate leaned around Montana to find a woman herding a group of twenty or more children in choir robes up onto the stage.

"They brought children to the gala?" she said softly. "Who authorized that?"

Mrs. Brantley's laughter filled Kate's ear. "They always have a children's choir sing at the gala. It makes the guests more aware of how important it is to protect them and help them when they are sick."

"But they're children," Kate said. "What if something happens?"

Mrs. Brantley didn't respond right away. "I didn't think about that. Really, I'd forgotten about the choir altogether."

Kate glanced at Montana. "We have to get them out of here."

The woman in charge of the choir smiled at Kate and proceeded to organize the children on the stage.

Kate gritted her teeth, her gaze sweeping the room as she prayed that whoever might attack her or anyone else present would consider waiting until the children sang their song and left the club.

All through the three verses of "Hallelujah," Kate worried. They finally finished, and the woman herded them down the steps and out of the club.

Kate released the breath she'd held. With her speech obligation complete, she had no reason to remain at the club. She descended the stairs with Montana close behind. No bullets flew, no bombs went off. If they were lucky, the entire gala, the coordinates and date would be a nonevent.

"Ah, Mrs. Brantley." A man with graying hair and

a slight paunch approached her, smiling. "Thank you for a moving speech. Your husband would have been so proud."

Montana moved closer, his eyes narrowing.

"This man is Nigel Carruthers," Mica said into Kate's ear. "He's a dear friend of Trevor's. They've known each other since they were roommates at Harvard. I usually hug him."

"Nigel. It's so good to see you." Kate hugged the man and then stood back, smiling. "Thank you for the kind words."

"I miss playing golf with Trevor. Just the other day, I walked by my clubs and wished I could have given him a call to go out and hit a few balls." The man sighed. "A shame to lose such a talented man."

Kate nodded and waited for Mrs. Brantley to feed her more information. For a long moment, she didn't speak. "My husband loved playing golf, but he wasn't very good at it. He did it to get outside in the fresh air more than anything. Nigel always won."

"Trevor would have loved to get out in this wonderful weather we're having lately," Kate said.

Carruthers nodded. "Although he'd been pretty busy with his latest projects, he made time to play a few rounds with me before he passed." The older man looked up and gave her a sad smile. "I imagine if he'd known he wouldn't be around much longer, he might have spent more time with his family. Emily might not have gone to New York and been abducted."

Mrs. Brantley gasped. "Trevor loved us more than himself. He wouldn't have committed so much time to his project had he not considered it important. He was devastated when Emily went missing. He dropped everything to search for her."

Kate stared at the man in front of her, wanting to kick him for being so inconsiderate. He obviously hadn't known the Brantleys as well as he thought.

"Family is everything," Carruthers continued. "You should know that now more than ever, right, Mica?"

"I don't know why Nigel is being so hurtful. He should know how hard it is for me. Nigel lost his brother several years ago in an embassy bombing. I remember how distraught he was. Trevor was there for him, helping him through the difficulty of having his brother's body returned to the States, and arranging for his funeral."

"Nigel, we both miss Trevor," Kate said, searching for words to say to the man who'd just insulted a grieving widow.

Carruthers grabbed her arm and squeezed hard enough to hurt her. "Trevor didn't tell you what he was working on, did he?"

"No, he didn't," Mrs. Brantley said.

"No," Kate repeated, twisting her arm in an attempt to free it from the man's grip.

Montana grabbed Carruthers's wrist and pulled it free of Kate's arm. "Please, don't touch Mrs. Brantley."

Carruthers glared at Montana and then turned to Kate. "I just wonder if he thought through whatever it was that he was doing and the implications it had on his family. If he had, would he have considered it worth it?" Carruthers stepped away from Kate and Montana, spun on his heels and left the ballroom.

"What the hell was that all about?" Montana stared at the man's retreating figure.

Kate rubbed her arm where a bruise was beginning to darken her skin. "I don't know. We need to check him out. See what his story is."

"He's been a bitter man since his brother's death," Mrs. B said. "Losing someone tends to change the ones left behind."

Kate could imagine. But that didn't give Carruthers the right to be so aggressive.

A band started playing in the far corner of the ballroom, the sound drowning out conversation.

If Kate could, she would have left at that moment. Her feet hurt, she was tired of pretending to be who she wasn't and her face itched from all the makeup.

But they were there in case something happened. At this point, it didn't appear as though it ever would.

A scream ripped through the air, the only sound that could be heard over the band being amplified through the speaker system.

One scream led to another, and the entire roomful of people surged toward the exit.

Kate craned her neck to see over the tops of people's heads. As the crowd thinned, she caught a glimpse of a group of people gathered in a circle, looking at something on the floor.

Kate pushed through the men and women heading for the door to get to the circle. Then she elbowed her way in to find a man lying on the polished marble tiles, his face gray, his eyes bulging and foam dripping from his mouth.

Well, damn. Even with all the precautions they'd

taken, they hadn't been able to stop someone from taking yet another life. No guns or bombs were used to eliminate the subject. Nothing so barbaric. No. This time the attack had been with what appeared to be poison.

Chapter Nine

Police stopped everyone from leaving the yacht club. An ambulance arrived within five minutes, and emergency medical technicians were on the scene so fast Montana suspected Royce had had them on standby.

Nothing they did helped the guy who'd been poisoned. Apparently the toxin used was fast-acting and permanent. Montana's fists clenched and he hovered near Kate, refusing to budge from her side. His team circled the throng, watching closely, ready to spring into action.

Royce conferred with the police and EMTs, but didn't make contact with any of the others. They'd have time back at the SOS alternate site to put their heads together, review the videos and discover where their logic had gone wrong.

Montana couldn't wait to get Kate out of the ballroom. He didn't feel that she was any safer with a roomful of police. If anything, the chaos of adding more people to the mix only made him more anxious to get her to safety.

"Stop worrying. I wasn't the one who was poisoned." She pushed him to the side. "And you can quit blocking my view. You're making me crazy."

He'd pretty much backed her into a corner and stood in front of her. It was the only way he could be certain no one would get a shot at her while attention was on the guy who'd been poisoned.

"Now would be the time to make another attempt," Montana said.

"Move." She shoved him to the side and stared at the first responders, firefighters and police. "What the hell? What's wrong with Royce?"

Montana's gaze shot to the last place he'd seen Fontaine and Tazer, standing beside the man in charge of the scene.

Fontaine was leaning heavily on Tazer, his face pale.

Tazer shouted for help.

EMTs converged on Fontaine and eased him onto a gurney. The emergency crew went to work stabilizing the leader of the SOS.

Kate started forward.

Montana's hand shot out, grabbing her arm. "We're not supposed to know him."

"But he's our friend. He's one of the team."

"What can you do to help?" Montana reasoned.

"I don't know. But I can't just stand here."

"What's going on?" Duff's voice sounded in Montana's ear.

"Fontaine is down," he responded. "Could be the same problem as the first victim."

Duff cursed. "Give me bullets and mortars any day. Poisoning guests is pure evil."

"Someone needs to go with Fontaine."

"Sawyer's on the outside of the building. He can go with Fontaine and Tazer to the hospital. In the meantime, you need to get Mrs. Brantley out."

Montana glanced toward the main exit, swarmed by at least a dozen police officers. "Can't get past the cops."

"Head toward the kitchen. There's a back exit they haven't completely closed off yet. We can create a distraction while you slip out."

Montana hooked Kate's arm. "Time to go."

"But what about Royce?" Kate dug in her heels and pulled against his grip on her arm. "What happened to *no man left behind*?"

"Tazer has his back. Sawyer is one of the security guards on the outside. He'll go with them to the hospital. Royce isn't being left behind. We can't do as much good as the doctors at the hospital can. Hopefully, he didn't get a full dose of whatever killed victim number one."

Kate allowed Montana to escort her through the crowd to the back of the ballroom and through a swinging door into the kitchen.

The state crime lab was already at work collecting evidence from the trays of food and champagne flutes. The caterers were being questioned and names were recorded.

"Never mind the kitchen," Duff's voice said from behind them. "Follow me."

He led them down a hallway lined with doors bearing gold nameplates. At the end of the hallway was another door labeled Yacht Shop.

Duff pulled a small metal file from his pocket, slid it into the keyhole and wiggled it several times.

Montana watched behind them, sure a police officer would find the hallway and haul them back inside the ballroom for questioning.

A metal click sounded and Duff chuckled. "Works every time." He opened the door and led the way into the shop.

Kate went next and Montana brought up the rear, closed the door behind them and twisted the lock.

Duff weaved through the racks of windbreakers, hats and life vests to the opposite end of the shop, where another door led to the dock outside.

He paused, his gaze fixed to a plastic box on the wall with a keypad. "Looks like a security system. Be prepared to run if we trigger it."

"Maybe we should go back inside and wait our turn to be questioned," Kate said. "I'd hate for Mrs. Brantley to have to explain why she bypassed investigation protocol to leave the premises of the yacht club."

A loud click sounded.

Duff smiled, tapped his ear and said, "Thanks, Geek. We owe you." He opened the door. "I don't know how he does it, but that man is a magician. And he said he could substitute footage on the video feed without leaving a trace." He waved Kate through. "Let's get you out of here."

Kate stepped through the door and out onto the wooden planks of the dock. A maze of platforms led away from the club into the marina, where dozens of yachts were moored.

Montana slipped his arm around Kate's waist and helped her navigate the boards to keep her heels from getting caught in the gaps. "We can't really go around to the front of the building. How do you propose to get back to SOS headquarters?"

Duff smiled. "Royce had that covered, as well." He

strode toward an intersection of the wooden walkway and turned left. Then he dropped out of sight.

Kate gasped and hurried toward the point where he'd vanished.

Montana followed. Below the decking was a small skiff tied to a ladder.

Duff grinned up at them. "Get in. We'll take this to the park on the Potomac that's only two blocks from our destination."

Kate removed her shoes and dropped them into the bottom of the boat. Then she lifted the hem of her dress and draped it over her arm.

"Tell you what. Let me go first," Montana said. "If you have any troubles, I can catch you."

"Why not let Duff?" she asked.

Montana shook his head. "I'd rather be the one. I'm your bodyguard, not Duff."

Kate's lips quirked upward. "You just don't want him ogling my behind."

Montana nodded, keeping his expression serious. "There is that."

She shook her head and moved to the side. "After you."

He hurried to get several rungs down the ladder before he paused. "Now you."

Kate eased her foot onto the first one and started down.

Montana waited for her to lower herself into the circle of his arms, and together they descended into the small skiff.

Duff sat at the tiller, his hand on the motor's start switch. "As soon as you take a seat, we'll get going."

Once Kate's feet touched the bottom of the boat,

Montana took her hand and helped her to sit on one of the benches.

Montana took his seat.

Duff started the engine and eased the small craft out of the marina and into the main channel of the Potomac River. Though the boat wasn't equipped with the required lights for night boating, the lights from the city were sufficient to navigate the river in that area.

Montana prayed they'd make it to the park without being pulled over by the river police and ticketed for boating without the proper equipment. If they were discovered, they might also be arrested for leaving a crime scene without permission.

Past caring, Montana stared at the smooth water ahead. Light from the buildings on both sides of the channel outshone the stars above. Navigating didn't require a light for them to see. The legally required lights were more to make the boat visible to others on the water, to avoid collisions.

"Anything on Fontaine?" Duff said behind them.

Montana glanced over his shoulder at his teammate in the rear.

Kate turned in her seat and looked, as well.

Duff cupped a hand over his ear, his eyes narrowed. Then he nodded. "On our way to the pickup location. Roger. Out."

He glanced up and shook his head. "Nothing yet. Fontaine made it to the hospital and was taken straight back. Tazer is with him."

Montana returned his attention to the river in front of them, his gaze trained on the banks, searching for any signs of movement.

They reached the park and slid up on the shore. Montana jumped out and reached for Kate's hand.

She stepped off the front of the boat, slipped on the muddy bank and fell into his arms.

He held her close, glad to have the excuse for however short the time. Even before the death in the ballroom, he'd been tense, worried and waiting for something to happen. He didn't like that Kate was the decoy, but he wasn't calling the shots for her. If she hadn't wanted to take on the assignment, she would have voiced her opinion. The woman had a mind and heart of her own.

He admired that about her. At the same time, he didn't want her heart to be pierced by a bullet or stopped by poison in her bloodstream.

"You might want these." Duff held out Kate's heels.

Kate took them, but didn't move out of Montana's arms. A shiver rippled through her.

The warm spring air had turned chilly after the sun had set. Montana shrugged out of his tuxedo jacket and wrapped the garment around her shoulders.

She smiled up at him. "Thank you."

He frowned. "You should have said something on the boat."

"I'm okay."

Headlights flashed above in the park.

"That will be our transportation." Duff led the way up the bank and past picnic tables, to where Fontaine's limousine was waiting for them.

A dark-haired man got out and held out his hand. "Glad to see you made it out of the circus. I'm Sam Russell, SOS. Royce had me waiting on standby. I would have been at the gala, but I just got back in town this afternoon from another assignment."

Duff and Montana shook hands with Sam.

Kate stepped up to him and held out her hand. "Nice to meet you, Sam."

"Wow," he said. "I've seen Leslie's work before, but this is amazing. I ran into Mica Brantley at HQ. You look exactly like her."

Kate nodded. "Leslie gave up her career in Hollywood too soon."

"To our benefit," Sam added. He held open the door for her.

Kate slid in.

Montana got in beside her.

"I'll ride up front with Sam," Duff said.

Sam drove the limousine out of the park and onto the main road leading back into the city.

Beside Montana, Kate shivered and hunkered deeper into his jacket.

He draped his arm over her shoulders. "Better?"

"Yes. These dresses weren't meant for running around outside in fifty-degree temperatures."

"No, they weren't." Montana pulled her closer.

"Do you think the man who was poisoned was a random killing?" she asked.

"Not at all. Hopefully, by the time we get back to headquarters, Geek and Lance will have the victim's identity. I would bet he ties into the other killings in some way."

"Yeah, but we have yet to figure out the connection between all those who've been targeted thus far." She leaned into him. "Why Trevor Brantley? Better still, why his daughter?" Kate shook her head. "I can understand wanting to take Mica out, since she's on a relentless hunt to find the ones responsible. But why Emily Brantley?"

"I don't know. Something Carruthers said tonight made me wonder. What project was Brantley working on? Was it what made him and his family a target?"

"It's worth digging into. Maybe Mrs. Brantley can shed some light on that."

"She said her husband had contacts that led her to the human trafficking chain in Cancun. Fontaine said he searched down that rabbit hole and came to a dead end. Mica's contacts were either killed or disappeared off the radar."

The limousine slammed to a halt, throwing Kate and Montana forward, tumbling across the floor.

No sooner had Montana righted himself than he lurched sideways, when the vehicle swerved.

"Hold on," Sam said. "We have two SUVs trying to hem us in."

Montana dived for the seat, strapped his seat belt and then reached for Kate. He grabbed her hand and yanked her up against his body as another vehicle rammed into them.

Refusing to let go, he held on as they rocked to the side, the SOS vehicle's left side leaving the ground, then crashing back down on all four wheels.

Sam gunned the accelerator, cut hard to the right, jumped the curb and drove down the sidewalk for several yards before bumping back onto pavement.

Montana pushed Kate into the seat beside him. Kate hiked her dress up, planted her knees in the seat and pulled her tiny gun from the strap around her thigh. Then she rolled down the window and leaned out.

"What the hell are you doing?" Montana shouted.

"Fighting back," she said.

Montana released his seat belt, pulled his pistol from his shoulder holster and leaned out his side of the vehicle.

One SUV flanked the limousine on the left. The other followed so closely behind, he could hit—

"Get down!" Montana grabbed a handful of her dress and pulled her back on the seat.

The SUV behind them rammed into their rear, while the other swerved to the left and raced up along the driver's side.

Kate rolled up on her knees, waited until the driver of the vehicle was in range and then fired into the tinted passenger-side window.

The driver jerked away and then came back.

Kate recoiled just in time.

The SUV rammed into the side of the limousine.

Kate tumbled across the floor.

As Montana bent forward to grab her hand, the trailing SUV clipped the corner of the limousine's left rear bumper.

The SOS vehicle spun to the right, ran over the curb and slammed into a covered bus stop.

Sam shifted and tried to back up, but the SUV that had been following pulled to a stop behind them, blocking that route of escape. The one that had blown past them was backing toward them at a fast clip, with no sign of slowing.

"Stay down," Montana said. He threw open his door, rolled out onto the ground and away from the limo as the second SUV backed into them.

Rage drove him to his feet, his gun drawn. He hunkered low behind the limousine, rounded the driver's side of the SUV and fired point-blank into the tinted window.

The glass shattered and Montana could see inside. He'd hit the passenger, but the driver was seated so far back, he'd only been grazed. He stomped his foot on the accelerator, sending the SUV leaping forward.

Montana fired into the vehicle, then leaped back to avoid having his feet run over.

The SUV that had backed into the limousine spun tires in an attempt to shoot forward. The back window slid down.

Montana didn't wait for it to make it all the way down before he fired his last five bullets into the vehicle. He released the clip and reached into his pocket for another, realizing at the last moment he didn't have one.

He was a sitting duck with no ammo. This couldn't end well.

WHEN THE LIMOUSINE had been hit by the backing vehicle, Kate had been slung sideways, slamming against a padded wall, her tiny pistol knocked from her grip. The *bang, bang, bang* sound of gunfire made her scramble to find the gun. Once she had it in her hand, she sat up, rolled over and out the open door Montana had escaped through.

Montana stood at the rear of the vehicle, firing at an SUV driving away from the fray.

The flash of relief Kate felt was short-lived when a man popped up over the top of the other SUV and fired at Montana.

Montana flung himself to the ground and rolled toward the limousine.

Kate couldn't see him, but was almost positive he wasn't behind any cover, which meant he was exposed to the man's gunfire.

Her heart leaped into her throat. She turned her little pistol toward the shooter and fired. The man ducked down and the SUV jerked forward, the tires smoking against the pavement.

Kate fired again, aiming for the driver. The bullet hit the rear windshield, but the vehicle kept going.

Duff staggered out of the limousine, blood dripping down his face from a cut on his forehead. "Are you all right?"

Kate nodded. "But I'm not so sure about Montana."

"I'm okay," Montana called out from the other side of the vehicle. "Thanks to whoever was shooting there at the end." He stood and glanced from Kate to Duff.

Duff held up his hands. "It wasn't me. You can thank Kate." He pressed his fingers to his injured forehead. "We need to get the limousine free of the bus stop."

"What about Sam?"

"He's okay, just shaken up." Duff handed his gun to Kate. "You cover while we push." He waved to Montana. "Come on. We don't have time to answer a bunch of questions. We need to get to headquarters."

Kate stood guard, watching for a return of the two SUVs, the heavier 9 mm pistol fitting nicely in her palm. She'd shoot to kill if either of the vehicles reappeared.

Montana and Duff leveraged themselves between the front of the limousine and the bus stop's metal pole and pushed.

Sam had the vehicle in Reverse, his foot on the accelerator. At first the tires only spun.

Montana bounced the front of the hood and eventually whatever was holding the limousine worked loose.

Sam blasted backward, off the sidewalk and back onto the street.

Duff, Montana and Kate dived into the limousine, and Sam drove away from the bent pole of the bus stop.

Kate would have felt guilty about leaving it a mess if she didn't have a raging headache and bruises all over her body from being bounced around the interior of the limousine like a ball in a pinball machine.

"How did they find us?" she asked, as soon as the doors closed. "We could have been anywhere in the city. How did they know we would be at that exact place, at that exact time?"

In the front of the vehicle, Sam shook his head. "I was careful to keep an eye on the rearview mirror. I'm ninety-nine percent positive they didn't follow me to the pickup location. If they had, you'd think they would have attacked sooner."

Kate didn't believe the attackers had accidentally found them driving on the streets of the nation's capital. The SOS vehicle was as nondescript as a limousine could be, and looked like any one of hundreds that moved about the city at any time of the day, carrying politicians, lobbyists and various celebrities trying to be seen or heard supporting their pet causes. And Royce seemed like too much of a professional to leave the same license plate on his car all the time. He'd have it changed each time he made use of the company vehicle.

"Could the limousine be tagged with a tracking device?" Kate asked.

"We swept it before I left HQ," Sam said. "Geek

is top-notch at encryption. Since we had the takeover last year, Geek's made it his mission to lock down access. No one can get into our system but him, Lance and Royce."

"Could one of us be tagged?" Montana asked.

Kate glanced down at her dress. "If I've been tagged, I don't know where they would have hidden it." She tugged at the bodice of her gown. "I barely have room in this dress for me."

Montana reached for his tuxedo jacket, which had ended up on the floor of the limousine.

He checked every pocket, carefully feeling for anything out of the ordinary, no matter how small. When he came up empty, he handed the jacket to Kate.

She repeated the search, while Montana checked his trouser pockets.

He dug deeply into each, checking every corner. Then he went still and his lips thinned into a straight line. "Son of a bitch."

Montana pulled his hand out of his pocket and held up a tiny metal disk the size of a watch battery.

Chapter Ten

"You found it?" Duff turned and stared over the back of the seat.

Kate took the device from Montana's hand. "Someone probably slipped it into your pocket in the crush of guests at the club."

"We need to ditch it before those goons circle back for round two of bumper cars," Sam said.

Kate lowered the window on the undamaged side of the limousine and cocked her arm.

Montana grabbed her wrist before she could throw the disk into the street. "Wait." He nodded toward the front windshield.

A street cleaning machine moved slowly ahead of them, brushes spinning in an effort to keep the city streets trash free.

"Switch places," Montana said.

Kate slid over his lap.

He caught her hips as she did so, squeezed gently and then let her continue to the other side of the vehicle. As they pulled up behind the street cleaner, Sam slowed to match the big machine's crawl. Montana jumped out of the moving limousine, ran up to the back of the cleaner and planted the tracker.

He returned to the limo in a matter of seconds and hopped into the backseat.

Sam drove around the cleaner and sped away, performing a number of switchbacks through the streets until they were confident they hadn't been followed.

Forty-five minutes after they'd left the yacht club, they pulled through the overhead door of the SOS building and parked in the underground garage.

Quentin, Hunter and Rip emerged from the building and surrounded the car.

"We were about to send out the posse to find you," Hunter said. "Why did you turn off your radios?"

Montana, Duff and Kate raised their hands to their ears.

"We must have dropped them in the crashes," Duff said. "No matter, we're here now. What's the news on Fontaine?"

"Last we heard, he was still in the ER," Quentin said. "Sawyer hasn't seen or heard from Tazer to know if Fontaine made it through."

Rip stepped forward and looked at the cut on Duff's forehead. "Looks like you were in a fight. What happened?"

"We'll explain inside," Duff said.

Montana pushed past the others, pulling Kate with him. "We want to know who the victim is and see for ourselves who planted the poison."

Hunter fell in step behind them. "Lance and Geek are combing through the video footage of the party, trying to determine the point at which the victim and Fontaine were poisoned."

Each person took a moment to glance into the security camera. After all of them had done this, the door lock clicked and Hunter pushed through. By the time they'd reached the computer room, Kate's head was throbbing. She could barely wait to trade the dress for a long, soft T-shirt. "I'll be right back." She hurried to the infirmary, riffled through the stores of over-the-counter drugs for ibuprofen and downed two with a bottle of water.

By the time she returned to the computer room, Lance and Geek had their heads together, staring at a screen depicting the ballroom as people began to filter in.

Slowly advancing the images, they pored over the forty-five minutes before Kate's speech.

Montana scanned the crowd, looking for the man who'd died that night.

Geek pointed at the monitor. "There's Royce and Tazer, entering the ballroom."

"Look behind them." Montana leaned forward, excitement rippling through him. "See the two men following them?"

Kate leaned over Lance's shoulder. "Is that the dead guy? The one on the left?"

Montana nodded. "The guy on the floor had on a dark purple cummerbund."

"So does he," Kate whispered. "Dark hair, longish sideburns. It has to be him." She turned to Geek. "Any idea who that might be?"

"You're kidding, right?" Geek glanced up at Kate and Montana. "That's the guy who died tonight?" He shook his head and turned to another keyboard and monitor, where he clicked several keys, entered some data and then waited. Images popped up of the man shaking hands with the vice president of the United

States, with the secretary of state and with a prominent member of the United Nations. And there he was sitting with the president in the Oval Office.

"Who is he?"

"Tarek Abusaid, the Syrian ambassador, here to ask the president for assistance in peace negotiations between his country and the Islamic State fighters attempting to completely overthrow the Syrian government."

"What the hell was he doing at the yacht club gala?" Montana asked.

Geek clicked on an image of Abusaid and the man who also appeared in the gala video.

"He's a personal friend and distant cousin of the man with whom he arrived, Nizar Sayid, a naturalized US citizen born in Syria, raised in Massachusetts. Their mothers are cousins. Says here that Sayid is a pediatric oncologist at the children's hospital."

"Are we dealing with Islamic terrorists?" Sam asked.

Geek shook his head. "Not all of the people who've died or have disappeared seem to have a connection to each other or Abusaid."

Lance stood and walked to a large whiteboard with a long timeline sketched across it. He drew a short, perpendicular line on it, assigned the current date and Abusaid's name. On another portion of the board, all the names were written, with lines drawn between them and notes that had been jotted.

Montana crossed to the board and stared at the drawing.

"From what Rand Houston told us when we were

in Cancun, he was working with the two CIA agents on the human trafficking issues."

Kate pointed at Rand Houston's name and followed the line connecting him to Marcus Smith. "He worked with Marcus Smith and Oscar Melton. My bosses." She pointed at Marcus's name. "Becca's father mailed her the disk with the dates and coordinates. He thought it important enough to mail it versus hand it to her in person."

Montana touched his finger to the board where Becca's name had been written. "Becca followed a lead about a certain mercenary heading to Cancun. Through her contacts, she came to believe the mercenary was the man who'd killed her father."

Quentin joined them at the board. "Mica Brantley showed up in Cancun following her lead about an auction selling women, in her attempt to find her stepdaughter, Emily." He pointed to Emily's name. "Trevor Brantley's daughter."

"Trevor," Kate added, "according to Nigel Carruthers, the man we met tonight, was working on a special project that was taking him away from spending time with his beloved family."

"Here's something interesting we learned today," Geek said. "Carmelo DeVita, the Mexican drug lord you ran into in Mexico, is involved in more than just drugs and selling women. We knew he sold arms as well, but we learned to whom today."

Montana turned toward Geek. "Who?"

Geek glanced over his shoulder. "Syrian rebels. ISIS. The Islamic State, who are terrorizing Syria, Iraq, France, England, Belgium, and who knows where they'll strike next."

"And the Syrian ambassador was murdered tonight." Kate lifted one of the dry-erase markers, wrote "Tarek Abusaid" on the board and then drew a line between Carmelo DeVita and the Syrian ambassador. "There's the Syrian connection here. Do you suppose they used the money from the sales of the women to fund the guns and fighting?"

Montana nodded. "And what better way to stir up more trouble in Syria than to kill the ambassador who had come to talk peace?"

"What do you want to bet there's a connection between Trevor Brantley, the CIA agents and the gun-running to Syria?"

Kate looked at the board. "Who's Cassandra Teirney?"

"She was heavily involved in kidnapping the women," Duff said.

"Cassandra is just one of her many names," Geek said, without looking away from the monitor. "She spent time in prison for identity theft. She's been seen in and around DC. Our sources think she bases out of this area and reports to someone. She's smart, but not necessarily smart enough to pull off something as big as murdering a dozen people and not leaving a crumb for us to—" Geek cursed. "Speak of the devil, check this out."

Montana crossed to the bank of monitors and followed the cursor Geek was using to point to a woman in the crowded ballroom.

He enlarged the woman's face, made a copy of it and dropped it into another program. "If it's who I think it is, we should have a hit in five, four, three—" He pointed to the monitor as a woman dressed in prison orange came up next to the face he'd pulled from the ballroom. Below the woman in orange was the name Carol Anthony, alias Catherine Tilley, alias Cassandra Tyler…and the list went on.

"Cassandra Teirney," Montana said. "She was there tonight and none of us saw her."

Lance snorted. "Her hair is a different color, but it takes a lot more to change the structure of her face."

Kate leaned close to Montana. "Follow her on the video. See who she came in contact with. Maybe she was the one who planted the poison."

Segment by segment, Geek moved through the video. Cassandra made a complete circuit around the room, avoiding the SEAL waiters and managing to remain on the opposite end of the ballroom from Montana and Kate.

"There." Kate pointed. "Is that Abusaid?"

Geek backed up the video several seconds and played it forward slowly.

"There it is again," Kate said. "She stopped to talk with Sayid and shook hands with Abusaid. She didn't shake hands with Sayid."

They watched it again to confirm, and then followed Abusaid as he stood quietly through Kate's speech and the children's choir. Then a waiter carrying hors d'oeuvres stopped beside Sayid and Abusaid. Sayid selected one of the fancy crackers from the tray and popped it into his mouth.

Abusaid declined and the waiter moved on.

The two men chatted and talked with others. Abusaid yawned, covering his mouth with his right hand, and then used the same hand to rub his eyes. He blinked and rubbed them again. He reached out with his left hand to his friend, as if in distress. Sayid hooked his elbow and had him tip his head back. Abusaid refused, seeming unable to open his eyes.

A moment later he clutched his throat and fell to his knees.

The crowd shifted around him, blocking the view.

"He didn't ingest the poison," Montana said. "He rubbed it into his eyes. His body absorbed it faster that way."

"What about Royce?" Lance said. "Back it up. See if he touched Abusaid's hand at any point."

They backed up the video to where Royce entered the ballroom with Tazer. Geek rolled the footage and they followed Royce through the room. He chatted with several people and at one point bent to retrieve something from the floor. When he straightened, Kate gasped. "It's Cassandra, and he's handing her what looks like a glove."

Montana's fists clenched. "The glove with the poison, I'll bet."

KATE COULDN'T BELIEVE this had all happened in front of them and she hadn't seen any of it. She'd been searching for someone carrying a gun or a detonator.

In the video, Cassandra snatched the glove and turned away as a man stepped up to speak with Royce.

"That's Nigel Carruthers," Mica Brantley said from behind Kate.

She spun to face the woman entering the computer room.

Mica smiled at Kate. "I can't get over how much you look like me." Then she turned back to the monitor. "Nigel was rude tonight. Kate, I don't know how you refrained from slapping his face. I would have, had I been there in person. He had no right to judge my husband."

"Mica." After having the widow in her head all evening, Kate couldn't bring herself to address her as Mrs. Brantley. "Carruthers mentioned something about a project your husband was working on. Did he share any details of his work with you?"

She shook her head. "When he retired from the financial industry, I knew it was a mistake. The man couldn't sit still for long before he was climbing the walls. He said he wanted to do something that made a difference, not just something that made money. He started going out for coffee more often. Said he was meeting up with friends." She smiled. "I thought he was having an affair."

Kate's heart constricted at the sadness reflected in Mica's eyes.

The widow continued, "When I confronted him with my concerns, he laughed and kissed me, telling me no one could take my place. I was what made everything he did worthwhile. He wanted me to be happy and proud of him. He swore he'd never have an affair with another woman. That he had all the women he wanted in his life with his daughter and me."

That was all any woman wanted to hear. Kate found herself envying what Mica had with her husband.

Mica shrugged. "I believed him. And I still do. He was a terrible liar. When he had secrets he didn't try to lie about them, he made himself scarce to protect us."

"Was he gone a lot?" Montana asked.

"Sometimes he'd leave in the middle of the night and be back in the morning. Other times he'd go out for coffee and not come back until late at night. He said he was working on a project and hoped to tell me all about it someday."

"Do you know who he was working with?" Kate asked.

She shook her head. "No. I was busy organizing sponsors for the gala. I didn't pay much attention after he assured me he wasn't having an affair. Trevor got phone calls. Some of them I answered, and they were from men, not women. Nigel would call as well, to see if Trevor wanted to play golf. Trevor always made time to play a few rounds with Nigel. Then Emily disappeared."

Kate shot a glance toward Geek.

Geek turned to his computer. "Checking phone records."

"I had gone to Paris the week Emily disappeared. I couldn't get a flight home because of weather delays." Tears welled in Mica's eyes. "Trevor and I talked every day, sometimes several times each day. By the time I got home, he was gone, too."

Tears ran down the woman's cheeks.

Kate's chest tightened. The woman had gone through so much, and had been a target herself. It was a miracle she had made it this far.

Brushing aside her tears, Mica straightened. "Trevor also had a cell phone he carried everywhere." She frowned. "I haven't really wanted to go through his things yet, otherwise I might have found it. After the funeral I was in a hurry to get away to find Emily. It was important to me to bring our sweet daughter home. My husband had dropped everything he'd been working on and focused his undivided attention on finding Emily. I'll continue the search until I bring her home."

"How did you find your way to Cancun?" Montana asked.

She brushed fresh tears from her cheeks. "My husband had some clients he'd told me about from his days as a financial analyst. He said they were connected to the Mafia." Mica glanced away. "I got into his records and looked up the names of those clients and paid a visit."

"Were they part of the DC Mafia?" Kate had heard about the crime family. They were reported to be incredibly dangerous. "You went there by yourself?"

Mica shook her head. "Oh, no. I took Rex." Her smile returned. "They were very nice and had nothing but good things to say about how Trevor helped them to invest their money wisely. When they found out I wanted their help to find Emily, they told me about the auction. I knew I couldn't get in as myself, so I had my new friends set me up as a potential client. A *male* client." She smiled across at Duff and Montana. "That's when I met the Navy SEALs. I'm sure I would have botched the whole effort if they hadn't come along when they did."

Kate's head spun. She felt like she'd missed half the conversation. So much more had happened. What had occurred over the past two days, though significant, had been just the tip of the iceberg. No wonder it took an entire whiteboard and timeline to keep track of what was going on.

A phone rang in the room and everyone looked around for the source.

Geek grabbed a receiver from the desktop and answered, "Yeah." He listened for a moment, said, "Will do," and ended the call.

Everyone in the room waited in silence.

He turned to face them. "That was Tazer. Royce is critical, but they think he'll make it. Apparently, he didn't absorb as much of the poison as Abusaid."

As one, they all heaved a sigh.

Montana broke the silence by clapping his hands. "Well, we're not getting paid to look pretty. Let's solve this case and make Royce proud."

Geek returned to his computer to look up phone records.

Kate pulled Mica aside. "Did your husband keep any records at your home?"

Mica shrugged. "Some. We have a safe in the wall. I rarely go in it, except when I need a certain piece of jewelry. He kept our will and the keys to our safe-deposit box at the bank in it."

"Have you cleaned out his files or the safe?" Kate asked.

The widow shook her head. "I really haven't been home since the funeral." She glanced down at her hands. "I haven't had the heart to go back. The house seems so cold and lonely without Trevor."

Kate took the woman's hands in hers. "Would you mind if I go there and have a look around?"

"And me?" Montana laid a hand on Kate's shoulder. "As your bodyguard, I can't let you go alone."

Mica shook her head. "Sure. Go. I'll even give you the combination. You're welcome to go through anything you want. I can't go back. It hurts too much. I keep going over and over in my mind what I could have done differently. I keep thinking that if only I had come home early from Paris, before the storms, Emily might have come to DC to meet me at the airport. She wouldn't have been abducted and Trevor would be alive and here with her. We'd go home as a family."

Kate slipped an arm around the woman's shoulders.

Mica straightened and wiped the tears from her eyes. "Maybe you'll find something the police didn't. A clue as to who did this to Trevor. And, please, look for anything that might point me to Emily. I can't imagine what she's had to endure."

Kate hugged the woman. "I won't make any promises, but we'll try. To the best of our abilities, we'll try." She looked over the top of Mica's head, her gaze capturing Montana's.

The SEAL nodded and, in that one glance, said it all. He was in it to finish it.

Hope swelled in Kate's chest. If anyone could find Emily and bring Trevor's murderer to justice, this team of SEALs and special agents could do it. Kate had to believe it. She didn't care about proving herself and reclaiming her career. Satisfaction would come from helping this woman and avenging the deaths of those who'd fallen.

Kate stood, ready to make it happen.

Chapter Eleven

Montana wasn't keen on going back out into the night after the latest attack, but the only way to solve this case was to take a few risks.

Kate refused to remove the makeup and wig, and claimed that entering the Brantley mansion as Mica would draw less attention or concern from nosy neighbors. However, she did change into dark jeans, a dark sweater and jogging shoes.

"I can't run in a tight dress and high heels, and you won't let me go barefoot," she said as she tied the laces.

Montana chuckled at her logic. He'd removed the torn tuxedo, hoping Fontaine wouldn't be out a lot of money for the damaged rental. He'd had to hit the pavement hard and fast to dodge the bullets aimed his way. Pavement wasn't kind to the fabric that made up a tux.

When they were both ready, he went in search of Geek and Lance, hoping they had some form of transportation they could borrow. He didn't trust a taxi, and the SOS limousine was out of commission.

Lance grinned when Montana approached him with his request. "Do I have some form of transportation you can take to the Brantley estate?" He crooked his finger. "Follow me." He led Montana out to the garage and used a remote control to open an interior overhead door. As the door rose toward the ceiling, Montana's pulse quickened. Inside was a sleek black Ducati motorcycle.

Lance faced Montana, his brows furrowing. "You do know how to ride a motorcycle, don't you?"

Montana nodded. "I learned to ride a motorcycle almost as soon as I learned to ride horses. We used to ride the trails around the ranch on dirt bikes for fun during the summertime."

"Good." Lance crossed to a cabinet, opened it and extracted a black leather jacket and helmet, handing them to Montana. "If those don't fit, there's more where they came from." He opened the door wider, displaying a rack of black leather jackets in all sizes and a row of helmets.

"Good, because Kate's coming with me."

"Has she ever been on the back of a bike?"

"I don't know, but we'll find out soon enough," he said.

Lance grinned. "I'll let her know you're ready and waiting."

Montana selected a jacket and helmet for Kate, guessing at her size. Then he pushed the bike out of the storage area and started the engine. Rather than roaring and rumbling like most of the motorcycles he'd ever ridden, this bike had a muffler system that made it sound like it was a big cat purring with ultimate satisfaction. The vibrations beneath him made him anxious to hit the road. He wished they had time to take the bike out in the country, where he could push it to its limits.

When Kate stepped out of the building, her brows dipped. "Is that our mode of transport?"

Montana, already wearing his helmet with the visor pulled down over his face, nodded. He tossed the jacket into her arms and held the helmet until she was ready for it. "Ever been on a bike?"

"Yes." She slipped her arms into the jacket and propped her fists on her hips. "Have you?"

"Yup." He held out the helmet. "You'll need this, if you're riding with me."

She slipped the helmet over her head and buckled the strap beneath her chin. "And what if I want to drive?"

Montana grinned behind the tinted face shield. Did the woman have any faults? She could take down a grown man, dress like a runway model and command a motorcycle. "I think I'm in love." The words came out before he could stop them. Once they were spoken, he couldn't take them back. Instead, he pretended they didn't mean anything, and scooted back on the Ducati's seat.

Kate climbed aboard. "My father was an avid cyclist. I think he wanted a boy, but he got me. So he taught me to trail ride by the time I was six and had me competing in motocross competitions by eight." She revved the engine. "You might want to hold on."

Any excuse to put his arms around her was good enough for Montana. He cinched his arms around her waist and molded his body to hers.

Lance raised the overhead door.

Even before it was all the way up, Kate drove through, racing out into the street.

Montana had to duck to keep from getting his head knocked off. "Hey! Remember, I'm a little taller than you are."

"Keep your eyes open, then." She didn't cut him any slack. He didn't really want her to.

If he believed in love at first sight, this would be what it felt like. Kate was amazing. He hoped that after this operation, he'd get to see her again.

KATE HADN'T BEEN on a bike since her father, riding his favorite Harley, was hit by a drunk driver and killed instantly. Her heartbroken mother couldn't stand the sight of her husband's collection of motorcycles. They reminded her too much of her dead husband.

Kate had been in training when her father died. They'd allowed her only a week off to come home for the funeral and then she'd had to report back, or agree to recycle and start all over.

By the time her training was over, her mother had sold all her father's motorcycles for pennies on the dollar and cleared his man-cave garage of all of his trophies. Her mother's grief had taken the form of anger at being left behind. When the anger cooled, she sold the house and moved into a condominium closer to town and went to work for a pediatrician.

Kate loved her mother, but she'd had a special bond with her father that had died when he'd died. Motorcycles would always remind her of him and the joy they'd shared when the wind blew against their faces on the open road.

Kate had committed the route to the Brantley estate to memory from the directions Geek had shown her on the monitor back at SOS headquarters. She leaned into each turn, taking them fast, but controlled.

The SEAL behind her leaned with her, their bodies in tune, like a well-choreographed couple on a dance floor. He knew how to ride. Not all men had experienced the rush of excitement or freedom one could feel on the back of a motorcycle.

All too soon she was gliding to a stop in front of the gated community in which the Brantley estate was located. She punched the code into the box and drove through the gate. A guard stepped out of the booth and waved her to a stop.

She pulled off the helmet, hoping her wig and makeup hadn't rubbed off.

"Oh, it's you, Mrs. Brantley. I didn't know you rode bikes." The guard smiled and backed away. "Good to see you again. It's been a while. Let me know if you need anything. I'm here all night."

"Thank you." Kate drove around the guard shack and turned left at the first street. The road curved past several massive mansions, each perfectly landscaped with designer bushes and trellises.

Kate pulled into the driveway at the end of the road.

Montana climbed off first and then helped her put the kickstand down.

They walked up to the door together. Montana inserted the key Mica had given Kate and they entered. Kate reset the alarm beside the door and looked around. The foyer was a large open area with marble-tiled flooring and a sweeping, curved staircase leading to the second floor. Kate turned to the right and entered Trevor Brantley's study. Lined in rich wood paneling, the room had bookshelves from the floor to the ten-foot ceilings.

"I'll check out what's in the safe," Montana said. "You take the file cabinet, since you have the key."

"Deal." Kate crossed the room to the built-in file

cabinet that blended into the wood paneling. The key unlocked the drawers, allowing her to open them one at a time.

She riffled through file after file, skimming, looking—for what, she didn't know. Were there any clients he'd had in the past who thought he'd taken advantage of them?

Kate searched for red flags, notes or something that would indicate trouble. Since Trevor had been found in that very study, the police concluded he'd been murdered by someone he knew. There were no signs of struggle. He'd been shot point-blank in the heart and had died instantly.

Kate noticed a dark stain on the Persian carpet in the middle of the floor. She suspected it was Trevor Brantley's dried blood. She wondered if he'd felt any pain or if he'd just ceased to exist. What had been his last thought as the monster who'd claimed his life pressed the gun to his chest?

After going through all four drawers, Kate concluded there were no clues to be found. Not any she could see. She turned to where Montana stood in front of the wall safe Trevor had hidden behind a painting of a racehorse. Her partner was removing documents one at a time, reading through them.

He glanced across at her. "Want to go through them in case I'm missing something important?"

She took the papers and scanned them quickly. One was a will. It had the standard wording, giving Mica everything, with a portion of his life insurance going to his daughter. A trust fund had been set up in Emily's name to pay her a monthly stipend for as long as she lived.

Kate's heart clenched. Emily could already have passed. But until they found her body, Kate refused to believe the young woman was dead.

"Other than the will, a stack of bonds and the key to their safe-deposit box, I don't see anything that raises a flag."

"Then just hand over that key and we can call it a day," a voice said from across the room.

Kate spun to face a woman wielding a pistol with a silencer affixed to the end.

Montana stepped a little ahead of her, placing his body between the woman and Kate. "Cassandra. Or is it Carol? Which did you prefer to go by in prison?"

She snorted. "They called me Bulldog because once I sink my teeth into something, I don't let go."

"I take it you sank your teeth into Brantley and didn't let go until he was dead," Kate said.

Cassandra shrugged. "He was the job. Nothing more. Just like you two are only a means to an end. Brantley refused to give me what I came for."

Kate held up the bank key. "Were you after this?"

Cassandra's eyes narrowed. "If that's the key to the safe-deposit box, yes."

"You know you can't get into it without me," Kate said, glad she hadn't removed her disguise.

"Yeah, well, I know how to get you to cooperate with me." She smiled like she knew a secret.

"And if I don't cooperate?" Kate said.

"Your precious stepdaughter dies." Cassandra lifted a shoulder. "Pretty simple, even for a rich bitch."

Kate's heartbeat rattled against her ribs. "How do I know you're not lying about Emily?"

She lowered her eyelids and gave Kate a sneering

smile. "Are you willing to risk her life for whatever's in that box?"

It was Kate's turn to shrug. "I don't believe you have her. I think you're bluffing."

"All I have to do is call and they'd slice her throat." Cassandra's eyes narrowed into slits. "Don't make me mad."

Kate lifted her chin and stared down her nose at the woman. "Give me proof of life and I might give you the key and take you to the bank to let you into the box."

Cassandra's eyes remained narrowed. "How about I just shoot you and take the key?"

"What part of 'you can't get in without me' did you not understand?" Kate asked. "That's how safe-deposit boxes work. You have to have the account holder present to get into it."

Cassandra glared at her. "Don't talk down to me. You're the one on the other end of a gun barrel." She wiped sweat from her forehead.

Kate studied the woman.

Her face was flushed, her eyes bloodshot and red-rimmed. Blood dripped from her left nostril. She raised her arm and wiped the blood away with the back of her sleeve.

"What do you want in the safe-deposit box, Cassandra?" Kate asked.

"*I* couldn't care less about what's in it. The man I work for wants whatever Brantley put in there."

Kate moved forward, holding the key out. "Cassandra—or is it Carol—you don't have to do what that man says. You're sick. You need to get to a doctor."

"I'm fine." She straightened, clutching the gun in

both hands. Her arms trembled, causing the gun to shake. "Just give me the key."

Montana held a slim box in his hand, still standing in the same position he'd been in when Cassandra made her presence known. "You're suffering effects from the poison," he said softly. "Turn yourself in and get some medical attention before it's too late."

"What's it to you? You think I don't know you're one of those muscle-bound jokers who got in my way in Cancun? You and your SEAL friends, living the easy life, vacationing at resorts, sleeping with your favorite flavor of female every day. If I turn myself in, what do I have to look forward to? Going back to jail?" She spat on the floor at Montana's feet. "No way. I make good money working for my boss. I'd rather die than go back to that hellhole."

"You might get your wish," Kate said. "The poison won't stop until you're dead. You saw what it did to Abusaid. If you want to live, you need to get to a hospital right away."

"Abusaid deserved to die. He says he wants peace, but all he really wants is the money to keep flowing, the guns to be delivered and the fighting to continue. As long as his country is at war, he'll continue to make a lot of money."

Kate pressed the woman for answers. "What does Abusaid have to do with Trevor or Emily Brantley?"

"What do any of you have to do with Abusaid, or Senator Houston, or those women I stood to make a crap ton of money on at the auction in Cancun? If you don't see how it all ties together, you deserve to die in ignorance." Cassandra raised the gun with the silencer.

By then, her arms shook so badly she could barely keep the barrel parallel to the floor.

Kate bunched her muscles. The woman would have to shoot one or the other of them, but she wouldn't be able to shoot both the way her hands shook.

"You don't owe your boss anything, Cassandra," Kate said, inching across the floor, trying to get close enough to throw herself at the woman. "Go now. Get to a hospital. Choose to live."

"Blah, blah, blah. That's all I hear. Don't you ever shut up?" Blood ran from Cassandra's nose as her gaze narrowed and she shifted her weapon to Kate. "Just die."

Kate dived for the floor, rolled to the right and came up on her haunches.

Something flew through the air, hitting Cassandra in the face. The gun went off and the next few seconds were a blur of motion.

Montana tackled Cassandra, knocking the gun from her hand. It skittered across the floor, well out of her reach.

The woman lay beneath Montana, her breathing ragged, foam bubbling from the corner of her mouth. "Doesn't matter. He'll get the money any way he has to. You can't stop what he's put in place."

Montana straddled Cassandra's hips, pinning her wrists above her head. "What who put in place?"

Cassandra coughed, blood mixing with the foam dribbling down the side of her face.

"Who are you working for, Cassandra?" Kate asked softly.

Cassandra snorted. "Doesn't matter. You're all going

to die." She laughed, the sound turning into a hacking cough.

Montana rose to his feet, kicked the gun farther out of Cassandra's reach and patted down her legs and sides.

Kate walked to the phone on the huge mahogany desk in the middle of the room and dialed 911. "Send an ambulance to this location. We have a woman down. We suspect she's been poisoned."

While Montana stood guard over Cassandra, Kate grabbed a woven throw blanket from a wingback chair and spread it over her. "The poison you used on Abusaid is extremely potent. You might not pull through," she said as she tucked the blanket around Cassandra.

"No one will miss me," she said, her voice cracking, filled with the rattling sound of liquid filling her lungs.

"Why protect the man you work for? He gave you the poison to use, didn't he? Did he tell you it could kill you, as well? Tell me his name, Cassandra," Kate pleaded. "Don't let him get away with killing you."

She stared up at Kate. "He was the only man who ever saw me as anything other than a criminal." Her body shook with the effort. Even after she stopped coughing, she continued to tremble.

Kate nodded. "He must have seen something special in you. Someone he trusted."

"He had to trust me. Anyone else would have turned him in." She smiled and closed her eyes. "Not me. He saved me from spending my life behind bars. He gave me a purpose."

"Who is he?" Kate asked again.

With her eyes still closed, Cassandra whispered, "Your worst nightmare. The judge, jury and executioner." Her words faded and her breathing became shallower.

Kate stared across at Montana, her heart hitting the bottom of her stomach. She couldn't help feeling sorry for the woman, even after she'd tried to kill her. No one deserved to die. Especially such a horrible death, with poison destroying her from the inside.

"What do you think she means by our worst nightmare?" Kate asked.

Montana's lips thinned. "He's been that all along."

Cassandra's mouth moved.

Kate leaned closer to hear the woman's last words.

"You ain't seen nothing yet."

Chapter Twelve

Montana and Kate waited until the ambulance took Cassandra away and the police had processed the crime scene. Nothing they could have done would bring the woman back to life. The poison had taken its toll and put the woman out of her misery and theirs.

Kate had called back to SOS headquarters, reporting what had happened with Cassandra. Becca had taken the call, promising to look more closely at the data they'd compiled on the woman. There had to be some small detail they'd missed that would link her to the man who called the shots.

When the room was clear, Montana held up the key to the safe-deposit box. "We need to touch base with Mica and see what she wants to do about this."

"I'd go to the bank for her," Kate said, "but I'm sure she'll want to see what's in the box herself."

"Either way, it'll be morning before the bank officials can open the vault. We should call it a day."

As they left the house, Kate seemed distant, almost withdrawn.

Montana wanted to pull her into his arms and hold her, but they'd had a long day and needed to make it back to headquarters and get some sleep. Tomorrow might turn out to be just as difficult. They needed rest to fuel their bodies for the fight.

He slipped his helmet on and waited for Kate to mount the bike.

She buckled her helmet and shook her head. "You drive."

He didn't argue, just took the front seat and waited for her to slide on behind him.

When her arms slid around his middle, he laid his hand over hers and squeezed gently. No words were spoken; just that little bit of skin-to-skin contact was enough for now.

Montana started the engine and drove out of the gated community. As he passed through the streets of DC he was careful to scan the road and side roads in front of him as well as check the rearview mirror. The last thing he wanted to do was lead the assassins back to the SOS building. One bombing in a week was enough.

In the silence of the drive back, he thought through what Cassandra had said. *You ain't seen nothing yet* implied more trouble to come. Possibly on a larger scale than what had already taken place. It didn't bode well for the city of DC.

As soon as he got back to HQ, he'd be sure to check the code dates and coordinates for the next event their tormenter intended to target. Perhaps they'd be better prepared this time and have poison-sniffing dogs there as well as those that sniffed out bombs.

How many ways would the man kill people? And how many mercenaries had he hired to do the job?

After a three-hundred-sixty-degree thorough check, Montana drove up to the overhead door leading into the garage of the SOS alternate site. Not certain how he'd get in, he pulled the helmet off so that the gatekeeper could identify him as one of the good guys. The overhead door opened and Montana drove in.

Once inside, they were met by Becca and Quentin.

"The rest of the gang has bedded down for the night," Quentin said.

"They've already been briefed on the Cassandra situation," Becca added. "Geek's got some information that may or may not be of use."

Montana parked the bike in the storage compartment, set his helmet on a shelf and hung the jacket in the cabinet.

Kate removed and stored her helmet and leather jacket and followed her friend Becca into the building.

Quentin hung back and waited for Montana. "How in the hell did Cassandra get past the gate guard and into the Brantley house?"

"Since we didn't hear her enter, I have to assume she was already there and waiting."

Quentin held the door for Montana. "What gets me is how she knew you two would be there."

"Maybe she didn't. Maybe she was there looking for something, just like us." Montana held up the key to the safe-deposit box. "She wanted this."

Quentin took the key and turned it over in his hands. "You'd think someone would have gone after the safe-deposit box sooner, if it was that big a deal that she'd shoot you for the key."

Montana shrugged. "I certainly don't have all the answers." As they entered the room with the computers, he glanced across at Geek. "What have you got for us?"

Geek pulled up several views on his array of monitors. "I was able to hack into the phone system and look at Brantley's records."

Montana shook his head. "Is there anything you can't get into?"

Geek grinned. "I'm still working on the Chinese military database. It might be easier if I could speak Chinese." He pointed to the monitor on the top right. "These are the phone numbers Brantley called most often. Mrs. Brantley's cell phone, his daughter Emily's cell and these four numbers show up most often. The first two I traced back to burner phones. The kind you throw away when you've used all the minutes. The last two were incoming calls from a local coffee shop."

"Why would a coffee shop be calling Brantley?"

"I asked the same question. I located the shop and looked around it for possible security systems with videos. I struck gold when I found a convenience store nearby that had a clear shot of the front entrance of the coffee shop. I was able to hack into the security system the convenience store uses. God, I love technology."

Geek pointed to another monitor with a blurry image. "On the days Brantley had incoming calls from the coffee shop, I was able to capture images of him arriving fifteen minutes after the call. That's Brantley."

Geek dragged the starting point of the video back twenty minutes. "I wanted to see who'd entered the shop right before the call to Brantley, so I backed it up about thirty minutes and ran it forward." He hit Play and ran the video in slow motion.

Several people entered and exited the coffee shop. Then one man in a jacket, wearing sunglasses and a baseball cap, approached from the opposite direction, his face in full view of the convenience store camera, but the sunglasses hiding his eyes.

"First of all, no one was wearing sunglasses that day, until this guy. That was my first clue he might be the one." Geek zoomed in on the man's face. "He had a scar on his chin that made it look like he had a dimple."

Geek zoomed in even more. "But if you look closely, it's a scar, not an indentation." He moved the cursor and zoomed in on the small, embroidered emblem on the left breast of the man's jacket that read Washington Golf and Country Club. "I could have spent the next two days searching through the registry of the country club looking for someone who could have some connection to Brantley, but Becca walked in about that time."

"What Geek's trying to tell you is that I recognized the jacket, the scar and the man." Becca drew in a deep breath. "That was my father." She bit down on her lip, her eyes suspiciously bright. "Brantley was meeting with my father. I gave my dad that jacket for his birthday last year. He got that scar playing rugby in college."

Quentin slipped an arm around Becca's waist and pulled her close. "We have to assume Brantley's project had something to do with what Marcus Smith and Oscar Melton were working on. Which includes the dates and coordinates, the human trafficking in Cancun and the hits on various, seemingly unrelated people."

Montana stared at the man on the screen. "Which comes back to the question, what did all these people have in common?" He moved to the whiteboard with the names listed, to find a line drawn connecting Brantley to the CIA agents.

"I'm still working on it," Geek said. "I feel like I'm

on the verge of connecting all the dots. That is, if we have all the dots on the board."

Becca laid a hand on Geek's shoulder. "Maybe if you get some sleep, you'll be fresh to start back at it in the morning."

Geek shook his head. "I don't need to sleep. I'm too wound up. I might as well keep going. I want to know who's responsible for all the trouble." His lips thinned. "The boss deserves to know."

Becca turned to Lance, who'd continued to search the internet the entire time Geek was talking. "What about you, Lance?"

"I'm with Geek. I want to know who did this." He and Geek exchanged a glance and nodded. They went back to work, combing through news articles and images.

"Is there anything we can do to help?" Montana asked.

Kate slipped her hand in his. "I can man a computer."

"No, we'd probably just duplicate effort," Geek said. "Besides, you two have been through enough tonight."

Montana led Kate to the office she'd been assigned as her sleeping quarters. "Need help getting out of that wig?"

She shook her head. "I can manage. But I could use some help a little later getting that bed out again."

Montana nodded. "Count on it." He left her in the hallway and continued to the room he was supposed to be sharing with the guys.

Becca stepped out of one of the offices and blocked his way.

He started around her, but she moved in front of him. "Montana, you got a minute?"

"Sure."

She led him into the office and closed the door behind him. "You and Kate seem to be hitting it off working as partners."

He stiffened. "Yeah. She's smart and knows how to take care of herself."

"There's a reason for that. She's been through a pretty nasty relationship."

He held up his hands. "Whoa. Wait a minute. Are you about to give me the warning about not hurting your friend?"

Becca's cheeks flushed pink. "Yeah. I guess I am." She touched his arm. "I know you're a good guy. I'm just worried about Kate. The mess with Alex nearly destroyed her career and her trust in men."

Montana's lips thinned. He'd like to put his fist through the guy's face. "I'm not Alex."

"I know that. Just don't break her heart. She's been there and done that."

"I've only known Kate for a couple days. When we're done here, I'll be headed back to Mississippi. She's got her work here in DC."

"My point exactly." Becca nodded. "Just keep that in mind. That's all I wanted to say."

Montana turned, reached for the door handle and paused. "How long did it take for you to realize you were in love with Quentin?"

Becca laughed. "Who said I was in love with the self-proclaimed Loverboy?"

Montana faced her, his eyes narrowing.

"Fine. I love the big galoot." Becca sighed. "I knew

the day he pulled me out of the alligator-infested swamp in Mississippi. Less than a week after we met. I would have known sooner if I hadn't been so determined *not* to fall for the guy. But our situation is different. We've known each other longer and I wasn't heartbroken by my first love. Kate is fragile."

Montana laughed out loud. "Kate, the woman who could take down a man with one hand tied behind her back and can drive the hell out of a Ducati?"

"I didn't say she was physically fragile. But you don't want to be her rebound guy."

"What do you mean?"

"You know. The guy a girl falls for right after being dumped. Those kinds of relationships don't last."

Montana shook his head. "And you have statistics to back that up?"

Becca shook her head in turn. "No."

"Just so you know, my father was my mother's rebound man after her first husband died from a fatal fall in a rodeo." Montana captured her gaze and held it. "They're still married and more in love than when they first got together. Rebound matches can work. And for the record, Kate's smart, sexy and genuinely good. I'd never break her heart." *But she might break mine.*

Becca gave him a brief smile. "That's all I wanted to hear. Thanks for letting me be a friend to Kate."

Montana hesitated, wanting to be angry with Becca, but understanding why she'd given him *the talk.* "You go right on being a friend. Kate needs them." Montana left the room and continued to the dorm where his stuff was stored. Grabbing a clean shirt and shorts, he headed for the shower and scrubbed away the feeling that he shouldn't go back to Kate's little office with the hide-a-bed. But he'd promised.

KATE HAD MORE trouble removing the wig and makeup than she'd expected. By the time she returned to her room as a natural blonde, it was close to two o'clock in the morning. She entered to find the bed had been pulled out, the sheets smoothed and no Montana.

Disappointment filled her chest. After all they'd been through that day, she'd imagined snuggling with him for the rest of the night. After being shot at, nearly poisoned and run off the road, she wanted…no, she needed the security of his arms around her. Short of marching down the hallway and demanding to know why he hadn't stayed, she didn't have any other choice but to sleep alone.

Kate crawled into the bed and pulled the sheet and blanket up to her chin, feeling more alone than she had since her father died.

Montana had fulfilled his promise to help her with the bed. He was probably supertired and knew if he stayed with her, they'd end up making love again.

Then a horrible thought occurred to her and she shot up to a sitting position. Had he been less than impressed by her lovemaking prowess? Rather than come back again for a second night, was he trying to tell her he wasn't interested?

Kate sank into the mattress. Funny how she hadn't noticed how lumpy it was the night before. She hadn't noticed anything but what Montana was doing to every inch of her body.

God, she missed him. What kind of fool would she be if she fell in love with the SEAL? She had her life as a CIA agent in Washington, DC. He was stationed in Mississippi, on call and highly deployable to some of the worst hellholes in the world. Any woman would be an idiot to fall in love with a man like that. And he'd be even dumber to fall for a CIA agent with a job such as his.

These thoughts went round and round in her head, keeping her awake for the next two hours. Exhausted beyond insanity, she finally fell into a troubled sleep filled with dreams of friends being poisoned, the people she should have trusted turning against her and the man she feared she was falling in love with walking away without saying goodbye.

By the time she woke the next morning, she felt more exhausted than when she'd gone to sleep. Rather than lie in bed and try to sleep longer, she jumped up, dressed in shorts, a sweatshirt and her running shoes, and went for a jog. Maybe the rush of wind in her face would blow the man from her mind and she could get back to work. *Yeah, and pigs really could fly.*

Chapter Thirteen

Throughout the night, Montana tossed in his bunk, praying he could get even an hour of sleep. By six, he was done trying. He got out of bed and slipped into jogging shorts, a T-shirt and running shoes. He let Lance know he was on his way out and slipped out a side door of the building into an alley.

A few minutes later he was running down the street, headed for the river, hoping for somewhere open and green amid the concrete jungle of the capital.

Once he reached the river, he ran for a couple miles until his body had reached its limit, then he turned around and ran back the way he'd come, pushing himself faster and faster. No matter how hard he worked or how fast he ran, he couldn't get Kate out of his mind. In fact, he could swear he was starting to hallucinate when he saw a woman ahead of him with the same sandy-blond, shoulder-length hair, trim waist and tight calves as Kate.

His pulse quickened and he ran faster. Not until he was less than a block behind her did he realize he was running after a perfect stranger. What would he have done if he'd caught up to her? She might have screamed for the police and accused him of being a stalker.

Montana slowed.

The woman ahead turned at a crosswalk.

Kate.

Montana's heart skipped several beats and then raced, shooting blood and adrenaline through his system like a fire hose at full pressure.

Kate stepped off the curb and jogged across the intersection.

Montana hurried after her, reaching the crosswalk as the red hand blinked a warning to stop. He ignored it and sprinted after her.

Horns honked and a car nearly clipped him as he reached the other side of the street.

Kate glanced over her shoulder at the traffic, spotted him and stumbled. She righted herself and continued to jog, not bothering to slow down and wait for him.

Montana supposed he deserved it for the previous night. She'd more or less invited him to share her bed and he'd been altruistic—sneaked in, pulled out the bed and ran back to his own room before she emerged from the shower. He'd known if he saw her again, he wouldn't be able to walk away.

He told himself he should let her return to headquarters at her own pace, and give her the space she needed. But his body had different ideas.

He ran faster.

Kate sped up, keeping ahead of him, until they were both running all out. By the time they reached the block where the SOS building was located, Montana's lungs and calves burned and he couldn't catch his breath. He slowed, finally giving up. If she didn't want to see him, he shouldn't bust his butt trying to force the issue.

Kate must have come to a similar conclusion at

about the same time. She stopped running and bent double, resting her hands on her knees, dragging in deep, gasping breaths.

"Go ahead," she said. "If this is a race, I concede."

Montana joined her and walked the rest of the way to the side entrance of the building. "I'm sorry."

She stiffened beside him. "For what?"

"For not waiting for you to get back from the shower."

Kate shrugged. "Why should you have waited? I asked you to help with the bed and you did. The end."

As they came to a stop in front of the door, Montana gripped her arms and turned her to face him. "I left because I didn't want to take advantage of you."

"Take advantage?" She knocked his hands from her arms. "What kind of man-logic is that?"

"I don't know." He shoved a hand through his sweaty hair. "I'm not a mind reader. I don't know what a woman wants."

"Obviously. When a woman says she wants you to help her with a bed, it's a sign she wants you to stick around to test the springs." Kate turned toward the door, entered the code and let herself in.

Montana followed. "You're still getting over the first man you fell in love with. I'm just your rebound lover."

Kate stopped and turned slowly, shaking her head. "Rebound? Sweetheart, I'm *way* over my first love. In fact, I'm not certain I ever really loved him. Now *you*, on the other hand, are a man and you think just because a woman sleeps with you, she's falling in love with you. Trust me. Just because I slept with you doesn't mean I plan on keeping you around or committing my life to you. I was just looking for a little fun."

Montana's chest tightened. "Is that all? You just want to have fun?"

"Yeah. Then when this is all over, you can go your way and I can go mine. No one gets hurt. Nobody's heart gets broken. Hell, we barely know each other."

"Darlin', you've read me all wrong. I'm not the kind of man who falls in and out of bed so carelessly. *You* might not want to fall in love, but maybe that's what *I* want." He gripped her arms and pulled her against him. "I thought we had a connection. I also thought I was rushing you, so I didn't come to you last night. Not because I didn't want to. Oh, I wanted to. But I didn't want to push you too soon after the hell you'd gone through. Damn it, Kate, I like you. Everything about you, especially kissing you and holding you close. I think you're special, and I want more than just to have fun."

Then he kissed her, his lips crashing down on hers. He pushed his tongue past her teeth and swept the length of hers in a kiss that stole his breath away.

When he was done, he stepped away, dropping his hands to his sides. "That's just who I am. So sue me."

Kate grabbed him around the back of his neck and pressed her finger to his mouth. "Don't you ever shut up?" Before he could answer, she kissed him hard, her tongue searching for and finding his. When she stopped, she backed away, turned and ran.

Montana shook his head. "I don't think I'll ever understand women."

BY THE TIME Kate showered and dressed in jeans and a T-shirt, her pulse had slowed and she could almost make sense of her thoughts again. But no matter how many times she replayed what had happened in the alley, she couldn't believe she'd heard Montana right.

He *wanted* to fall in love?

Most men in his position just wanted to love 'em and leave 'em. Not strings-attached sex. From the beginning, she'd known Montana was different. That's what she loved about him.

Kate passed on breakfast and hurried to the conference room, where she found Geek and Lance hunkered over their keyboards. By the stubble on their chins and the dark circles beneath their eyes, she knew they'd been up all night.

Geek glanced over his shoulder. "Kate. I'm glad you're here. Where's the rest of the gang?"

Becca entered the room. "I'm here. Who else do you want?"

"Everyone. I have something to show you."

Becca left the room and returned with six SEALs, Sam Russell and Natalie. "This is everyone but Fontaine and Tazer. Show us what you've got."

"I knew there had to be a connection to everyone on that board. I just couldn't seem to find it." Geek clicked the keyboard and brought up a view of the Syrian, Abusaid, standing among a group of Caucasians with an American flag on display behind them.

"I did a search on the internet for Abusaid and found this image, taken three years ago at the American embassy in Turkey. Abusaid worked there as a liaison between the Americans and the Syrian government. It was right around that time when there was a car bomb attack at that embassy. Several people were killed in that attack, including this man." Geek pointed to the figure standing beside Abusaid. "That's Patrick Skinner."

Montana shook his head. "Who the hell is Patrick Skinner?"

"Bear with me," Geek said. "I asked the same thing. But I focused my attention first on the Syrian. I found articles about Abusaid visiting Mexico..." Geek pulled up a media picture of Abusaid standing in front of a huge building in the bright sunshine. "This is him at the Mexican parliament building, and there he is again in Cancun, greeting Mexican officials at one of the posh resort hotels. If you look at the man in the background, surrounded by guys in black shirts, you might recognize him."

Montana's gut clenched. "Carmelo DeVita."

"DeVita, the Mexican drug lord?" Kate asked, leaning close to Montana, her gaze on the monitor.

"He believed in diversifying his portfolio of illegal operations to include drug running, arms sales and human trafficking." Montana's fists clenched. "So Abusaid could have been involved in DeVita's activities."

"Not only *could* he, he *was*. I verified it by going back to DeVita's foreign bank accounts and tracing a link between them and Abusaid's in Turkey. Then I noticed large sums of money moving from Abusaid's account to a Swiss bank account ultimately traceable back to Patrick Skinner."

"Who the hell is Patrick Skinner?" Duff stepped up beside Montana.

"That's where it gets even more interesting." All traces of fatigue seemed to vanish from Geek's face as he warmed to his tale. "Patrick Skinner was the son

of multibillionaire Thomas Skinner and his wife, Angela. And get this, Angela brought a son to that marriage and a considerable fortune from her family and
her first husband's holdings. You might have heard one
of her names. Angela Preston *Carruthers* Skinner."

Montana leaned closer. "Carruthers. Isn't he the man
who was all in Kate's face last night at the gala?"

"*Mica's* face. He thought he was talking to Mica,"
Kate corrected. She walked to the whiteboard and
wrote Carruthers's name in the middle of the diagram
and drew a line between him and Brantley. Then she
wrote Skinner's name and drew lines between Skinner and Carruthers, Skinner and Abusaid, and Abusaid
and DeVita. "Carruthers could be our missing link that
pulls all of the events together." A chill rippled across
her skin and she shot a glance toward Montana. "He
could be the one orchestrating this whole operation."

"He could be the one who had been working with
assassins to steer the CIA away from what was happening in Cancun."

"Do we have enough evidence to go after him?"
Sawyer asked.

Geek shook his head. "Lance and I have been at it all
night. All we have are loose connections between Carruthers, Brantley and this Patrick Skinner. We haven't
traced any money movement from Carruthers's bank
accounts to any of the others."

"All we do know," Lance said, "is that three years
ago, he was worth a lot of money. His bank account
today is looking pretty bare."

"Do you think he was getting his money to pay the
assassins through his connections with DeVita's ille-

gal activities?" Kate asked, feeling excitement building. This could be the break they'd been searching for.

"We don't know at this point."

"We need to find out what's in that safe-deposit box that he wanted so badly," Montana said. He held up the key.

Kate frowned. "I thought you gave that to Quentin last night."

"I did, to keep it safe for the night." Montana glanced toward the door. "Where's Mrs. Brantley?"

"I'm here." Mica entered the room. "What safe-deposit box?"

"We found the key in your home safe last night."

Mica nodded. "Duff was good enough to fill me in on what happened at my house. I'm glad you and Kate made it out all right." She held out her hand.

Montana dropped the key onto her palm.

She studied it. "I hadn't even thought about the safe-deposit box."

Kate's heart twisted. "You had more important things on your mind." She moved to stand in front of the widow. "If you want, I can go to the bank as you and look inside the box."

"No." Mica curled her fingers around the key. "I'll do it. I've relied too much on you already."

"I don't mind at all."

"Let me guess." Mica smiled. "It beats desk duty." The widow pushed back her shoulders and lifted her chin. "I'll go. But I'll need someone to be my Rex."

"I'll go with you," Rex said, stepping into the room behind her. He was still pale and he held his arm close to his side as if he was in a lot of pain from the wound there.

Mica patted his cheek. "Thank you, Rex. You're wonderfully loyal, but I need someone who can run if he needs to. I need you to get well so that you can take up your duties again in the near future."

Rex frowned.

Mica laughed. "Don't worry. I have no plans to replace you. I like having you around." She returned her attention to Montana. "Since you did such a good job protecting my doppelgänger last night, I'd like you to accompany me to the bank. Do I need to call for my car?"

Montana cast a glance toward Kate.

She grinned and nodded.

Turning back to Mrs. Brantley, Montana asked, "How are you at riding on the back of a motorcycle?"

Chapter Fourteen

It was obvious Mrs. Brantley had never been on the back of a motorcycle. Despite the quick briefing he'd given her, she still didn't understand the concept of leaning into the curve.

They managed to get to the bank unharmed, and Mrs. Brantley met with Mr. Carmichael, the bank manager, to gain access into the vault. She insisted Montana accompany her.

Once inside, they located the box number. The bank manager used her key to unlock it and pull it out of the slot, setting it on a table in the middle of the room.

"Take all the time you need, Mrs. Brantley." The bank manager backed toward the door. "When you're done, use the intercom to let me know you're ready to come out."

"Thank you," she said, her attention already turned toward the contents.

"My husband was a big believer in savings and investments," she said as she lifted out dozens of bond certificates, setting them in a neat stack beside the box. "I guess it's natural for a man who made his living as a financial planner for some of the wealthiest people in this country and abroad." She bit her bottom lip and pulled out a ring box. "Oh my. I thought he'd sold this a long time ago."

"What is it?"

She opened the box. A modest diamond engagement ring nestled in the black velvet. The band was a little dull, but the diamond sparkled, reflecting the overhead lights in a tiny rainbow of colors. "It was my first engagement ring. He'd had to take out a loan to purchase it. When he started making more money, he bought me this one." She held up her hand. On her ring finger was a large square diamond that had to be at least three carats. "I never told him that I preferred the original. He was so proud of himself that he'd done well enough to give me the ring he thought I deserved."

She set the box aside and lifted more papers out. Some were deeds to properties. There were more bonds and stock certificates.

At the bottom of the box was a plain, yellow, legal-sized envelope.

Mica removed the envelope and folded back the metal brads. Two sheets of paper were inside. The first, she handed to Montana. "It appears to be a list of banks and account numbers. By the look of the names, they're Swiss."

Montana studied the paper while Mrs. Brantley read the second document.

Silence stretched between them. When Montana glanced toward the widow, his heart contracted.

Tears streamed down her cheeks and silent sobs shook her body.

He stepped toward her and slipped an arm around her shoulders. "What is it?"

She didn't say, just held out the sheet of paper and pressed a hand to her mouth, the tears continuing to fall as Montana took it from her.

Dearest Mica,
If you're reading this letter, I'm either comatose or have passed. In either case, I'm not around to answer questions. You always left the finances up to me, trusting me to do what was right. You loved and trusted me completely. I hope I've lived up to your trust.

In the event of my demise, I want you to know how very much I love you and wish you to be happy. I don't want you to suffer in any way, and wish for you to go on living a full and happy life. If it means falling in love again, I hope that you will. You are the light of my life and everything I could have dreamed of in a lifelong partner.

Take care of yourself and continue to love Emily like you always have, like the mother she needed.

Give her my love and know that I love you, too. You will be forever in my heart.

Love,
Trevor
P.S. The accounts listed in this packet are where you can find the proceeds from some of my more lucrative investments. I put aside the earnings for a rainy day. There's enough there that you shouldn't have to worry about money for the rest of your life.

Without uttering a word, Montana pulled Mrs. Brantley close.

She buried her face in his shirt and sobbed. For several minutes she poured her heart out in grief. When she had soaked his shirt through, she straightened and looked up at him through red-rimmed eyes. "I'm sorry."

"Don't be. You're allowed to grieve."

"I didn't let myself cry through the viewing or his funeral. I held it together when my heart was breaking into a million pieces. It was the promise I made to myself that I'd find Emily and bring her home that kept me strong." She sniffed and more tears slipped down her cheeks. "And I've failed so miserably."

"It's not over yet," Montana assured her. "We have a lead now. Hopefully, it'll help us find your daughter."

She nodded. "In the meantime, we should take this with us. The stocks and bonds aren't nearly as liquid as Swiss bank accounts. If Cassandra was after something of value, it would be these."

Montana helped Mrs. Brantley replace the paper certificates of stocks, bonds and deeds in the drawer.

Mica slid the ring box into the envelope with the letter and the account numbers, and crossed to the intercom. "We're ready to leave," she said into the speaker.

A moment later the vault door opened and Mr. Carmichael escorted them out.

The ride back to the SOS building was uneventful. Mrs. Brantley held on to Montana, the envelope tucked into her jacket for safekeeping.

Rex met them in the garage, wrapped his good arm around Mrs. Brantley and ushered her inside, where he supplied her with a cup of hot tea and made her eat some crackers.

After Montana stowed the bike and gear, he returned to the conference room, his heart heavy, his body tense with the need for action.

"How did it go?" Kate turned as he entered.

"It was hard," he said, his jaw tight, his fists clenched. "From the little I know about Trevor Brantley, he was a good man who loved his wife and daughter. He didn't deserve to die."

"Agreed." Kate turned away, but not before Montana saw the mist in her eyes. She stared over Geek's head at the computer monitors. "So what are we going to do about it?"

"We need to check into Carruthers," Montana said.

"Meaning?"

"We need to get inside his house, his business, his anything and find out what he's all about."

"That's breaking and entering," Kate pointed out. "You could go to jail for that."

"Do you think I give a damn about breaking the law? If that man had anything to do with all of the murders, he needs to be stopped before another life is lost."

"So when do we leave?" Duff stepped up beside Montana.

"We need to know where he lives and where his businesses are."

Geek hit a key on his keyboard and a printer spit out a sheet of paper. "Carruthers's home address in Alexandria, his office and warehouse."

Montana's lips quirked upward. "Is there anything you can't do, Geek?"

"I never was much good at tennis," he said, and turned back to his computer.

Duff laid a hand on the computer guru's shoulder. "You and Lance should get some rest. We need you alert and ready to go when we ship out."

Geek nodded. "About to hit the shower, shave and drop for a few Zs. When do I need to be back?"

Montana's eyes narrowed as his resolve strengthened. "Tonight."

KATE SPENT THE day at the computer, monitoring the searches Geek had set up to run automatically. When there was a hit, she checked the data and determined whether it was useful or superfluous. Another application ran in the background, trying every combination of passwords to break into Carruthers's many bank accounts, both personal and corporate.

On the desk beside her, she'd selected an H&K .40 caliber pistol as weapon of choice for the reconnaissance that evening. She'd assembled, disassembled and reassembled it four times. Then she'd cleaned, oiled and fitted it into a shoulder holster she'd strap on when they were ready to move out.

Becca leaned over her shoulder and set a steaming mug of coffee in front of her.

The aroma filled her senses and she inhaled deeply. "You read my mind."

"Have you talked with Mica since she returned from the bank?" Becca asked.

Kate shook her head. "She looks so sad, I'm afraid I'll make her cry again if I ask her how she's doing."

Becca's lips tightened. "I take it you read the letter."

Kate nodded. Every time she thought about it, her

throat constricted and her eyes stung. "We need to find Emily."

"Mica's spent a fortune chasing leads. What makes you think we'll have any more luck?" Becca asked.

"She didn't look right here at home." Kate lifted the pistol and weighed it in her palm. She'd had one like it in her apartment. Her father had given it to her for her nineteenth birthday and spent the day at the range with her, teaching her how to handle it properly. "That poor girl has been gone for weeks. Can you imagine what she's had to endure?"

Becca shook her head. "I don't want to."

"I don't, either." Anger burned inside Kate. "She needs to be home with her mother."

"I'm afraid to leave Mica here tonight."

Kate looked up into her friend's face and read the concern etched into the lines on her forehead. "Why?"

"I'm afraid she might take matters into her own hands and go after Carruthers."

"We don't know for certain Carruthers is our man," Kate argued.

"Exactly." Becca's lips twisted. "And going outside these doors without Rex or another bodyguard is too dangerous."

"What do you propose?"

"One of us needs to stay with her at all times."

"What about Rex?" Kate asked.

"Mica insisted he take a painkiller. I think he's down for the night."

"What about Geek or Lance?" Kate didn't want to stay behind and look after Mica when the others would be out in the field, possibly cornering the bastard who'd put them all through hell.

"Geek will be manning operations from here. Lance and I are operating the communications van." Becca smiled. "I'm driving."

Kate sighed. "Which leaves me." She glanced at the gun, knowing it wouldn't be used that night. "Why me, and not one of the guys?"

"Fair question. I think she would appreciate a female shoulder to lean on right now."

"Tazer?"

Becca shook her head. "She refuses to leave Royce in case the poison attack on him wasn't just an accident of picking up the glove." Becca laid a hand on Kate's shoulder. "You've been Mica. You've had her inside your head. You practically know what she's thinking."

Much as Kate hated to admit it, she was the logical choice to stay with Mica. If the woman was contemplating making an attempt to see Nigel Carruthers, someone had to be there to stop her.

"So, will you stay?" Becca asked.

"We'll see." Though her answer was noncommittal, she knew what she had to do.

The six SEALs and SOS agent Sam Russell prepared a battle plan. Geek and Lance would provide the tech support they'd need for communications and to bypass security.

Geek had already hacked into Carruthers's security service and was prepared to shut it down for the time needed for the SEALs to get in and out of the man's house.

The men dressed all in black and wore soft-soled dark shoes and ski masks. They carried pistols and stun guns, prepared to use whichever the situation warranted.

"Just remember," Sam reminded them, "this isn't a foreign country, and we aren't under wartime rules of engagement. If we're caught, we face the possibility of going to jail for breaking and entering. Anyone who wants to opt out, do so now. Once we go in, we're committed."

None of the men left the room.

Becca must have let them know that Kate would be staying behind to assist Geek and protect Mica, because they didn't include her in the planning.

She wanted to be a part of the team that found the evidence that would nail the guy who'd killed so many. She wanted to be there when they took him down.

"And, men," Sam continued, "if you locate Emily, bring her home."

The team loaded into the communication van. Becca would drive while Lance manned the electronics. Once they were within half a mile of their target, Sam and the SEALs would disembark and continue on foot.

Montana was the last to climb into the van.

Kate caught his arm before he stepped in. "Hey."

He paused with one foot in and the other on the ground. "Hey, yourself."

"When you get back, we should talk." Kate wanted to say so much more, but the guys were waiting. "Okay?"

Montana nodded. "You bet."

She started to back away, but Montana grabbed her arm and pulled her close, capturing her mouth with his. His kiss was brief, but warm, and promised more when he got back.

Quentin, Sawyer, Duff, Hunter and Rip whistled and teased him as he climbed in and the door slid shut.

Kate didn't care what anyone thought but Montana. She hadn't known him long, but one thing was sure, she could very easily fall in love with the man, and might already be halfway there. The thought of him going to a place that could be teeming with assassins made her wish she had gone along. She could have had his back. Mica had taken care of herself thus far, and could make do for one more night.

Then again, Mica hadn't read the letter before today, nor had she allowed herself to grieve for her dead husband until now. Grief made people do things they wouldn't normally do, like sell every last motorcycle in her husband's treasured collection.

Kate returned to the conference room, where Geek was talking into his mic, performing a comm check with each member of the team. When Montana checked in, Kate's pulse quickened.

She told herself he'd be back soon enough. They'd talk. They might even make love, if she convinced him she really wanted him to stay for the night, and that he wouldn't break her heart.

Yeah, they had a few things to discuss. Number one on the list was where their relationship was going.

Kate wandered out into the corridor in search of Mica. Rex was as Becca suspected, passed out in the men's dorm, doped up on pain medication.

She found Mica in the little kitchen, sitting at a table, nursing a cup of tea and rereading the letter her husband had left.

Kate poured a cup of coffee, carried it over to the table and sat across from her.

Mica sniffed. "He really did love me."

"Yes. He did," Kate agreed. "I hope someday to

find a man who loves me as much as your husband loved you."

Mica glanced up with bloodshot, red-rimmed eyes. "Until now, I hadn't stopped long enough to consider living life without Trevor. Today is the first day it really hit me."

Kate didn't know what to say to her. How did you console someone who was deeply and utterly heartbroken? She reached across the table and placed her hand over Mrs. Brantley's.

"I miss him," she whispered.

"My dad and I were really close," Kate said. "When he passed away, I couldn't imagine life without him in it. He was my rock. I always knew he would be there to catch me if I fell. When he died, it took a long time for me to regain my balance, but I did."

Mica looked up. "How did you get over the loss?"

Kate smiled and shook her head. "I didn't. He's still that big part of my life that I will never forget. He's with me every day." She patted her chest. "I carry him in my heart. The memories we shared, good and bad, are all there. I take them out and examine them occasionally when I run across something that reminds me of him."

They sat for a long while in silence.

When Mica drank the last drop of her tea, she stared into the cup as if wondering where it had all gone. Then she sighed. "I think I'll go lie down for a while. You will come get me if you hear anything, won't you?"

"You bet," Kate said. She took both their cups to the sink and rinsed them, then walked Mica to her room. "If you need me for anything, even an ear to bend, I'm here for you."

Mica smiled. "Thank you. You've been more than kind to a woman you didn't even know."

"I just wish I could do more."

Mica hugged her, tears filling her eyes. She hurried into her room and closed the door.

Kate returned to the conference room, her heart hurting for the woman who'd lost her entire family.

Geek was staring at a monitor with several green dots, each with a name assigned. "They're on the Carruthers estate grounds, moving up to the main house."

Kate leaned close, her pulse rushing through her veins. What she wouldn't give to be with them. She could almost smell the gardens and taste the night air.

Geek pressed some keys. "Security system has been disabled at the house with a false signal feed to the security provider." Geek sat back. "Now all they have to do is get inside without being detected, find some evidence and get back out without being shot." He shook his head. "God be with them."

Kate sat on the edge of her chair, her breath caught in her throat. The silence stretched between them as they watched the green dots move into the mansion.

A sound behind her made Kate jump. She turned to find Mica standing in the doorway, her face pale, her eyes wide.

Kate leaped from her chair and ran to the woman. "What's wrong?"

The widow held up her cell phone. "He wants to make a trade. Emily for the Swiss accounts access codes."

Chapter Fifteen

Montana moved through the house, treading lightly,
careful not to bump into anything or make a sound.
From all Geek and Lance could find online, Carruthers
didn't own a dog. There were no payments made to a
veterinarian and nothing they could find that indicated
he spent money on dog food bills. That didn't mean he
didn't have one. So far, they hadn't been attacked or
had an animal barking to raise the alarm.

Once inside, the team split up. Duff and Sawyer
went up the sweeping staircase. Rip and Hunter had
the main floor, while Montana headed to the basement.
Quentin and Sam Russell had bypassed the house to
check the outbuildings and the additional three-car, de-
tached garage. Their goal was to be in and out in less
than ten minutes. With an office building and warehouse yet to visit that night, they had a lot of ground
to cover.

Montana found the doorway to the basement tucked
beneath the staircase leading up to the second floor.
The door had a keyed lock on the outside, which made
the hairs on the back of Montana's neck stand on end.
He pulled out his Swiss Army knife, unfolded the thin,

hardened, stainless steel file and inserted it into the keyhole.

After several twists and feeling his way around, he found the sweet spot and disengaged the lock. Pushing his night-vision goggles down over his eyes, he descended the steps into the basement.

Halfway down, one of the boards creaked. Montana paused and listened for any sign that the basement was occupied. Nothing moved and complete silence reigned.

Continuing to the bottom, he paused and looked around. His goggles picked up a heat source, which turned out to be the water heater. Another source was the pilot light for the central heating unit. Other than that, the room was cold.

Montana pushed the goggles up and clicked on his small flashlight. The floor space equaled the size of the first floor, with eight-foot ceilings and a massive system of wine racks lined up to the back wall. Most of the racks were empty and laced with cobwebs. The two windows the basement sported had long since been bricked over.

Other than stacks of old furniture and boxes, Montana didn't see much that interested him. Still, he checked behind the furniture and boxes, careful to search for hidden doors. The boxes and crates contained vintage clothing and knickknacks from what appeared to be the sixties or seventies. Thankfully, he didn't find any skeletons or bodies among the refuse.

Montana checked the wine racks one by one, finding nothing but dust and spiderwebs. Strangely, the main path leading past them had many footprints, displacing the layers of dust.

Adrenaline spiked in his blood as Montana eased forward, his weapon drawn. He clicked off the flashlight, lowered his night-vision goggles and passed the last rack, to find another door at the very back of the room, tucked behind it. Only this door was short, only five feet tall at the most, and it, too, had a lock on the outside and several shiny new dead bolts, all engaged.

Whatever Carruthers stored in here, he didn't want getting out.

Montana pressed his ear to the solid wood door, but couldn't detect any sound inside. Raising his night-vision goggles again, he clicked on his flashlight and checked all around the seams for anything that might trigger an explosion.

When he was fairly certain it hadn't been booby-trapped, he unlocked the dead bolts, one at a time, careful not to make noise. Again he applied his file to the door lock. This one took a little more time, but he finally found the right spot and disengaged the lock.

Stepping out of the entryway, he pulled open the door and aimed his weapon at the interior. His breath caught and held as he waited for movement, but none came.

With one hand holding his gun and the other a flashlight, he shone light into the tiny space. The majority of the room was filled with a cot bolted to the concrete floor. On it was a thin mattress and a single blanket. In one corner was a gallon tin bucket, in the other a collection of empty water bottles and food wrappers. Hanging on hooks screwed into the wall was a pale pink blouse, covered in dirt and grime. A Washington Redskins hooded sweatshirt hung beside it.

Montana swore and then spoke softly into his radio

headset. "I think I found where the bastard has been keeping Emily."

Within seconds, three of the six other men converged on the basement.

Montana snapped pictures of the blouse and sweatshirt. He'd have Mica verify whether or not they belonged to Emily.

Looking closer, they discovered several long, blond hairs on the blanket. Montana was confident if they ran a DNA test on those hairs, they'd prove the person held captive in this room had been Emily Brantley.

They were all very careful not to touch the evidence. Montana and the rest of the SEAL team had worn gloves to avoid leaving any fingerprints or destroying other fingerprints throughout the house.

Carruthers wasn't home and, based on how fresh some of the food wrappers were, Emily hadn't been gone from her cell for long.

As they emerged from the house into the open, the team converged and moved toward the fence they'd scaled on their way in.

"We need the police on this house ASAP and an all-points bulletin out on Carruthers," Montana said into his mic. "Lance, any idea where Carruthers could be right now?"

"He might have moved her to one of his other buildings. Since the office building is in downtown DC, my bet would be he took her to the warehouse."

"Uh, gang, we have a problem," Geek said into Montana's ear.

"What?" Montana asked, his stomach clenching.

"Mica and Kate are on their way to meet with Carruthers."

"Say again?" Montana demanded. "I thought Kate was going to keep Mica there."

"Yeah, well, as of five minutes ago, they left, asking me to give them a head start. Carruthers called Mica and offered a trade. Emily for the Swiss bank account codes. She's to arrive alone. They took the bike."

Montana swore, his heart pounding against his ribs as he imagined Kate racing through the night toward what Montana was certain would be a trap.

The SEAL team reached the eight-foot-tall concrete block fence and assisted each other over the top, one by one. The van waited on the other side of the street.

Once they were all inside, Montana leaned over Lance's shoulder, stared at his computer monitor and spoke into his radio headset. "Tell me you sent them with trackers."

Geek responded, "Absolutely. Bringing them up now."

Lance's screen blinked and two green dots appeared amid an outline of the Washington city streets.

"They're headed toward the river," Lance said.

"On it," Becca called out from the driver's seat.

They raced toward the capital, headed north from Carruthers's estate in Alexandria.

"Not good," Lance said. "Look, they're following the river, but heading due south toward the convergence of the Potomac and the Anacostia Rivers."

"Carruthers's warehouse isn't in that direction," Geek said.

"What else *is* there?" Montana asked.

"I believe Carruthers owns a boat or a yacht," Geek replied. "They could be headed for the James Creek Marina. Want me to call in the police?"

"They might get there before we can," Duff said.

"And you said she's supposed to show up alone." Montana didn't like it. "Calling in the police could put them in even more danger." He looked down at the map on Lance's screen. "Where's the closest marina to us?"

Lance brought up another screen and searched for marinas. "There. Two miles ahead on the right."

"Head for it. We can get to the James Creek Marina quicker by water," Montana said. "And if Carruthers takes them aboard his boat, we can pursue in one of our own."

"And where do you propose we get one at this hour?" Duff asked.

Montana's jaw hardened, but he didn't respond.

Duff sighed. "That's what I was afraid of. We can add grand theft watercraft to breaking and entering on our rap sheet." He clapped his hands together. "What are we waiting for?"

Becca drove like a wild woman, coming to a screeching halt at the marina.

Montana pointed to his teammates. "Duff, Sawyer and Quentin, you're with me. The rest of you try to make it to the marina by road and head them off if Carruthers makes a run for it by land." Montana was first out the van door.

He'd gone boating in Montana in an old fishing boat his grandfather kept together with spit and glue. He'd had to manually start the engine on more than one occasion, which was pretty much what he'd had to do for most of the old farm machinery around the ranch. He had skills that weren't part of his résumé, and he planned to use them to rescue Kate, Mica and Emily.

Montana sprinted toward the last row of boats, hoping to get away before an alarm was sounded. A locked chain-link gate blocked his entrance to the boat slips.

"Want me to go back to the marina and see if I can find bolt cutters or a pry bar?" Duff asked.

Montana shook his head. The van had left as soon as the team of four had disembarked. They'd spend more time looking for something to break through the combination lock on the gate than going around. He shrugged out of his gear, shirt and shoes, and handed everything to Duff, including his radio headset. "I'll be right back."

"Uh-huh," Duff said. "And we'll be waiting here as your accessories to the crime."

Montana dived into the murky water of the Potomac River and swam around to the boat slips, where he pulled himself up onto the dock. He looked for the fastest craft that could carry the four of them and climbed down onto the bow. Before he attempted starting the engine without a key, he checked the glove box and beneath the seats. Luck shone down on him when he found the keys to the boat in the storage well beneath a bench seat. In seconds, he had the boat untied, engine running and pulled around to the ramp where the others of his team waited.

A quiet *hoo-yah* sounded off and they all piled in.

Duff took over driving the boat as Montana dried his face with his shirt and reestablished communications with headquarters and the comm van.

"Where are they now?" he asked, shivering in the cool night air.

"They stopped at the marina," Geek replied.

"The van's ETA is about fifteen minutes the way

Becca drives," Montana reported. "Four of us are going by water. ETA less than five minutes."

"Good," Geek said. "I'll let you know when they're moving again."

Montana fought the urge to take the helm from Duff. But Duff was the best boat driver on SBT-22. Instead, Montana moved to the front of the ski boat and searched the water ahead for boats coming or going. Since they were in a stolen boat, Montana hadn't wanted to turn on the running lights and alert harbor police to their presence. They didn't have time to be stopped, and he had no desire to play hide-and-seek with the authorities any sooner than he had to.

"You should see the light on Hains Point coming up, dead ahead," Geek said into Montana's headset.

The moon shone down on the water, giving Montana a clear view of the convergence of the two rivers. He could see the spit of land separating the Potomac from the Anacostia. "I see it."

"Steer right of the point and you'll see the next one, Greenleaf Point," Geek instructed. "James Creek Marina is just past it."

"Got it." Montana counted the seconds, praying they got there in time. With Carruthers's ruthless disregard for life, he might decide to shoot all three of them, take the codes and leave the country.

Montana couldn't let that happen. He liked Mica. The woman was strong, dedicated to her family and genuinely good. And Kate…

He was already halfway in love with her. He needed more time to convince her she could love him, too. Yeah, his career in the Navy would make it hard to date, but he really wanted to see Kate. He'd make the sacrifices necessary, if given the chance.

KATE STOPPED SHORT of the James Creek Marina, the last place the man who'd called Mica had given them on their scavenger hunt through the city. Since Mica was supposed to arrive by herself, she'd have to go in on foot. Kate would ditch the bike and follow at a little bit of a distance, swing around and try to come at the kidnapper from the side.

She'd bet the man was Carruthers. After listening to the instructions with the phone on speaker, she would recognize that voice as Carruthers's from his rude remarks at the gala. The man was insane, which didn't bode well for Emily.

Mica couldn't be dissuaded from delivering the codes herself. She didn't want Carruthers to have any excuse to execute her stepdaughter. Kate suspected Carruthers had no intention of letting either one of them leave alive. He'd killed, or paid to have killed, too many people to leave any loose ends running around with his name on their lips.

Dressed in dark jeans and a dark shirt, with her hair stuffed up into a black hat and her skin covered in black camouflage paint, Kate hugged the bushes and buildings, moving swiftly and quietly through the shadows. She carried the .40 caliber H&K pistol, and a sniper scope and rifle with a removable butt she'd reassembled once she'd dismounted the bike.

Mica walked down the road toward the marina, carrying the page of account access codes tucked into her back pocket. Though shaken by the call, she'd held up pretty well, with the chance of getting Emily back giving her the hope and determination to face the killer.

Mica had promised to move slowly, giving Kate time to position herself to take a shot if the need arose. The caller had instructed her to walk out on the dock and wait for additional instructions.

Geek had equipped Kate with a single-lens, night-vision monocular. As she moved toward the wide-open space on the approach to the marina, she lifted the monocular to her eye and scanned the area for the telltale green heat signature of a warm body.

Immediately, she noted a figure leaning against the far side of the marina and another on the closest corner.

"Damn," she muttered beneath her breath. It would take some doing to reach either one without alerting them to the fact Mica that was not alone. All Kate could hope for was that their attention would be on Mica.

Swinging wide, Kate came at the marina on the far side, hopefully sneaking up behind the man on the back corner.

Clouds skittered across the half-moon, giving Kate additional concealment as she raced across an open area and ducked behind a storage shed. Rather than confront the sentry guarding that end of the marina, she slipped behind the building and peeked around the corner toward the dock.

A large man stood on the wooden planks, his arm wrapped around the neck of a young woman.

Emily.

Kate's pulse quickened.

"Don't do it, Mom," the girl called out. "He's lying about letting me go."

"Shut up," the man said, and clamped a hand over her mouth.

Emily bit his palm.

The man hit her in the side of the head and she went limp.

"Emily!" Mica said, increasing her pace until she was running toward the man who held her stepdaughter.

When she was within ten yards of the two, the man said, "Stop."

Mica slowed to a stop, breathing hard. "Don't hurt her. I have the codes. Let her go, and I'll give you them."

"How do I know you have the codes?" the man asked.

Mica dug in her back pocket and pulled out the sheet of paper, then held it over the side of the wooden dock. "Let her go, or they go in the water."

"If you do that I have no reason to let you or the girl live."

"Nigel," Mica said, her voice clear and calm. "She's done nothing to hurt you."

"My brother did nothing to hurt you and your family, but your husband was determined to smear his name, even after he was dead."

"I don't know what you're talking about. What Trevor did has nothing to do with Emily. She's innocent."

"Nobody is innocent. Nobody comes out of this world alive. We all die."

"Nigel…" Mica spoke in a soft, insistent voice. "It's over. You can't continue to kill people."

"Why not? Abusaid's people killed my brother. Our government didn't protect him. Patrick was my only family member. Everyone who had a hand in what happened needs to pay for what they did, or what they refused to do. And they're going to pay with their lives and those of their families. They should have cared."

"Please, let Emily go," Mica begged.

He tightened his grip on Emily and his voice grew harder. "Give me the codes."

Mica stepped closer. "Release Emily."

"Not until I have the money," Carruthers said.

Kate lifted the rifle to her shoulder and set her sight on Carruthers. Emily's head and body were in the way of a clear shot at the man.

"That will take time," Mica said. "You'll need access to a computer."

"Then you'll have to come with me." He spun and dragged Emily toward the long, sleek yacht behind him. A man emerged from the shadows, grabbed her and tossed her on board.

Emily scrambled to her feet and rushed toward the side of the vessel. As she bent to spring out into the water, a man grabbed her from behind. She screamed.

The man clamped a hand over her mouth and dragged her inside.

"Emily!" Mica rushed forward.

Carruthers grabbed her arm and twisted it up between her shoulder blades. "Come on, Mica, we're going for a little ride." He yanked the page of codes from her hand and shoved her toward the yacht.

Kate aimed at the back of Carruthers's head as he shoved Mica toward his waiting henchman.

"I wouldn't do that if I were you," said a coarse voice

behind her. She turned to look down the long barrel of an AR-15 rifle, with a tall, mean-looking man at the other end, ready to shoot. "Drop the weapon and get up."

Kate laid the rifle on the ground, but as she rose, she brought it up with her and slammed it into the man's groin.

He cursed and swung a meaty fist, hitting her in the side of the head. She staggered backward and into the arms of another one of Carruthers's goons.

He clamped his arms around her, pinning her arms to her sides, and lifted her off her feet. Kate kicked and fought, but the guy had her in a pinch she couldn't wiggle her way out of. Between the two men, they carried her on board the yacht and the boat pulled away from the dock.

Carruthers waved his hand toward the interior of the yacht. "Throw her in the room with the other women, bring my laptop and get us the hell out of here."

The men carried Kate through a doorway and down a stairwell to the cabin area below. One of them opened a door, and she was tossed into a small room.

Mica held a dirty, disheveled Emily in her arms. Tears streamed down both their faces.

As soon as she hit the floor, Kate scrambled to her feet and ran back to the door. But it shut in her face, and she heard the sound of a lock clicking in place.

She didn't waste time trying to twist the knob. She had to find something with which to pick the lock or pry the door open. The cabin consisted of two bunks, one over the other, and a built-in dresser. Kate ran for the dresser and yanked out a drawer.

"What are you going to do?" Mica asked.

"Get us out of here." Kate slammed the drawer against the bunk, breaking it into pieces.

Mica let go of Emily and straightened. "How can we help?"

Chapter Sixteen

As the ski boat approached Greenleaf Point, a yacht passed them, fifty feet away on their starboard bow.

"Kate and Mica are on the move again." Geek's excited voice filled Montana's headset. "They just passed you on the river, headed the opposite direction."

Duff waited for the yacht to clear them, staying close to the bank. The clouds chose that moment to provide concealment from the other vessel. Once the big yacht passed, Duff swung wide and fell in behind it.

"Montana and Quentin, get ready to board," Duff called out. "Sawyer, cover."

The men took their places. Montana and Quentin hunkered low in the front of the boat until they were right behind the yacht, riding in the bigger boat's wake. The roar of the yacht's engine covered their motor noise. With luck, the occupants wouldn't ever expect someone to board them while they were moving.

Duff eased up in the churning wake. When they were close, he shoved the throttle forward a hair more, practically riding up on the back deck.

Montana leaped from the bow and landed on the yacht's back platform. Quentin landed beside him and

Duff slid away to the rear and swung wide, coming up on the starboard side.

Sawyer yelled, loudly enough for the yacht occupants to hear, "Hey, jerkface! Wanna race?"

While the attention was on Sawyer, Montana climbed onto the deck. A man carrying a gun looked over the side at the ski boat keeping pace with the yacht in the dark.

Montana sneaked up behind the man and hit him hard on the back of the head with the butt of his .45 caliber pistol. The man went down.

Quentin was there to zip-tie his wrists and ankles and jam a cloth into his mouth. Together they lifted him up and stowed him in a rubber dingy, covering him with several life vests.

Montana and Quentin eased around the port side, while Duff, in the ski boat, zigzagged close to the yacht's starboard side, with Sawyer yelling like a drunk man.

Montana found an open, sliding glass door leading into the luxury yacht. He eased up to it and peered in.

Across the lounge, a man wearing a tailored suit and carrying a gun stood beside a thin man in thick glasses hunched over a computer, cursing. Montana recognized the suited man as Nigel Carruthers.

The computer guy cursed again. "Damn it! These codes aren't getting me in."

"You better hope they do," said Carruthers. "If you don't get the money transferred by midnight, we don't get the activation key."

"I'm working on it. Give me time."

"You said you could make it happen if you had the

accounts and passwords. What's the holdup?" Carruthers demanded.

"In addition to the codes and passwords, there are prompt questions I don't have the answers to."

Carruthers waved toward the door where Montana was standing. Two men stepped forward. Each was dressed like a member of an elite military force, in matching black outfits, and they carried military-grade AR-15 rifles.

"Get Mrs. Brantley," Carruthers ordered.

Both men executed an about-face and walked out of Montana's view.

Once Carruthers turned back to the man at the computer, Montana dared to stick his head through the door. He saw the hired guns descending a staircase into the lower level of the big yacht.

A voice sounded over an intercom. "Sir, we might have a problem out here."

Montana held his breath, praying Quentin or the disabled guard hadn't yet been discovered.

Carruthers hit a switch on an end table. "Can't you handle it? We've got bigger fish to fry in here."

"We have company off the starboard bow. A small boat, running without lights."

"Authorities?" Carruthers asked.

"No. It appears to be a couple of drunk guys on a joyride."

"Run them over, shoot them. I don't care. Just get rid of them."

Montana almost laughed at the description of Sawyer and Duff. Their diversion had bought the two SEALs on board precious time to locate their opponents and neutralize them.

Montana was certain he could handle those inside the yacht. He only hoped Quentin didn't run into heavy resistance on the outside.

Since the men went down under to retrieve Mrs. Brantley, it stood to reason the other two ladies were below, as well.

Gunfire sounded from below.

"Damn it! We don't need this now. They're going to bring every member of the port authority out to investigate." Carruthers kicked the back of the computer guy's chair. "We're running out of time." He glanced toward the stairwell. "What the hell is going on down there?" Louder, he yelled, "You better not shoot Mica Brantley! I need her to break this code!"

KATE HAD STRIPPED a metal slide off the broken drawer and rammed it into the door casing. Unfortunately, the builder had spared no expense and built the framing strong enough to withstand a pirate attack. After bending two slides, she searched for something small enough to slip into the lock. The only thing she could think of was the underwire on her bra.

She stripped off the bra and ripped the wire out. Kate had the wire in the lock when a key pushed in from the other side.

"Someone's coming in," Mica whispered.

Kate spun away from the door, grabbed one of the long splinters from the broken drawer and hid it behind her back.

Mica released her grip on Emily, and the two women grabbed other strips of wood, tucking them behind their backs, as well.

The door slammed open.

A big guy dressed in all black pointed at Mica with a pistol. "You. Upstairs."

Mica shot a glance at Kate, who was standing closer to the door and the man with the gun.

Kate gave a slight nod. When Mica passed her, she edged forward.

The man half turned to leave, giving Kate her opportunity.

She leaped forward and stabbed her splinter into the man's hand holding the gun.

He cursed, flung the weapon to the floor and clutched his hand to his chest.

"Mica, Emily, drop!" Kate yelled, as she dived for the gun.

Mica and Emily dropped to the floor as another man burst into view with his pistol.

Mica stabbed the guy in the calf.

Grabbing the gun off the floor, Kate turned onto her back and fired at the man, hitting him in the chest.

He staggered backward but didn't go down, indicating he was wearing protective body armor. Kate fired again, hitting the guy in the neck.

The man whose hand she'd stabbed reached down and grabbed a hank of Mica's long black hair and dragged her to her knees.

Kate didn't hesitate; she pulled the trigger. The bullet hit Mica's assailant square in the face. He fell backward and lay still.

Mica jumped up and ran for Emily, pulling the younger woman into her arms.

Kate rolled to her feet and ran for the door. Their only hope was for her to fight her way out of this. After she'd killed Carruthers's thugs, Kate knew he wouldn't let her live.

MONTANA STARTED ACROSS the lounge toward Carruthers when the man at the computer shouted, "I'm in!"

"Quick! Transfer the money." Carruthers slammed his palm against the back of the man's chair. "Hurry, damn you!"

"Doing it now." The computer guy pressed a button and stared at the screen. "Transferred!" He pounded the keys again and sat back. "We have the firing key."

"Enter it! Do it!" Carruthers screamed.

Montana stepped up behind the man and pressed his gun to Carruthers's head. "Stop whatever it is you're doing or I'll shoot you."

The computer guy jerked around in his seat so fast he fell backward.

Carruthers swung, slamming his hand into Montana's arm, but didn't succeed in dislodging the gun.

Montana brought his fist upward in a powerful uppercut, caught the man in the chin and knocked him flat on his back. Then he straddled him and pressed his .45 to his captive's cheek. "It's over, Carruthers. You're done terrorizing others."

Lying on his back, Carruthers smirked. "You're right, I'm done. In exactly two minutes, all of DC, its crooked politicians, lobbyists and political action committees will be blown off the map."

"What are you talking about?" a female voice said from behind them.

Out of the corner of his eye, Montana could see Mica, Emily and Kate. His chest swelled, filling with joy. Kate held a gun on Carruthers. Mica and Emily held splinters of wood like battle swords.

Carruthers looked past Montana to Mica, and his smile became a sneer. "You thought you could save your stepdaughter, but what you didn't know is that you would be dying with her. The irony is I used *your* money to purchase the key to activate a dirty bomb located so close to the capital, nobody will get out alive." He laughed. "You have less than two minutes. Say your goodbyes."

Kate stepped forward. "What have you done?"

The man on his back shook his head. "What someone should have done a long time ago. I'm taking a bomb straight to the nation's capital and it's too late to stop it."

Montana's heart stopped for a second and then raced ahead. "You have a bomb on this boat?"

Carruthers chuckled. "Even if you find it, you can't disarm it."

Montana leaped to his feet. "Kate, take him. We have a bomb to find."

About that time, the yacht came to a stop. Quentin appeared in the doorway. "Guards have been neutralized and the captain is unconscious." His eyes narrowed. "What's going on?"

"Carruthers has a dirty bomb on board. We have a minute to find and disarm it."

Montana ran toward the staircase leading below. "Mica, get Duff and Sawyer up here. Now! Take the lounge, helm and deck. Look in and under everything."

"I'm going with you below," Quentin said.

As Montana ran for the stairs, he said over his shoulder, "Kate, if he moves, shoot him! And in case we don't make it out of this alive, I think I love you."

He leaped to the bottom of the stairs and ran straight for the galley, searching through anything large enough to hold a dirty bomb. Hell, he didn't know what a dirty bomb even looked like. All the while, he counted down. One thousand one, one thousand two…marking each second of the remaining minute.

When he didn't find anything in the galley, he threw open the door marked Engine Room. He stood for five seconds, staring at all the parts that made up a yacht engine. Finally, his gaze landed on what he thought was a toolbox, but it was duct taped to the wall. On closer inspection, he noticed an electronic timer displaying the number 21, then 20, then 19…

"Found it!" Montana shouted, and dropped to his knees, studying the contraption, his heart slamming against his ribs, his mind racing through a thousand different scenarios. As a SEAL, he'd been trained in demolitions. Some bombs were set up to explode if tampered with. If this was one of them, he could doom them and all of DC to death if he pulled the wrong wire.

The numbers clicked by…11…10…9…8 and he was no closer to figuring it out. When it came down to 5…4…3 he grabbed all the wires leading from the clock to the bomb and yanked as hard as he could. Three of the five came loose, but the clock didn't stop. In the last second, Montana sent a prayer heavenward, ripped out the last two wires, took what he thought might be his last breath and held it.

Quentin slid to a stop beside him, breathing hard. "You found it?"

Montana nodded and held up a handful of wires, unable to say anything.

Quentin looked from Montana to the bomb and back to Montana, then dropped to his knees and bent over, his shoulders shaking.

Montana frowned. "Hey, dude, I think we're okay. It didn't explode."

Without looking up, Quentin reached out and touched Montana's arm, his shoulders still shaking. "Oh, Montana. I wish you could have seen your face." When Quentin raised his head, his own face was wreathed in a huge smile and tears were running from his eyes. "I know I shouldn't laugh, but the expression on your face was the funniest thing I've ever seen." He bent again and his shoulders shook, the laughter making its way up to burst from his throat.

Montana stood, pulled his friend to his feet and suffered through a bone-crunching hug.

"Thanks, man. You saved our butts." Quentin rubbed the tears from his eyes and clapped his hand on Montana's back. "Let's go clean up the rest and call in the Feds. I'm sure they're going to want to dispose of the bomb."

Montana led the way up to the lounge, where Kate was applying zip ties to Carruthers's wrists and ankles, while Duff did the same with the computer guy.

"Mind telling us what's going on?" Lance said into Montana's ear. "We just got to the marina. Where are you guys?"

Montana glanced at Duff. "You want to fill him in and get this ball rolling? I'd like to get back to HQ by morning."

Kate stepped in front of him and held out her hand. "Care to take a stroll on the deck?"

Montana took her hand in his and held on tight. Together, they stepped through the sliding glass doors onto the deck. The clouds had completely cleared from the sky, and the lights of the capital shone like a brilliant crown.

Kate leaned against him. "Thanks."

"For what?" God, he loved her body resting against his. He couldn't wait to get her alone. And naked.

"For saving us and the city."

Montana shrugged. "All I did was pull a few wires."

She shook her head and held out her other hand. "Must have been a little bit more intense than that. You still have the wires in your hand."

He glanced down and laughed. She was right. He'd been so intent on keeping Kate and the rest of his friends alive, he didn't remember to put the mass of wires down.

Kate took them from his hand and laid them on the deck. Then she turned to face him. "About what you said before we were almost obliterated from the map… Did you mean it?"

Montana knew what he'd said, but now that they were going to live, he didn't know what it would mean to Kate. "Look, I don't want you to feel like you have to commit to anything or say anything you don't mean. All I want is the chance to see you again."

She nodded. "Fair enough. And if I decide there's something more than amazing sex between us, then what? How would a relationship between a CIA agent and a Navy SEAL ever work?"

"I could ask to be transferred to Little Creek in Virginia. It's a lot closer than Mississippi," he said, his hopes rising dangerously. He'd known Kate only a few days, and in that time frame they'd lived a lifetime. He knew what he wanted, but he'd need time with Kate to convince her she wanted the same.

"Why move to Little Creek? Your team is in Mississippi. You've been through so much with them."

He had, and it would be hard starting over on another team. "Kate, you're worth it. I'd rip the wires out of a thousand bombs to get to spend even one more day with you."

Tears welled in Kate's eyes. "Damn you, Ben."

His heart swelled at her use of his first name. "That's the first time you've called me Ben." He gathered her in his arms. She didn't pull away. Hell, maybe he had a chance with her.

"Damn you." She laid her hand on his chest and tears ran down her cheeks. "I didn't want to. But you're making me."

He chuckled, his chest filling with hope. He rested his forehead against hers. "Making you what?"

Kate raised her hand and cupped the back of his neck. "You're making me fall in love with you."

Joy exploded inside him and he felt he could light up the sky with it. He tightened his arm around her waist and tipped her chin up to his. "Is that such a bad thing?"

"It's bad. Very bad." Kate leaned up on her toes and brushed his lips with hers. "I lose control when I'm around you."

"From my perspective, that's a very good thing. And kissing you is even better." He bent to take her lips in a heart-stopping, soul-defining kiss that only ended when the port authority's boat pulled up beside them and shone a spotlight on them. Even then, Montana didn't want to let go.

"Put your hands up and hold them high where we can see them."

Slowly, he released her and backed away. As he raised his hands, he said, "I surrender my heart to you, Kate McKenzie."

She smiled and raised her hands, as well. "And I surrender mine to you."

* * * * *

Don't miss the previous books in Elle James's exciting SEAL OF MY OWN series:

NAVY SEAL TO DIE FOR
NAVY SEAL CAPTIVE
NAVY SEAL SURVIVAL

Available now from Mills & Boon Intrigue!

Give a 12 month subscription to a friend today!

Call Customer Services
0844 844 1358*

or visit
millsandboon.co.uk/subscription

MILLS & BOON®

Why shop at millsandboon.co.uk?

Each year, thousands of romance readers find their perfect read at millsandboon.co.uk. That's because we're passionate about bringing you the very best romantic fiction. Here are some of the advantages of shopping at www.millsandboon.co.uk:

* **Get new books first**—you'll be able to buy your favourite books one month before they hit the shops

* **Get exclusive discounts**—you'll also be able to buy our specially created monthly collections, with up to 50% off the RRP

* **Find your favourite authors**—latest news, interviews and new releases for all your favourite authors and series on our website, plus ideas for what to try next

* **Join in**—once you've bought your favourite books, don't forget to register with us to rate, review and join in the discussions

Visit **www.millsandboon.co.uk**
for all this and more today!